Meet two women who face life's challenges in their own unforgettable ways...

Dannie Treat, from *A Widow in Paradise:*

"I eat when I'm stressed out," Dannie said defensively. "Food fixes everything."

"If you treat your body like a vehicle, and give it only the best fuel, you'll get the most mileage out of it," Guy said.

"Yeah, well, I don't drive much. I just idle at the curb. So what's this all about, Mr. Loughran?"

"Call me Guy." He leaned in, staring into her eyes.

A little shiver ran up her spine, and she entertained the notion of biting his full bottom lip.

Until he said, "I believe your husband and my wife had an affair."

***

Grace Becker, from *Suburban Secrets:*

"Nick, I have a confession."

Grace decided that since this was a game of Truth or Dare she'd just tell him the truth. "Do you see those women over there?" She pointed to her friends. They all stared back as if they were watching a bad reality-TV show. "They dared me to come over here and give you something."

"Like what?"

"Like my underwear."

Dear Reader,

The two books in this volume, *A Widow in Paradise* and *Suburban Secrets,* take place following a girls' night out and a crazy game of grown-up Truth or Dare.

Dannie and Grace are both women whose lives didn't turn out exactly as they planned, and they've had to improvise to find a new place in the world—something many of us can relate to. I hope you enjoy their journeys.

I have to thank Rebecca J. Hysell, Director of Marketing, Westin Hotels & Resorts, Key West, Florida, for her help with questions about hurricane preparedness. Of course, they do things much differently in Cuatro Blanco than they do at the Westin, where severe weather events are taken very seriously and their guests are treated with the utmost importance!

Thanks also to Anthony Serrao, State Farm Insurance Agent, who answered my questions about insurance investigations.

Any mistakes or liberties taken for plot purposes are purely my own!

Also, I want to thank my wonderful critique partners Anita Nolan, Joy Nash, Sally Stotter and Ellyn Bache for their support, criticism and suggestions. I don't know what I'd do without them!

And of course, my agent Jenny Bent, my wonderful editor Ann Leslie Tuttle and assistant editor Charles Griemsman for his patience and deft touch!

Wishing you lots of love and laughter,

Donna Birdsell

DONNA BIRDSELL

A Widow in Paradise

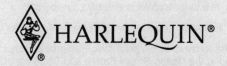

TORONTO • NEW YORK • LONDON
AMSTERDAM • PARIS • SYDNEY • HAMBURG
STOCKHOLM • ATHENS • TOKYO • MILAN • MADRID
PRAGUE • WARSAW • BUDAPEST • AUCKLAND

Recycling programs
for this product may
not exist in your area.

ISBN-13: 978-0-373-23079-2

A WIDOW IN PARADISE
Copyright © 2010 by Harlequin Books S.A.

The publisher acknowledges the copyright holder of the individual works as follows:

A WIDOW IN PARADISE
Copyright © 2010 by Donna Birdsell

SUBURBAN SECRETS
Copyright © 2006 by Donna Birdsell

Printed in U.S.A.

CONTENTS

A Widow in Paradise

For Jodi,
a great friend and fellow neurotic mom

Chapter One

DANNIE TREAT BRACED herself for the news. As she suspected, it wasn't good.

"I'm sorry to have to tell you this, but she's dying. I did what I could, but she won't last long." The man in the white coat spoke in a solemn tone.

Dannie bit her lower lip to keep from crying. "There's no way to save her?"

"I'm afraid not."

Dannie's five-year-old son, Richard, reached up and took her hand. "Is it my fault, Mommy?"

"Not this time, honey. She's just old."

Dannie gave the ancient water heater a pat and followed the technician from Plumbing Doctor up the basement stairs into the kitchen.

Richard ran off into the living room and Dannie said a silent prayer to the angels who protect all things breakable.

"So you want to replace her?" the plumber asked.

Dannie sighed. "I don't really have a choice, do I? Hot water isn't exactly a luxury."

"Only when you're camping."

Which was exactly what she and the kids were going to have to do in a few months when she couldn't afford luxuries like hot water, groceries or the mortgage anymore.

Every day the bills piled up and the balance in her bank account went down. She had to do something fast if she was going to keep a roof over their heads.

The insurance company was dragging its feet, refusing to pay on her husband Roger's policy since his death eight months before. They claimed they needed a death certificate from the authorities on Cuatro Blanco, the island where Roger had drowned, but those so-called authorities apparently moved at the speed of a mentally challenged slug.

She'd even had her lawyer contact them several times, until she realized he was charging her three hundred an hour to argue over the phone with a Cuatro Blanco coroner's clerk.

Roger had also owned a ton of stock in the accounting firm where he'd worked, which automatically reverted back to the company on his death. This should have meant a big fat check for Dannie. But Wiser-Crenshaw's human resources manager had been dodging her calls, too.

So she'd gotten a job at Wee Ones Art Studio, teaching pre-school art classes a couple times a week while a neighbor watched the kids. But her paycheck was barely enough to keep them in breakfast cereal.

So no more eating out, no more weekly trips to the ice cream parlor, no new toys except on birthdays. Steaks on the grill had become hamburgers, they got their books from the library instead of the bookstore, and she'd turned off the premium channels on cable.

Dannie had given up things she'd become accustomed to, as well, like expensive perfume and pretty new shoes and decent chocolate. Hell, she'd given up cheap perfume, functional shoes and bad chocolate, too.

But she'd be damned if she was going to give up hot baths. They were one of the few luxuries she had left in this world. Come hell or cold water, she was going to find the money to buy a new water heater.

Dannie pushed an unruly blond curl behind her ear. Her in-laws would lend her the money if she asked. God knew they had enough of it. But there would be strings attached. There always were.

No, she was going to do this herself. She just had to figure out how.

She'd already sold most of the paintings she'd done in her life before Roger—before she'd closed her paint boxes to become a good wife and an attentive mother. The ones she'd saved either weren't good enough to sell or she couldn't bear to part with them.

She had to find another solution.

As she was shutting the basement door, something at the bottom of the stairs caught her eye. The exercise bike.

And next to the exercise bike, a box of paperback novels. And next to that the Ping-Pong table. Stuff she was never going to use again. Stuff she could sell at a yard sale!

With the Columbus Day weekend coming up, it was perfect timing.

Dannie smiled. "Hello, new hot water heater."

HALF AN HOUR LATER she had a pile of junk by the front door, mined from the recesses of the basement, dusty but still functional. She was about to tackle the garage when she heard her eighteen-month-old twins, Erin and Emma, babbling on the monitor.

Nap time was over.

She braced herself for the afternoon onslaught, which included lunch for four kids—Dannie's own consisted of the crusts from four peanut-butter-and-jelly sandwiches, a rubbery stalk of celery and one soggy bread stick—a mad dash to get Richard to afternoon kindergarten, and a quick trip to the vet to dislodge the arm of a toy robot from the throat of her lovable but senseless behemoth of a dog, Quincy, who had a tendency to eat shiny objects.

Thus it was two o'clock before she could get back to her hunt for salable items.

She put the twins up for their afternoon nap, put her four-year-old daughter, Betsy, in front of the TV and set off for the garage.

It was a chilly and dark space, a place Dannie had avoided since Roger's death.

Roger had transformed it into a workshop and had been re-storing an old sailboat there, before he died.

The boat still sat upside down on crude wooden stands in the middle of the garage floor. The length of it reached across the entire three-car garage, with just enough room to walk on either side. Its hull almost touched the ceiling. At twenty-two feet, it wasn't a large boat. But it sure was pretty.

The lines were clean and unfussy, the deck still in excellent condition. Roger had hoped to get it into the water by the end of the summer. Unfortunately, summer had never come for him.

Dannie picked a piece of sandpaper up off the floor and

rubbed it over the side of the boat, blowing off the dust it produced. Tears welled in her eyes.

The name of the boat was lettered on the back, outlined in black but not yet painted in. *Treat's Dream.*

She supposed she should sell it, but she just couldn't. Not yet.

Maybe she'd try to finish it, and put it in the water. A tribute to Roger. She wasn't much of a sailor—was a little scared of the ocean, to be honest. But it seemed like a fitting tribute. Maybe Roger's best friend, Lyle, would help her.

Turning her attention to the business at hand, she set about finding stuff she could sell at the yard sale.

Against the far wall of the garage, forgotten sports equipment stood as disheveled and dirty as seventh-grade boys lined up for gym class. A scarred ice-hockey stick, a torn badminton net, an unstrung tennis racquet.

She gathered it all up in her arms and pushed the button for the automatic garage door with her elbow. It went halfway up, then stopped.

Great. Fabulous. One more thing to fix.

She tried again, but the door got stuck at the same place. She peered up into the rafters of the garage, and noticed something wedged there. A leather bag of some sort was stopping the door.

She dropped all the stuff she'd been holding and lowered the garage door. Dragging a ladder over, she set it up beneath the rafters and climbed up. She reached for the bag, her hand catching a tangle of spiderwebs.

"Mommy?"

Dannie nearly fell off the ladder. "Jeez, Bets. You scared me. What is it?"

"Can I have a snack?"

"Sure."

"What?"

"Something good for you."

"Is candy good for me?"

"No."

"Marshmallows?"

"No, they're just like candy."

"A Popsicle?"

"No, honey. Popsicles aren't good for you."

"Then what *is?*"

"Carrots. An apple. Celery."

Betsy rolled her big blue eyes. "All the gross stuff."

"Okay. I'll be there in a minute, and I'll get something for you."

Betsy lingered by the door.

"Is there something else?"

"Quincy ate a bug."

Dannie wiped the sweat from her forehead with the back of her arm. "Good. We can't afford the exterminator anymore."

Betsy kicked the doorjamb with her toe. "Are we poor, Mommy?"

Dannie sighed. "No, we're not poor. Not yet, anyway. And if we get enough stuff together for this yard sale, maybe we'll get rich. Now, go back in the house. I'll be there in a minute."

Betsy disappeared, leaving the door wide open, the heat sucking into the cold garage.

Dannie reached up and grabbed the leather bag, trying to pull it down from the rafters. It wouldn't budge. She climbed up the next step of the ladder, and could now see that it was a golf bag, wedged lengthwise between two beams.

She untangled the shoulder strap, giving it a yank. Just then Quincy bounded through the open door and into the garage, charging straight for her.

"No, Quincy. No!"

The dog flung his giant, shaggy tan body at the ladder, grabbing for the leg of Dannie's jeans. The ladder toppled over, leaving Dannie swinging from the golf bag strap. The rafters creaked ominously.

"Oh, shhhh—"

The bag pulled free of the beams, sending Dannie plummeting to the floor and landing on top of her with a thud.

"—it."

Dannie blinked, and then blinked again, certain she must be seeing things. It wasn't possible.

Money.

It was all over her.

She sat up slowly. A cascade of hundred-dollar bills slid off her body and pooled around her like a chalk outline. Quincy picked one up in his mouth and danced around her.

"Quincy, no. Bring that here."

Quincy wagged his tail and gave her a mischievous look, then trotted around the perimeter of the garage with the bill hanging out of his mouth like a green tongue.

Dannie corralled him between the boat and the wall and grabbed his collar. She pried his jaws open and took the money from his mouth. Then she herded him back into the house, pulling the door closed behind him.

She stared at the hundred in her hand.

This was a dream. It had to be. Who finds thousands of dollars in golf bags in the rafters of their garage?

She rounded the boat and saw the bag lying on top of the pile of money.

Apparently *she* had.

She knelt, raking the money together with her fingers, then forming tidy stacks of ten on the cold floor. Lots of stacks.

She counted them twice.

Thirty-one, plus the six hundred she held in her hand.

"Thirty-one thousand, six hundred dollars." She said it out loud, just to make it real.

Questions roared through her mind at the speed of a freight train. Whose golf bag was it? As far as she knew, Roger had never played a round of golf in his life, much less owned a golf bag.

Why was it filled with cash? Roger, a CPA, wasn't one to be careless with money. She doubted he knew it was there.

In that case, where had it come from?

It *was* an old house. Perhaps it had been there since they'd bought the place, and the garage door had shaken it loose from the rafters. But how could she never have noticed it?

And finally, what was she going to do with it? If she deposited it in the bank, would there be questions? Would she have to claim it on her income tax?

She needed some time to think. To research. To roll around naked in all those bills.

She gathered up the money in two fists, took it into the house and put it in a plastic freezer bag. As an afterthought, she took one of the bills out and tucked it into her bra. She deserved a finder's fee, didn't she?

She emptied a box of freezer-burned hot dogs into the trash and stuffed the money into the box. There.

Betsy ran into the kitchen wearing nothing but fairy wings and hiking boots.

"What's that, Mommy? Are we having hot dogs for a snack?"

"Nope. It's the answer to our prayers." Dannie pushed the box to the back of the freezer, behind a pile of ice pops. It would have to suffice until she figured out what she was going to do with it.

"What did you pray for?" Betsy asked.

"A new water heater."

"That's boring. I would pray for a Moon Bounce. And Emma and Erin are awake."

"Okay. I'll get them."

Betsy stood in the doorway, twisting her hair around her finger. It was a habit she'd picked up from Dannie.

"Was there something else?" Dannie said.

Betsy pointed past her.

Dannie turned around. Quincy had his big head in the trash can, scarfing down frozen hot dogs.

"Hey, save some room for the caviar we're gonna be having tomorrow, Quince."

He looked at her and burped.

"Gross," Betsy said. Then she ran off, her bare bottom the last thing to disappear around the corner.

Dannie pulled the hundred-dollar bill out of her bra and stared at it, still unable to believe she had three hundred and fifteen more just like it in her freezer.

The answer to their prayers.

BY THREE O'CLOCK, Erin had thrown up in the car, Emma had drawn a mural in permanent marker on the bathroom wall and Quincy had knocked over the potted palm in the sunroom.

Betsy was still naked.

By three-thirty, Richard had stuffed a tennis ball into the garbage disposal, ripped seventeen pages out of the phone book and melted a plastic army guy in the microwave.

Betsy was still naked.

By three forty-five, Quincy had eaten the melted army guy, Emma and Erin were fighting and Richard had attempted to climb the living room drapes while dressed in his Spider-Man Halloween costume.

Betsy was still naked.

By four o'clock, Dannie knew exactly what she was going to do with the money in her bra…

Spend it on margaritas.

She picked up the phone and called her friend Roseanna at work. "Rosie, it's Dannie. We're going out tomorrow night."

Chapter Two

ROSEANNA PULLED INTO the parking lot of Caligula, a club in center city Philadelphia, just after Dannie did. They smiled at each other through the windows of their cars—Dannie's beat-up minivan, Roseanna's beat-up Mustang convertible.

"Hey," Dannie said as they climbed out of their cars.

"Hey, yourself," Roseanna said in her husky Greta Garbo voice. "How did you come up with this place?"

Dannie laughed. "One of the girls I work with had her birthday party here a couple of months ago."

"Eighties night is supposed to be awesome. You ready to party?"

"Sure. But if I fall asleep at the table, wake me up, okay?"

Roseanna gave her a sympathetic look. "How's everything going?"

"It's okay. Some days are harder than others. But when you've got four kids under six, it's never easy."

"Where are the little monsters tonight?"

"My in-laws are keeping them until after lunch tomorrow, so I'm a free woman for the next fifteen hours or so."

Roseanna flung her arm over Dannie's shoulder. "Did I ever tell you you're my hero?"

Dannie grinned. "Are you going to start singing Bette Midler songs to me now?"

"You know I don't sing. I just write about the people who do."

"You're a great singer, Rosie. At least, you were in high school."

Roseanna shook her head. "That boat sailed. I'm just a hack now."

"You're a hack who gets paid to write about something you love. I've got a master's degree in fine arts and I'm teaching toddlers how to paint."

"Hey, you're doing what you have to do right now," Roseanna said. "It'll get easier."

"Oh, yeah? When?"

Roseanna was silent for a minute, and then they both burst out laughing.

"Don't listen to me," Roseanna said. "My kid is almost thirteen, and I still don't have a clue."

They got in line behind a group of twentysomething girls in tiny T-shirts who were having a heated discussion about who was the hottest guy on some new reality show.

"Did you call Cecilia?" Roseanna said.

"Yeah. She sounded pretty desperate for a night out, too."

At the door, Roseanna flashed her ID from the music magazine she worked for and the bouncer let them in without paying the cover charge. A moment later they stepped out of a twenty-first-century parking lot and into ancient Rome. That is, if ancient Romans played eighties music.

Hard-bodied waiters and waitresses crisscrossed the room in

togas and leafy headpieces, serving drinks to kids who looked as if they might still play with Barbie dolls and baseballs on occasion.

Rick James's "Super Freak" blared over the sound system. Dannie spied Cecilia at a table, smoking a cigarette and ogling an achingly hot waiter whose biceps looked harder than the marble columns littering the room.

Roseanna grabbed Dannie's arm and dragged her toward the table. "We're going to have a good time tonight if it kills you."

A few minutes later a waiter with a gorgeous butt, wearing a tiny toga, brought the first round of drinks. Luscious-looking pink concoctions called Gladiators.

Cecilia removed the pineapple wedge and took a sip. "Why do they call this a Gladiator?"

Dannie gave her an evil grin. "Because it's gonna kick your ass."

After two rounds the women were on the dance floor, shaking it down to The Escape Club, the Go-Go's and Wang Chung. In the middle of a Madonna song, Roseanna pointed to someone who'd just come in the door.

"Look."

A tall woman in a red silk jacket scanned the crowd. She looked familiar.

"Oh. My. God. It's Grace Poleiski," Dannie said.

"I saw her at Beruglia's when I went there for lunch today," Roseanna said, grinning. "I didn't think you guys would mind if I invited her."

"Are you kidding!" Cecilia laughed. "It's gonna be just like old times."

TURNED OUT TO BE MORE LIKE old times than any of them had imagined it would be.

After a couple more drinks, a few rounds of shots and a nostalgic game of Truth or Dare, Roseanna was passed out, her head resting on a pile of napkins on the table.

Dannie sucked on an ice cube. She needed to cool down after Cecilia's dare, in which she'd talked their waiter, whom they'd lovingly dubbed "Spartacus," into giving her a lap dance. Dannie had been treated to the full frontal view, and she couldn't help noticing Spartacus had more in his toga than starch.

"Tonight's going to go down in history as the best Truth or Dare game ever," she said.

"It is, isn't it?" Cecilia puffed on a cigarette, making tiny smoke rings by tapping on her cheek. She glanced over her shoulder at Grace, who was sucking face at the bar with a scorching-hot stranger. A much, much younger stranger.

They'd dared *her* to give him the undies she was wearing. And by the looks of things, he was hoping to get more.

"I don't believe it," Dannie said. "Look at her. She actually did it."

"She always had guts," Cecilia said, a twinge of envy in her voice.

"She sure did." Dannie wished she had half the guts Grace had, a quarter of Cecilia's self-assurance and a pinch of Roseanna's full-out craziness.

If she had, maybe she could have stood up to Roger better. All the times she wondered where he was, and what he was doing.

And maybe she could stand up to Lyle now. Tell him she just wanted to be friends, nothing more. But it wasn't in her nature. She'd always been a people pleaser. In second grade, when Timmy Burke's dog had died, she'd shown him her underpants just to cheer him up.

"Okay, we've lost Grace," Dannie said. "And Roseanna's no good anymore."

"Doesn't matter," Cecilia said. "You're the only one who hasn't had a turn, and I can handle it. Truth or Dare?"

Dannie slid down in her chair and sucked on the straw of her drink. "I dunno. You pick for me."

Cecilia crushed out her cigarette. "Okay. Truth. I want to know what's going on with you."

"What do you mean?"

Cecilia leaned in. "I know you, Dannie. Something's wrong. Are you missing Roger?"

Dannie snorted. "Yeah. I don't know what I miss more, the lying or the cheating." She stopped herself and shook her head. "Oh, God. I'm sorry. I know I shouldn't speak ill of the dead, but he could be such a shit." She began to cry.

Cecilia pulled a cocktail napkin out from beneath Rose-anna's head and handed it to Dannie. "He cheated on you?"

Dannie nodded. "At least twice that I know of. But probably more than that." She sighed. "He was a good father, though."

And he was. He took the kids to the park almost every weekend. He read to them at night. He changed diapers and wiped noses. She knew from talking to other women that was no small thing, and it gave her something to focus on during the rough times.

She'd always figured they'd get back on track someday. She'd loved him so much when they'd first met, it seemed impossible that they would ever grow apart. But they had, and now it was too late to fix things.

Dannie shrugged. "He just made me feel…small."

"I'm so sorry," Cecilia said. "But you know you could have talked to me about it. Anytime."

"I guess I was embarrassed, which is just silly. Life would be so much better if we could all just share our secrets and get them off our chests. Don't you think?"

"Hmm." Cecilia chewed on an ice cube. "As a matter of fact…"

Dannie dabbed her eyes with the now-soggy napkin. "What? You have a secret, too?"

Cecilia pushed her shot away. "I *have* to sober up."

Dannie squeezed her hand. "Come on. I'm your friend. Maybe I can help."

"Well, the thing is, I'm…" Cecilia sighed. "Well, I'm flat broke."

"Broke?"

Cecilia, with the eighty-thousand-dollar SUV? Cecilia with the five-thousand-square-foot house on the golf course? Cecilia with the closet full of designer clothes and three-hundred-dollar shoes?

Before Roger's death, Dannie had lived comfortably. But Cecilia was *rich*. For her to confess something like this, she must really be hurting.

Dannie considered offering Cecilia some of the cash she'd found, but thought better of it. She was still uncomfortable about not knowing where it had come from.

Face it—she was punking out on the Truth. She wasn't going to tell anyone what was really bothering her. Not the money, or her rocky relationship with Roger, or even her desperation for a new water heater. What was the point? No one could help her. She had to get through this on her own.

So she was going to violate the conditions of the game. Conditions they'd set long ago, when they'd all sworn on their posters of Jon Bon Jovi that they would never lie in a game of Truth or Dare, under severe penalty.

Damn. Now she was going to have to hand over all her Duran Duran albums.

The lap-dancing waiter reappeared, and Dannie motioned him over. "Can we take care of our tab?"

He pulled a leather billfold out of the folds of his toga and handed it to her. She opened the billfold and examined the sales slip inside, completely unable to focus on anything except the waiter's cute butt as he cleared the empty glasses from the table.

Oh, screw it.

She reached into her bra and fished out the hundred-dollar bill, unrolling it before she gave it to him. "Keep the change, Spartacus."

Cecilia raised her eyebrows.

Dannie shrugged. "Mad money."

The two of them danced and sang until they'd sobered up. Then Cecilia went to check on Grace, who was still sucking face with the hot guy.

Behind the bar, Spartacus powwowed with a bartender. He pointed at Dannie, and she gave a little wave.

"Grace is okay," Cecilia said, returning to the table. "She's going to get a cab."

Dannie and Cecilia slung their arms around Roseanna and dragged her through the crowd toward the door.

"Come on, gorgeous," Cecilia said. "Let's try to get you home before you lose your cookies."

They'd just about made it to the door when a man in a dark suit and slicked hair grabbed Dannie's arm.

"Miss, can I speak to you for a minute?"

"I'm not interested," Dannie said, shaking off his grip.

"That's good, because I'm not hitting on you. I'm the club's manager." He leaned close, speaking directly into her ear. "It's about that hundred-dollar bill you gave the waiter."

Chapter Three

DANNIE'S STOMACH DID a little flip. Cecilia gave her a questioning look.

"It's okay. I forgot something at the table," Dannie said. "Can you get Roseanna home?"

"We'll have someone help your friends to their car," said the manager, waving a bouncer over.

Dannie gave Cecilia a quick peck on the cheek. "I'll call you soon, okay?"

The club manager took Dannie's arm, gently but firmly escorting her to the rear of the club, where they ducked behind one of the marble columns. Like magic, they were back in the twenty-first century.

The manager guided her down a long, narrow hallway to a small room she could only assume was his office. It was little more than a converted broom closet—polar opposite to the lavish decor of the club.

Two beat-up filing cabinets on one wall leaned against each other for support, sagging beneath the weight of their contents. A torn desk chair was pushed beneath a scarred wooden table that served as a desk. An old *Playboy* calendar from 2003 hung on the wall above a copy machine.

Spartacus and the bartender he'd been talking to earlier stood beside the desk.

"My name is Patrick, by the way. Patrick Baldwin," the manager said. "No relation to the Baldwin brothers."

He said this seriously, as if he thought he might actually be mistaken for one of "the" Baldwins.

Slim chance of that. This guy resembled a Baldwin brother the way Elvis on velvet resembled a Renoir.

"Mr. Baldwin, may I ask what's going on? I really need to get home."

Baldwin snapped his fingers and held out a hand.

The bartender handed Baldwin a bill, which he smoothed out on the surface of his desk.

"Drew, is this the bill the lady gave you to settle her tab?" Baldwin asked the waiter.

Spartacus nodded.

"Kenny, is this the bill Drew gave you?" Kenny was, apparently, the bartender.

"Yeah," Kenny said.

Baldwin tapped the bill with a manicured finger. "Our procedures require we test all bills of fifty-dollar denominations and greater. We tested this one, and it failed."

"Failed?" Dannie's voice cracked.

"It's counterfeit. You see, we have this pen, and we draw on the bills. If the paper turns brown—"

"It fails."

Baldwin nodded. "We're supposed to call the police and the FBI when something like this happens."

"The police? The FBI? Really?" The blood pounded in Dannie's eardrums.

"They'd probably want to question you."

"But how could I help them? I have no idea where that bill came from." Dannie swallowed, but her throat was as dry as her mother-in-law's Thanksgiving turkey.

"You got a hundred-dollar bill and you don't know where it came from?" Drew asked.

"Do you keep track of where all your money comes from?" Dannie said.

"But this is a hundred-dollar bill," Baldwin said. "There aren't many places you get a hundred-dollar bill, am I right? That's not chump change."

Dannie twisted the strap on her handbag, trying to think. What would she tell the authorities? *I found it in a golf bag in my garage, and I have three hundred and fifteen more just like it?*

It couldn't go that far. It just couldn't.

"Listen," she said. "I probably got it from my boss. I get paid under the table for watching her kids. I can't tell the cops it's from her, though. I'll get fired if I bring her into it, and I really need that job, you know?"

Baldwin shrugged. "Not my problem."

"Can you just…" Dannie took a deep breath. "Can't you forget about it? I can pay for the drinks on my credit card, and we can just tear that money up."

"Sorry. No can do."

He seemed amused, as if he was enjoying making her squirm. Dannie gave Drew and Kenny a pleading look.

Drew took pity on her. Or maybe he was bucking for a

better tip. "What's the big deal, Mr. Baldwin? Why can't we just let this slide?"

Baldwin sucked something out of his teeth, and glared at Drew. "We're supposed to fill out an incident report."

"You hate filling out reports," Kenny said, clearly irritated.

Dannie was beginning to think this wasn't so much about her as it was about Baldwin's management skills. Or lack of them.

His employees obviously couldn't stand him.

"Now that I think about it," Drew said, "I can't really be sure this lady's the one who gave me that bill."

"Yeah," Kenny said. "And I'm not positive Drew's the one who gave it to *me*."

Baldwin's face turned red. "That's bull. You just told me it was her ten minutes ago." His thick neck bulged over the collar of his shirt.

"I think I made a mistake," Drew said. "Sorry."

"It's really dark in the club, man," said Kenny. "Honest mistake."

Dannie sensed Baldwin weakening. Confusion setting in. She went for the kill.

"Mr. Baldwin, do you really want to call the police? Some of those people drinking out there seem awfully young. Are you sure they all have ID?"

Baldwin looked stricken. "I guess the police have better things to do on a Friday night than waste their time on something like this."

Dannie held her breath.

The room was silent except for the beat of the music they could hear through the walls—Billy Idol's "Dancing with Myself."

Dannie had a feeling a guy like Baldwin could relate intimately to that song.

Finally Kenny said, "Yo, can I get back to work now? Maria's in the weeds out there."

"Go ahead," Baldwin said. "You, too, Drew. I'll take care of the lady's bill."

Dannie gave Drew and Kenny grateful looks as they filed past her out of the small office.

Baldwin shook his head. He was clearly a man who hadn't figured out how to use his power yet. "What the hell just happened here?"

Dannie gave him a small smile. "You gave a hardworking mother a break?"

Baldwin chewed on that for a minute. "I guess I'm a pretty nice guy, huh?"

Wow, did he have issues.

"The nicest," Dannie said sweetly.

Baldwin picked up the hundred-dollar bill and ripped it in half, and then in half again. "Go on. Get out of here."

"What about my drinks?" Dannie asked.

Baldwin grinned. "Don't worry about it. They're on the two nimrods who just left."

Dannie pushed blindly through the club and out into the damp darkness of the parking lot, thinking only of escape. But when she climbed into the car her hands shook too badly to turn the key in the ignition.

She started laughing uncontrollably. Didn't it just figure?

Turned out the answer to her prayers was counterfeit.

THERE WAS NO WAY she could sleep.

Dannie pulled the last of Roger's suit jackets off its hanger and dug through the pockets.

Empty.

She threw the jacket onto the bed with the others she'd already searched. Out of nine suits—forty-five pockets in all—

she'd found seventeen cents, three toothpicks, a receipt for a ten-dollar cigar and one fuzz-covered mint.

She sank to the floor of the closet and buried her face in her hands. She had no idea what she was looking for. A business card from Joe Counterfeiter, maybe?

It was almost morning. Thank God her in-laws had the kids. She didn't think she could deal with dirty diapers and Saturday-morning cartoons after the night she'd had.

Quincy wandered into the closet, flopped down next to her and started chewing on a hanger.

Dannie stretched out, resting her head on Roger's gym bag. She had to find something. Some sort of clue as to where the money had come from.

Where should she look next? The attic? The basement? Roger's underwear drawer?

Or maybe she should just call Lyle.

Lyle knew Roger as well as she did. Maybe better. They'd been best friends since they were in college. If Roger had been involved in something, Lyle would know about it.

She fished her cell phone out of a pocket of the sweats she'd changed into when she'd come home from the bar. The time flashed in bright green on the screen: 5:19 a.m.

Too bad for Lyle, because there was no way she was going to wait for a more decent hour. Still lying on her back, she punched in the speed-dial code for his home number.

"Mungh?" Lyle slurred, his voice rough with sleep.

"Lyle, it's Dannie. Sorry to wake you, but I have to ask you something."

"Mmm. Dannie. What time is it?"

"Early. Listen, was Roger involved in anything illegal?"

"What?"

She heard rustling, and imagined Lyle sitting up in bed in a pair of blue pajamas, fumbling for his glasses, his thinning brown hair sticking up.

"What do you mean, anything illegal?" he said.

She tapped the phone with her fingernail, debating how much she should tell him. "I found something…unexpected when I was going through Roger's stuff. I'm not sure what to think."

"Like what? Drugs?"

Dannie bolted upright, bumping her head on the shirt bar. "He was doing *drugs?*"

"No! No, of course not."

"Then why did you say drugs?"

Lyle exhaled into the receiver. "It's just the first thing that came to mind, I guess."

"Oh." Dannie flopped back onto the gym bag.

"You want to tell me what it is you did find?" Lyle said.

"I'm not sure."

"You're not sure what you found, or you're not sure you want to tell me?"

"I'm not sure I want to tell you."

Lyle was silent for a few moments. "Dannie, you know you can tell me anything. I'm here for you. You can trust me."

"I know." She pulled a string dangling from the pant leg of her sweats. It kept unraveling. "Okay. All right. I found some money."

"Money?"

"A lot of money. But…"

"But what?"

"It's not real."

"What do you mean, it's not real?"

"It's fake money. Counterfeit."

"Jesus. How do you know?"

Dannie twisted the string around the tip of her finger. "I tried to use some. Last night, when I went out with some friends. I gave the waiter a hundred-dollar bill, and the manager stopped me at the door on the way out of the club."

"What did he do?"

"He read me the riot act. Threatened to call the police and the FBI and everything, but I convinced him not to."

"Did he take your name?"

"No."

"So he can't trace you? Doesn't know where you live?"

"I can't see how he would."

"Good. Great." Lyle's breathing quickened on the other end.

"Are you okay?" Dannie said.

"Yeah. Of course. I'm just worried about you, Dano. I don't want you to get in trouble."

Dano.

That's what Roger used to call her. Lyle had started using the name after Roger's death. In fact, he'd filled the void left by Roger's absence in lots of ways.

He was the man around the house, fixing the things he could, finding others to fix them when he couldn't. He was the date she always had. The shoulder she could always cry on.

He was great in almost every way.

The one exception was his discomfort around the kids. He just didn't seem to know how to act around them, which wasn't, she supposed, unusual for a forty-two-year-old bachelor. Otherwise he'd done a very respectable job of taking care of them.

She'd be lost without him.

Dannie knew Lyle would like to become more than a friend. He'd begun to introduce the idea, gently but persistently, over the past couple of months.

She just couldn't do it. It would feel as if she was betraying Roger. And as much of a jerk as he'd been, she still missed him. A lot.

But although she couldn't bring herself to get closer to Lyle, she couldn't let him go, either. She needed the comfort he provided too desperately.

"I'm coming over," he said.

"No, Lyle. Please. The kids are with Elizabeth and Albert, and I just want to sleep." Dannie twisted the string tighter around the tip of her finger until it turned purple.

Lyle hesitated. She could tell he was deciding whether or not to press the issue. Finally he relented. "Okay. But call me later. We should talk about all this."

"Okay. Will do."

She closed the phone and unraveled the string from her finger, letting the blood circulate. It throbbed with relief.

She wished there was a string to unravel from her heart.

DANNIE WOKE to the sound of the phone ringing.

She opened one eye to find herself facedown on Roger's suits on the bed. Quincy still lay in the closet, snoring, a mangled patent-leather pump between his paws. She checked her watch. Eight forty-five.

She rolled over and grabbed the phone, clearing her throat before she spoke.

"Hello?"

"Is this Mrs. Roger Treat?" The voice was male. Calm, but intense.

"Yes. Who is this?"

"Does your husband belong to Main Street Gym?"

"He did. But he passed away in February."

"We need to talk."

She rubbed her eyes. "Listen, if this is about his membership fees—"

"It's not about that. I have some information that might interest you."

Dannie sat up on the bed. "What kind of information?"

"I'd rather not talk about it over the phone. Can we meet at the gym in half an hour or so?"

"I don't think so. I don't make a habit of meeting men I don't know in places I don't know."

"You name the time and place, then."

She sighed. "What is this about again?"

"Your husband. And my wife. And what they were doing together."

The blood drained from Dannie's head. She felt woozy. She lay back down on the suits.

"Mrs. Treat?"

"Myrna's Diner, on Bethlehem Pike. Nine-thirty," she said, and hung up.

Myrna's was a functional brick box with functional square windows evenly spaced across the front of the building. Diners framed in each window could have been paintings in a gallery installment, with titles like *Couple Arguing Over Patio Furniture,* or *Grandma Stealing Sugar,* or *College Students with Hangovers.*

Dannie wasn't doing so hot herself. Too many Gladiators, not enough sleep. She slipped on her sunglasses and crossed the lot, taking the concrete stairs two at a time. She had no idea how she was going to recognize the caller, who she'd discovered was G. Loughran, according to her caller ID.

An elderly man with a cane exited the diner, holding the door open for her with shaking hands. Chivalry was not dead. Just really, really old.

Warm, greasy air leached out around her, luring her in. Dannie drifted through the door as if in a trance, drawn less by curiosity than the smell of bacon.

Stress always made her hungry.

She took a calming breath, telling herself that no matter what the outcome of this meeting, nothing would change.

So she might have proof that Roger had been cheating on her again. So what? She'd known it on some level anyway. Having proof wouldn't change the fact that he was dead. That she'd loved him, despite his flaws. That the kids had loved him.

She really didn't even know why she was here.

She was about to turn around and leave when the hostess caught her.

"Hiya. Seat for one?"

"I'm meeting someone, actually." Dannie scanned the tables. "I'm not sure what he looks like."

"Ah." The hostess winked an eye thick with black liner and mascara. "A blind date."

"Not exactly. Do you have any single men?"

"I wish."

"I mean at the tables."

"Oh! Gotcha." The hostess pointed to a table in the far corner. "Just him."

G. Loughran. It had to be.

The man was lean and rumpled, twisting a paper napkin between his fingers. His hair was thinning; his eyes bore the haunted look of a husband scorned.

Dannie took a deep breath to bolster her nerve, but before she could move she heard a voice behind her.

"Mrs. Treat?"

She turned and found herself up against a solid wall of muscle wrapped in a pink T-shirt that read "Hair Technicians Do It with Style."

She looked up, into the most unusual eyes she'd ever seen.

Light blue at the edges, deepening to green in the center. Warm and exotic and exciting, like a cruise to the Caribbean.

His hair was blond and he would have been perfect, except that his nose was crooked, as if it might have been broken once, giving him a sort of bad-boy-surfer look. It was all finished off with a heart-stopping dimple on the cheek.

He had to be gay. The universe seemed determined to play those kinds of jokes on women.

His voice was low and rumbly, like distant thunder. And when he shook her hand? Lightning.

Definitely lightning. And definitely not gay.

"I'm a guy," he said.

"No kidding."

He gave her a quizzical look. "Guy Loughran. I called you this morning?"

"Oh! Not *a* guy. Your *name* is Guy! Well, it's fitting, isn't it? I mean you're tall, and with that voice, and you have…wow… really nice muscles and—okay, I'm babbling. I'm sorry. Can we sit? I'm really hungry."

"Sure."

Guy motioned to the hostess, who stood beside Dannie drooling slightly, clutching a menu to her chest.

"Nice manicure," Guy told the hostess. "Who did it?"

"A girl at Kim's Nails. Her name's Terri."

Guy nodded knowingly. "She's good."

The two chatted about local salons as the hostess led them to a table. Dannie thought how odd it was to listen to a man who looked like a professional football player talk so knowledgeably about hair and manicures.

Obviously it didn't bother the hostess. She giggled like a thirteen-year-old at her first school dance.

Guy squeezed his sizable frame into one side of a booth at

a window, and Dannie slid into the other. They opened their menus. Dannie wondered what they looked like from outside. What their title might read, if they were a painting. Maybe *Man and Woman Stare at Menus in Awkward Silence*. Or *A Meeting About an Affair*.

A waitress wearing an itchy-looking blue nylon blouse appeared to take their orders. Fresh fruit, plain yogurt and orange juice for Guy, the logger's breakfast for Dannie.

"You can eat all that?" Guy asked, sounding impressed. Or was it repulsed?

"I eat when I'm stressed out," Dannie said defensively. "It's a little trick my mother taught me. Food fixes everything."

"If you treat your body like a vehicle and give it only the best fuel, you'll get the most mileage out of it," Guy said.

"Yeah, well. I don't drive much. I just idle at the curb."

The waitress, who giggled almost as much as the hostess, brought a pot of coffee. Dannie nodded. Guy declined. Apparently caffeine wasn't an acceptable form of fuel, either.

"So what's this all about, Mr. Loughran?" Dannie said when the waitress had gone.

"Call me Guy." He leaned in, staring into her eyes.

A little shiver ran up her spine, and she entertained the notion of biting his full bottom lip.

Until he said, "I believe your husband and my wife had an affair."

The spell was broken. She leaned back in her seat. "Really? What makes you think so?"

Guy reached into the back pocket of his black pants and withdrew a folded a piece of paper. He spread it out on the table and pushed it toward her. It was a grainy photo, printed on plain white copy paper, of a man and a woman kissing beside a rack of free weights.

"It's from the Main Street Gym's security camera," Guy said. "I know the owner, and he was good enough to print this out for me."

The man's face was clear in the picture, but only the back of the woman's head was visible.

Dannie nodded. "It's Roger."

"And that's Lisa," Guy said. "And I'll tell you something else. I think it's still going on."

Dannie sighed. "I told you on the phone, my husband died in February. He was washed overboard from a fishing charter, and drowned."

Guy shook his head. "I don't think so."

Chapter Four

DANNIE FELT HER STOMACH clench. "That's just...just *sick*."

Guy was silent.

"How dare you disrespect my husband's memory like that?" She stood, but Loughran grabbed her wrist.

"Did they ever find his body?" he asked.

Dannie wrenched her wrist from his grasp. "Are you crazy?"

"I'm sorry," he said, a note of pleading in his voice. "Just hear me out."

Against her better judgment, Dannie sank back onto the red leather seating.

"I know this is a shock, but just listen." He leaned over the table. His voice was low and even.

"My wife worked at the Main Street Gym. She was a trainer. About a year ago she introduced me to your husband. I didn't pay much attention at the time because she was always introducing me to people, but when I heard that a local guy had drowned in Cuatro Blanco, I remembered the name."

"Yeah? And?"

"And it still didn't mean much. But my wife had taken off two days before your husband drowned. And a couple of days ago, when I was at my mother-in-law's house, I happened to see a package waiting to be mailed. To Cuatro Blanco."

"So what? I don't understand what that has to do with Roger. I'm sorry your wife left you, but she wouldn't be the first disgruntled spouse to run off to a tropical island."

"Look at the facts. My wife and your husband knew each other. They were probably having an affair. My wife takes off. Then your husband drowns two days later on some obscure island in the Caribbean, but they don't find his body. And then I find out my mother-in-law is sending a package to that same obscure island. Don't you think that's a little odd?"

The waitress reappeared with a tray. She set the lumberjack's breakfast—two eggs, two pancakes, two pieces of toast and two slices of bacon—in front of Guy, and the yogurt in front of Dannie. They waited for her to leave before they switched.

"I find *you* to be very odd, Mr. Loughran. You didn't know my husband at all. You obviously don't know how devoted he was to me and our children. He would never do something like you're suggesting."

Guy stabbed a chunk of melon with his fork. "I've learned never to say never, Mrs. Treat."

Dannie shoveled a forkful of eggs into her mouth.

"For instance," he went on as he picked the blueberries out of his fruit salad, "I never thought The Who would get back together for a reunion tour. I never thought that after I earned a master's degree in business management I'd be cutting hair.

And I never thought that when I opened my safe one day, all my cash would be gone, replaced with counterfeit."

Dannie nearly choked on a piece of bacon. "What did you say?"

Guy looked up from his breakfast. "What? About The Who reunion tour?"

"No. The other thing. The counterfeit money."

Guy shook his head. "It doesn't matter."

"Go ahead. Tell me."

He leaned back and stretched one arm across the padded back of the booth seat. "I had money in a safe. Money I'd saved to put toward building my own salon. A day spa, actually. And then a couple of months after Lisa left me, I go to pay my contractor with that money, and he comes back a few days later and tells me it was all counterfeit."

"Counterfeit?" Dannie had never actually fainted, but she was pretty sure that was about to change.

"Fake. Copies from a copier. Damned good ones, but fake just the same."

Dannie took a slug of her coffee, and held her mug up to signal the waitress to bring more. "Wait a minute. You pay your contractor in cash?"

Guy stared out the window at the parking lot. "Yeah, well. We have a little arrangement. It's not exactly…"

"Legal?"

"Right. But he's cheap and he's good, so I don't ask too many questions."

Dannie dabbed the corners of her mouth with her napkin. She leaned in. "Was Lisa…into anything? Drugs or anything like that?"

"Drugs? No, I don't think so. She was into men. And the beach, and clothes and shoes. But drugs? No."

Dannie stared out the window at the traffic speeding past.

Guy tapped his fingertips on the table. "Listen, I just have a feeling they're together. With my money. And I need to find her, because I need to get that money back."

"To pay for your salon?"

"Day spa," he corrected.

"Why don't you just hire a private investigator?"

Guy shook his head. "I don't have that kind of money. Do you?"

"No." Not *real* money, anyway.

"I'm going down to Cuatro Blanco to look for her. I'm using my frequent flyer miles, and I have enough to get you a ticket, too, if you want to go with me."

"Why in God's name would I want to do that?" she said.

"To help me look for them. With two of us, we could cover more ground. You'd know where to look for Roger. What he likes to do, places he'd most likely go."

"How about the bottom of the ocean?" she said. "Because that's where he is." Her eyes filled with tears.

"Oh, jeez. Don't cry, all right? I'm sorry. I didn't mean to upset you."

"What did you think would happen? That I'd be thrilled to hear someone tell me he thinks my husband faked his death to get away from me?" She filched a tissue from her purse and blew her nose.

"Hey, I'm just calling it like I see it. A little dose of reality."

"Well, thanks." She tossed her tissue onto her plate. "I almost confused my life with paradise, what with four kids to support on minimum wage, the insurance company that won't pay up and the two-hundred-year-old house falling down around me that I can't sell because I still haven't received a death certificate from the Caribbean Keystone Cops." Her voice had risen almost to a pitch that could be heard only by dogs. "I really needed a dose of reality."

"I'm sorry," Guy said. And he looked as if he meant it. "I guess it's been a difficult time for you since your husband's…"

"Death."

"Right. Forgive me." He pulled his wallet out of his back pocket and threw two tens on the table. "I hope everything works out okay for you."

And then he just walked away, leaving Dannie alone with half a lumberjack's breakfast and an ache in her chest that felt as if she'd just lost Roger all over again.

As soon as Dannie got home, she ran up to the closet and found Roger's duffel bag from the gym. She ripped open the zipper and dumped the contents out onto the floor of the closet.

The odor from Roger's eight-month-old sweaty socks hit her like a frying pan to the face. When she recovered from the smell, she examined the pile.

Shorts. T-shirt. Sneakers. Deodorant. Hairbrush. Mouthwash. A receipt for bottled water from the juice bar.

With a phone number written on the back.

She grabbed her cordless phone and scrolled through the numbers in the caller ID box.

Dear God.

The number on the receipt matched the last one on her phone—G. Loughran.

Dannie stumbled down the stairs to the kitchen and poured herself a tumbler of scotch. A very large tumbler. Then she went out onto the patio and called Lyle.

"Tell me what he said again, exactly."

Lyle grilled her on the other end of the connection as Dannie lay on a lounge chair with a damp towel over her eyes, trying to get rid of the persistent headache she'd had since her meeting with Guy Loughran.

It was a warm October day, and she should have been getting some work done around the house before her in-laws brought the kids home. Quincy lay beside her, drool pooling on the flagstone beneath his mouth.

"It's not even worth repeating," Dannie said to Lyle. "He's crazy. To think Roger's still alive, abandoning his kids like that. It's insane."

"Absolutely," Lyle said. "Still, maybe you *should* go down there. Try to get the authorities to issue you a death certificate. It's the only way you're going to get the insurance company to pay you."

"I wish I'd gone down there when Roger died."

"Dano, we talked about that. Your lawyer and I agreed there was nothing you could do there. You were needed more here."

It was true. The twins had been so young, and still nursing. It would have been hard to leave them. And, of course, she'd had to plan a memorial service. Roger had been well liked around town. People expected something nice.

Dannie took the towel off her eyes, blinking against the blinding sun. "What am I going to do with the kids, and Quincy? I can't just hop on a plane."

"Sure you can. Your in-laws could watch them for a couple of days."

"Elizabeth hates Quincy."

"Well, I'll watch him for you. Or maybe I should come with you."

"Come with me?"

"Yeah." Lyle hesitated. "Dannie, this whole thing stinks. The counterfeit thing. The authorities dragging their feet on the death certificate. I don't know about you, but I would love some answers. The sooner the better, too."

Dannie could picture Lyle's face, puckered into a frown, the tiny lines forming on his forehead above his wire-rimmed glasses.

"You'd really go with me?"

"Of course. Roger meant the world to me. You do, too. I want to help you. I'm your friend."

And I want to be more.

Lyle's unspoken words hung in the dead air of the phone connection. Dannie knew his feelings. He'd confessed them to her once, when they'd both had a little too much wine.

"Lyle…"

"No strings. I'll get on the phone right now and get us some tickets. Okay?"

Dannie sighed. "I'll talk to Elizabeth when she brings the kids back today."

IT HADN'T BEEN HARD TO convince her in-laws to take the kids again. And her friend Cecilia had come through in a pinch to take Quincy. Although Cecilia had looked just a tiny bit terrified when Dannie had shown up with him.

Now, less than twenty-four hours after she'd met Guy Loughran at Myrna's, she was standing in the Philadelphia International Airport, on her way to the island where her husband had drowned.

"How much did you have to pay for these tickets?" Dannie asked as she and Lyle stood in line at the Air Caribbean ticket counter early Sunday morning. "They must have been expensive on such short notice."

"Don't worry about it."

"I'm going to pay you back." She had no idea how, but she would.

"I know you will." Lyle threw his arm around her shoulder

and gave her a brotherly hug. "Let's just hope we can accomplish something while we're there. We have a little less than two days. I have to be back to work on Tuesday."

Lyle was the regional manager for an office supply company, a job that had him traveling two or three days a week. Dannie was sure the last thing he wanted to do was spend half his long weekend on a plane.

"You're sweet," Dannie said, and gave him a peck on the cheek.

"That's what they all say."

"You know, I never asked you. You're a member of the Main Street Gym, too. Did you know Lisa Loughran?"

Lyle shifted from foot to foot, clearly uncomfortable with the question. "I'm not sure. I guess I'd have to see a picture of her." He pulled a twenty out of his wallet and handed it to Dannie. "Why don't you stock up on magazines and gum while I check our luggage?"

"Okay."

She'd let him off the hook this time. She knew he was caught in the middle, not wanting to be disloyal to Roger's memory.

Men would always stick together, even when death do them part. They were more faithful to each other than to their wives.

Dannie turned around, bumping into a dark-haired woman in big black sunglasses.

"Going to Cuatro Blanco?" the woman asked.

"Yes."

"I hear it's beautiful. Have you ever been there before?"

"No. This will be my first time."

The woman gave her a little smile. "Have fun."

Dannie headed for the newsstand, but stopped short. Guy Loughran stood near the magazine rack, thumbing through a copy of *Cosmopolitan*.

His blond hair was gelled into spikes in the front, and he

wore a long-sleeved pink oxford shirt—what was with him and pink shirts?—and jeans. In profile, his nose looked perfectly straight. He chewed on his lower lip as he read.

Dannie didn't know if she wanted to punch him or kiss him.

She sidled up next to him, but he was so absorbed in the magazine that he didn't notice her.

"Good article?" she said.

He looked up, startled. "Mrs. Treat!"

"Call me Dannie." She pointed to the magazine. "Do you read *Cosmo* often?"

"All the time. I have a subscription, but I didn't get to read this issue yet."

Not a hint of embarrassment. She wondered what in the world could possibly threaten a man's masculinity more than reading about managing PMS.

She shook her head, reaching past him for the latest issue of *Sports Illustrated*.

"Do you read *Sports Illustrated* often?" he countered.

"It's not for me. It's for a friend."

"Sure it is." He grinned, that sexy little dimple appearing on the side of his mouth. Dannie's heart nearly stopped.

She had to get away from this man. This infuriating, irritating, annoyingly attractive man. But just then, Lyle materialized behind her. "Hey. I couldn't get two seats together, but they're close."

"Lyle." Dannie hooked her elbow through his. "This is Guy Loughran. Guy, this is Lyle Faraday. He was a good friend of my husband's."

"And a good friend of Dannie's," Lyle said, proffering his hand.

Guy shook it. "Nice to meet you." He turned back to Dannie. "What are you doing here? Did you change your mind? Are you going to Cuatro Blanco?"

"*We're* going to Cuatro Blanco," Lyle said. "I convinced Dannie that she needs to go, to settle things once and for all."

Guy gave a half smile. "I take it you don't believe Roger is alive, either."

"Not a chance," Lyle said.

Guy shrugged. "Well, I guess I'll see you around." He took his *Cosmo* and headed for the check-out line.

"So that's the guy you met yesterday?"

"Uh-huh."

"He's big."

"Yep."

"He reads *Cosmopolitan?*"

"Apparently so."

"What a fruitcake."

Dannie opened her mouth to protest, but what could she say? The man wore pink shirts. He talked to hostesses about manicures. He wanted to open a beauty parlor. He read *Cosmopolitan,* and didn't seem the least bit embarrassed by any of it.

He was a man truly in touch with his feminine side, which made him insanely appealing. She didn't need to witness the drooling looks he got from every female under the age of a hundred to realize that.

She snagged a *Vanity Fair* from the magazine rack for herself. "Come on. I need some chocolate."

Chapter Five

AS IT TURNED OUT, Dannie had a window seat beside Guy on the plane, while Lyle sat directly behind them.

Lyle poked his head around Guy's seat and talked over him, addressing Dannie. "Everything okay up here?"

"Don't worry, man. I'm not going to attack her," Guy said.

"I wasn't suggesting you would," Lyle said. "But Dannie doesn't like to fly."

"Really?" Guy turned to her. "Why not?"

"It's a control issue," she said.

Guy nodded. "That makes sense."

"What is that supposed to mean?"

"I don't know." Guy flipped through the pages of his *Cosmo.* "You seem like the controlling type."

"I am *not* the controlling type! Far from it. Tell him, Lyle."

"She's not the controlling type," Lyle said.

"Okay."

Dannie opened her mouth to give Guy a piece of her mind, then snapped it shut. What was the point? She slouched down in her seat.

"So what sort of things did your husband like to do?" Guy asked her.

"Why do you want to know?"

"Just looking for a jumping-off point."

Dannie huffed. "He's not alive."

Guy shrugged.

Lyle leaned around Guy's seat again. "Dannie, do you want your magazine?"

"The *Sports Illustrated?*" Guy said.

"That's mine," Lyle said.

"Really?" Guy sounded as if he might not believe this.

"Lyle is a huge sports fan," Dannie said.

"Huh," Guy said. "I wouldn't have guessed that."

"What's *that* supposed to mean?" Lyle's face turned red.

Dannie reached across Guy and took her magazine from Lyle, giving his hand a little squeeze. "Thanks."

Lyle sat back in his seat, but Dannie knew he was fuming. An image of him as the skinny little guy in the back of the comic books she used to read when she was a kid popped into her head. The guy who always got sand kicked in his face.

She gave Guy a nasty look, but he was too engrossed in an article about the pros and cons of bikini waxing to notice.

The pilot's voice filtered out from the overhead speakers.

"Good morning, passengers. I hope you're enjoying your flight. At this time we're working with the FAA to chart a different course to Cuatro Blanco, due to a tropical storm picking up strength over the western Caribbean."

Dannie sat up straight in her seat.

Lyle leaned forward, peering around Guy to give her a reassuring look. "Don't worry. This happens all the time."

The pilot continued. "Please pay attention to your flight attendants as they explain some important safety precautions."

A few minutes later a pretty flight attendant with red hair and long legs began the safety orientation, which most of the other passengers ignored. But not Guy, Dannie noticed with some satisfaction. His eyes were riveted on the flight attendant.

He was afraid, too! He just didn't want to admit it.

Dannie glanced out the window. If the plane went down, was there any chance a floating seat cushion would save her? Jesus, she hated the ocean.

When the flight attendant finished her spiel, Guy waved her over.

"I couldn't help but notice your hair color," he said. "Is that a henna rinse?"

"As a matter of fact, it is! How did you know?"

"He's opening his own hair salon," Dannie said bitterly.

"Day spa," Guy corrected.

The flight attendant, who introduced herself as Bunny, crouched down beside Guy's seat. He ran his fingers through the ends of her hair, suggesting a treatment for her dry ends, complimenting her on her makeup.

She pulled a pen out of the pocket of her jacket and wrote a phone number on Guy's hand. "I'll be in Cuatro Blanco overnight. Here's my cell number if you want to get together."

She gave him a little wave as she went off to serve beverages.

Lyle poked his head around the back of Guy's seat again. "Do you need anything, Dannie?"

Lord, yes. She needed sugar. Desperately. "I'll take a candy bar."

Lyle handed it to Guy to pass to her, but Guy held it just

out of her reach. "I have an extra granola bar, if you'd rather have that."

"I don't think so." She grabbed the chocolate.

Guy shook his head. "If I were you, I wouldn't eat that."

"Why don't you leave her alone?" Lyle said. "She's a big girl. She can make her own decisions."

Guy shrugged. "Whatever. But eating sugar and drinking alcohol while you're flying is going to give you a headache."

TURNED OUT GUY WAS RIGHT. Dannie did have a headache when they landed, but she suspected it was mostly because of the turbulence. That, and Guy and Lyle bickering through most of the flight.

When they disembarked in Cuatro Blanco, the tarmac was little more than a narrow strip of black in the middle of a sea of sand, worn shiny by airplane tires and the shoes of tourists eager to start their Caribbean vacations.

It was hot. Ungodly so. And humid beyond anything Dannie had ever experienced in Philadelphia, which was really saying something.

By the time they reached the tiny airport terminal, Dannie wanted nothing more than to peel her clothes off and stand naked in front of an air conditioner. Too bad the one in the terminal wasn't working.

The place bordered on chaotic as tourists, natives and small farm animals jostled for space against the walls while golf carts pulling flatbed wagons piled with luggage inched toward the baggage claim area.

A television bolted to the wall near a waiting area showed a weather map in motion. The big green swirl that had formed off the coast of Florida the day before had moved west across the Caribbean, and now lingered near the tip of Cuba.

Little green ovals dotted the blue expanse of ocean.

"Which of those islands is Cuatro Blanco?" Dannie asked Lyle, pointing at the screen.

"I don't know. But thank God we only have carry-on," Lyle said. "Did you see the line at the baggage claim?" He grabbed Dannie's hand. "Come on. We don't want to miss the shuttle bus to the hotel."

"Where are you staying?" Guy asked, his long strides keeping him effortlessly beside them.

Lyle glared at him. "El Pelícano. Not that it's any of your business."

"Hey, that's where I'm staying, too. I guess we'll be on the same shuttle."

"Great," Dannie said in a tone that clearly indicated it wasn't.

"Maybe we can hook up tonight. Compare notes," Guy said.

"I don't think so," Lyle said. "Come on, Dano. Let's find a taxi instead."

"See you around." Guy headed toward the shuttle desk.

"There's something about that guy that gets under my skin," Lyle said.

"Mine, too." Dannie watched him walk away, loath to admit she enjoyed the view. And not only because he was moving away from her.

She and Lyle reached the far end of the terminal, stepping out onto a tiny slab of cracked cement. A breeze had kicked up, swirling gritty dust around their ankles.

A native Cuatro Blancan, a dark-haired, brown-eyed Antonio Banderas look-alike, stood at a small wooden stand near the street.

"Can we get a taxi?" Lyle asked.

"A taxi. Sí. In one hour."

"In an hour? Why will it take an hour?"

"It is siesta now."

"Jesus," Lyle muttered.

The man at the taxi stand grinned. "Do you know our saying on Cuatro Blanco? 'Take it easy, amigo!'"

Lyle turned red. He wasn't the kind to take it easy.

"Why don't we just get the shuttle bus?" Dannie suggested.

They wheeled their luggage back to the shuttle desk, where dozens of tourists snaked through a rope maze, fanning themselves with brochures, sitting on their suitcases. There was no one behind the desk.

"Siesta time," said the guy in front of them, nodding his head knowingly. He wore a blue-and-red Hawaiian shirt. Sweat poured from his forehead, soaking the brim of his khaki fishing hat.

"What do they do, sleep behind the counter?" Lyle said.

"I don't know if they actually sleep," the guy said. "I think it's more like a long coffee break."

"You'd think if they drank that much coffee, things would move a little quicker around here." Lyle dropped his luggage in disgust.

Dannie grabbed a hair band out of her giant purse, raked the curls off the back of her neck and twisted them into a small bun. Then she pulled out two bottles of water and handed one to Lyle.

"I can't believe the stuff you've got in there," he said.

Dannie took a swig of her water. "Look. There's Guy, over by the waiting area."

He spotted her and motioned her over.

She pretended not to see him, until he started shouting her name.

"I'll be right back." She left Lyle and her luggage in line and went over to Guy.

"Bad news," he said. "The lady at the shuttle desk told me that tropical storm just got upgraded to a category 1 hurricane."

"So?"

"So it was tracking to the north, but it took a sudden turn about an hour ago. Right now it's heading straight for Cuatro Blanco."

BY THE TIME THEY BOARDED the hotel shuttle—a dented, rust-eaten blue school bus with a cross-eyed pelican painted on the hood—the wind had kicked up.

Palm trees bent low across the unpaved roads, the green fronds brushing the roof of the bus as they bumped toward the hotel. Dust swirled up around them, making it almost impossible to see the surrounding countryside. Just as the bus rolled up to El Pelícano, fat raindrops pelted the windows, picking up frequency as their group disembarked.

Two men carrying a large sheet of plywood disappeared around the corner of the hotel. Dannie held her suitcase over her head and ran for the door, Guy and Lyle trailing behind her. They'd almost made it to the wide blue doors when the skies opened up.

Guy shook the rain from his hair. Lyle shed his sport jacket and flung it over his shoulder.

"Is this the hurricane?" Dannie asked.

"Not yet," said Guy. "It's still a few hours away. This is just a pop-up storm. They have them all the time in tropical climates."

The lobby of El Pelícano looked much like the terminal at the airport—crowded, noisy and chaotic. Bellhops in red uniforms pushed carts piled with luggage through knots of people. Everyone seemed to be discussing the same thing—the hurricane.

"Maybe we can get something accomplished before the

storm hits," Lyle said. "Why don't you go see what you can find out while I check us in?"

Dannie worked her way to the concierge desk. A pretty young woman, her dark hair piled into a thick ponytail on top of her head, smiled at her from behind the counter. "Welcome to Cuatro Blanco!"

"Thanks. Listen, I need to get to a town called El Cuello. What would be the best way to get there?"

"The ferry would be fastest, but you just missed the last one. It won't run again until the storm passes."

"What about a taxi, or a bus?"

The young woman shook her head. "I'm afraid you won't be able to get anywhere very easily until the threat of the hurricane has gone."

"Okay. Thank you."

"Take it easy, amiga!"

On her way back to Lyle and Guy, a sleepy-looking teenager in cutoff denim shorts and a red shirt, sporting a hotel name tag, handed Dannie a flyer.

"Hurricane party in the Playa Lounge! Complimentary food, Cuatro coladas and dancing! Take it easy, amiga!"

"Shouldn't we stay in our rooms during the storm? I mean, won't it be dangerous?" Dannie asked.

"Our lounge is the safest place in the hotel, *señora*. Very sturdy. Besides, it's going to be a great party!"

"Wonderful," Dannie muttered. She crossed the lobby to where Lyle still waited in the check-in line, which hadn't moved an inch. He looked even more aggravated than when she'd left.

"The concierge said public transportation has stopped running for today. I don't think we're going to make it." She handed the flyer to Lyle. "Look at this."

"Where are you trying to go?" Guy asked.

"None of your business," Dannie said.

Guy's face was carefully neutral.

"He isn't alive," she said.

Guy shrugged. "Okay. He isn't alive."

Lyle gave Guy a dark look and picked up Dannie's suitcase. "Come on. Let's go up to our rooms."

After letting themselves in, Lyle set Dannie's suitcase down next to the bed in her room. They looked out the window, which faced the ocean. The rain had already stopped, but the water looked as if it were starting to churn. Even so, the scenery was spectacular. Until two men climbed a rickety scaffolding and nailed a piece of plywood over the window.

"Nice view," Lyle said.

"Very funny."

Someone had spray painted a semi-lewd picture on the side of wood that was visible through her window.

Dannie flopped onto the bed. "I just wish we could get something done. Maybe we should call the police in El Cuello."

"I don't know. Seems to me they might respond better if they saw you in person."

"Why?"

He raised an eyebrow.

"What?"

"Come on. Cute blonde woman in distress?"

"I'm cute?"

"You know you are. You're more than cute. You're adorable."

"Please. Koala bears are cute. Babies with chocolate cake on their faces are adorable. I'm a thirty-nine-year-old widow who just wants all of this to end, so she can maybe get on with her life."

Lyle sat down beside her on the bed. "Do you really want to get on with your life?"

"Yes! I've spent the last eight and a half months trying to hold it all together, and now I find out that Roger was cheating on me with some fitness instructor, and he had a bag of counterfeit money in the garage, and he was involved in God knows what. And meanwhile I can't even get the insurance check so I can get a new hot water heater."

Lyle hooked a finger under her chin. "I'm sorry Roger was such a jerk."

"It's not your fault," Dannie said.

Lyle closed his eyes, touching his lips to hers.

Dannie kept her eyes open, staring at a freckle on Lyle's cheek, surprised that she felt so little when he kissed her.

Scratch that. She felt absolutely *nothing* when he kissed her. Like when she was twelve, and had practiced kissing on a pillow, or a balloon with a face drawn on it. Lyle was a kiss-test dummy.

He slid an arm around her waist and deepened the kiss. She wriggled out of his grasp and sprang from the bed.

"I…ah…I really could use some time to freshen up," she said.

"Of course." If he was embarrassed, or if he felt rejected, he gave no indication. Then again, maybe he thought she wanted to freshen up for *him*.

On his way to the door, Lyle said, "I'll stop by in an hour or so, and we can go grab something to eat and figure out what we're going to do tomorrow. We'll have to get back to the airport by five tomorrow afternoon, so we'll only have a few hours."

"Sure. Sounds good." She closed the door behind him, sliding the safety chain into place.

Maybe it had been a mistake to come here with Lyle. But the thought of coming by herself—or worse, with Guy—was just plain scary. She wasn't usually the fragile type, but the chance that she might learn the gory details about Roger's death without having a friend to lean on made her glad to have Lyle there.

Besides, he had loved Roger like a brother. If anyone wanted to get to the truth as much as she did, it was Lyle.

So she'd simply have to avoid being alone with him, and when they got back to Pennsylvania they would have to have a serious talk about the state of their friendship.

ALTHOUGH IT WAS ONLY four o'clock in the afternoon, the Playa Lounge was packed with hotel guests in varying states of inebriation. A group of college-aged kids were bent backward over the bar while the bartender poured tequila and lime juice into their mouths, creating instant margaritas.

On stage the house band, Los Cangrejos, had just finished up an Elvis medley. A disorderly table of fiftysomething ladies yelled out drunken requests from the rear of the lounge.

A waitress walked by and offered them drinks with little umbrellas speared through chunks of pineapple. "Cuatro colada?"

"Why not?" Dannie took one from the tray. It wasn't as if they were going to get anything accomplished during a hurricane, anyway.

Lyle took one, too, and they touched glasses before they drank.

"To Roger," he said.

"To Roger." Dannie took a sip. "These are delicious."

Lyle scanned the bar. "I guess everybody wants to party through the hurricane."

"Guess so."

They squeezed into a small table for two just as another couple vacated it.

"You hungry?" Lyle asked.

"Is that a rhetorical question?"

Lyle smiled. "There's a buffet over in the corner, if we can get through the crowd."

"That's not a crowd, it's a feeding frenzy. Let's just listen to the band for a while, until the line gets a little shorter."

They were working on their third Cuatro colada when Lyle pointed to the door. "Great. Look who's here."

Chapter Six

GUY LOUGHRAN STOOD in the doorway, filling it up like a big pink door. The red-haired flight attendant clung to his arm.

"Doesn't he own a shirt that isn't pink?" Lyle said. "What a girl."

Dannie took a chug of her Cuatro colada. Guy definitely was *not* a girl, as evidenced by the lustful stares he was getting from every female in the place. Though she couldn't see them from where she sat, Dannie knew his sexy, ocean-green eyes were analyzing hair, makeup, nails, skin.

And there was a *lot* of skin.

Dannie became suddenly self-conscious of the conservative blouse and skirt she'd worn. She unbuttoned the bottom three buttons on her blouse, tying it into a knot just beneath her bra.

Lyle gave her a look.

"What? It's hot in here."

Lyle sucked down the rest of his drink, waved the waitress over and took two more Cuatro coladas from the tray.

"Maybe we should slow down a little," Dannie said. "We haven't eaten all day, and you're not much of a drinker."

"I can handle it." Lyle slurped down half of his fresh drink.

"Well, I'm starting to feel a little drunk. I'm going to get some food," she said. "Are you coming?"

"I'll hold the table."

"I'm sure nobody will take it—"

"Go ahead. I'll get something when you get back."

Dannie watched Guy out of the corner of her eye as she made her way through the buffet line.

The flight attendant had disappeared. Guy stopped to talk to the group of ladies who were yelling at the band, and pretty soon they were all having their pictures taken with him, in poses that could have been on the covers of romance novels.

After that he chatted up a couple of waitresses, admiring their jewelry, looking at their nails.

What a jerk.

When he spotted Dannie, he smiled that sexy smile—the one he presumed would send any woman to her knees.

Well, not *her.*

Dannie braced herself against the buffet table. Man, was it hot.

"Hey! What are you doing here?" Guy said.

"Not that it's any of your business, but Lyle and I are having a few drinks, and something to eat."

"No kidding. Where is good ol' Lyle?"

Dannie jabbed a thumb over her shoulder. "He's holding the table."

Guy laughed. "Looks more like the table is holding him."

Dannie turned around. Lyle was slumped over, passed out with an empty Cuatro colada glass in his hand.

"Great."

"Here," Guy said, taking the plate—piled high with tostadas, enchiladas and tamales—from her hand. "I'll run this back to the table for you. You get something for him to eat."

"How do you know this plate isn't for him?"

Guy looked at her with raised eyebrows. "We had breakfast together, remember?"

Muttering, she shoveled more food onto another plate and worked her way back to the tiny table, which now seemed even smaller with Lyle's head on it.

"Looks like he's out cold." Guy grabbed Lyle by the hair and picked up his head, letting it fall back onto the table with a thump.

"Lyle." Dannie shook his shoulder. "Lyle!"

Nothing.

Dannie put the plate of food on the table. Guy was sitting in her seat.

"Do you mind?" she said.

"Not at all." He leaned over and grabbed an empty chair from the next table, squeezing it between his and Lyle's. "How's that?"

"Great."

The sarcasm was lost on him.

"I guess he won't be needing this." Guy took the extra plate of food.

"Please. Help yourself." She pushed Lyle's head out of the way and began to eat.

Guy poked the food around on his plate with a fork. "There's nothing good here. How do you eat this crap?"

"It's delicious."

"It's full of sodium and fat."

"That's what makes it good." Dannie shoveled refried beans and cheese into a tortilla and rolled it up. "Hey, don't you have a stewardess to harass?"

"Flight attendant. And she hooked up with a pilot."

"Aww. Too bad."

"Not really. She wasn't my type."

Before Dannie could ask him what his type was, Guy waved a waitress over, speaking to her in perfect Spanish.

"You speak Spanish?" Dannie said.

Guy shrugged. "There are a lot of Spanish-speaking clients at the salon I work for. Besides, I think everyone should speak a second language."

Dannie agreed, but she wasn't about to tell Guy that. She'd taken French in college, but could remember only about enough to order a meal.

"Let me ask you a question," Dannie said. "Why are you so sure Roger is still alive?"

Guy leaned back in his seat. "I have my reasons."

"Would you mind sharing?"

For a minute she wasn't sure he was going to tell her. But then he said, "For one, my friend at the Main Street Gym said Lisa had training appointments with Roger almost every day for the two weeks before she left."

"That's hardly a reason," said Dannie. "She was his trainer."

"She was his lover."

Dannie couldn't deny that one. "So they saw each other a lot. That doesn't prove they ran off together."

"Listen, I know Lisa. It would never occur to her to run away to a tropical island by herself. It would never occur to her to run away to the *Jersey shore* by herself. She's never been able to do anything without a man, and Roger was the man of the moment."

Dannie mulled this over, and dismissed it for what it was. A man's homegrown psychoanalysis of a wife who'd realized she didn't have what she wanted at home, so she ran away.

"Maybe Roger told her he was coming to Cuatro Blanco

for a business trip, and it sounded good to her. Maybe she came down to meet him, and then he had his accident."

"Maybe," Guy acquiesced. "But let me ask *you* something now. Why are you so sure he didn't fake his death?"

Dannie opened her mouth to speak. Guy held up a hand. "Save the stuff about him being Super Dad, and about how he loved you too much. Give me a theory. Give me something solid."

"Okay," she said. "You really want to know what I think?"

Guy nodded.

"I think Roger was murdered." There, she'd said it.

Guy looked at her as if he expected her to go on.

She twisted her napkin around her finger. "I don't think the accounting firm he worked for was completely ethical."

"No?"

Dannie wondered if she should keep her mouth shut, but then she thought screw it. She didn't owe Wiser-Crenshaw an ounce of loyalty. They'd done nothing for her, nothing at all, since Roger's death.

"Roger used to tell me stories about some of the clients," Dannie said. "How the firm would help them launder money. Their biggest client was Jimmy Duke. You know him?"

"I've heard of him."

"Then you know what kind of a 'businessman' he is."

Guy shrugged. "I guess."

Dannie nodded. "Well, some of the things the firm was doing didn't sit well with Roger. He was an honest man."

"Except when it came to being faithful to you," Guy pointed out.

"Thanks." Tears stung behind her eyes.

"Sorry. Listen, I…"

Just then the band came back from their break, and started off the set with a Jerry Lee Lewis number. The waitress returned, too, bringing a club soda and a Cuatro colada, along with a plate of skinless chicken, vegetables and fresh fruit for Guy.

"Don't you let yourself have any fun?" Dannie asked, taking a big bite of tamale and washing it down with a slug of colada.

"I have plenty of fun," Guy said. "I just believe you should treat your body like a temple, not an amusement park."

"Wow. Mr. Excitement. No wonder your wife left you. You never let her go on the rides."

Guy shook his head. "I suppose your sex life was great?"

Okay. Was this really an appropriate conversation to be having with the husband of the woman Roger had cheated with?

Maybe not. But she couldn't think straight. In fact, everything had gone a little fuzzy around the edges.

Guy was staring at her.

Dannie pointed to her plate. "Why do you think I eat all this crap? I replaced sex with food years ago, when Roger started treating my body more like a fast-food drive-through than an amusement park."

Guy gave her a strange look.

"What? Too much information?"

"No. It's just a damned shame. I mean, you're a beautiful woman. You've got great skin, great hair, a killer body for someone…"

"Go ahead. Say it. Someone as old as me." She took another bite of her tamale.

"I was going to say 'for someone who spends so little time working on it.'" He reached over and tucked a curl behind her ear.

She swallowed. "I exercise."

"You do?"

"Sure. I lift kids, I run to the grocery store, I chase the dog."

"Do you dance?"

"Dance?"

"Yes, dance." Guy stood up and held out a hand.

Dannie gave Lyle a desperate look. Completely ineffective, seeing as he was still facedown on the table. She gave him a kick, but he only moaned.

"He's not going to save you this time," Guy said. "Come on."

Dannie gave in and took Guy's hand. He led her to the dance floor in front of the band, which was already packed with people doing the merengue.

"Now, this is good exercise," Guy shouted over the music.

"Where did you learn to dance like this?" Dannie shouted back.

"My mother was a dance instructor. I spent every Saturday in her studio from the time I was three until I was seventeen."

"No kidding? My grandfather worked for Arthur Murray. He gave me lessons whenever we visited."

"Really? Then you should be familiar with this move."

He dropped her into a dip so low, her hair brushed the dance floor. His eyes were inches from hers, and for an instant she felt as if they were completely alone, moving in slow motion at the bottom of the sea. Then he pulled her up and took her hands, and for the next half hour they danced as she hadn't danced since those afternoons with her grandfather.

They did the jitterbug, the twist, the swing and the fox-trot before the band slowed things down, launching into the Spanish version of "Unchained Melody." Dannie headed off the dance floor, but Guy spun her back into his arms.

The smell of his cologne, something fresh and beachy, like an ocean mist, enveloped her. His arms closed to form a barrier between her and the other couples on the dance floor, most of whom did little more than stagger to the beat.

Dannie felt woozy from the heat and the lights and the spinning. And, okay, if she was going to be completely honest, from Guy's muscles.

She couldn't help it. Something about well-formed biceps and a solid wall of chest to lean on appealed to her on a purely animalistic level. Guy might have been the exact opposite of her idea of the perfect man, but he was right on the money as her perfect fantasy—a straight man who liked to talk hair and makeup, could dance like Fred Astaire and looked like the quarterback of her college football team.

He held her close, swaying in time with the music, lulling her into a false sense of security before he said, "So what was the name of the fishing charter Roger hired?"

She pulled away. "I don't believe it. You don't give up, do you?"

He dragged her back into his arms. "It was just a question."

"He isn't alive, Guy. I know—I *knew* my husband. He wasn't capable of what you're suggesting."

"Well, you're lucky, then. I thought I knew what Lisa was capable of, but obviously I didn't."

Dannie softened in Guy's arms, suddenly feeling very sorry for him. It couldn't have been easy to lose his wife and his dream at the same time.

"You'll find her," Dannie said. "You'll get your money back."

"I better. Time is running out."

"What do you mean? What time?"

Guy shook his head. "It doesn't matter."

The song ended, but just as they were about to leave the dance floor, the hotel's activities director—Majorca, according to her name tag—took the microphone.

"Everyone, please stay right where you are. We're about to start our *Dirty Dancing* contest!"

The crowd on the dance floor hooted and yowled.

"Oh, no," Dannie said, heading toward the table. "This is my stop."

"Come on." Guy laughed. "It'll be fun."

He grabbed her elbow and pulled her back onto the floor.

"We have some great prizes," Majorca shouted. "All you gotta do is show us what you got. Be sex-y-y-y!"

The band broke out into The Contours' "Do You Love Me?" and the couples on the dance floor started bumping and grinding. Guy grabbed Dannie's hips and pulled her to him. Her bare belly brushed the buttons of his now-damp shirt. She wrapped her arms around his neck, tightening her grip as he swung her backward.

Everything around her faded to a blur as she and Guy danced. He drew her closer, fitting himself into her curves, rubbing his body against hers and leaving her senses raw and on edge. Every brush of his skin set her nerves on fire.

Guy slid his hands down her back and over her rear end to the back of her thigh, hoisting her knee up to his hip as he gyrated his pelvis against hers. A bead of sweat trickled down her neck and into her bra. She closed her eyes.

Los Cangrejos worked their way through the *Dirty Dancing* soundtrack as couples all around them were tapped out of the competition. Dannie hardly noticed. She was Baby Houseman and Guy was Johnny Castle, and he had taken her out of the corner and was showing her the time of her life.

She and Guy were so lost in their own world that when the music stopped and Majorca announced the winners of the competition, they were still dancing. It wasn't until the activities director waved an envelope between them that they finally realized the competition was over. And they had won.

"Congratulations!" Majorca shouted into the mike, handing the envelope to Dannie. "As our *Dirty Dancing* champions, you've both won a free stay at El Pelícano!"

All around them, the other guests clapped and whistled. A couple at a table near the dance floor stared at Dannie as if they knew exactly what had been going through her mind while she'd danced with Guy.

Dannie's face burned. She looked toward her own table, but Lyle was gone. Then she saw him out of the corner of her eye, heading for the door of the club.

Just then, the lights went out.

"Here." She shoved the envelope at Guy. "I have to go."

She pushed her way through the crush of people, most of whom felt compelled to either congratulate her or grab her butt. By the time she made it out into the hotel lobby, it was too dark to see where Lyle had gone.

Chapter Seven

A few minutes later, the emergency generators kicked in, lighting emergency lights in the lobby and hallways.

The elevators were down, of course, so Dannie took the stairs three floors to Lyle's room—just a few doors down from her own. In the near darkness, with all the hotel windows covered with plywood and the wind and rain picking up, the place was downright spooky.

The only other person in the hallway was a woman in a sarong and a big straw hat, carrying a drink in a coconut shell. She looked familiar, but Dannie couldn't place her. She supposed she'd seen her in the lounge. Just about everyone in the hotel had been there.

The woman disappeared into the stairwell.

Dannie knocked on Lyle's door, the sound echoing in the empty hallway.

"Lyle?"

No answer.

She knocked again. "Lyle? Are you in there?"

She pressed her ear to the door. She could hear him moving around.

"I know you're in there. Come on. Open up."

The security chain rattled, and the door opened a crack.

"Hey," Dannie said. "Can I come in?"

"I'm trying to sleep—"

"You just took a two-hour nap at the bar," she joked.

Apparently Lyle didn't think it was funny.

"What were you doing with Guy? I mean, I open my eyes, and you're practically climbing on him on the dance floor."

"It was a *Dirty Dancing* contest."

"I could see that."

"Come on, Lyle. Let me in."

He hesitated, then the door swung open. And there he stood in a pair of light blue boxer shorts. His legs practically glowed.

This was a man who desperately needed a tan. Too bad the beach was currently being pummeled by ninety-mile-an-hour winds.

Dannie followed him into the room, leaving the door open for light. "The activities director announced that Cuatro Blanco is only supposed to catch the edge of the storm. It should all be over by midnight or so. Still, it would be safest if we waited it out in the lounge."

"I'm not going back there." His voice held a bitter edge.

"Lyle, nothing happened between me and Guy. You know I can't stand him."

"That's not what it looked like."

That wasn't what it felt like, either.

She sat on the edge of the queen-size bed, smoothing the

yellow bedspread with her palm. "I guess I've had a little too much to drink, and I just got carried away with the dancing. It's been a long time since I've been out dancing with a man."

"*I'll* take you dancing," he said, his words still a little bit slurred.

She sighed. "You don't have to do that."

He sat down beside her and grabbed her hand. "I don't feel like I *have* to do things for you. I *want* to do them. Roger would have wanted me to take care of you, Dano."

Dannie shook her head. "I know you and Roger were close, but you're not responsible for my happiness."

"But—"

"Lyle, really. I appreciate everything you do for me. But I think it's time I stood on my own two feet. Roger's been gone for eight and a half months, and it's time I got on with things."

"This is about the kiss, isn't it?" He sounded miserable.

"No, it's not about the kiss. It's about me taking charge of my life."

Outside, the driving rain sounded like marbles hitting the side of the hotel. The wind moaned against the plywood-covered windows.

Lyle looked down at their hands, and unlaced his fingers from hers. "Can I still help you while we're here? I'd like to know myself how Roger died. And I'd like to make sure you go home with that death certificate."

She smiled. "Of course you can help me. I'm counting on it."

"Good." He got up, went to the minifridge and took out a Coke. "You want one?"

"Why don't we go have one in the lounge? I promise we won't go anywhere near Guy Loughran."

She and Lyle went back down to the bar, standing in a corner by the door, listening to the band—which had reverted to acoustic—and sipping Cokes until Majorca announced that it was safe for them all to return to their rooms.

"Call me when you wake up tomorrow, okay?" Lyle said when they stopped at his room.

"Okay." She gave him a peck on the cheek. "Get some sleep."

Dannie rooted through her handbag for her room key. The lady with the hat and the coconut drink was still wandering up and down the hall. Dannie finally placed her as the woman she'd spoken to in the line at the airport back home. The one who told her to have a good time in Cuatro Blanco.

Fat chance.

Dannie gave her a little wave as she opened the door to her own room and went inside, not exactly eager to face a night alone, filled with darkness and wind and rain.

AS IT TURNED OUT, the weather wasn't what kept Dannie up half the night. It was Guy Loughran.

Or rather, thoughts of him.

Every time Dannie closed her eyes, Technicolor visions of Guy's blue-green eyes and sexy, crooked nose filled the darkness, and she imagined the hard muscles of his chest and belly pressed against hers as they danced.

The bed spun.

By two o'clock she realized she wasn't going to get a moment of sleep. She grabbed a bottle of water from the fridge and sat in bed, listening to the storm.

By three, the wind and rain had died down, along with the thoughts of her dancing partner. Dannie drifted off to sleep.

Now, just a few hours later, she was wide awake, looking forward to accomplishing what she'd come here for and getting back home to her kids. She hopped into the shower, which was ice-cold, and then realized she had no way to dry her hair. It was not going to be a pretty sight. She found a scarf in her purse and tied it around her head.

She waited until seven to knock on Lyle's door.

"Time to get moving," she said through the door. Lyle grunted in response. She heard him clump to the bathroom.

He had to be hurting. He wasn't much of a drinker to begin with, and the Cuatro coladas had packed a wicked punch. Dannie still suffered a dull throb in her temples, even after a couple of aspirin and a bottle of orange juice from the minibar.

She returned to her room and paged through the *Vanity Fair* she'd bought at the airport while she waited for Lyle. She wondered what Guy was doing.

Would he find Lisa? And if so, what would he do? Would he ask her to come back to the States with him? Would he beg her?

She felt a pang of sympathy for Guy. It must be hard to feel abandoned. Unwanted. Duped.

A knock on the door roused her from her thoughts, and she grabbed her purse. Time to get to work.

"WHAT DO YOU MEAN, nothing is running?"

"I'm sorry, *señora*. The storm has disrupted all transportation on the island. No taxis, no ferries, no buses."

"But I thought it wasn't that bad."

The concierge shrugged. "Not too bad. The main road is flooded, and the ferry broke loose and hit something. Got a big hole in the side."

"What did it hit?"

"The other ferry."

Dannie bit her lip.

"How are we supposed to get to El Cuello?" Lyle's face was turning red again.

The concierge smiled. "You could walk."

"How far is it?" asked Dannie.

"About nine kilometers."

"Six miles?" Lyle said. "We can't walk that far in this heat."

"Why don't you take it easy, amigos?" The concierge looked down at Lyle's pale legs. "You should check out the beach. It's all cleaned up, and the staff is serving Cuatro coladas."

Lyle looked ill. "No, thanks."

"I'm going to go down there," Dannie said. "Check it out. See if I can find anyone who could get us to El Cuello."

She left Lyle in the lobby and followed a set of narrow stone steps through a rocky outcropping and down to the beach. The sun was bright and, aside from a few stray palm fronds and sticks, the beach was beautiful. White sand, wispy clouds, blue waters. Well, almost blue. More like the color of Guy's eyes—

"Dannie?"

Think of the devil. He lay there on a hotel towel in the sand, in pink swim trunks and black T-shirt, zinc oxide covering his crooked nose.

"Guy. How are you?"

"I'd be better if I could get something accomplished."

"I know. I just came down to see if I could find someone with a boat who'd be willing to take us to the other side of the island."

"To El Cuello?"

She opened her mouth to answer, then clammed up.

"It was just a question, Dannie. Don't read anything into it."

She sat down beside him and stretched out her legs. The warmth of the sand seeped into the backs of her calves. "Roger chartered the fishing boat in El Cuello. I was going to go talk to the owner of the boat, and try to get the authorities to issue a death certificate while I'm here."

"Good luck."

She gave him a look.

"What? I just meant because everything moves so slowly here."

She leaned back on her elbows. "I guess it doesn't matter, anyway. We're not going anywhere today. Both ferries are out of commission, and the main road is flooded."

They stared out over the water for a few minutes.

"It's beautiful, isn't it?" Guy said.

"Yes," she said quietly. "Yes, it is."

She could feel Guy watching her as she watched the waves. Roger was out there, somewhere.

Tears gathered in the corners of her eyes.

"Watch my towel for a minute," Guy said. "I'll be right back."

She lay back in the sand and put her head on her bag, closing her eyes. If only she wasn't here to find out about Roger's death. If only she could take it easy, as the natives kept suggesting, and just lie on the beach all day, working on nothing but a tan and a drink.

She opened her eyes when she felt a shadow loom over her. Guy.

She sat up.

"This is Pedro." Guy nodded toward the waiter standing beside him with a tray of Cuatro coladas. "He's got a boat, and said he'd be willing to take you to El Cuello on his break, for the right price."

Pedro nodded.

"Are you kidding me?" Dannie jumped up and brushed the sand from her skirt. "When's your break?"

Pedro shrugged. "Whenever."

"How long is your break? Will you have time to take us there and back?"

Pedro shrugged again. "Sure."

"Oh, wow. Great. Okay, let me go get my friend." She picked up her bag. "I suppose you're going, too?" she said to Guy.

He shook his head. "This one is all yours."

She smiled, rising on tiptoe to kiss his cheek. "Thank you."

Was it her imagination, or did he blush?

Nah. It was probably just the sun.

She ran back up to the hotel. Lyle was slumped in a wicker chair in the lobby, his hat pulled down over his eyes.

She shook his shoulder. "Come on, hurry up! We've got a ride to El Cuello."

He jumped up and followed her toward the stairs. "Wow, that was fast. How'd you do it?"

"Actually, I didn't. It was Guy."

Lyle came to a dead halt. "Is he coming along?"

"Nope."

"You're kidding."

"Nope."

Lyle took off his hat, wiping the sweat from his forehead with the back of his hand. "Damn, it's hot."

"Don't worry. In a few hours we'll be on an air-conditioned plane back to Philadelphia with Roger's death certificate and a nice tan, and we'll never have to see this place again."

TWELVE HOURS LATER they were on a plane, all right. Except it wasn't moving, and the air-conditioning was broken, and they didn't have the death certificate. They weren't tanned, either.

At least, Lyle wasn't. He was burned, a deep lobster-red.

"Didn't you have sunscreen on?" Dannie asked, pressing a finger onto his leg. The white mark it made faded quickly back to red.

"I was so hungover I forgot." He looked absolutely miserable.

Indeed, it had been a miserable day.

Pedro's boat had turned out to be a motorized skiff, which took the residual waves left by the hurricane about as well as a Hollywood actress took cellulite.

Dannie clung to the sides for dear life, wearing two life jackets. Pedro babied the tiny engine around the south end of the island as it plowed over three-foot swells. The ride took more than half an hour, and by the time they arrived in El Cuello, both Dannie and Lyle had retched up everything they'd eaten for breakfast.

Pedro dropped them off at the end of a long dock, promising to return for them when his shift was over.

"When is that?" Lyle asked.

Pedro shrugged. "Whenever."

They asked a fisherman the way to the El Cuello police station, and he pointed to a small yellow building at the end of the narrow beach, fronting onto a street that looked like something out of a Tijuana postcard.

The place was locked when they arrived. They wandered through streets littered with debris from the storm, asking everyone they saw where they could find the owners of the local fishing charters. No one seemed to know.

Eventually they went back to the police station and waited in front of the building, playing four games of gin rummy with a deck of cards Dannie had found in her purse. They waited for more than two hours, but no one returned.

When they heard the spastic drone of the engine on Pedro's dinghy, they ran back down to the dock. The fisherman said he'd forgotten to tell them that all the police officers had gone to a neighboring town for a meeting about the hurricane cleanup.

So here they were twelve hours later, sitting on the narrow tarmac at the Cuatro Blanco airport, waiting for clearance to fly back to the States without having accomplished anything.

Well, that wasn't entirely true.

Lyle had managed to get first-degree burns on his legs, and she'd won a *Dirty Dancing* competition with a man she both lusted after and despised.

Okay, maybe she didn't despise him so much anymore. Not since he'd found a boat to take them to the other side of the island. Maybe he'd finally realized he'd been wrong about Roger.

Still, she wished she could have uncovered some information about Roger's death. Even she could see there had to be *some* connection between Roger and Lisa besides the affair. The counterfeit money had to be more than a coincidence.

Was it possible Roger had been framed for something? Killed for something Lisa had done? Or maybe Lisa had killed him herself?

A shiver ran through her, despite the suffocating heat in the airplane's cabin.

Dannie got up to put her bag in the overhead compartment. A woman peered at her from the rear of the plane.

It was the same woman who'd been in the hallway of the hotel the night before. The one from the line at the airport.

She was one of the lucky ones, like them.

The airline had double booked every flight out of Cuatro Blanco for the next four days, so it was pretty much now or never.

She and Lyle had considered extending their stay by a day or two, but the airline couldn't guarantee them a flight before Friday, and Lyle had an important meeting to attend on Wednesday.

She settled back in her seat. Lyle was snoring beside the window.

The "fasten seat belt" light went on above her head, and Dannie closed her eyes. She wondered if she'd ever know the truth about Roger.

Chapter Eight

"MOMMY, I MISSED YOU!" Betsy, still wearing her pink baby-doll pajamas, clung to Dannie's leg.

It wasn't quite eight in the morning. Dannie had come straight from the airport after nearly three hours of waiting on the runway in Cuatro Blanco—apparently typical for the island—and an overnight stay in Miami because they'd missed their connecting flight. She couldn't wait to see the kids.

Richard paraded in front of her, showing off every gift Elizabeth and Albert had given them the whole weekend.

The twins sat on her lap, and Dannie buried her nose in Erin's hair. Nothing like the scent of baby shampoo to put everything into perspective.

"How did it go?" Elizabeth poured Dannie a cup of coffee as they sat in her mother-in-law's immaculate living room.

Dannie noticed several pieces of Elizabeth's bric-a-brac had gone missing. She wondered if her mother-in-law had put them away to save them, or if Richard had already reduced them to rubble.

"It was a bust," Dannie said. "A hurricane swept through the island Sunday evening, and the roads were a mess on Monday. We got to El Cuello, but couldn't talk to the authorities because everyone was busy with the cleanup. In fact, we were lucky to get out of there at all."

"So you didn't find anything out?" The disappointment was raw in her voice. She and Albert wanted closure, too.

Dannie shook her head. "I'm sorry."

Elizabeth sighed. "Maybe next time."

"There won't be a next time. I'm not going back to Cuatro Blanco." Dannie stood, hoisting the twins onto her hips. "All right, guys. Tell Grandma and Grandpa thank you."

"Thanks, Grandma. We liked it here, even though you don't have Cocoa Crunchies." Richard turned to Dannie and made a face. "We had to eat oatmeal for breakfast."

"Yeah," said Betsy. "And we had *fruit* for dessert. Mommy, tell Grandma what you always say. If it doesn't have chocolate in it, on it, or under it, it's not dessert."

Elizabeth raised her eyebrows. "Is that what you say?"

Dannie's face heated. "Something like that. Listen, I really appreciate your help."

"We enjoy having them."

"I'm sure you do. But I know they can be a handful."

Elizabeth touched Dannie's arm and gave her a little smile. "You're doing a good job with them, dear."

Tears stung Dannie's eyes over this praise from a most unlikely source. "Thank you."

Albert tore himself away from the history channel in the living room long enough to see them off. He kissed the kids, telling Dannie to bring them back soon as she hustled them out the door.

Still, Dannie thought she saw the tiniest expression of relief on Elizabeth's and Albert's faces through the big bow window of the living room.

Exhausted Grandparents Waving Goodbye.

THE FRONT DOOR SWUNG open when Dannie touched the doorknob. She stepped over the threshold into the house, crunching on shards of broken glass that littered the foyer, glittering in the sunlight.

Quincy sniffed around the front door, whining and barking.

"Nobody move!" Dannie grabbed Richard's shoulder and turned him around. "Get back to the car."

"How can we get back to the car if we're not allowed to move?" Richard said.

Dannie pushed him out the door. "Get going. Back to the car. Hurry."

She called the dog and herded the kids back to the van, locking the doors when they were all inside. She started to dial 911 on her cell phone, but then remembered the hot-dog box full of counterfeit money in her freezer.

What if the police found it?

Or what if that was what the thief had been after?

She debated going back into the house to see if it was gone, but she didn't want to leave the kids in the car alone. And she certainly wasn't bringing them in there.

The police would have to wait until she knew for sure where the funny money was.

She dialed the first few digits of Lyle's number, but then thought better of it. She needed to stop treating Lyle like Roger's replacement.

As she pondered her options, her cell phone rang.

G. Loughran.

Her heart gave an involuntary flutter.

She waited four rings before answering.

"How did you get this number?"

"Lyle gave it to me."

"I highly doubt that."

"Actually, I got it off his cell phone when he was napping on the table in the lounge."

She had to smile at that one. "What do you want?"

"I called to see if you found anything out in El Cuello."

She sighed. "If you must know, no. I didn't."

"I'm sorry." He actually sounded sincere.

"Yeah, well. Things seem to be heating up here at home."

As they talked, she backed the van out of the drive and headed toward her in-laws' house.

"What do you mean, heating up?" he asked.

"Somebody broke in to my house."

"Oh, my God. Are you okay?"

"Yeah. Just a little shaken up. It happened while we were gone, thank God. I'm going back to my in-laws', I guess."

"Why don't you come here?" he asked.

"Cuatro Blanco?"

"No. My house."

"You're *back?* How did you get back?"

He hesitated. "A friend got me onto a private plane."

"Would that friend happen to be a redheaded flight attendant?"

"Actually, it was the redhead's pilot. He flies a charter back and forth from Philly, and there was an extra seat. I got in around seven this morning."

Two hours sooner than she and Lyle had.

"So what do you say? You wanna come over?"

Did she?

She did. And before she could analyze why, she said, "What's your address?"

TEN MINUTES LATER Dannie was sitting at Guy's kitchen table while Quincy and the kids played in his tiny backyard.

The house was small, with a country-cottage decor that had to be Lisa's doing. Dressed in black spandex shorts and a sweat-soaked T-shirt, Guy looked completely out of place amidst the gingham and lace.

"We interrupted your workout," Dannie said.

"No, it's fine. Just let me grab a quick shower. Do you want anything while you're waiting?"

"How about some coffee?"

He pointed to the corner of the kitchen. "The machine is right over there. Coffee's in the cabinet above it. You'll have to make it yourself, though. I don't know how to work it."

"No problem. I can operate a coffee machine with my eyes closed and one arm wrapped around a toddler."

Guy smiled. "I'm glad you're here."

So was she.

He disappeared down a hallway, while Dannie busied herself with the coffeemaker. She looked out the kitchen window into the backyard. Quincy chased Betsy around the pole of a bird feeder while the twins played on a blanket Guy had taken off the bed in the spare room. Richard was blowing dandelion seeds all over the grass. Guy would be so pleased.

She found a mug with a handle shaped like a pair of scissors, which she held under the dripping stream of coffee, unwilling to wait for it to fill up the pot. She downed an entire scorching-hot cup in ten seconds, then refilled the mug and went outside to the deck, stretching out on a mesh lawn chaise.

Caffeine coursed through her veins, clearing the fog that had settled on her brain over the past twenty-nine sleepless hours. She realized she had to get to the bottom of all this. Maybe if she helped Guy find out what had happened to Lisa it would give her some kind of clue as to what Roger had been involved in.

Her cell phone buzzed in her pocket. She took it out and looked at the caller's number.

Lyle.

She took another swig of coffee for fortification before she answered it.

"Are you okay?" Lyle said on the other end. "I went by the house and saw a broken window by the front door."

"I'm fine. The neighbor's kid hit a baseball through the window," she lied. "No big deal. I called a glass place, but they can't fix it until tomorrow."

"Why don't you bring the kids and stay here tonight? You can't sleep at your place with that window. It isn't safe."

"I appreciate the offer, but we're at Elizabeth and Albert's. We'll be fine."

"You know I'd be happy to have you," Lyle said.

"I know. Thanks. I'll call you tomorrow, okay?"

She hung up just as Guy stepped out onto the patio.

"You need more coffee?" he said.

She shook her head. "One more cup and I'll be wired enough to light up Times Square. What are you drinking?"

He raised his mug. "Rooibos tea. It's great for the digestive system."

"So are Twinkies."

"Are you hungry?"

Dannie rubbed her forehead. "I don't know. I guess so. My body can't even tell what time it is anymore."

"You need some sleep—"

"Richard!" Dannie yelled. "Get your face out of that bird-bath! And Betsy, put your shirt back on."

"Interesting children." Guy took a sip of his tea. "How are they taking Roger's absence?"

Dannie sighed. "Richard is acting out a bit. He asks about his father all the time. Betsy's in her own little world, and the twins are just too young to realize what's going on."

"At least they have Lyle."

Dannie couldn't tell if he was being sarcastic.

But how could he know that Lyle really wasn't into kids? Or animals.

He tried. He really did. But Lyle was particular about his house, and his suits, and his car. And being particular didn't coexist very well with chocolate-smeared fingers and dirty diapers and slobbering dogs.

Guy, on the other hand, seemed impervious to the fact that her son had broken the hat off a garden gnome, the twins had spit up on his blanket and the dog had already dug a hole in the patch of black-eyed Susans near the fence.

Betsy was sitting up in a rhododendron bush and chirping like a bird. And chirping. And chirping. And chirping…

"So you want to tell me what's going on?" Guy said.

Dannie settled back into the chaise. "I told you. Someone broke a window in the house."

"Any idea who?"

"Probably just some kids. I don't know."

"Did you call the police?"

She hesitated. "No. Not yet." She could feel him looking at her.

"Come on, Dannie. Level with me."

"About what?"

"Whatever it is you're hiding. I can hear the tension in your voice. You're scared."

She sighed. It was time to come clean. She needed help with all of this, and for whatever reason, her gut was telling her that Guy was her man.

"You know the counterfeit money you found in your safe?" she said.

Out of the corner of her eye she could see Guy's body tense. "What about it?"

"Are you sure Lisa put it there?"

"Positive. She was the only other person on earth who knew the combination to the safe."

"Do you know where she got it? The money, I mean."

"No." Guy crossed his legs at the ankles. "Why, do you?"

"I might."

He sat up, focusing his full attention on her. "You gonna tell me?"

She swung her legs off the chaise and turned to face him. "Okay. A couple of days before you called me, I was going through some things in the garage, and I found a golf bag full of hundred-dollar bills."

"Yeah?"

"Yeah. And Roger never played golf in his life. Then when I tried to use some of the money to pay for a round of drinks with some friends, the manager informed me it was counterfeit."

"No kidding. What happened?"

"I convinced him not to call the police."

"How much money was in the bag?" Guy asked.

"Thirty-one thousand, six hundred dollars."

Guy whistled through his teeth.

"How much was in the safe?" Dannie said.

"A hundred and fifty."

"Dollars?"

"Grand."

"A hundred and fifty *thousand?* I don't understand. Why would you have that much money in a safe? Why wouldn't you put it in the bank?"

Guy scratched his chin. "Let's just say the origins of the cash were somewhat suspect."

"You *stole* it?"

"No! Nothing like that."

"Then what?"

Guy shook his head. "I'm not a thief, Dannie. I couldn't get another loan from the bank, so I borrowed the money from…another source. And now, obviously, I have no way to pay it back. So I'm screwed, unless I find Lisa and get my money back."

Dannie exhaled the breath she'd been holding. "Did you find out anything in Cuatro Blanco?"

"Not a thing."

"So why didn't you stay?"

"There was a problem with one of the permits for the spa that had to be taken care of immediately."

"It couldn't have waited another day or two?"

"Only if I wanted to pay a plumbing crew to sit around for that long."

"So what are you going to do?"

He was silent for a moment. "I don't know."

"Mommy! Emma smells bad," Richard yelled. "Do you want me to get the diaper bag?"

Guy got up. "I'll take care of it."

"If you're trying to turn me on, it's working," Dannie said.

Guy flashed her his famous dimples before he went off to handle diaper duty. There was a side to him that was really very sweet. And sweet was something she could use right now.

She only hoped she hadn't made a mistake in telling him about the counterfeit bills. But really, who else could she turn to about this if she wasn't going to turn to Lyle?

Chapter Nine

QUINCY LAY PANTING on the rug beside the couch, exhausted from a day of chasing kids, squirrels and sticks that Guy had thrown.

The children were in the spare bedroom—the twins in the portable playpen Dannie had in the car, Betsy in the single bed and Richard on a pile of blankets on the floor. He'd balked at first, but when Guy had told him that was how the cowboys did it, Richard had been sold.

Now Dannie sat on the couch with Guy as he flipped through the television channels, looking for a movie for them to watch.

He had convinced her to stay at his place instead of going back to her in-laws. It hadn't been difficult.

He might drive her crazy, but she did feel safe with him. It was probably all that muscle.

"You're good with kids," Dannie said. "Where did that come from?"

"I have five nieces and nephews. I was hoping Lisa and I would have a few, but I guess that won't be happening."

Once again Dannie was struck by how much Guy had lost, too. She touched his hand. "You'll have it someday. You'll find someone."

"Right. I can't even find a decent movie." He handed her the remote.

She flipped through the channels. "Have you ever seen *Escape from Zombie Island?*"

"Sounds great."

Dannie yawned. "It is."

They settled back to watch, but before the opening credits finished rolling, Dannie had drifted off to sleep.

She dreamed she and Guy were dancing naked on a beach, their bodies slick with suntan oil, the ocean waves licking their toes.

When she woke up, she was sprawled across Guy's chest, her face pressed against his neck. Guy's arm was draped across her back, his big hand cupping her rear end. Quincy was licking her toes.

She stirred, and Guy tightened his grip, groaning in his sleep. Her insides went liquid at the sound. Dear God, she just wanted to peel his clothes off and get the suntan oil.

She pressed her lips lightly to his neck, a night's worth of razor stubble rough against her lips. She closed her eyes, breathing in the beachy scent of his that drove her insane.

Guy stirred and kissed her, his eyes still closed.

Dannie's heart rate sped to dangerous levels. Was he even awake? Did he know what he was doing to her?

Did she care?

She closed her eyes and drifted into the kiss—a warm, lazy morning kiss. The kind that usually led to warm, lazy morning sex.

Guy moved her hips against his. *Dirty Dancing,* just like her dream, only horizontal—

Wait a minute. This was a man who drove her insane—and not in a good way. What in hell was she *doing?*

She'd never been able to think straight before her coffee.

She scrambled to her feet.

Guy gave a disappointed moan. "What's the matter?"

"It's morning," she said.

"What time is it?"

"Almost eight. I have to get out of here. The window guy is coming at nine."

He sat up. "I'll go with you."

"No!" She raked her fingers through her curls. "No, that's okay. Really."

Guy rubbed his eyes. "The kids aren't up yet?"

"I think you wore them out yesterday. They haven't played like that since…"

"Since Roger?"

She nodded.

He cleared his throat. "Listen, if you want to leave them here until you get your window fixed, I'd be happy to watch them."

"That's nice of you, but they're really a handful."

He laughed. "I can handle them. Now, Quincy on the other hand…"

Quincy had spied a squirrel outside in the yard, and was flinging his sizable body against the sliding glass door.

"He was dropped on his head when he was a puppy." She opened the door and let him outside. "Guy, listen. I appreciate your letting us stay here last night, but we really do have to go."

"All right. Do you want to have dinner with me tonight?"

"I can't."

"How about tomorrow night?"

"I don't think so."

"Then when?"

She was silent.

His smile faded. "Ah. I see. You want to say, 'never,' but you're too polite."

She blew a curl off her forehead. "I don't want to hurt your feelings. But I can't go out with a man who keeps insisting my dead husband is alive."

"What if I don't say that anymore?"

"Guy—"

"Dannie, I like you a lot. I'm attracted to you, and I think you're attracted to me."

"So what if I am? It doesn't change anything. I'm not ready to be with anyone right now. Especially not the husband of the woman Roger had an affair with."

"So you believe he had an affair with Lisa?"

"That issue was never in question."

"Then why don't you believe there might be more to the story? Especially since you found that money."

"How are we supposed to find out?" She paced in front of the couch. "I've scoured the house for something, anything that could give me a clue as to what was going on. But I didn't find anything. I'm assuming you haven't, either, or you wouldn't have come to me."

"So we'll work together—"

"No, Guy. I'm done. Roger is dead, and I'm going to get on with my life. I suggest you do the same."

"Don't you want to know who's breaking in to your house? Somebody is looking for something."

Dannie shook her head. "I don't know that the broken window had anything to do with this. Maybe it was just a random break-in."

"You don't really believe that, do you?"

Dannie gave him a small smile. "I'm trying to."

She left him sitting there and went into the guest room. Betsy was sitting up in bed. Richard looked up at her from the makeshift bed on the floor. "Do we have to go?"

He looked so sad, it nearly broke her heart.

She knew just how he felt.

"I'm afraid so, honey. Come on, get up. We have to get our stuff together."

"Are we going to see Guy again soon?" Betsy asked.

"We'll see." Dannie bent over the portable crib and shook the twins awake.

"That means no," Richard said.

"That means we'll see," Dannie argued.

Why was she giving them false hope? Why couldn't she just say it? Why couldn't she tell her children they were probably never going to see Guy again, ever?

Maybe because she didn't want to believe it herself.

LYLE CALLED JUST AS the glass repair truck pulled out of the driveway.

"Is your window fixed?" he said.

"The repairman just left," Dannie said. "Why?"

"We need to talk."

"About what?"

"Guy Loughran."

At the sound of his name, her stomach did a little flip.

Okay, enough with the schoolgirl crush.

"Lyle, I just want to relax. I have to go back to work tomorrow, and I want to give the kids a bath—"

"Ten minutes, that's all. Can I come over?"

She sighed. "Okay. Come on over."

Luckily she'd already straightened up the mess the intruders had left.

Furniture overturned, drawers rifled, pictures pulled off the walls.

But the chaos ended at the dining room. The kitchen—including the hot-dog box—hadn't been touched. It was almost as if they'd been interrupted.

Was it possible they'd still been in the house when she and the kids got back yesterday? She gave a little shiver.

A few minutes later the doorbell rang. She peeked out the newly fixed window. Lyle stood on the front step, hands in his pockets.

She opened the door. "That was fast."

"I was picking up my dry cleaning around the corner," he said. "Can I come in?"

She nodded.

He stepped inside, shutting the door behind him. "I don't want to freak you out, but I think I'm being followed."

"What makes you think that?"

He pointed out the window. "That blue car. I've seen it at least three times this morning."

A dark blue Chevy was parked half a block down from Dannie's door.

"There's nobody in it," she said.

Lyle pulled her away from the window. "It was a woman driving."

"What did she look like?"

"I don't know. She had dark hair, and sunglasses."

Dannie thought about the woman from the airport with the straw hat, and her heartbeat quickened. "Why would someone be following *you?*"

"I don't know. Maybe it has something to do with Roger…"

Richard and Betsy ran into the room. "Uncle Lyle! Uncle Lyle!"

When Betsy grabbed Lyle's legs, he gave her an awkward pat on the head.

"Hey, what's going on, kids?"

"Somebody broke our window," said Richard. "And it wasn't me."

"I heard."

"And we had a sleepover," Betsy said. "We went to G—"

"Kids," Dannie interrupted, "your uncle Lyle and I are having an important conversation. Go play."

"But—"

"Go!"

Richard and Betsy ran from the room.

"Do you want something to drink?" Dannie started for the kitchen.

Lyle stepped in front of her, blocking her way. "Where were you last night?"

"I told you. Elizabeth and Albert's."

Lyle raked his fingers through his hair. "Don't lie to me, Dano. I went there to see you. They said you'd left at eleven yesterday morning and they hadn't heard from you since."

Maybe she should have felt guilty for lying to a friend, but she didn't. Instead, she was mad.

"Why did you insist on looking for me after I told you I was okay?"

"I wanted to talk to you about something I found out.

Something important. But you weren't there." His voice held an accusatory tone.

"Okay, fine. I was at Guy Loughran's house. I didn't tell you because I knew you'd overreact."

"*Guy's?* Please tell me you're not serious."

"I don't really see where it's any of your business," Dannie said. "My relationship with Guy has nothing to do with you."

"Relationship? Jesus, Dannie. You've got to stop this infatuation with him."

"I'm not infatuated with him! He's a friend, that's all."

"He's involved with Jimmy Duke."

Dannie sucked in a breath. *"What?"*

Lyle nodded. "I did a little bit of asking around about Guy yesterday. Word is Jimmy's a partner in Guy's 'spa.'"

Jimmy Duke was Wiser-Crenshaw's biggest client. Roger had spent years regaling Dannie with reports of all the underhanded schemes Duke and the firm had devised to launder Duke's millions, which had come from God knew where.

Duke had dozens of businesses around town that served as fronts for illegal activities—offtrack betting, gambling, drug running. The list was endless.

Almost everyone who was involved in dealings with Jimmy Duke was a thug or a con man. Or a sucker.

Roger had hated the man. And now Dannie had gone and slept with one of his flunkies. Well, slept *on* him, anyway. But the idea was the same.

"It has to be some kind of mistake," she said, more to herself than to Lyle.

"It's not." Lyle's expression softened, and he touched her cheek. "Just stay away from Guy Loughran, okay?"

She nodded, pulling away from his touch. "Is that what you wanted to tell me?"

"That's it."

"Well, then, I guess I better go take care of the kids. Good-bye, Lyle."

It was only after he'd left that Dannie remembered what Lyle had said about being followed. She looked out the window. The blue car was gone.

She didn't know what to think. Lyle being followed? Guy in bed with Jimmy Duke? Was his salon just another one of Duke's fronts?

What if Roger had discovered something about Guy and Jimmy Duke, and confronted one of them? Had Jimmy Duke killed Roger?

Had Guy?

Maybe this story about Roger having an affair with his wife was all a cover for something. Maybe Guy had had Roger killed, and was trying to find out how much Dannie knew.

No. Impossible.

She might not have liked Guy in the beginning, but Dannie prided herself on having good judgment when it came to people.

She'd figured out that it was Timmy Quentin who'd told all the boys in tenth-grade gym class that he'd gone to third base with her. Her ears always itched around him.

And she'd taken an immediate dislike to Richard's peewee football coach, a man who'd run off with the team's treasury halfway through the season. Her palms always itched when he was nearby.

Nothing had itched around Guy.

Still, as much as she didn't want to admit it, Lyle was right.

If she knew what was good for her, she'd stay away from Guy Loughran altogether.

Maybe nothing itched when she was around him, but it did tingle. And that meant nothing but trouble for a lonely widow with four kids.

Chapter Ten

"Don't forget to take your bees!" Dannie held up a stack of paper bumblebees her preschool art class had painted the week before.

The children mobbed her as she passed the projects out, then they filed out into the hall, one by one, where their parents waited.

Dannie shed the smock she'd been wearing over her clothes and slumped into a tiny plastic chair.

Kelly Smith, one of three other instructors at the Wee Ones Art Studio, sat down beside her.

"Thanks for taking my classes yesterday," Dannie said.

"No problem. How was Cuatro Blanco?"

Dannie picked a fleck of paint off her fingernail. "There was a hurricane the day I got there, and I didn't get the chance to talk to anyone about Roger. Everyone was too busy cleaning up. So I came home."

"Wow. That sucks."

"Yeah. And then when I got home, my house had been broken in to. Two hundred and fifty bucks to replace the window they broke."

"Wow, that *really* sucks."

"You're telling me. I had to take the money out of the water-heater fund." Dannie got up and hung her smock on a hook near the door. "I've got to get going."

"I'll walk out with you," Kelly said, hanging her own smock next to Dannie's.

They chatted until they reached Dannie's minivan. Kelly pointed to one of the tires. "Looks like you have a flat."

"Great." Dannie looked at her watch. "I've got to pick up Richard at school."

"You want me to drive you?" Kelly said.

Then she'd have to bring Richard back here while she changed the tire? No way.

"Actually, if you could pick Richard up and take him to my neighbor's house, that would be a big help." She gave Kelly the address of the woman who was watching Betsy and the twins, and then she called the elementary school to let them know what was going on.

After Kelly had gone, Dannie opened the back hatch of the van. What was she looking for exactly? A tire and a jack, right? Why was that so difficult? She poked around the back, but couldn't find either one.

She never should have let her AAA membership lapse.

After ten minutes of searching, she located in a side compartment something that might have passed for a jack, but the spare tire was nowhere to be found.

"Hey, there."

Dannie froze. She knew that voice.

Guy.

She turned around.

His elbow stuck out of the driver's window of his black Mustang. He wore a black leather jacket, and his hair was perfectly disheveled.

Damn. He had no business looking that good.

"You look upset," he said. "Is something wrong?"

She pulled the jack from the trunk. "I have a flat."

"Need some help?"

"No."

"Dannie, what's wrong?"

"Nothing. I just need to change this tire. So if you'll excuse me…"

Guy pulled his car into a parking spot a few spaces down and walked over to her. "I've been trying to call you."

"I know."

He grabbed the jack from her hand and slid it underneath the van near the flat tire. Then he used the lug wrench to unscrew something under the frame.

"They keep the spare under here," he said.

"Oh."

He handed her his jacket before squatting to loosen the lug nuts on the flat. His jeans stretched taut over the solid mass of his thighs. The muscles in his back and arms flexed beneath his neon-pink T-shirt as he worked the tire off the wheel and replaced it with the spare.

Dannie folded his jacket over her arm and held it to her nose, breathing in the scent of his cologne mixed with the alluring smell of leather. She closed her eyes.

"Hey, you okay?"

Her eyes popped open. "I'm fine."

"Good. Because you looked like you were ready to pass out or something."

Irritated that he'd caught her sniffing his jacket, she said, "What's with you and pink shirts, anyway?"

"It's my signature, I guess."

"Like Charles Manson's swastika tattoo."

"More like Buddy Holly's glasses."

He rolled the flat tire toward the back of the van and leaned it against the rear bumper. He bent down, running a finger over the rubber.

"What are you doing?"

"Come here," he said.

She hunkered down beside him, feeling the heat of his leg against hers, trying hard not to think about waking up in his arms on his couch.

He took her hand, pushing one of her fingertips into a slit in the tire.

"Feel that?"

She nodded.

"That was no accident. Your tire was slashed."

She jerked her hand away. "Slashed?"

Guy nodded. He took his jacket from her arm and put it back on. "Do you know anybody who'd want to do that?"

"No. I... No." She pressed a palm to her forehead. "Wait a minute. How did you know where to find me?"

"I didn't. I was just driving by."

"Just driving by a strip mall that contains nothing but a preschool art studio, a lingerie store and a Vietnamese restaurant?"

"As a matter of fact, yes. I love the *Canh Chua Ca*."

"The what?"

"*Canh Chua Ca*. It's a sweet-and-sour fish soup."

Guy threw the jack and the tire into the back of the van.

"Uh-huh." Dannie slammed the hatch shut. "Well, thanks so much. See you around."

"Wait!" He stepped between her and the car door. "What's going on? You seem…angry."

"Do I?"

"Yes, you do. And I don't get it. I thought we'd put our differences aside. I thought we, you know, made a connection."

"That wasn't a connection. It was misplaced attraction."

"Misplaced?"

"Yes. Misplaced." She pushed past him and got into the car, rolling down the window. "Why didn't you tell me you were partners with Jimmy Duke?"

He seemed startled by the question. "Where did you hear that?"

She ignored the question and started the car. "When we were in Cuatro Blanco, I told you that Roger's firm handled Duke's finances, but you didn't say anything. You live in this town. You know Jimmy Duke's reputation."

"Dannie, let me explain—"

She held up a hand. "Don't bother. It's your business. Really. I just don't want to know about it."

She backed out of her parking space. Guy stepped into the void left by her van and watched her drive away.

DRIVING HOME, she was just angry enough to do what she'd wanted to do for the past eight months.

She was going to walk into Wiser-Crenshaw and give them a piece of her mind.

But when she arrived at the cool, gray-brick office building, her confidence wavered. It might have had something to do with the imposing decor—ultramodern, black and silver, lots of granite and steel. Or it might have been because—as she realized too late—she was disheveled and smudged with dirt from the tire incident.

But most likely it was the bitchy receptionist, Monique, who greeted her with a cool smile when she walked into the lobby, making it clear she was no longer welcome at Wiser-Crenshaw.

Well, screw it. She deserved some answers. She deserved to know why she had to worry about the hot water heater, and about her kids' futures, when Roger had more than paid his dues working for this company. As a matter of fact, she and the kids had paid their dues, too.

Wiser-Crenshaw owed her. Owed all of them.

"How may I help you, Mrs. Treat?" Monique spoke in a smooth, cultured tone Dannie knew for a fact was fake. She'd heard Monique's thick south Jersey accent in the ladies' room at the firm's holiday party two years ago. The receptionist had drunk one cup too many of the hard cider, and was fighting with her husband on her cell phone in one of the bathroom stalls. *Whaddayah want from me, Toneee…?*

"Hello, Monique. I'd like to speak to Rob Goody."

"Let me see if he's in—"

"Don't bother. I'll see for myself." Dannie marched to the elevator and, once inside, pressed the button for the third floor, where the human resources office was located.

Dannie knew Monique would be on the phone with Rob's secretary, warning her of Dannie's impending arrival. The bastard hadn't taken her calls in months.

She stormed off the elevator, which opened directly onto the reception area of Rob Goody's office. Rob's door was closed, but she could see him sitting at his desk through the frosted glass panels in the door.

"Dannie, what a surprise." Rob's secretary, Veronica, at least had the decency to look guilty. Dannie had always liked her.

"I need to see Rob."

"I'm sorry, he's busy at the moment. Can I leave him a message?"

"Yes, you can. You tell him that he better get his ass out here and talk to me, or I'm going to key the paint on his goddamned Porsche."

Veronica gave her a sympathetic nod. "I'll go see if I can get him off the phone."

Veronica slipped into Rob's office, and Dannie could see them talking. The secretary put her hands on her hips, wagging a finger at Rob. Seconds later Rob stood. He caught Dannie's eye through the window, hesitating, but Veronica pushed him toward the door.

"Dannie Treat! What a pleasure." He stepped out into the small reception area.

"Cut the crap, Rob. I need to talk to you about the money for Roger's stock holdings."

Rob cleared his throat. "I guess we'd better speak in my office, then."

He held the door open. Dannie stalked by him, trying not to be intimidated by the expensive crystal bric-a-brac or the huge mahogany desk. Rob gestured to a chair, but Dannie shook her head. She needed to stand for this.

"Rob, I'm not going to beat around the bush. My kids and I need the money for Roger's stock holdings. The insurance company hasn't paid off his life insurance yet, and we're living on a shoestring. If I don't get that check soon, I'm going to have to sell my organs, among other things."

Rob tented his fingers under his chin. "I'm sorry, Dannie, but there's nothing I can do. These things take time."

"That's bull, Rob. The company issued a check to Alice Peterson less than a week after Stan died."

"Those were different circumstances."

"What circumstances? He died on top of a toothless hooker in a thirty-five-dollar-a-night hotel room."

Rob squirmed in his high-backed leather chair. "Believe me, if I could help you I would. My hands are tied."

"So who can untie them? Who can I talk to about this if you can't help me?"

Rob shook his head. "Nobody. It just has to go through the channels."

The *channels?*

"Roger was dedicated to this company, Rob. He died on a goddamned Wiser-Crenshaw retreat. Three of your executives watched him fall overboard and drown. You're lucky I haven't tried to sue all of you."

"Don't go there, Dannie," Rob warned. "If you know what's good for you, you'll go home and wait it out."

"Don't treat me like a child."

"Then don't act like one."

"Maybe I need to speak to Ben Wiser."

Rob took a deep breath and splayed his hands out on his desk. "Listen to me. I'm telling you that if you mess with the bull, you're going to get the horns. Ben Wiser is not going to give you what you want. Nobody is."

"But *why?* Just tell me what's going on."

"I can't." He said it quietly, but with a conviction Dannie knew she wouldn't be able to break.

She ran out of steam. Clearly she would accomplish nothing here today. She rubbed her forehead. "Right."

"Hey. Hang in there," Rob said. "It's going to get better." He was a bigger fake than Monique.

Dannie slouched out of Rob's office. Veronica looked up at her with sympathy in her eyes.

"You okay?"

Dannie's voice cracked. "I just wish I knew what was going on."

Veronica glanced around. She took a key out of the top drawer of her desk. "Come with me."

Dannie followed Veronica to the executive washroom. Veronica opened the door, and when they were inside, locked it behind them.

The restroom decor was similar to the rest of the building—lots of chrome and black. Veronica leaned against the dark marble sink. "You can't tell anyone I told you this, but I know why they're not giving you your money."

Dannie's pulse quickened. "Why?"

Veronica bit her lower lip.

"Go on. I can take it."

"They think Roger embezzled some money."

"What?"

Veronica nodded. "About six months before he died, Roger got the Jimmy Duke account. Inherited it from that old horn-dog Stan Peterson."

"What?" Dannie said in a daze. "Roger never told me."

"Well, it happened. A few weeks before the Cuatro Blanco retreat, Jimmy Duke started complaining to Ben Wiser that he thought some money was missing from one of his accounts. But before anyone could audit Roger's books—" she lowered her voice "—you know, the *real* ones—he up and died."

"Wait." Dannie ran a hand through her tangled curls. "You mean to tell me they think Roger was stealing from Jimmy Duke?"

Veronica nodded again. "Some money earmarked for the Greenwood Mall project was funneled into an account that nobody can find."

Dannie's stomach rolled. "How much?"

Veronica hesitated. "Jimmy's business receipts are sort of... inexact."

"How much?"

"A quarter of a million dollars."

Dannie's mouth formed an *O*. She started sucking air, unable to get a breath. Veronica grabbed a paper towel out of a basket on the sink and ran it under cold water. She pressed it to the back of Dannie's neck.

"I hate to be the one to have to tell you this, but I thought you deserved to know. They're not going to pay you a dime until they figure out exactly how much Roger stole. Which they can't do until they find his records."

Dannie's breathing evened out. She tossed the wet paper towel into the trash and smoothed her hair, checking herself in the mirror. "Thank you, Veronica. I appreciate your honesty."

Veronica smiled. "You always struck me as the kind of woman I'd want for a friend."

Dannie hugged her. "You got it."

Veronica checked her watch. "We'd better get out of here. Old man Crenshaw had Mexican for lunch. He'll be looking for this key any minute."

Dannie drove home in a daze.

Roger had the Jimmy Duke account? Why hadn't he told her?

Come to think of it, Roger *had* been spending an awful lot of money before he died. He'd bought the old boat in the garage, and some expensive new suits. And a diamond tennis bracelet for Dannie on their anniversary.

Dear God. Could it be true? Had Roger been stealing from Jimmy Duke?

Dannie's blood turned to ice in her veins. She was more convinced than ever that Roger had been murdered.

Chapter Eleven

TWO WEEKS LATER, Dannie was standing at the stove making spaghetti when Quincy came running through the kitchen, a Barbie doll tied to his back.

"Giddyap!" Betsy ran after the dog, wearing felt chaps, a cowboy hat and nothing else.

"Put some clothes on!" Dannie yelled after her. "It's almost time to eat."

After half a dozen unreturned calls to the police in El Cuello, a brief and unfruitful conversation with one of the men from Wiser-Crenshaw who'd been on the fishing charter with Roger, and a meeting with the owner of the Main Street Gym, Dannie was no closer to knowing what had happened to Roger than she had been in Cuatro Blanco.

She needed a clue. A lead. Something.

She dumped a jar of spaghetti sauce into a pan and took a

loaf of garlic bread out of the oven. As she sliced bananas for the twins, she suddenly got the feeling she was being watched.

She'd been getting that feeling a lot lately.

She ran to the back door and looked out into the yard, but it was empty. The unlatched gate swung on its hinges in the breeze.

Had Richard just left it unlatched again? Or had someone been there, looking in at her? She shivered and pulled the curtains closed over the window.

This was getting ridiculous. She felt like Jamie Lee Curtis in *Halloween*. Any minute a man in a mask was going to jump out at her from behind the shrubbery.

But who? Why?

It had to have something to do with the counterfeit money and Guy's wife and Jimmy Duke. Maybe even Guy himself.

The spaghetti boiled over, the water splashing on the coils of the burner with a hiss. She turned off the stove and picked up the phone, dialing as she stirred the sauce.

"Can you come over?" she said. "I need to talk to you."

An hour later Guy horsed around in the living room with the kids while Dannie cleaned up the dishes from dinner.

She dried her hands on a towel and stood in the doorway, watching. Her heart squeezed at the expression of joy on Richard's face. He really had missed having a man around the house.

He remembered throwing a ball around the backyard, and Roger tucking him in at night, and this. This roughhousing that a mother could never duplicate.

Guy stood up. Richard hung from his biceps. "Hey! I've been looking at your paintings. You're good."

"Was good. I don't paint anymore."

"Really? Why not?"

Dannie sighed. "No time, I guess. No energy."

"No inspiration?"

"Maybe." She looked around at the works she'd completed in college, and in her twenties and early thirties. *Flowers in Orange Vase. Man Feeding Pigeons in Franklin Park. Woman with Scarf.*

After she'd married Roger, it had seemed so frivolous to spend her time in the studio. They always had other, more important things to do. Wiser-Crenshaw outings and charity events.

And then the children had come, and she'd put away her paints for good.

"You all done in the kitchen?" Guy asked.

She nodded. "I'm going to put Erin and Emma down, and then we'll talk."

"Right." Guy set Richard back on his feet. "Until then, be prepared to fight the Mud Monster. Aarghhh!"

Richard and Betsy ran screaming into the kitchen, Guy and Quincy on their heels.

When the twins were in bed and Betsy and Richard were in the den watching a movie, Dannie poured herself some wine, Guy a glass of orange juice and sat down beside him at the kitchen table.

"Okay. I want the truth," she said, setting the juice in front of him.

"What do you want to know, exactly?" Guy asked.

"I want to know everything," Dannie said. "Starting with how you're involved with Jimmy Duke."

Guy wrapped his hands around the juice glass and stared down into the liquid.

"Guy?"

He exhaled. "It's not what you think."

"You don't know what I think."

"Yes, I do. You think I'm one of Jimmy's employees. I'm not."

He leaned back in his chair, looking her straight in the eye. "It was a mistake."

"Oh, boy. I can't wait to hear this. You became partners with Jimmy Duke by mistake?"

He shrugged. "I ran out of money. I was in the middle of building the spa, and it ran over budget. *Way* over budget."

She took a sip of her wine, waiting for him to continue.

"The bank wouldn't loan me any more money, so Lisa introduced me to Jimmy. She'd met him at the gym. And to make a long story short, I asked him for help."

"But you know how he operates!"

"Believe me, I had no other choice. I tried everything, and if I had stopped construction, I'd have gone bankrupt. It was the only way."

"So he loaned you the money?"

"Two hundred and fifty thousand dollars. With the stipulation that if I didn't pay him back within three years, he'd become a permanent partner in the spa." Guy pushed his juice glass away. "Needless to say, I'm way behind schedule. The spa isn't even finished yet, much less making money. There's no way I'm going to be able to pay him back on time."

"So the money Lisa took was Jimmy Duke's money?"

Guy nodded. "So then Lisa sets me up with this contractor, who'll do the work for cash. The contractor tries to use the cash he got from me to pay for his girlfriend's boob job at some cheap, cash-up-front chop shop. The so-called surgeon's office discovers it's counterfeit. Now the contractor's girlfriend is threatening to tell the contractor's wife about their affair if he doesn't get her new boobs soon. And the contractor is leaning on me, threatening to tell Jimmy about the money being stolen if I don't pay him soon. And if Jimmy finds out…"

Guy looked miserable. Defeated.

Dannie slid a hand over his and gave it a squeeze. "So basically, this is all because of a boob job?"

Guy laughed and shook his head. "I guess you could say that. I've been looking for Lisa for months. This Cuatro Blanco thing was my only lead."

"But why do you think Roger had anything to do with this?" she asked.

"There are too many coincidences," Guy said. "Their affair. The fact that he...died in Cuatro Blanco. The fact that they both knew Jimmy Duke. And now the counterfeit money."

"Maybe Jimmy got to both of them," she said. "Maybe he made them disappear."

"I thought of that, but it didn't make sense. Why would Lisa have stolen the money from the safe if she didn't know she was going to disappear? And why would her mother be mailing packages to Cuatro Blanco?"

Dannie finished her wine and poured another glass, pacing the kitchen. "So the only person you know who has had any contact with Lisa since she left was her mother?"

"Yes. Lisa tells her mother everything. I'm sure she knew exactly what was going on."

"Have you gone back to her mother's house? Looked for more evidence?"

"No. But I still have the key from Lisa's key chain. I could get in there anytime I want."

"Then what are we waiting for?"

THEY PLANNED A STAKEOUT for the following evening, when Guy knew that Lisa's mother, Rose Hoffstetter, would leave the house for her regular Thursday-night bingo game and they could use Guy's key to get in.

Guy arrived early to Dannie's house and helped her clean up the dinner dishes, commenting, of course, on the lack of a vegetable.

"We had ketchup on the hot dogs," Dannie said. "That counts as a vegetable."

"Says who?"

"The U.S. government."

Dannie's regular babysitter couldn't make it, but the girl had recommended a friend, Kristi, who showed up fifteen minutes late. Not a good omen.

Kristi had an earring through her eyebrow, a stud in her nose and she chewed her gum with her mouth open. She looked bored as Dannie explained the rules of the house and the bedtime procedure.

"Betsy and Richard can have pretzels before bed, but not ice cream. They'll get too hyper. The twins get a little bit of yogurt, or some grapes. I've cut some up and put them in the fridge."

Kristi cracked her gum. "So what should I *do* with them? This is, like, my first time babysitting."

Dannie bit the inside of her cheek. "Well, there's a movie in the DVD player. Erin and Emma have some wooden puzzles in that drawer over there. They go to bed at seven-thirty. Betsy and Richard can stay up until eight-fifteen. Their pajamas are in the dryer, so they should be dry by bedtime."

Kristi pulled her gum into a long string, and twirled it back into her mouth with her tongue.

What a talent.

"My cell phone number is on the table," Dannie continued, "along with a list of emergency numbers. Okay?"

Kristi shrugged. "Whatever."

"Do you have any questions?"

Kristi took the gum out of her mouth. "Like, how much do you pay? I'm saving up for a tattoo."

Dannie felt a twitch forming in her left eyelid. "Guy…?"

He grabbed her hand and pulled her toward the door. "Come on. It'll be fine. She can call you on the cell if she needs you. We'll be less than five miles away."

Dannie glanced over her shoulder. Kristi was twirling her gum around her finger, looking at the kids as if she was trying to figure out how to turn them off.

Dannie knew from experience there was no switch for that.

"We'll take your car," Guy said when they reached the driveway. "Rose would know mine."

Dannie tossed him the keys and slid into the passenger side, sitting on a half-melted chocolate bar. She peeled the wrapper off her butt and stuffed it into a plastic grocery bag on the floor.

"Not to sound rude," Guy said, "but do you ever clean this thing?"

Dannie pulled the seat belt over her lap. "Roger used to handle that. I guess I haven't really thought about it."

"Maybe it's time." He unstuck a piece of gum from the gear-shift and threw it into the bag.

They'd just pulled out of the driveway when Dannie's cell phone rang.

Kristi popped her gum into the phone. "Um, like, who did you say couldn't have ice cream? Because the boy is saying he can have some, but I thought you said he couldn't."

"That's right. *Richard* is not allowed to have ice cream. Betsy isn't, either. They can have pretzels or an apple."

"'Kay. See ya."

"The babysitter?" Guy asked when Dannie hung up.

"If you can call her that." Dannie resisted the urge to demand he turn the car around and take her back home. She sighed.

"At least she didn't give Richard ice cream. He'd be up all night."

A few minutes later Guy drove slowly past a small white house with green shutters.

"That's it."

Lights blazed in the kitchen, the living room and a bedroom upstairs. A cat sat tucked up into itself on a windowsill over-looking the street.

"Looks like she's still home," Dannie said.

"Huh. Must be running late. Bingo starts in ten minutes, and she likes to get there early so she can get a beer and a plate of hot wings."

"Beer and wings? Where is this bingo game, in the back room of a bar?"

"Close. At the firehouse."

Guy pulled the van up to the curb a few doors down from Rose's house, and cut the engine.

"What now?" Dannie said.

"We wait."

They sat in silence for a few minutes, staring at the house, with no sign of movement from Rose.

"Can we at least listen to the radio?" Dannie said.

"Sure. Why not?"

Guy turned the key in the ignition just enough to start the power in the car. Dannie tuned the radio in to the eighties station. REO Speedwagon's "Keep on Lovin' You" drifted from the speakers.

"I love this song," Dannie said. "I had my first kiss to this song."

"Oh, yeah?" Guy said. "Tell me about it."

Dannie leaned back in her seat. "I was almost thirteen, and I was at my first boy-girl birthday party. It was the middle of summer. Really hot. We were dancing in the basement, and all the lights were out except for one of those tabletop disco lights. This song came on, and the boy I'd had a crush on all year asked me to dance. I couldn't believe my luck."

Guy leaned back in his seat, turning his head toward hers. "Go on."

"The heat was terrible in the basement. He'd unbuttoned his shirt, and I thought I had died and gone to heaven. He pulled me close. I don't think we were dancing really. We weren't moving, just sort of rocking back and forth. And then he leaned down and kissed me."

Guy reached out and gave one of her curls a tug, letting it spring back into place. "Did you like it?"

"Are you kidding? I was too scared to like it."

"What were you scared of?"

"I don't know. Love, maybe. Or lust. Both were way beyond my control at that point."

"And what about now?" He slid his fingers into her hair, burying them in her curls.

"I…" The words caught in her throat. She fought for a breath, but it seemed as if the air had been stolen by the rising temperature in the car.

Guy touched his lips to hers, softly, tentatively. So much like that first kiss, her throat constricted. She closed her eyes. She could see the spinning lights. Hear the music echoing off the painted cinder-block walls…

"I guess they're both still way beyond my control," she whispered.

Guy groaned, crushing her chest against his, running a hand over her back, her hip, her thigh. The melted chocolate on her backside.

They struggled to get closer, blocked by the center console and the steering wheel. Guy smacked his head against the window as he climbed into the passenger seat. He groaned again, probably in pain, but it still managed to turn her on.

Everything about him turned her on, and not just physically. Spending time with him had an addictive quality. A little bit of Guy was never enough. And it was getting dangerous.

Dannie lifted her hips and twisted around until he was sitting on the seat and she was straddling him. Before she knew it, he'd peeled off her jacket and blouse, and was working on the button of her jeans.

"Died in Your Arms" by Cutting Crew came on the radio and Dannie thought there might not be a truer song for that moment. Her body fit against Guy's as if they were two parts of a puzzle, separated only by a pink T-shirt and an eighth of an inch of denim.

She moved her hands over his face, touching his eyelids, his crooked nose, his lips. She slid against him and pulled up his shirt, touching her bare stomach to his.

"You are so sexy," he breathed. "I want you so bad, it hurts."

"That's probably the door handle."

He held her face in his hands. "I'm not joking, Dannie. I feel things for you I haven't felt in a long, long time."

"You're just nostalgic from the music," she said, pulling away.

But he wouldn't let her off so easily. His arms circled her waist and he pulled her back to him. "The music has nothing to do with it."

"Guy, we can't do this."

"Why? What's stopping us?"

"How about the fact that we're in a car outside your mother-in-law's house, trying to get information about your wife and my dead husband?"

Guy's arms fell away from her body. "You're right. We shouldn't be doing this in a car."

"That's what you got out of that? We shouldn't be doing it in a *car?* What about the other stuff?"

Guy picked her blouse off the driver's seat and held it up to her. She slipped it on, and he buttoned it as he spoke. "Look, Lisa left *me.* She stole from me, knowing full well that I'd be in deep trouble because of it. Jimmy Duke is not a man you mess with."

"I realize that, but you're still married."

"Marriage isn't just a piece of paper. It's the commitment behind the paper that counts. Doesn't seem to me like Lisa was very committed. Roger, either, for that matter."

"Roger was a good husband."

"Yeah? You didn't seem too surprised when I told you he was cheating on you with my wife. I'm guessing it wasn't the first time."

She shook her head. "But there are other measures of a marriage. He was a great father."

"That's admirable. But what does that have to do with you and me? Are you going to be loyal to a man after he's been gone nine months because he was a crappy husband but a good father? What about what *you* want?"

She was silent.

"Do you want me, Dannie? Or am I just in this thing alone?"

How could she answer that?

There were so many things to consider. Too many things. She wasn't the kind of woman who had idle affairs, especially not with married men. And guy was still married, whether Lisa had left him or not.

Roger was only the third man she'd ever been in love with in her life, after two long-term boyfriends, one in high school and one in college.

And then there was Lyle.

If she hooked up with Guy, it would surely cause a rift in her friendship with Lyle. And she cared about him, she truly did.

But you don't want to have sex with him, the devil on her shoulder whispered. *Isn't it time you let yourself have a little bit of fun?*

Before she could commit to anything, her cell phone rang. She exhaled, both in relief and frustration. "Yes?"

"Okay, like, now they're fighting. What should I do?" Kristi sounded decidedly less cool than she had twenty minutes ago.

"Send Richard to his room and stick Betsy in the corner for five minutes. Let the twins listen to a *Sesame Street* CD while they're having their snack."

"Right. Okay. Like, this is a lot harder than taking care of my neighbor's guinea pigs."

"No kidding?" Dannie gave Kristi a few words of encouragement and flipped the phone shut.

"Now I'm worried," she said. "Maybe we should go back."

"Too late." Guy pulled her down in a slouch behind the dashboard. Lights flashed against the fogged-up windshield as a car drove past. Dannie cleared a spot with her fingertips, and peeked out. "Was that her?"

"That was her." Guy opened the door. "Let's rock and roll."

Chapter Twelve

THEY WENT AROUND TO the back of the house, dodging decorative land mines—a shiny ball on a pedestal, whirligigs, ceramic bunnies.

A koi pond gurgled at the edge of a small concrete slab that apparently served as a patio, on which two white plastic chairs sat.

Guy fumbled with the key, opening a door that entered on a small kitchen. A plastic night-light glowed on the wall beneath the cabinets. Even in the dim light, Dannie could see the harvest-gold appliances and gold-flecked Formica countertops of her youth.

The kitchen bore the smell of sauerkraut. Or rather, it secreted the smell, which seemed as if it had been steeped into the dark paneling and worn linoleum floor.

Guy switched on a light, turning the dimmer as low as it could go. In the corner of a kitchenette sat brown vinyl-covered chairs and a fake wood table piled high with mail, circulars, newspapers, coupons and other detritus.

"That's where I saw the package," Guy said. "Maybe we should go through these piles."

Go through someone's private stuff? It just felt wrong. But Dannie was desperate to find out what was going on. Or rather, desperate to fix it. And if she had to shuffle through some lady's junk mail to do it, then that's what she'd do.

"I'll take the table—you take the rest of the house," she said. "You know the place. Where she'd be most likely to keep things."

"Right." Guy pulled a penlight out of his pocket before disappearing into the living area, which was separated from the kitchen by a half wall topped with a wrought-iron trellis that went up to the ceiling.

Dannie picked through the piles of paper, taking care not to disrupt things too much. As if anyone would possibly notice.

A heap of *Parade* magazines held no interest. Nor did a teetering mountain of coupons, most of which had expired. But the stack of telephone bills did.

She picked the pile carefully off the table and shuffled through the bills, skimming all the long-distance charges for foreign phone numbers.

In a phone bill from January, three weeks before Roger had died, there were several calls to one number in Costa Rica. The following month, February, included half a dozen calls to a number in Cuatro Blanco.

Dannie pulled a small notebook and pen out of the pocket of her jacket and jotted down the numbers in Costa Rica and Cuatro Blanco. Then she moved on to the credit card bills.

After nearly fifteen minutes of searching, she could find nothing else that definitively linked Rose Hoffstetter to Cuatro

Blanco. She was just about to go looking for Guy when she heard him calling her from upstairs.

She followed the sound of his voice, feeling her way through the dark until she discovered a flimsy railing that creaked beneath her hand as she made her way up the steps. A light shone from the back bedroom, illuminating the upstairs hall.

The first bedroom she passed was done up in pink gingham, with white furniture and about a hundred teddy bears on the bed, all staring out at her with little black plastic eyes.

The second room was, apparently, a television room, with a TV set and an old VCR on a stand, and a love seat pushed against the far wall.

Guy stuck his head out of the last bedroom, motioning to her.

"Did you find something?" she asked from the doorway.

"Maybe. And I need you to check something for me."

"What?"

"Her underwear drawer."

Dannie held up a hand and backed away. "No way."

"Come on. I can't do it," Guy said. "I can't. She's my mother-in-law, for chrissake."

"I can't do it! I don't even know her!"

Guy gave her a look. "Does that even matter? You went through her mail." He slid the top drawer open. "C'mon. Just do it."

Dannie suppressed a shudder. She stuck her hand into the drawer, touching something that had an awful lot of elastic. A bra, maybe. Or a girdle. "Ugh."

She pushed her hand around a bit more, looking for anything that felt as if it wasn't an undergarment. And then she felt it. Something long and bumpy and definitely rubbery…

"Oh, dear God." She whipped her hand out of the drawer and slammed it shut.

"What?" Guy said.

"Nothing."

"Did you find something?"

"Shut up! I don't want to talk about it! Let's just get out of here."

Guy's gaze lingered on the drawer. "What was it?"

"Trust me, you don't want to know." She grabbed his hand and dragged him from the room, throwing the light switch as she went.

They descended the stairs in darkness, and were heading for the dim light of the kitchen when they heard the knob on the back door rattle. They hunkered down in the shadow of the staircase, watching the door through the railing.

A woman Dannie could only assume was Rose came through the door, a bag from Royer's Pharmacy in one hand, her keys in the other. The cat that had been in the front window jumped up on one of the kitchen chairs and meowed loudly. Rose patted the cat on the head.

"Snickerdoodle! I could have sworn I turned this light out when I left." Her voice was raspy. She coughed a loud, hacking cough. The cat took off.

Rose puttered around the kitchen for a few minutes in her coat and hat, fishing a bottle of pills from the pharmacy bag, running a glass of water.

Dannie grabbed Guy's arm. "What do we do?" she whispered.

"We'll have to go out the front door," he whispered back. "Wait for my cue."

To get to the front door they'd have to run directly in the line of sight of the kitchen.

Rose opened a can of cat food and dumped it into a dish on the floor. Then she sat down at the kitchen table and started sifting through her mail.

Guy nodded. They moved for the front door, crawling, staying below the half wall. Dannie's heart pounded in her ears.

Halfway across the darkened living room Dannie's cell phone rang. Out of habit, she'd stuck it in her jacket pocket.

Rose leaped to her feet. "Who's there?"

Dannie and Guy reached the front door. Guy fumbled with the doorknob, only to realize the security chain was in place. The world shifted into slow motion. Dannie watched Guy fumble with the chain as Rose moved toward the light switch in the living room.

Dannie's cell phone was still ringing.

Guy and Dannie burst out onto the front stoop just as the living room light came on, and they took off across the yard at breakneck speed. Halfway to the car Dannie ran smack into a cement donkey pulling a flower cart. A blinding pain exploded in her shin. Her teeth rattled in her head.

She kept going, spurred on by the sight of Guy's back moving farther ahead of her with every step.

Rose was out on the stoop now, yelling. Dannie couldn't hear what, and wasn't about to stop and try to figure it out.

Guy jerked open the door to the van. Dannie flung herself in the driver's side door, tumbling over both Guy and the center console as Guy jammed the key into the ignition and peeled out.

Dannie looked in the rearview mirror at Rose, who squinted out into the night.

"What if she gets my plate number?" Dannie said, panting. She held her shin, biting her lip against the pain.

"She won't," said Guy, his words coming in staccato spurts. "She's blind without her glasses, and the car was a good distance away."

"Do you think she recognized you?"

"I don't think so. But if she did, I'll hear from her."

Dannie's phone rang again. She hadn't been aware it had ever stopped. Maybe it had happened when she'd maimed herself on the cement donkey.

She answered the phone. "Yes, Kristi?"

She tried to keep her voice even. Not give away the fact that she'd been out breaking and entering. Or at least entering.

"So now I can't find the kids' pajamas." There was a note of hysteria in her voice. "The big girl said they usually sleep naked, but you don't seem like the kind of mother that would allow that. Am I right, or what?"

Dannie closed her eyes. "You're right. The pajamas are in the dryer, remember?"

"Cool." Kristi hung up.

Guy squeezed her hand. "I'll take you home."

"Screw that. I need a drink."

Chapter Thirteen

"I'LL HAVE A MARGARITA. Frozen, please." Dannie gave her order to the waitress at Finnegan's, one of those fake Irish pubs that had popped up like blemishes in recent years near every shopping mall. It had been the first place they'd come across after leaving Rose's.

The waitress, a twentysomething in black pants, a visor and a purple shirt covered with collectible pins, wrote Dannie's order on her pad in painstaking, curly handwriting. She smiled shyly at Guy. "Something for you?"

"I'll have a Toasted Almond," he said.

"A Toasted Almond?" Dannie said. "First of all, you're putting alcohol in your temple?"

"I think I deserve it tonight, don't you?"

"Why not? But a *Toasted Almond?* Couldn't you order something a little bit more manly?"

"Hey, what can I say? I don't know the names of many

drinks. Lisa used to drink Toasted Almonds, and I know I like them. You have a problem with that?"

The waitress patted Guy's arm. "I personally think it's nice you're so secure in your masculinity."

"What is this, psych 101?" Dannie said. "Just get our drinks, okay?"

The waitress gave Dannie the mental finger, winked at Guy and sauntered off in the direction of the bar, her size-zero hips swinging as seductively as size-zero hips can swing.

"Do women hit on you everywhere you go?" Dannie said, annoyed with herself for being so annoyed.

"Apparently so."

Dannie gave a frustrated sigh.

Guy grabbed her hand. "Hey. It's not like I take them up on it. I just have a way with women. That's why I'm in the spa business."

"Not yet," Dannie said. "Not until you get your money back."

"Right." Guy drummed his fingertips on the high wooden table. "So let's take a look at what you found at Rose's."

Dannie pulled the little notebook with the phone numbers out of her pocket and tossed it on the table between them. She pointed to one of the numbers. "This exchange is Cuatro Blanco. Even if it didn't say it on the phone bill, I'd recognize it from all the calls I've had to make there since Roger died."

"What about the other one?" Guy said.

Dannie shook her head. "The phone bill said Costa Rica. I don't recognize that one."

Guy pulled his cell phone out of his pocket. "So let's call it."

The waitress arrived with their drinks, serving them along with another shy, flirty look for Guy. She hovered around the table as he took a sip of the Toasted Almond.

"Is it okay?" she asked.

"Very good."

"Thank you for your concern," Dannie said sarcastically. "Now, can we have a moment, please?"

The waitress stalked away.

Guy took a healthy slug of his drink before punching the Costa Rican phone number into his cell. He motioned Dannie over.

She climbed down from her tall stool and stood beside him as he held his phone out for her to hear. She leaned her head close to his, listening.

A recording, in Spanish, streamed out from the phone.

"It's a bank," Guy said.

"A bank?"

Guy nodded.

"Why would Rose call a bank in Costa Rica? There were at least four calls to that number."

"What month was the phone bill?" Guy said.

"Last January." A lightbulb went off in her head. "A month before Lisa left."

"Exactly."

"So Lisa could have made those calls."

"I'm betting she did." Guy drained his Toasted Almond. "Let's call the other number."

She resumed her position near his phone, and they listened in as another recording in Spanish played.

"Disconnected." Guy raised a hand to summon the waitress. He caught her attention—or perhaps had never lost it—and pointed to both his and Dannie's glasses.

"Wow, do you really think you should?" Dannie said. "Those Toasted Almonds are wicked."

"Okay, smart-ass. So do you want to see what *I* found?"

"Absolutely." Dannie sucked frozen margarita through her

straw until she had brain freeze. She wasn't about to get out-lapped by a man drinking Toasted Almonds.

Guy pulled a business card out of the back pocket of his jeans and flicked it onto the table. It slid to a stop under Dannie's pinkie finger.

She picked it up, blinking. "I…I don't understand."

Guy shook his head. "I don't, either."

"Why would Rose have one of Lyle's business cards?"

"You tell me."

Dannie thought for a moment. "Maybe Lisa got it from Roger."

"So why would Roger give Lyle's card to Lisa?"

"I don't know. Maybe she needed some office supplies."

Dannie tried to make light of it, but her stomach churned. Why *would* Rose have Lyle's card? Even she didn't buy her own explanation.

The waitress showed up and set their drinks on the table. She slid the black leather billfold with their tab in front of Dannie, and touched Guy's shoulder. "My shift ends in ten minutes, so if you want anything else, let me know. Anything at all."

"Excuse me," Dannie said. "You can see me sitting here, right? Me, his date?"

"Oh, sorry. I didn't realize you were a couple. You don't really look like his type." She walked away, giving Guy a little wave over her shoulder.

"How rude," Dannie said.

"Are we really on a date?" Guy asked.

"Of course not. But *she* didn't know that."

"Well, we'll have to do that sometime," Guy said.

"Do what?"

"Have a date."

She felt slightly dizzy. She hadn't eaten much dinner—she'd been too nervous—and that first margarita had gone straight to her head. "We have to figure all of this stuff out first."

"What stuff?"

"All of it. Like where Lisa is, and what really happened to Roger."

"You're starting to believe me, then?" Guy asked. "That he might still be alive?"

"Of course not. But I do think something suspicious happened. That's probably why I can't get a death certificate. They're still investigating everything in Cuatro Blanco."

"Why wouldn't they just tell you that, then?"

Dannie took a sip of her drink. "You've seen how they operate. Everything moves in slow motion. If they told me they were investigating, they'd probably worry that I'd come down there and try to make them hurry."

Guy stared into his drink. "Maybe you're right."

"I know I'm right." She finished her drink. "We should get out of here."

"Your place or mine?" Guy said.

"Mine. I have to get home and make sure my kids are still in one piece."

Guy tucked some money into the leather billfold the waitress had left. "I think you should be more worried about whether the babysitter is still in one piece."

WHEN THEY ARRIVED BACK at Dannie's, Kristi was lying on the couch with a pillow over her head.

Richard, wielding a pair of kitchen tongs dripping with water, emerged from the bathroom. "I'm sorry, Mommy."

Oh, boy. That was never good. "What are you sorry about?"

"I was playing with my submarine, and it got stuck in the pipe."

"Oh, God. What pipe?"

"The one in the potty."

"I'll take care of it." Guy followed Richard into the hall toward the bathroom.

Betsy, dressed in nothing but a clear raincoat and galoshes, ran past, pulling Quincy by his leash, who in turn was pulling the twins in a plastic laundry-basket carriage rigged with jump-rope reins.

"You gave them ice cream, didn't you?" Dannie said.

Kristi teared up. "Okay. This job is *so* not fun. I'm, like, completely wiped."

"Welcome to my world." Dannie grabbed Betsy by the hood of her raincoat as she ran past, stripped her naked and told her to march upstairs.

She scooped the twins out of the laundry basket and handed one of them to Kristi. "Come on. I'll show you how I do things."

Forty minutes later the kids were all in bed, Guy was driving Kristi home and Dannie was the one lying on the couch with the pillow over her head.

The phone rang. She was tempted not to answer it, but it went against her nature.

"Hello?"

"Dannie. Where have you been?" It was Lyle, sounding annoyed.

Dannie's blood pressure shot up. How dare he act annoyed with *her?* She was tempted to ask him about the business card Guy had found at Rose's house, but how would she explain being in Rose's house? Plus, it would bring up the whole thing about Guy again, and she wasn't in the mood.

"What do you want, Lyle?"

He was quiet for a moment. "Are you okay?"

"Not really, no. I'm tired, and I have a headache."

"Let me come over and take care of you. I'll make you something to eat, and we can watch a movie or something."

The doorbell rang.

Guy.

She got up and hurried to the door.

"Was that the doorbell?" Lyle asked.

"No. I'm picking up the kids' toys. One of them made a noise." She opened the door and held a finger to her lips so Guy wouldn't talk. She mouthed "Lyle," and pointed to the phone.

"So how about it?" Lyle said. "I can be there in ten minutes."

"I don't think so. Not tonight."

Guy leaned in and kissed her neck. She closed her eyes. It was hard to breathe.

"Okay, then. How about tomorrow night?" Lyle said.

"Maybe. I'll call you," she mumbled.

Guy's tongue swirled in her ear. Her knees went weak, and he caught her around the waist to hold her up.

Wow. A couple of Toasted Almonds brought out the animal in him.

Lyle exhaled. "Are you sure you're okay?"

"I'm fine. I just… I want to go to bed."

Her voice trailed off as Guy took the phone from her hand and pressed the off button. The phone clattered to the hardwood floor. Guy pulled her against him and kissed her hard on the mouth.

"What are you doing?" she mumbled.

"Just continuing what we started in the van."

"I thought we agreed we wouldn't."

"I never agreed to that. Besides, aren't you the one who told me to loosen up and let somebody get on my rides?"

"Ah, yes. The amusement park."

"So what do you say? You wanna try the Wet 'n' Wild?"

All reason left her. Especially the reason telling her this was a bad idea.

So the man was the complete opposite of her idea of what a man should be. He cut hair. He wore pink. He drank Toasted Almonds. So what?

And he was partners with Jimmy Duke—the man who just might have killed her husband. But she had no proof of that. And it sure seemed as if he wasn't thrilled to be tied to Jimmy Duke in any way.

And he was the husband of *her* husband's lover. Was there anyone more appropriate to sleep with, really? An eye for an eye, right?

Besides, he was such a good kisser. She could only imagine the rest of his game was just as good. And she was slightly tipsy, and very horny, and really, really lonely.

She might regret this tomorrow morning, but she sure as hell wasn't going to regret it tonight.

"You want to go to bed?" Guy whispered.

She nodded.

He picked her up in his arms, turning the switch for the living room light out with his elbow on his way up the stairs.

"I CAN'T BELIEVE THIS." Guy lay on his back, staring at the ceiling.

"I'm sorry," Dannie said. "When it came down to it, I guess I just wasn't ready."

"It would have been nice if you could have told me that downstairs," he said.

"I didn't know it downstairs. I thought…" She sighed. "I like you, Guy. Very much. But this is so strange. And we're here, in the bed I shared with Roger, and I just—"

"Stop," he said, touching her mouth with his index finger. "You don't owe me any explanations. I was being a jerk."

"No, you weren't. I led you on."

"Hey, once you get all your hair cut off, you can't put it back on. At least, not without paying some serious money for extensions."

"What?"

He rolled over and propped himself up on his elbow. "You changed your mind, that's all. At the salon, women change their minds all the time. But once they get their hair cut off, they can't get it put back on. And once we sleep together, we can't undo it. So we'll wait until you're ready."

Dannie gave him a grateful look. "Okay. So what are we going to do next?"

"Well, I guess I should go home…."

"No, I meant what are we going to do about this whole thing with Lisa?"

Guy played with her hair, his breath soft on her cheek. Dannie was sorely tempted to ignore her misgivings and just sleep with him. She knew it would be good. Really good. And God knew, she needed something good right now.

"We should go back to Cuatro Blanco," Guy said.

Dannie rubbed her eyes. "I can't. My in-laws just watched the kids for that long weekend. Besides, I don't have the money."

"You know your in-laws won't mind. And we don't need money. Not much, anyway. We can hitch a ride on the charter with my new friend. And we can use the free week we won in the dance contest."

"What if there aren't any rooms?"

"I doubt that will be a problem, considering it's hurricane season."

"I don't know…"

"It's the only way. We'll never find anything out by calling the Cuatro Blancan authorities."

It was true. She'd gone that route for the past nine months and it had gotten her nowhere. If she was going to accomplish anything, she was going to have to go back to Cuatro Blanco.

Only, this time she wasn't taking Lyle. She wouldn't even tell him until she got back.

"Okay," she said. "We'll go."

"Good. I'll call and make the reservations at El Pelícano tomorrow." When he rolled out of bed, Dannie got a good look at his amazing body.

It was tempting—too damned tempting—to invite him back into bed. But she made a silent vow that she would control herself.

At least until all this was over. Then all bets were off.

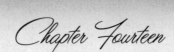

Chapter Fourteen

THEIR PLANE LANDED fifteen minutes earlier than scheduled, which Dannie took as a good omen. Anything that happened ahead of schedule in Cuatro Blanco was a small miracle.

She and Guy made their way through the tiny airport and onto the shuttle bus—no delusions about a comfortable, air-conditioned taxi ride this time—and squeezed into one of the bench seats.

Guy's thigh bumped against hers every time they hit a rut in the road, which was about every three seconds. His T-shirt clung to every damp, sculpted muscle, and the scent of his cologne was driving her crazy. Her mind kept flashing back to the night in her bedroom, when she could have felt his entire body move against her, not just his thigh.

What would it be like to be with a man other than Roger? The thought was both exhilarating and frightening.

By the time they got to El Pelícano, Dannie was hot and cranky and completely turned on.

At the desk Guy presented the certificate they'd received from the dance contest. "I called a few days ago and made reservations."

"Ah, *sí!* Our dirty dancers!" The woman behind the desk tapped on a keyboard. "Welcome back. I hope the weather is much better for you this time."

"Yes, let's hope so," Guy said, flashing his sexy little dimple.

"Okay. Everything is ready." The desk clerk pushed two keys across the counter. "Fourth floor."

Guy handed one of the keys to Dannie as they made their way to the elevator.

"What do you think we should do first?" Dannie asked.

"Let's get settled into our rooms, and then we can meet by the pool to hammer out a game plan."

"Sounds good."

They exited the elevator, and both headed in the same direction. Dannie checked her key. Room 403. Guy's room was probably right next to hers.

Great.

There would be no way to avoid him. She would probably be able to hear him breathing right through the thin walls. How was she going to keep her promise to herself of no hanky-panky when she could hear him breathing through the walls?

"Well, this is me," Guy said, stopping at a door.

Dannie looked at the number—403.

"This is *my* room," she said. "Let me see your key."

Guy handed it over—403.

"There must be some sort of mistake," Guy said. "They gave us keys to the same room."

"Gimme that." Dannie grabbed Guy's key and dropped her suitcase. "I'll be right back."

In the lobby she waited in line for twenty minutes behind

a crowd consisting mostly of fat, balding men, all wearing blue T-shirts that said "Fishermen Have Bigger Rods." Dannie shuddered at the image.

They were a noisy group, telling jokes and punching one another on the arms. By the time Dannie reached the desk, she had a splitting headache.

She slid the two keys across the counter. "We have a little problem. You seem to have given my friend and me keys to the same room."

The clerk tapped the keyboard. "The dirty dancers, no?"

"Yes."

"That is your room, miss—403."

"*Our* room?"

"*Sí*. Your room."

"You mean we only get one?"

"Of course. You won only one contest, no?"

"Yes. But we're not a couple. We can't share a room."

"Would that be such a bad thing? Your friend is, how do you say, *muy guapo,* no?" The clerk grinned.

"*Muy guapo?*"

"Very handsome."

"Yes, he is very handsome. But he's not my boyfriend."

The clerk winked. "No one will tell on you."

Dannie felt her blood pressure rising to critical levels. "Can you please just give me another room? I'll pay for it."

"I wish I could, miss. But the hotel is full." She swept a hand toward the men in the blue T-shirts. "Fishing competition."

"You don't have one room available?"

"Not one. Sorry."

"So what am I supposed to do now?" Dannie asked, realizing she was dangerously close to whining.

The clerk shrugged and smiled. "Take it easy, amiga!"

GUY WAS SITTING on his suitcase, leaning back against the door to room 403, when Dannie got back upstairs.

"Uh-oh. What happened?"

"Move." She shoved the key into the lock and opened the door. Guy tumbled backward into the room.

"Hey!"

Dannie stepped over him. "Did you bother to read the fine print on that certificate?"

"What fine print?"

"The fine print that said we get one room. *One.*"

"Oh. I must have missed that."

She glared at him. "Isn't that convenient?"

"Hey. Wait a minute. Are you suggesting I did this on purpose?"

"Did you?"

"No."

"I don't believe you."

Guy marched over and pinned her against the wall with his body, pressing his palm against the wall above her head. "Listen, lady. You're not *that* hot. I don't lie. And I don't have to manipulate women to get them into bed."

Dannie's heart pounded in her chest, as much from Guy's proximity as from her residual fury.

"Apologize," he said.

"I'm sorry you're such a dolt."

"Very funny. *Apologize.*"

"I'm sorry you're such an ass."

"Apologize."

"I'm sorry you're such a—"

She never got to finish the sentence. Guy captured her last word with a kiss that sent lightning bolts ricocheting through her body. She couldn't even muster a token resistance. She'd been thinking about this moment since they'd last kissed, that night in her bedroom.

She and Guy clung to each other in the humid heat of the room, pulling ineffectually at each other's clothes, which stuck to their bodies as if they were glued there.

"We need to turn the air-conditioning on," Dannie said.

"We need to take our clothes off," Guy said. He licked her neck, and if he hadn't been holding her up, she would have melted into a puddle on the floor.

"Guy…"

He groaned. "Don't, Dannie. Don't even think about it. Just go with it."

"Go with it?"

"Yes. You know how to do that, don't you? Just put your misgivings aside for a minute. An hour. A day. We want each other, right?"

"But Roger…"

"Roger is gone. Lisa is gone. You're not hurting Roger's memory by being attracted to another man. Weren't you ever attracted to anyone else while you were married to him?"

"Of course."

"But you didn't act on it because it would have been wrong."

"Exactly."

"So what would be wrong with it now?"

All these questions. Too many questions. And no answers. All she knew was that it *didn't* feel wrong to be here with Guy. It felt right. Very right.

He sensed her hesitation and kissed her—a long, soulful kiss filled with expectation and need. A kiss that held its breath.

She sighed, and it was as if Guy had been released. He took

her hands, entwining his fingers into hers. He had great hands. It was something she always noticed on men.

"Is that a yes?" he asked softly. Hopefully.

She nodded, and without a word he picked her up and carried her to the bed.

"Wow." Guy flopped onto his back. "That was…"

"Yeah," Dannie said, trying to catch her breath.

"Do you think we could slow it down a little this time?" Guy asked.

"What? You're ready to go again? So soon?"

He rolled over and slung a leg over hers. "Visiting the temple isn't so bad, is it? The amusement park might give you a quick thrill, but nothing beats a religious experience."

She smiled and kissed his chin. "Teach me, O Master of Love."

Three hours later Dannie lay exhausted on the floor beside the bed, wrapped in a sheet. Guy nibbled her earlobe.

"Please. No more. My heart can't take it."

Guy lay back and stretched his legs. "If you'd eat better and get a little exercise, we could do this forever."

"You mean we didn't just do that?"

"Not by a long shot. Did you ever hear Sting talk about Tantric sex?"

"Please. Who hasn't?"

"Well…"

Dannie struggled to her feet and crawled onto the bed. "Call me conventional, but four hours is enough for me. I have to ease back into this, you know."

"Hey, so do I." Guy climbed up onto the bed beside her.

"You mean to tell me with all the flirting you do, you haven't slept with anyone else since Lisa left you?"

"Nope."

"You're lying!"

"No, I really haven't. And Lisa was only the third woman I was ever with."

"In your life? You're kidding me."

He shrugged. "I don't take relationships lightly."

"So I'm number four?"

"That's right. What number am I for you?"

"Uh. About that." Dannie exhaled. "I don't get you."

"What?"

"You're this gorgeous, sexy, smart, funny, completely strange guy."

"How am I strange?"

Dannie looked at him with raised eyebrows.

"Okay. So I'm strange. But I'm a pretty good guy when you get to know me. And I like you, Dannie. A lot."

"I like you, too. But you're married. Just because your wife is missing, you still have one. And I recently lost my husband. I don't even have a death certificate yet, so I'm not even officially a widow. I'm just… I guess I'm almost a widow."

"None of that matters. We can't plan who we fall in love with."

"Whoa, there. Hold on. Who said anything about love?"

"All right, don't panic. What I meant to say is that we can't help who we're attracted to, and when. Neither of us has any real attachments. Why shouldn't we see where all this goes?"

"Because it's distracting us from finding Lisa, and finding out what happened to Roger."

"It's not distracting us." He stroked her cheek.

She pushed his hand gently away. "Yes, it is. We spent the last four hours…you know…when we should have been talking about what we're going to do next."

Guy sat up. "I refuse to feel guilty for spending an afternoon doing something I've wanted to do since I met you."

"You have? I mean, you did?"

"Absolutely."

Dannie allowed herself a moment to feel flattered, but then the practical side of her reared its head.

"It was nice," she said. "Very nice."

"Yeah? Like vanilla ice cream nice?"

"Like New York Super Fudge Chunk nice. But we have to get going if we're going to get anything accomplished today."

Guy sighed. "All right, already. I can take a hint. But I'm warning you, once you get religion, the lure of the temple is hard to resist."

Chapter Fifteen

A VEIL OF CLOUDS had drifted over the sun by the time the ferry reached the other side of the island, but the humidity hadn't abated any. In fact, it seemed worse than it had that morning, which Dannie hadn't thought possible. Could you have a hundred and ten percent humidity?

Guy's shirt was sticking to his back, but his hair was, as usual, perfect.

"What kind of product do you use in that hair?" Dannie said with envy.

"It's my own creation. All natural," he said. "I'll let you use it when we get back to the hotel."

Great. Until then she was going to look like a bush woman.

They disembarked the ferry at a wide whitewashed dock in the middle of nowhere. No taxis, no buses. Just a beat-up moped leaning against the ferry terminal. The sign above it read "M p ds for Re t. $15."

They stepped into the dim building. A big fan spun lazily on the ceiling, pushing the humid air from one side of the room to the other. Behind a counter someone was just closing a shade over the ticket window.

Guy ran over and knocked on the glass. A young woman who could have been on the cover of *Vogue* opened the shade. Was *everyone* in this country good-looking?

She flipped her long dark hair over one shoulder and smiled at Guy. *"Sí?"*

He spoke to her in Spanish, but Dannie recognized the words *taxi* and *bus*. The woman shook her head. She pointed outside and said, "Moped."

Guy walked over to where Dannie sat. "It's siesta time. If we don't want to sit here for the next hour, we've got to take the moped."

The woman with the hair came out of a door next to the ticket window. "Moped?"

Guy looked at Dannie, and she nodded.

"Sí," he said. "Moped."

They all walked back out to the side of the building, where the motorized bicycle stood. Or rather, leaned.

"I don't know," Dannie said. "Have you seen how crazy the traffic is on these roads?"

"It's all we've got," Guy said. "Unless you want to take a long nap on one of those wooden benches in there."

"Oh, all right."

"You sure?"

Dannie nodded.

Guy paid the woman fifteen dollars and swung a leg over the seat. He looked at Dannie.

She made the sign of the cross and climbed onto the moped behind Guy. "Don't orphan my children."

Guy puttered up the dirt drive from the ferry station to the island's main road, into the flow of traffic.

Their rear wheel shimmied as they picked up speed. The moped was missing a foot peg, so Dannie had to hold her left foot up. The bike also refused to go over thirteen miles per hour. Cars and trucks whizzed past them, honking.

Didn't these people know it was siesta time?

Dannie wrapped her arms around Guy's waist, burying her face in his back. If she was going to die, she didn't want to have to witness it.

"What town are we looking for again?" Guy asked.

"El Cuello."

"The neck."

"The what?" she yelled into the wind.

"Neck. That's what El Cuello means."

Well, that made sense. When she and Lyle had been there last time, they'd been able to see the ocean on both sides from the middle of town. El Cuello sat on a very narrow stretch of land.

They watched for road signs, but it was at least ten minutes before they found one. It was barely legible. El Cuello was either two kilometers ahead or twenty.

Considering how her butt felt on the tiny seat as they bumped over the road, Dannie sincerely hoped it was two.

A few minutes later the four-lane road narrowed to two lanes, and the traffic slowed. Dannie recognized the tiny police station on the right, at the edge of town.

"Pull in there," she told Guy. "That yellow shack."

He swung the moped into the dirt parking lot. "What's this?"

"The police station."

"You're kidding me."

"Nope." Dannie eased off the bike. Her left leg was numb

from having to hold it up the whole time. She limped toward the building.

"Don't sneeze," Guy said. "You might knock it down."

The screen door squeaked as they entered.

A uniform-clad officer watched an American soap opera dubbed in Spanish on a small TV as he ate something out of a plastic container. The back of his wooden chair leaned against a wall. His feet were propped on his desk.

He didn't even look up when they walked in.

"Excuse me," Dannie said. "May I speak to Officer Palmas?"

The police officer held up one finger, his gaze glued to the TV. A couple was arguing. They glared at each other as the background music climbed to a crescendo. When a commercial came on, the officer turned off the TV, shaking his head.

"Bronson's wife is pregnant, but it is not his baby," he explained, throwing the plastic container into a trash can beside the desk.

"It's probably Slate's," Guy said. "They hooked up after Nikki's party last month."

Dannie looked at him with her mouth open. "How do you know these things?"

Guy shrugged.

"I think it is Peter's," the cop said. "Alyssa has been secretly in love with him for two years."

"Yeah, but he had a vasectomy," Guy said. "Remember? Last year he couldn't make it to the town picnic because he was on bed rest."

"Oh! *Sí!* I forgot."

"I hate to interrupt," Dannie said. "But I'm actually trying to get some information about Roger Treat?"

"Who is he?" the officer said. "Was he married to Nikki?"

"No," Dannie said, trying not to get hysterical. "He was married to me. He was… He drowned here in February."

"Ah!" The cop turned a dark shade of red. "Sorry."

"Is Officer Palmas here? I spoke with him on the phone several times."

"Wait one minute, please. I will see if I can get him on the radio."

He fiddled with a desktop unit that sat on a credenza, speaking into the microphone in rapid Spanish.

Guy looked over at Dannie, his expression grim. He shook his head.

The young police officer returned to the desk. "I am sorry, but I was not able to find Officer Palmas. If you wish to leave your name here, and the hotel where you are staying, I will have him contact you." He pushed a blank pad of paper and a pen toward Dannie, giving her an apologetic smile.

Dannie wrote down her information and thanked him before she and Guy went back out to the parking lot.

"He was lying," Guy said quietly when they reached the moped. "That was Palmas he was talking to on the radio."

"Why didn't you tell me?" Dannie said. "We could have called him on it."

Guy shook his head. "I thought it would be better if they didn't know I speak Spanish. We might learn more that way. Palmas will be back here in an hour, so we'll come back then. In the meantime, I think we should do a little investigating of our own."

They hopped onto the moped and puttered another quarter of a mile, to the docks where Pedro the waiter had dropped her and Lyle off last time. Unlike the day after the hurricane, today the docks bustled with activity.

Fishing boats motored in and out of slips, picking up bait and charters and dropping off catch packed in huge ice chests. The humid air reeked of fish.

Guy parked the moped in a gravel parking lot above a small stretch of sand. They walked down a set of wooden stairs to a path that led to the docks.

"Do you know who you're looking for?" Guy asked.

"The name of the charter company was Alejandro's Fishing Tours."

As they walked, Dannie got butterflies in her belly. Roger had taken this same path almost nine months ago. He'd talked to some of these people. Perhaps one of them was the last person he'd ever spoken to.

She wished she had come to Cuatro Blanco when they'd called to tell her Roger had drowned.

Ben Wiser had assured her the authorities on the island would handle everything—that when they found Roger's body, they would inform her immediately.

Frankly, she'd been so shocked and grief stricken that she couldn't even have imagined making the trip. Now that she was here, though, it all hit her.

These were the last sights Roger had seen before his life ended. The last people he'd spoken to.

It hadn't really sunk in last time, because everything had looked so jumbled after the hurricane. But now… Now it was a day like any other. A day like the day her husband had lost his life.

"I think we should split up," she said. "You go ask around about Lisa, and I'll find Alejandro's Fishing Tours. We can meet back at the moped in half an hour."

Guy gave her a puzzled look. "All right. If that's what you want."

"It is."

"Then I'll see you back at the bike."

Guy headed off to the left while Dannie stayed on the path,

which ended at a small unpainted bait shack. A bait bucket filled with sand and cigarette butts held open a rickety screen door.

Dannie stuck her head inside. "Hello?"

A man popped up from behind a small counter, scaring the crap out of her.

He had to be close to eighty, his skin leathery from the sun, his eyes still bright and alert.

"Alejandro's Fishing Tours?" she said. "This dock?"

"No."

"Which dock?"

The man shook his head, and ran a finger across his neck.

Dannie felt the blood drain out of her. "Alejandro is dead?"

The man shook his head again. "No, Alejandro no is dead. Just his tours."

"He quit taking tours?"

"Jes."

"When?"

The man puckered his face in thought. "February."

"Thank you." Dannie's voice shook. She stepped backward out of the bait shack, nearly tripping over the makeshift ashtray.

Poor Alejandro. He must have so been distraught over Roger's accident that he quit taking charters.

She wandered onto the dock and watched a boat go out, loaded with men from the fishing club at El Pelícano. She imagined Roger in the back of the boat in his yellow polo shirt, sunglasses and that stupid wide-rimmed canvas fishing hat he liked to wear.

What had he been thinking when he woke up that morning? When he'd stepped onto the boat, looking forward to a day of fishing on the beautiful blue ocean?

She fought back a spate of tears before heading back toward the moped to wait for Guy.

"What'd you find out?" Guy trudged up the path. The picture of Lisa that he usually kept in his wallet was in his hand.

"Alejandro isn't running fishing tours anymore."

"No?"

Dannie shook her head. "He quit in February."

"Oh."

Guy stuck the picture of Lisa in the back pocket of his khaki shorts.

"Did you have any luck?" Dannie said.

"A little. A guy on one of the pleasure boats on the far dock says he saw her in a bar a couple months back. He described the tattoo on her shoulder."

"What bar?"

"It's called Carlito's. It's a couple of towns over."

Dannie climbed onto the back of the moped. "We should check it out after we go back to talk to Officer Palmas."

THE SOAP-OPERA-WATCHING desk cop seemed surprised to see them again.

He motioned to an Erik Estrada type through a window that looked into a small office. The desk cop gave him a look as if to say, "What should I do?"

The cop in the office shook his head, and came out to greet Dannie and Guy.

"May I help you?"

Dannie stepped forward. "I'm looking for Officer Palmas."

"You found him." His accent wasn't as thick as the other officer's and had a slight Boston twang. Dannie remembered him telling her once on the phone that he'd spent a year in the States as an exchange student.

"I'm Dannie Treat. I've been speaking on the phone to you

about my husband, Roger. He drowned offshore while fishing in February."

"Of course. I remember."

"I wondered if I could talk to you, or the coroner, or who-ever is responsible for issuing a death certificate."

Officer Palmas looked at Guy, and then at Dannie, and said to her, "We should speak privately in my office."

Guy nodded. "Go ahead. I'll wait out here."

Dannie followed Palmas into the little office. It smelled like lemon Pledge and microwave popcorn. He motioned to a chair, and she sat. Instead of sitting behind the desk, he sat in the chair beside her.

"Mrs. Treat, how much do you know about your husband's death?"

"Just what you and the people at Wiser-Crenshaw told me. That Roger went out on a fishing charter with a few other Wiser-Crenshaw executives, that the boat hit a buoy and Roger fell out, that there was a forty-eight-hour search, and that you never recovered his body."

Officer Palmas nodded. "We thought it was a routine acci-dent investigation at first. But now…"

Dannie's heart picked up speed. "Now what?"

The cop gave a little frown. "Things came up."

"What *things?*" Dannie demanded.

"For one, the charter boat captain—"

"Alejandro."

"Yes, Alejandro. Alejandro hasn't run a charter since that day."

"I know. I heard. He must feel just terrible about the accident."

Officer Palmas suppressed a smile. "I don't think so. You see, around here we can't afford to let our feelings keep us from making a living. Our families depend on us to support them. Alejandro's family depends on him."

"So he's not distraught?"

"I highly doubt it. In fact, he's never seemed so…*un*distraught."

Dannie stood up, pacing around the tiny office. "I don't understand what you're trying to tell me. Just *tell* me."

"It would seem Alejandro is having no problem supporting his family these days."

Dannie gave him a blank stare.

"He's got a new BMW. And a new fishing boat, too, just for himself. No charters."

"And you think all of this has something to do with Roger's death?"

Officer Palmas shrugged. "It's quite a coincidence, no? Your husband drowns, and suddenly Alejandro's financial situation is vastly improved."

Dannie sank back into her chair. "What are you saying? That someone paid Alejandro to hit that buoy? That he killed Roger?"

"Perhaps. Or maybe…"

The rest of his sentence faded to a buzz in her ears. Dannie's stomach rolled. She buried her face in her hands and took deep breaths. She felt dizzy.

No, she felt faint. Oh, hell. She *was* going to faint.

She slumped sideways, and the floor hurtled toward her face.

Chapter Sixteen

WHEN SHE WOKE UP, Dannie was lying on her side on a small cot in the police shack. Guy hovered over her like a mother hen, touching her hair, her arm, her hip, pressing a washcloth to her bloodied nose.

"What happened?" he said when he noticed her eyes were open.

"I don't know. I guess I passed out."

"Do you feel sick?"

Dannie shook her head. "It must be the heat."

Officer Palmas, who leaned against the wall behind Guy, nodded. "You need to rest. You should go back to your hotel for a while. Have something to eat. I assure you, Mrs. Treat, as soon as there are any further developments in your husband's case, we will contact you." He gave her a pointed look.

"I will take you back to the ferry," the other cop said. "You shouldn't ride a moped in your condition."

"Thanks," Guy said. He helped Dannie to her feet. "Can you walk?"

She nodded.

Guy escorted her outside. Soap Opera Cop pointed to a small pickup. Dannie got in, while Guy and the cop loaded the moped into the bed of the truck. The men squeezed in on either side of her.

Guy and the cop chatted as they drove to the ferry dock, but Dannie hardly heard a word they said. All she could think about was Roger and Jimmy Duke and the missing money. And whether the two other Wiser-Crenshaw people on the boat had been in on all of this.

It seemed likely.

Guy returned the moped and bought tickets for them back to the dock that was within walking distance of El Pelícano.

She and Guy spoke little on the ferry. It was nearly dark by the time they arrived at the hotel. The band played under a thatched gazebo on the edge of the beach.

"Why don't we grab something to eat before we head back up to the room?" Guy said. "You've hardly eaten all day."

"I don't think so."

He grabbed her hand. "Come on. Some nice, greasy, salty food?"

She had to admit that did sound good.

Dannie allowed Guy to lead her to the dining area on the terrace near where the band played.

The moon was rising over the ocean, and if she hadn't been preoccupied by everything that was going on, it would have been a beautiful night. A romantic night.

Guy ordered her a drink with an umbrella in it, and a sparkling water for himself. She sipped the drink, feeling the tension in her shoulders ease just a little.

What had she really found out today? She'd already suspected that Roger's death might have been foul play.

Why hadn't he told her he'd gotten Jimmy Duke's account? There had been a time they'd talked about everything. But that time had long passed. Since she'd caught him having an affair with a colleague five years ago, just after she'd had Richard, things had changed.

Roger said he'd just been freaked out by Richard's birth, by his new responsibilities as a father. He wasn't thinking straight. He swore it would never happen again.

Maybe she'd turned a blind eye, or at least hadn't looked very hard for proof that he'd gone back on his word, but she'd always believed him to be a basically honest man.

For him to have embezzled money from Jimmy Duke? It seemed so unreal.

"Are you okay?" Guy's voice pulled her back to the present, to the music of the band. To the moonlight riding the waves onto the beach.

"I was just thinking how little I actually knew Roger. I used to think I knew him inside out. But in the end...I mean, who was he?"

Guy gave her a sympathetic smile. "I used to think of Lisa as the other half of me. People joke about their spouse being their better half, but that's honestly how I thought of her. I trusted her completely."

"So this all came out of the blue? You had no idea?"

Guy leaned back in his chair. "I guess in retrospect there were signs. Late nights out with the girls. Her staying overnight at her mother's. A dwindling sex life."

Dannie nodded. "With Roger it was business trips, client dinners, long hours. And a dwindling sex life."

They sat without talking for a while, each lost in thought about life B.C.B.—Before Cuatro Blanco.

The band struck up a slow song, the lead singer crooning in Spanish.

"Want to dance?" Guy said.

"Sure, why not?"

He held her gently, as if she might break.

As if he knew how difficult it had been for her to stay strong all these months.

How could she feel so safe in his arms when she knew she was treading on dangerous emotional ground?

As they swayed to the music under the moonlight, she rested her head on Guy's shoulder and closed her eyes, wishing they were there just to enjoy themselves like everyone else around them.

Everyone except...

Behind a palm tree growing at the edge of the terrace, Dannie spotted a familiar figure. A dark-haired woman in a wide-brimmed hat. The woman from the Air Caribbean line at the airport. And the lounge, and the hotel hallway, and the airplane...

And the blue car outside her house?

The woman caught Dannie looking at her and quickly turned away, hurrying off into the darkness of the beach.

"I'll be right back." Dannie kicked off her sandals and took off across the terrace, hitting her stride when she reached the sand.

For a moment Dannie lost the woman in the dark, and then she reappeared, silhouetted against the moonlight reflecting off the water.

"Hey!" Dannie yelled. "Come back here!"

The woman kept walking.

"You, near the water. I want to talk to you!"

The woman hesitated, then stopped.

Dannie was out of breath by the time she reached her. "Do I know you?"

"I really don't think so."

"I think I do. I saw you last time I was here, a couple of weeks ago. And again in the airplane."

"Oh, that's unlikely," the woman said, with a definite Philadelphia accent.

"Exactly. Which is what makes it so weird."

The woman removed the floppy-brimmed hat. Dannie could see her face clearly now, illuminated by the moonlight.

"Are you following me?"

"I think it's the other way around. *You're* following me. *You* chased me out onto the beach."

"You were running away from me!"

"You're crazy." The woman tried to get around her, but Dannie grabbed the sleeve of her blouse.

"You're not going anywhere until you tell me what's going on." Dannie's voice had reached a fevered pitch. "What do you want from me? Did you kill my husband?"

"You're out of your mind."

"What's going on here?" Guy appeared out of the shadows. "Dannie, are you okay?"

"No, she's not okay," the dark-haired woman said. "She's harassing me."

"Dannie, come on. Let's get you something to eat," Guy said.

"No! I'm telling you, she's been following us. Spying on me."

"Dannie, please—"

"I can't believe you don't believe me," Dannie said to Guy.

"She hasn't eaten all day," Guy explained to the woman. "She's a little off balance."

"I'm not *off balance.* Listen to me. I saw her at the airport in Philly when I was with Lyle. I saw her at the hotel when we won the dance contest. I saw her on the plane on the way back home. And now she's here."

Guy looked at the woman, who looked away.

"There's a security guard on the terrace," he said. "Maybe we should go speak to him."

The woman exhaled. "Don't do that. Damn." She pulled a wallet out of her big straw bag and handed a business card to Dannie. "My name is Judy Finch. I'm an insurance investigator."

"An insurance investigator," Dannie repeated.

"With World Fidelity."

"Why in the hell are you following *me*? What are you investigating?"

"Fraud."

Dannie laughed, without humor. "How can I possibly have committed fraud? You people haven't given me a dime yet."

"Actually, it's not you we're investigating. It's your husband. We believe he faked his death."

"Oh. Oh, God." Dannie bent over, trying to breathe. "Why? Why are you doing this to me? I talked to you people three times and no one ever said anything about *fraud*."

"We couldn't tell you, because we suspected you might be in on it."

"In on it—? This is insane." Dannie squatted down, putting her hands over her mouth, trying hard not to hyperventilate.

"Dannie, are you okay?" Guy moved toward her, but she held up a hand to ward him off.

"I'm sorry," Judy said. "I understand this might be something of a shock for you."

"You think?" Dannie's head began to spin.

"Let's go back to your room," Judy said. "We can talk about this in more detail."

"Right," Dannie said. But when she tried to stand up, for the second time that day everything went black.

WHEN SHE WOKE UP this time, she was in the elevator with Guy and Judy, and a bellhop in a red polyester uniform.

Dannie's arms were flung over the shoulders of Guy and the bellhop. Guy held her up by the waist.

"She'll be okay as soon as we get her into the air-conditioning," Guy said.

The bellhop nodded and smiled. Dannie was guessing he didn't speak English.

The men helped Dannie down the hall to room 403, where Guy handed Judy the key. She unlocked the door, then they all filed inside.

"You two have a room together?" Judy asked.

"There was a mix-up at the reservations desk," Dannie said.

Judy looked at the rumpled sheets on the floor. "Uh-huh."

Guy gave the bellhop a ten and the man nodded his way out of the room, closing the door behind him.

Guy retrieved a bottle of water from the minifridge. He opened it and handed it to Dannie. "You okay?"

"I feel woozy."

"You've hardly eaten all day," Guy said. "We've been running around all over the island in the heat. You probably have sunstroke."

"Sunstroke? At night?" Dannie plopped down on the edge of the bed. Guy sat beside her.

"Maybe it's heat exhaustion." Judy dragged a chair over and pulled a spiral-bound notebook out of her oversize straw handbag. "You mind if I ask you a couple of questions?"

"What if I say yes?"

Judy shrugged. "The investigation will continue anyway."

Dannie gave a tired sigh. "You may as well ask away, then."

"Who is Lyle Faraday to you?"

Guy glanced sideways at Dannie, as if he might be interested in the answer, too.

"Lyle is a friend. Just a friend. He was my husband's best friend, as a matter of fact."

"Do you make a habit of taking vacations with your husband's best friends?"

"You mean a couple of weeks ago? We weren't on vacation. We came down here to try to find out what happened to Roger."

"Why would you do that, if you thought he was dead?"

Dannie stood up. "I still *do* think he's dead. I came down here to get the details. And to get your goddamned death certificate so my kids and I don't have to worry about how we're going to afford groceries next month."

Judy hunched over, writing furiously in her notebook in microscopic handwriting.

Dannie lunged for her, but Guy grabbed Dannie's arm and pulled her back down on the bed before Judy noticed.

Judy looked up from her tiny writing. "Do you know anything about an offshore bank account?"

A little lightning jolt passed through Dannie as she remembered the phone number to the bank in Costa Rica she'd found at Rose's house. She forced herself not to look at Guy. "No."

"Does the name Randy Jarvis ring a bell?"

"Nope."

But it did. Only, Dannie couldn't remember where she'd heard it before.

"How about the name Lisa Lewellyn?" She gave a pointed look at Guy.

He didn't flinch.

"I don't know a Lisa Lewellyn. Guy's wife is Lisa Loughran and, as I'm sure you've already found out, she and Roger had been having an affair. But I can't see how that has anything to do with insurance fraud."

Judy squinted and scribbled some more, then tucked her pen into the spiral of the notebook.

"That's all?" Dannie said.

"That's all."

"If you're through, then I'm going to have to ask you to leave," Guy said. "Dannie's obviously not feeling well."

"Of course." Judy stuck her notebook back into the straw bag and arranged her hat over her dark hair. "Sorry to have interrupted your evening. You make a nice couple out there on the dance floor."

Guy ushered Judy Finch out of the room. Dannie flopped back on the pillow, hardly able to keep her eyes open, but at the same time feeling as if she were wound tighter than the string on a yo-yo.

"I want to call my kids," she said.

"We should talk first—"

"I just want to call my kids."

"Sure. All right." Guy picked up the phone in the room. "What's your in-laws' number?"

Dannie recited the number as he dialed. He handed her the phone when it rang on the other end.

"Elizabeth, hi." Dannie's voice cracked.

"Dannie! What did you find out?"

Dannie choked back the tears. "Nothing yet. Maybe tomorrow. Hey, can I talk to the kids for a minute?"

Chapter Seventeen

When she hung up, Guy was gone. In fact, he'd left as soon as Elizabeth had answered the phone.

She had to admit he was polite. The bastard.

She couldn't believe what had happened on the beach. How Guy had made excuses for her. How he'd treated her like a crazy person.

Until Judy Finch had dropped the bomb. Then he was all ears.

Could it be that they were both right? Was Roger alive? Had he faked his death?

No, it couldn't be.

Officer Palmas had as much as told her it was foul play. Or had he?

She reviewed their conversation in her mind, and realized he hadn't really committed to any theory. Was it possible he thought Roger was still alive, too?

Dannie was wide awake now.

She paced, twisting a curl between her thumb and forefinger as she listed all the facts she knew.

One: Roger and Lisa Loughran had been having an affair. That fact was undisputed.

Two: She'd found counterfeit money in the garage, which she had to assume Roger had known about. Not so coincidentally, Lisa had replaced the money in Guy's safe with counterfeit.

Three: Roger allegedly stole money from Jimmy Duke and hid it in an offshore account.

Four: Someone called a Costa Rican bank from Rose's home just weeks before Roger died.

Five: The charter boat captain responsible for the accident that killed Roger was suddenly a wealthy man, at least by Cuatro Blanco standards.

Six: The insurance company believed Roger might still be alive.

And finally: Roger's body had never been found.

Dannie sat on the end of the bed, tangling her fingers in her hair. None of these facts led her to believe, without a doubt, that Roger had faked his death. There was just no irrefutable evidence.

There was only her heart, telling her that the man she'd known for more than a dozen years would never do something like this to her. To the family they'd built together.

The door to the room opened quietly. Guy came in with a foam container in hand. He set it down on the table beside the bed.

"I brought you something to eat."

"Thanks. I'm starving."

She opened the container to find fresh pineapple, scrambled egg whites and sliced tomato.

"Great," she said with an utter lack of enthusiasm. "Couldn't you find anything fried?"

"You need to put something healthy into your body," Guy said. "But if you're a good girl and eat everything there, I have a little treat for you." He pulled a candy bar out of his pocket. "Voilà!"

"It's a deal." Dannie dug in to her food, which was surprisingly tasty considering the lack of fats and sugar. When she'd finished she said, "Okay. Hand it over."

Guy tossed her the candy bar. She bit into it as if it was manna from heaven.

"Wow," Guy said. "That's just obscene."

"What's obscene?"

"The noises you're making."

"I'm making noises?"

"Sex noises. Over a candy bar."

"I am not."

"You are. And I'm wishing I was that candy bar."

Dannie finished chewing. "Listen, about this afternoon…"

Guy groaned. "Here come the regrets."

"No regrets. Just…let's put it down to an experience, and leave it at that."

"An experience? Dannie, I'm in lo—"

"Stop! Don't say it."

"But—"

"I'm serious." Dannie finished off the candy bar and tossed the wrapper into the trash can. "I can't talk about this right now."

"Why not?"

"Because I'm really pissed off at you."

"At me? Why?"

"Because of your attitude. You refuse to believe there can be more to the story than what meets the eye. I told you that woman was following me, but you didn't believe me."

"I'm sorry. I was wrong."

"So why can't you possibly believe that someone murdered Roger? That he might be dead?"

"I hate to point this out, but I'm not the only one. The insurance company doesn't think he's dead, either."

"Because they don't want to have to write me a check for half a million dollars."

Guy sighed. "Do you really believe that?"

"I do."

Guy shook his head. He peeled off the T-shirt he'd been wearing, then started on the buttons of his jeans.

Dannie bit her lip. Did he have to get undressed *here?* Right in front of her?

"What are you doing?"

"Getting ready for bed. Why?"

"Where are you going to sleep?"

Guy looked at the bed.

"Oh, no. I get the bed. You can sleep over there." She pointed to the wicker love seat near the sliding glass door to the balcony.

"You can't be serious," he said. "I'll never fit on that thing. I need a bed."

"I guess you should have thought of that when you were making the reservations."

"Are you really mad about that? Or are you punishing me because you're thinking I might be right about Roger after all?"

Dannie glared at him.

"I'm not sleeping on that thing."

"Hey, feel free to take a pillow down to the couch in the lobby."

Guy put his hands on his hips. "Is that how it's going to be?"

"Yep."

He stewed in silence for a minute. "Fine. Great. I'll sleep on the damned love seat."

Dannie slid under the covers and pulled off her shorts. Then she unhooked her bra, threading it out from beneath her shirt through the armhole, a trick she'd learned way back when from the movie *Flashdance*.

Guy grabbed a pillow and yanked the bedspread off the bed, then dragged them over to the love seat, muttering under his breath. He flashed her a dirty look, which she caught as she turned off the bedside lamp.

As exhausted as she was, though, she couldn't sleep.

Her mind was a centrifuge, sorting thoughts and emotions and theories by how much weight they held.

Memories of Roger spun to the top. She watched them pass…. Roger at their wedding reception, drunk on shots of Wild Turkey, toasting his new bride. Standing in the kitchen in a suit on his first day of work at Wiser-Crenshaw. Holding the twins, one in each arm, moments after their birth.

Making out with Lisa Loughran on the videotape from the gym…

Dannie rolled to her other side.

Now thoughts of Guy spun into her mind. Guy in his pink shirts. Arguing with him on the airplane. Finding her and Lyle a ride to El Cuello after the hurricane. Dancing with her. Making love to her.

Bringing her chocolate.

She hadn't felt so conflicted about a man since she found out John Travolta was a Scientologist.

She rolled onto her back, listening to the wicker squeak and groan beneath Guy's weight as he tossed and turned, trying to get comfortable on the love seat. She almost felt sorry for him.

Almost.

She closed her eyes. Tomorrow, come hell or a hurricane, she was going to find out what had happened to her husband.

GUY WAS IN A FOUL MOOD the next morning as they walked to the ferry after breakfast. For the first time since Dannie had known him, his hair wasn't perfect.

She felt a pang of guilt. "I'll sleep on the love seat tonight."

Guy just shook his head.

They pushed through the throng of sport fishermen on their way to El Cuello for the fishing competition.

"Where are we going this morning?" Dannie said.

He unfolded the map he'd been carrying. "Right here," he said, pointing to a spot on the map. "Where the guy I met yesterday said he saw Lisa in that bar, Carlito's."

"Is a bar going to be open at this hour?"

"I don't know. We'll see."

The ferry docked a couple of miles away from Carlito's, so they rented another moped.

The countryside was beautiful. The fog that had gathered in Dannie's head overnight cleared with the wind in her face and the perfumed scent of the lush greens and tropical flowers that flew past them in a blur.

As it turned out, Carlito's *was* open. There were even customers at the bar.

As Dannie's eyes adjusted to the light, she saw a couple of tourists with sunburned noses sipping Bloody Marys, nursing hangovers from the night before. The local drunk, hugging a beer bottle, chattered away in slurred Spanish to the bartender.

A group of women in housekeeping uniforms, who looked as if they might have just finished their shift at a local hotel, laughed in a corner booth.

Dannie followed Guy to the long, unembellished bar. The bartender ambled over, smiling in welcome.

He laid two napkins in front of them. "What you want?"

"Just pineapple juice for me," Guy said.

"Coffee, please," said Dannie.

The bartender returned with their order in half a minute. Guy handed him a large bill, and when he came back with the change, Guy pushed the picture of Lisa across the bar. "Have you seen her?"

The bartender hesitated, then shook his head.

Guy tapped the bills on the bar. "Take another look."

The bartender looked at the money, and then at Guy. Guy nodded.

"She been in here."

Guy straightened. "When?"

"The day before the hurricane was the last I see her. She drink Toasted Almonds. She with a man."

Now Dannie sat up. "What did he look like?"

The bartender shrugged. Guy pulled another bill out of his wallet and laid it on the bar.

"He have blond hair. Beard. Earring."

Dannie took a deep breath and relaxed back into the seat. Definitely not Roger.

"Does she live around here?" Guy said.

The bartender motioned to the drunk, who staggered over. Guy showed him the picture of Lisa while the bartender questioned him in Spanish.

He mumbled a response before returning to his long-lost beer, greeting it with a big openmouthed kiss.

"He say she used to come in after scuba diving," the bartender said.

"Scuba diving? Where do they scuba dive around here?"

"Fernando Pico, he give lessons and tours. His boat is docked at the pier."

"Thanks." Guy pushed the money across the bar.

"Gracias." The bartender stuffed the money into his pocket. "Take it easy, amigos!"

FERNANDO PICO WAS HARD to miss.

As tall as Guy, with long black hair and sexy dark chocolate eyes, he was by far the most gorgeous of all the gorgeous people Dannie had met on Cuatro Blanco. When he shook her hand, she actually giggled.

Guy shot her an irritated look.

"We're looking for someone," Guy said.

"Everybody's looking for somebody, brother." Fernando's accent was a cross between Cheech Marin and a California surfer. He winked at Dannie.

"Yeah, well, we're looking for someone in particular." Guy handed Fernando the picture of Lisa.

Fernando nodded. "I've seen her, man. She took lessons from me a while back, and then went out on a couple of my tours after that."

"Was she with anyone?"

Fernando smiled. "Hey. Like I told the other dude who came looking for her, maybe she don't want anybody to know her business."

"Someone else came looking for her?" Guy said. "When?"

"Yesterday."

"What did he look like?" Dannie asked.

Fernando held a hand up to his shoulder. "This tall. Light brown hair."

"Beard?" Dannie said. "Earring?"

"No. But he had a scar across his eyebrow. Right here."

Dannie and Guy looked at each other.

"Lyle?" Dannie said.

"Sounds just like him, doesn't it?"

"It can't be him," Dannie said. "He didn't even know Lisa."

"Are you sure? We did find his card at Rose's house."

Dannie felt sick to her stomach. "Do you think he followed us here?"

"I don't know. But if he got here first, he isn't following us anymore."

"Then maybe we should follow him," Dannie said. She turned to Fernando. "What else did you tell him?"

"Not much. She likes to party. She wears expensive clothes. She had her own equipment."

"Do you have her address?" Guy asked.

Fernando shook his head. "I don't get into all that stuff, man. If somebody wants to dive with me, that's cool. As long as they're certified, I don't care where they live."

"You don't even have a town?" Dannie said. "Please. It could be a matter of life and death."

Fernando scratched the back of his neck. "I think she said she lives somewhere on the other side of the island."

"Great. That narrows it down." Guy ran a hand through his hair.

"Listen, man, go to a place called The Tiki in Chipita. Ask for a guy named Paco. He knows everybody on that side of the island."

"Great, thanks." Dannie shook Fernando's hand again. He held it just a little too long.

For a minute Dannie considered taking scuba lessons, despite the fact that she hated the ocean.

Chapter Eighteen

THE TIKI TURNED OUT TO BE a surf shop that had been flattened by the hurricane.

Not surprising, since it appeared to have consisted of little more than a few sheets of plywood, a thatched roof and a few strings of lights. An old cracked toilet was the only thing still standing amidst the ruins.

Of course, no one milling about in the town could tell Dannie and Guy where to find Paco. Guy's typically cool demeanor was rapidly eroding, so Dannie decided it was time to take charge.

She directed Guy to pull into a little taqueria near the waterfront so they could grab a bite to eat and get out of the scorching midafternoon sun.

In typical Cuatro Blancan style, it took forever for their food to arrive, so they sipped lemon sodas while they waited.

"What do you think Lyle is doing on the island?" Guy asked her.

Dannie chewed on her straw. That was the question of the day, wasn't it? "I'm guessing the same thing we are. Trying to find out what happened to Roger. And maybe Lisa."

"So you think he knew her?"

She rubbed her eyes. "He told me he didn't. But honestly, I don't know what to believe anymore."

"Do you think we should try to find him?"

"Maybe not. It might be better if he doesn't know I'm here. Especially here with you."

Guy nodded in agreement.

When their food arrived, they ate in silence. Dannie wondered what their next move should be. Honestly, she wanted to do nothing more than go back to the hotel, get into bed and stay there for the rest of the day. And then she wanted to get on a plane and fly back to Philadelphia.

She was sick of the heat and the siestas and the searching. Sick of the dead ends. She just wanted to go home and see her kids.

A bell on the door jingled. A man the size of a jockey, his hair sticking up in all directions, sauntered in.

"¡Paco! ¿Cómo va?"

"¡Ay, Paco!"

"¡Paco! ¿Dónde has estado?"

Everyone in the place greeted him at once.

Guy's fork stopped halfway to his mouth. "It couldn't be."

"It seems unlikely," Dannie said, afraid to hope.

"There are probably fifty Pacos on this island."

"At least."

Guy wiped his mouth. "Thing is, he does seem to know everybody."

Dannie nodded. "Fernando said he knew everybody."

"It has to be him."

"Give me Lisa's picture," Dannie said. "There's only one way to find out."

Turned out it *was* him. The Paco they'd been looking for.

Sometimes life pelted you with lemons, then topped them off with a nice, fluffy meringue.

Paco said he knew the lady in the picture. Lisa Lewellyn. She'd taken surfing lessons from one of the guys at The Tiki, and hung out on a beach not far from there. In fact, he'd seen her there just the day before.

He gave them directions to the beach.

Dannie and Guy thanked him and paid for his lunch before heading out to the moped.

Dannie handed Guy the picture of Lisa, and he looked at it for a few moments before sticking it back into his wallet.

"You miss her?" Dannie asked quietly.

Guy sighed. "I don't miss *her* as much as I miss what I hoped to have with her. You know?"

Dannie knew.

She'd envisioned a life of togetherness with Roger—coffee on the patio, family bike rides, picnics by the lake—that never materialized. Not that she had expected it all to be perfect, just…happier. She knew exactly how Guy felt.

She climbed onto the back of the moped, wrapping her arms around Guy's waist, pressing her cheek to his back. In many ways, he was the kindred spirit she'd always hoped Roger would be. She felt a wave of sadness that her time with him might soon be over.

Who knew what would happen when they found Lisa.

THE BEACH PACO sent them to was hardly more than a football field long, but it was packed. It was obviously the place to be.

Bodies lay side by side on towels like pastels in a box. Children splashed in the surf as their parents lounged on the sand, thumbing through the pages of gossip magazines and the latest spy thrillers.

Umbrellas dotted the landscape like striped mushrooms popping up in a garden of suntanned flesh.

Dannie surveyed the scene with dismay. "How are we ever going to find her here?"

"You start at one end, and I'll start at the other. If you see anybody that looks remotely like her, wave. Most of these people are Cuatro Blancans. With her fair skin and red hair, she should be easy to spot."

"Okay," Dannie said. "We'll meet in the middle near that purple-and-white-striped umbrella."

Guy cut left, Dannie right. She started at the far end of the beach, where rocks and rough surf made swimming and sunbathing impossible. She snaked her way through the crowd, dodging sand castles and fat, hairy men in Speedos.

She tried to get close enough to everyone to rule them out, but much like the ocean, a beach crowd was a fluid thing, always moving and shifting.

Out on the water, fishing charters dotted the deep blue seascape, their white hulls and chrome reflecting the afternoon sun.

For some reason the name Randy Jarvis popped into Dannie's head. Judy Finch, the insurance investigator, had mentioned it, but Dannie hadn't been able to place it.

Now it niggled at the back of her mind.

She shaded her eyes, peering out over the water.

Randy Jarvis. Randy…

Jarvis! He was the host of one of the fishing shows Roger used to watch. *Big Game Fishing with Randy.*

How in God's name would an insurance investigator know about that? And why would she care?

It seemed as if every piece of the puzzle to this mystery just led to more pieces.

And every lead led to a dead end.

She'd made it to the middle of the beach with no sign of Lisa. Guy was nearing the middle as well, his bright pink shirt a beacon against the white sand. The way he picked his way through the sunbathers told her all she needed to know.

He'd had no luck, either.

They met and walked to the edge of the water. Kicking off their shoes, they waded into the surf up to their knees to cool off.

"Now what?" Dannie asked.

Guy stared out into the waves. "I guess we'll just have to wait and see if she shows up. I don't want to pass her picture around too much, in case she gets wind of it and gets spooked."

"Good point. I hope that hasn't happened already."

"That was a chance we had to take, right? I mean, we had to at least know where to start looking."

Dannie nodded. "Too bad we didn't bring a towel or something. It could be a long wait."

Guy grabbed her arm. "Maybe not as long as we think. Look." He pointed to a woman on the far end of the beach, near the rocks where Dannie had begun her search.

"Is that her?"

Guy squinted. "I think so."

"Let's get closer."

Guy held Dannie's hand, as much for a sense of support as for show, Dannie suspected.

The woman stood a few feet away from the surf behind a small pile of rocks, the breeze from the water blowing her cover-up away from her like a superhero cape flying in the breeze. *The Incredible Body.*

Her sunglasses covered more territory than her bathing suit, and she didn't have an ounce of fat on her.

Dannie tugged her own shorts as far down on her thighs as possible. "Well?"

Guy's jaw was tight. "It's her."

"I don't know how I missed her," Dannie said.

They quickened their pace.

Lisa had gathered up her things and was making her way up a path through the rocks. They reached the path just as she climbed into a small red car with a white roof.

Guy pulled Dannie by the arm. "The moped!"

But they were parked clear at the other end of the beach.

They ran until they were breathless, reaching the moped in two minutes. Still, Dannie feared they weren't quick enough. By the time they passed the parking area near the south end of the beach, Lisa's little red car was gone.

"She didn't pass us, so she must have gone in the opposite direction," Guy shouted over his shoulder. "Maybe she's still on the main road."

He pushed the moped to its limit, taking the turns on the road like a motocross racer. Dannie clung to him for dear life.

Soon they spotted Lisa's car in the distance, slowed by heavy traffic. There were several cars and a bus between them. A bus that seemed to stop at the corner of every side street and alley on the island.

"Come *on*," Guy complained when the bus stopped for the tenth time.

It was impossible to pass without risking certain death. And it was impossible to see around the big pink bus. By the time they were moving again, Lisa's car was gone.

They drove for a while without any luck, leaving the main road to putter past a row of cute little shops.

When they passed a place called Tienda de Empeño, Dannie smacked Guy's arm. "Look!"

It was Lyle, in yellow Bermuda shorts and a white golf shirt, carrying a paper grocery bag as he hurried down the steps of the shop. He hopped into a waiting taxi, and it sped off. Guy tried to follow, but he couldn't work his way into the endless flow of traffic on the main road. Apparently it was rush hour in Cuatro Blanco.

Like Lisa's red car, in a few minutes Lyle's cab disappeared, too.

Guy turned the moped around and pulled into a space in front of the building Lyle had come out of.

"It's a pawnshop," he said.

"How do you know?"

"Because 'Tienda de Empeño' means 'pawnshop.'"

"Oh."

"Maybe we should see what he sold," Guy said.

"Or bought. He was carrying a bag."

They ran up the steps and hurried into the shop, kicking up a swirl of dust motes in their wake.

An old woman sat knitting behind a glass case that held an odd assortment of wares—jewelry, tools, cell phones, china. She squinted up at them from her chair.

Guy spoke to her in Spanish, and she gestured to the end of the glass case.

Dannie and Guy walked down there.

"What? The false teeth?" Dannie asked.

Guy translated.

"No, no!" The woman limped down to the end of the case and pointed.

"Uh-oh," Dannie said.

Guns. Piled up in a cardboard box as if they were toys at a toy store.

"*¿El compró un arma?*"

The old woman nodded.

"He bought a gun," Guy said to Dannie.

"Oh, no." Dannie's palms started to sweat. What in the hell did Lyle need with a gun? Did he even know how to shoot one?

"I think we have to assume the worst," Guy said. "If Lyle was looking for Lisa and now he bought a gun, he must be going after her."

"No! Lyle would never do that," Dannie said.

"Are you sure?" Guy's gaze was steady, but tense. "Because if you're wrong, it really could be a matter of life and death."

Dannie hesitated only a second. "Let's go find him."

Guy gave the old woman some money, and he and Dannie ran back out to the moped.

"Which way?" Dannie said.

"I think we should drive through all the neighborhoods near the beach where we found Lisa. I would think she'd live nearby if she goes there."

Dannie nodded. She couldn't even speak. Things had gotten so strange it was as if they were caught in a bad, bad dream.

They sped back toward the beach. The traffic had lightened considerably, so it took only minutes to locate the beach again. Since the strip of land between the beach and the main road was narrow, there were no houses on that side road. Just beach and rock and more beach.

"We'll start north and work our way south," Guy said. "You keep an eye out for Lisa's car."

He turned left into a neighborhood of small cinder-block houses painted in pastel colors, each sporting white shutters and doors. They motored slowly through the streets. There were red cars aplenty, but none with a white roof.

They made their way painstakingly through a half-dozen neighborhoods just like it, with the same results. Dannie's rear end was numb. Guy slumped over the handlebars of the moped.

Dannie was just about to suggest they take a break when she spotted a red car with a white roof outside a neat, white-shingle bungalow with green shutters. She squeezed Guy's arm and pointed. "Over there."

Guy drove slowly past the house, pulling over when they'd rounded the corner.

"Looks like her car," Dannie said.

Guy swiped the sweat from his brow with his forearm. "We have to get a closer look."

"Stay here," Dannie said. "I'll walk past and check things out."

Guy looked as if he might argue.

"She doesn't know me," Dannie said. "If she sees you, she might take off."

He exhaled. "All right. But be careful."

Guy kept his eyes glued on her as she walked around the corner.

She tried to appear as if she were out for a casual walk. She tried to whistle, but her mouth was too dry. Then again, whistling might have been overkill anyway.

She counted her steps.

One hundred eighty-eight, one hundred eighty-nine…

The car was parked in a narrow driveway beside the house, which boasted a neatly trimmed yard in the back, littered with lawn ornaments—whirligigs, birdbaths, a big black kettle overflowing with bougainvillea. If the phrase "Like mother, like daughter" held any water, this had to be the place.

Dannie's suspicions were all but confirmed when she saw the sticker in the back window of the car.

Casually she turned back toward the corner, picking up the pace when she was out of sight of the house.

"Well?" Guy looked nervous.

He actually looked ill.

"I'm ninety-nine percent sure it's her place," Dannie said. "She's got lawn crap all over. And a sticker for Fernando's Dive Shop in the rear window of the car."

"It's gotta be her."

"I'd say so."

"So what should we do?" he said. Clearly he was in no shape to take charge.

"I think we should approach the house from the rear," Dannie said. "Try to get a look in one of the windows, just to be sure."

"Right."

They went around to the opposite side of the block, cutting through the yard that abutted Lisa's. In the grand tradition of seventies cop shows, they ran in a crouch until they were directly below an open window on the side of the house. Guy pointed up, and they slowly stood until they could see in.

The television was on, tuned in to a rerun of *Hawaii Five-O,* but no one was in the room. As they peered through the window, the doorbell rang.

"You gonna get that?" A woman's voice, coming from the back of the house.

Dannie looked at Guy. He nodded.

Suddenly a man rose into their line of sight, scaring the crap out of Dannie and Guy. He'd obviously been sitting on a couch beneath the window.

Bleach-blond hair, wrinkled red T-shirt. Baggy shorts hung on his hips. Dannie would bet he had a beard and earring, too.

He carried a beer in one hand, the remote control in the other as he shuffled in bare feet through the small living room toward the front door.

The doorbell rang again.

"What?" the blond guy barked.

"I'm looking for Randy Jarvis," said a voice through the door.

Randy Jarvis? The fishing show host?

The guy muttered under his breath, taking another swig of his beer before reaching for the doorknob. Before he could turn it, the door burst open.

Lyle stood framed in a rectangle of afternoon sun, holding the paper sack he'd carried out of Tienda de Empeño.

Angry Man with Gun in Bag.

Lyle pushed his way into the living room. "Where is she?"

The blond guy yelped, and backed away.

Lyle ripped open the bag and pulled out the gun. "I said where *is* she?"

"No!" Dannie shouted through the window. "Lyle, stop!"

Lyle looked up at the window, startled.

The blond guy's head whipped around. "Dannie?"

She'd guessed right. He did have a beard. And an earring. But there was one thing about him that was completely unexpected.

"Roger."

Chapter Nineteen

SHE'D SPOKEN HIS NAME in a whisper, but she'd meant it as a scream.

Guy grabbed her around the waist, obviously afraid she was going to faint again. But the danger of that was slim.

She wasn't faint. She was furious.

Dannie stormed around the side of the house and through the open front door, pushing past Lyle until she reached Roger.

"You son of a bitch!" She took a swing, but Guy was right behind her. He grabbed her arm before her fist connected with Roger's face.

"Can't you turn down that TV—" Lisa rounded the corner and stopped short. "Holy sh—"

"Everybody sit down!" Lyle waved the gun wildly.

Nobody sat down.

"Goddamn it, I said sit down, all of you!"

"Hey, calm down, man," Guy said, moving toward Lyle.

"Don't 'man' me, you hairstyling freak. I said sit down." Lyle pointed the gun at Guy's chest.

Guy held up his hands and sat on the floor.

Roger and Lisa followed suit.

"Lyle, please," Dannie said. "Give me the gun."

"Sit down, Dano. I'm running the show this time."

Dannie sat on the rug between Roger and Guy.

"Good. Great." Lyle pushed his glasses up the bridge of his nose. He was sweating like a cold can of beer on the beach. "Each of you is going to get a chance to answer for what you did. And I think we're gonna start with…you."

He pointed the gun at Roger.

"What do you have to say for yourself, old *friend?*"

Roger was silent.

"What, all of a sudden you can't talk? Well, I'll start for you. How about, 'Hey, Lyle. I'm really sorry I stole Lisa. I'm sorry I stole your fake money, and your big idea, and your god-damned *life.*"

"Lyle, it wasn't like that. I needed—"

"Shut up," Lyle snapped. "It's always been about what you need. Well, now it's about what *I* need."

"Listen," said Roger. "If it's any consolation, Lisa is no prize. She ran through all the money. All she does is gripe all day. It's like being married all over again."

"Gee, thanks," Dannie said.

Roger turned to her. "I didn't mean it that way—"

"I said shut up." Lyle pointed the gun at Dannie. "And you. You're nothing but a tease. We could have been good together, but you had to fall for Mr. Hair Salon."

"Day spa," Dannie and Guy said at the same time.

"You and Dannie?" Roger said incredulously. "You sure didn't waste any time moving in on her, did you, *friend?*"

"I thought you were dead," Lyle said. "At least until your wife found my golf bag in your garage."

"I'm sorry, Lyle. I had to do it," Roger said.

"You had to do it? It took me months to plan this thing, and then you just step in and take it all. Twenty years of friendship, and you screw me for some gym whore. Well, guess what? I'm screwing you now. I went to Jimmy Duke when I figured out you were still alive. He told me if I can get the books you kept on him, he'll pay me well. So you're going to tell me where they are, because I may not have gotten the girl, but I'm going to get the money."

Roger shook his head. "I can't do it. Those books are the only insurance I have that Duke won't kill me."

"What makes you so sure he won't?"

"Because I'm the only one who knows where they are. If he kills me, he'll never know where or when they might turn up."

Lyle turned the gun on Lisa. "What about you? What do you have to say?"

"Nothing."

"That's it? You were supposed to run away with *me*. You told me you loved *me*. You got nothing to say?"

Lisa shrugged. "Roger had more money. More than you, and a hell of a lot more than him." She jabbed a thumb in Guy's direction.

"Gee, thanks," Guy said.

Lisa shrugged again.

Lyle leveled the gun at Guy. "And you. You've been a pain in my ass since before we met. I hated you before I ever even knew you, and now I can finally do something about it. In fact, I can do something about all of you."

"Lyle, let's talk about this," Roger said.

"The only thing I want to hear is where those books are. You better tell me, or I'm going to start popping these people. Only question is who should go first." He moved the gun from one to the other to the other. "Eenie, meenie, miney, moe…"

There was no way Dannie was going to die without finding out exactly what had happened. She'd gone nine long months believing Roger was dead, and she wanted a damn explanation.

With hardly a thought she rolled onto her hip and kicked out hard, clipping Lyle in the kneecap. He screamed in pain.

The gun went off, the bullet splintering the ceiling fan above them.

Guy leaped for Lyle, tackling him at the hip. Lyle landed with an "oof." The gun flew out of his hand, skittering under the TV stand.

Lisa scrambled for it, but Lyle grabbed her legs. She kicked him in the face, bloodying his nose. Lyle countered with a wild slap that glanced off Lisa's thigh. He twisted violently, trying to shake Guy off his knees. It was a no go. Guy outweighed Lyle by at least thirty pounds, and those thirty pounds were all muscle.

Dannie came up with the gun. Borrowing a line from every cop show she'd ever seen, she said, "Everybody, freeze!"

Only, nobody froze.

She pressed the gun to Lyle's back. "I said freeze."

Lyle stopped struggling, lying facedown on the carpet. Lisa crawled away from him, wiping blood from the side of her mouth with the back of her hand. Her red hair blazed around her face like a firestorm.

"Jesus Christ, Lyle. What's your problem?" she screamed.

"What's my problem?" Lyle shouted into the carpet. "You

use me to get your fake money, and then you take off with another man. You women are all alike."

Roger still sat in the center of the room, as if he were unsure what to do. Guy grabbed Lyle by the back of his collar and hauled him to his feet.

"Tie him up," Dannie said.

"With what?" Guy asked.

Dannie looked at Roger.

"There's some duct tape in the garage."

"Go get it," Dannie told him.

Roger disappeared. He was gone so long, Dannie feared he wasn't coming back. But he finally returned, carrying a roll of silver tape and a half-empty beer. "Sorry. It took me a while to find it."

"Looks like you had no trouble finding the beer," Dannie said. "By the way, you look like crap."

The Roger she'd known had always been the healthy outdoorsman type. But sometime in the past eight months he'd turned into a character from a Jimmy Buffett song. Dannie had no doubt he'd blended his share of margaritas.

Guy taped Lyle's wrists behind his back, then moved to his ankles, and finally stuck a piece over his mouth for good measure. When he was finished, he picked Lyle up and plopped him on the couch.

Dannie slid the safety into place on the gun before she stuck it into the waistband of her shorts. "Guy, would you and Lisa mind excusing Roger and me? We have a few things to talk about."

Guy nodded. "So do we."

He picked Lyle up and threw him over his shoulder, following Lisa out of the room. When they'd gone, Dannie looked at Roger.

He took a long haul on his beer.

"What happened?" she said quietly. "Whatever possessed you to do something like this?"

Roger gave her a pleading look. "I had to. You have to understand. Ben Wiser thought I was embezzling."

"Were you?"

"Not exactly. I mean, I took the money, but Jimmy Duke is a scumbag—"

"So you embezzled from a scumbag. What does that make *you*?"

Roger took another pull on his beer.

Dannie felt herself falling apart, and she didn't want to. At least, not until she knew every single detail of what had happened.

"How did you do it?" she said with a calm she certainly didn't feel. "How did you make everybody believe you were dead?"

Roger shrugged. "I paid Alejandro big bucks to hit the buoy while I was standing at the front of the boat. I fell overboard and swam beneath the buoy. Lisa was waiting there with a diving tank and scuba gear. We swam underwater to shore while they searched for my body. Lisa had come down a couple days earlier and had already rented us a place. We just got in the car and drove away."

God, it was like a movie. Or a nightmare. Dannie actually pinched herself.

Roger continued. "I'd sent the money I took from Jimmy Duke's account at Wiser-Crenshaw to a bank account in Costa Rica. Lisa had it transferred into an account here, under a fake name. Lisa Lewellyn. I used an alias, too."

"Randy Jarvis."

He nodded. "I dyed my hair, grew a beard, got my ear pierced. People aren't too suspicious around here. There are lots of drifters. Fugitives escaping their boring stateside lives. We pretty much blended in."

"You left us," Dannie said, unable to keep the anguish from her voice. "You left me. You left your *children*. Do you know how much we missed you? Do you have any idea how I mourned for you? You bastard."

She couldn't help it. The tears came, raw and bitter and uncontrollable.

Roger stood, and reached out to touch her shoulder.

"Don't," she said. "Don't you dare touch me."

"Dano…"

"My life has been hell since you've been gone. Do you know somebody broke in to the house? Slashed the tires on my car? I refuse to go through the rest of my life fearing for my kids' safety. You embezzled money from a thug. You faked your death. You left us with nothing. *Nothing*."

"That's not true. I left you well taken care of. You have the insurance money and the money from my stock at Wiser-Crenshaw."

Dannie laughed. "The joke's on you. Or on us, I guess. The insurance company won't pay out because we can't get a death certificate from the Cuatro Blancan authorities, because they couldn't find a body. And Wiser-Crenshaw found out about the money you stole, so they won't give us a dime, either."

Roger sat on the couch and put his head in his hands. "Jesus. I had no idea. What have you been doing for money?"

"Certainly not using the stuff you left in the garage, that's for sure. And by the way, why the hell was it there?"

Roger blew out a breath. "Lyle made it on one of his high-end copiers. He and Lisa were going to steal the money in Guy's safe and replace it with the counterfeit. Only, she wasn't sure exactly how much was in there, so Lyle made extra. I didn't get a chance to destroy it before I left."

"So that was the big idea you stole from Lyle? Taking Guy's money and running away with his wife?"

Roger nodded. "How have you been paying the bills?" he asked.

"I've used just about everything we had saved. I got a job, too, but it doesn't pay much. I came down here to try to talk the police into giving me a death certificate."

"Dannie, I'm sorry. I really am."

"Tell it to the kids."

Roger's voice cracked. "I can't go back until things cool off, Dano. Christ, if I do I'm a dead man. Jimmy Duke will kill me. Do you understand that?"

"Oh, I understand, all right." The question was, did she care?

She looked at her husband. Or rather, the man who used to be her husband but was now Randy Jarvis—embezzler, fugitive, fraud and escapee from his boring stateside life. To say she didn't know him anymore was an understatement.

But while he might not have been the man she always thought he was, he was still the father of her children. She didn't want to see him dead, but she did want him to live up to his end of the bargain.

Dannie wiped the tears from her cheeks with the back of her hand. Her heart felt as if it had withered in her chest. "I do understand, Roger. But guess what? You're not getting out of this without giving me and the kids what we need."

Roger's cheeks reddened. "Jeez, Dano. I wish I could give you some money. But we're almost broke here. She's… She ran through almost everything I had. The bitch—"

"I don't want money," Dannie interrupted. "I want the books."

"The books? What books?"

"You know what books. The books Lyle is looking for. The books you kept on Jimmy Duke's illegal income."

Roger exhaled and dragged a hand down over his face. "I can't tell you where they are. They're the only thing that might save my ass."

"So you're telling me your own safety is more important than your children's?"

"Of course not—"

"Because if you don't tell me where those books are, Jimmy Duke's men will be breaking in to our house and harassing us for the rest of our lives while you hang out drinking beer and working on your tan."

"Jesus." He rubbed his face again. "Okay, okay. I'll tell you where they are."

Dannie waited, but he didn't say anything. Finally she said, "Well?"

"They're in the boat."

"What boat? Alejandro's?"

He shook his head. "The boat in our garage."

Dannie's mouth fell open. "What made you think I wouldn't get rid of that thing? That I wouldn't sell it?"

"Well, I didn't know you'd need the money." He smiled at her. "And I know you, Dano. You're sentimental."

"What does that have to do with anything?"

"Come on. You saved the cork from the bottle of wine we had on our first date."

"It was a good bottle."

"You also saved the mint we got with the check."

"What's your point?"

"My point is that I knew you wouldn't get rid of anything that meant a lot to me."

"Eventually I would have."

He sighed. "I planned on doing some traveling, getting back to the States eventually, with a new identity. In fact, I've been trying to get a passport for months, but even the forgers around here are slow."

Dannie rubbed her temples. "Let me ask you this. Were you planning on letting me know at some point that you were still alive?"

Roger finished off his beer and stared down at the carpet. "I thought about it."

Dannie fought back a fresh spate of tears.

"Listen," he said. "Don't tell anyone you saw me here, okay? Give me a fighting chance."

"I'll think about it."

TEN MINUTES LATER Dannie and Guy walked out of Roger and Lisa's bungalow. Alone.

Lyle was still tied up on the kitchen floor. They left it to Roger and Lisa to figure out what to do with him, which only seemed appropriate.

Dannie and Guy agreed that reporting Roger to the authorities, at least for the time being, could be detrimental to their plans.

Dannie didn't tell Roger that the Cuatro Blancan police suspected he was still alive. Nor did she tell him about the insurance investigation. A girl had to have her secrets.

They drove the moped back to the docks to catch the ferry. On the way, they spotted Judy Finch talking to Paco outside the taqueria. Guy pulled the moped over to the side of the road. Dannie removed her sunglasses to get a better look.

Judy was scribbling furiously in her notebook in her microscopic handwriting.

"You think she'll find Roger?" Guy asked.

"Probably," Dannie said.

"What should we do?"

Dannie put her sunglasses back on. "Screw it. It's every man for himself now."

Chapter Twenty

MOST OF THE PASSENGERS on Dannie and Guy's flight were asleep, but Dannie couldn't have closed her eyes if she'd tried.

Aside from the three cups of coffee she'd downed at the airport, she was running on adrenaline and indecision. She still had no idea what she was going to do with the books.

It wasn't as if she could turn off her feelings for Roger just like that. She'd loved him for a long time. Probably still did, in some way that begged for in-depth analysis.

If she went to the police, he'd be in a lot of trouble.

On the other hand, Judy Finch had probably found him, and if that was the case, he was already in a lot of trouble.

As if he'd read her mind, Guy said, "So what are you going to do?"

Dannie switched on the overhead lamp. A small cone of light shone down on them, cocooning them in the relative dark of the plane, creating a strange sort of intimacy. It was as if they were the only people who existed in that moment.

"I should probably take the books to the police," she said.

"It would be the right thing to do."

He didn't sound so sure. And then she realized why.

"If the police get hold of Roger's books, they'd probably find out you're involved with Jimmy Duke. That your spa is one of his 'investments,'" she said.

Guy nodded.

"Why didn't you say something to me? Why are you even letting me consider going to the authorities with this?"

Guy looked tense and exhausted. "Because it isn't my decision. You've got the most riding on all of this."

She reached over and curled her fingers around his. "I'm sorry."

"For what?"

"For not believing you when you told me Roger was alive. For getting you into this mess in the first place."

Guy rubbed his thumb over hers. "I got myself into this mess. I'm the one who made a deal with the devil." He sighed. "I just really thought I could make it all work. I had some great ideas for that spa."

He pulled her closer, tucking the scratchy airline-issue blanket under her chin. "I get no big thrill out of being right about Roger, you know."

"I know."

"And I love you."

She looked up into his eyes. She wanted to say something back. Not the Big *L*—she couldn't go there yet—but something to show how much he'd come to mean to her. But all she could muster was a heartfelt "I know."

"Listen, you do what you have to do to protect yourself and

the kids, okay? If that means going to the police, I'll take my lumps."

She kissed his lips softly. Then she laid her head on his chest and fell into a fitful, dreamless sleep.

THEY LANDED IN Philadelphia just after sunrise. It was four days before Halloween. The air was sharp, the sky overcast. Harbingers of November.

As they walked to the car, Dannie said, "I made a decision."

"Yeah?"

She could tell he was trying to sound casual.

"I've decided to give the books to Wiser-Crenshaw."

He looked at her, puzzled.

"In exchange for what's rightfully mine. I want the money for the sale of Roger's stock. I mean, technically the books are their property, right?"

Guy nodded.

"They wouldn't want them to get into the wrong hands. Like the D.A.'s, maybe?"

"Definitely not."

"They can figure out what they're going to do about Duke. But I'm going to strongly suggest they terminate their business dealings with him."

The tension in Guy's shoulders seemed to ease a bit. He grabbed her hand as they walked across the long-term parking lot. "Sounds like a plan."

The expressway was all but deserted, and they reached Dannie's house in the suburbs in no time at all. As soon as they walked in the front door, she knew something was wrong.

Woman Reclining on Blue Bed, the painting that hung above the little table near the front door, was gone.

Dannie went straight to the freezer.

"The money's gone, too," she said, holding the empty hot-dog box. "Let's go check on the books."

As they hurried through the house toward the garage, Dannie could see that the place had been thoroughly searched this time around, although nothing else seemed to be missing.

In the office, the filing cabinets and desk had been broken in to, the contents of the closet strewn all over the floor.

"Duke must be getting desperate," Guy said.

"You think it was him for sure?" Dannie asked.

"That would be my guess. He wants those books."

Guy followed Dannie into the garage, and she switched on the light. Broken glass lay on the floor beneath a window on the far side.

"Looks like that's where they came in," she said.

Guy nodded. "Where did Roger say the books were?"

She pointed at the boat, which lay like a beached whale in the middle of the floor, pushed off the blocks on which it had rested. Duke's men had obviously searched it.

Dannie grabbed a flashlight and a hammer and walked around the hull to the topside of the craft.

Ignoring her claustrophobic bent, she climbed into the cabin, shining the flashlight over the wreckage in the eerie darkness. It was like searching the *Titanic*. Only, *Treat's Dream* was a much, much smaller boat. And it hadn't hit an iceberg. And it wasn't underwater. And of course, nobody had made a movie about it.

She stepped over torn-up carpeting and broken decking to get to the small galley kitchen in the front of the cabin. The doors of the cabinets had been unlatched, and hung open above her head.

Dannie went to the second one and swung the hammer, splintering the back panel inside the cabinet. She cleared the broken wood with the claw of the hammer, exposing a hollow space about six inches deep between the cabinets and the fiberglass hull of the boat. Inside, just where Roger had told her, a paper grocery bag was taped to the fiberglass with duct tape.

Roger sure loved his duct tape.

Dannie freed the bag, crawling backward out of the cabin. Guy helped her to her feet.

They tore open the bag to reveal two slender red journals.

Dannie exhaled. "Wow."

Guy opened one of the books and skimmed the contents. "Jackpot."

THEY WALKED INTO Wiser-Crenshaw, the books in a big pink beach bag slung over Dannie's shoulder.

Monique looked up from the reception desk, giving Dannie an exasperated little smile. "Hello, Mrs. Treat."

"Hello, Monique. I'd like to see Ben Wiser, please."

"Mr. Wiser?" Droll amusement steeped her cultured tone.

"Yes, Mr. Wiser."

"Mrs. Treat, I'm terribly sorry, but you're on the list."

"The list?"

Monique nodded. "The list of people who have been banned from the premises. After what you pulled last time, forcing your way into Mr. Goody's office…"

"I didn't hear about that one," Guy said to Dannie.

"Slipped my mind," Dannie said. She turned her attention back to Monique. "Listen, Jersey girl. Just call Wiser and tell him I have something he might be interested in. Something that will make some very interesting reading."

Monique shook her head. She opened her mouth, but Dannie put up a hand. "So help me God, Monique, if you don't call him right now, I'm going to kick your nonexistent ass."

Monique's mouth snapped shut. She picked up the phone and savagely punched a button.

"Liliana, yes. Listen, Roger Treat's wife is here. She's insisting she speak with Mr. Wiser. Yes, I told her she's on the list. But she says she has something Mr. Wiser would be very interested in."

Monique hung up and gave Dannie a hostile look. "She's sending an escort. Just so you don't pull any stunts."

Dannie was about to say something smart when her phone rang.

"Dannie, where are you, dear?" It was Roger's mother. "Are you back in Pennsylvania?"

"As a matter of fact, I am," Dannie said. "My plane just got in a couple of hours ago. I'm taking care of a couple of errands, and then I'll be by to pick up the kids."

"Oh, I wish I had known! Some nice men stopped by earlier, asking for you."

A frisson of fear ran down Dannie's spine. "What nice men?"

"They didn't say their names, actually. They were looking for a book Roger had borrowed."

"Oh God, Elizabeth. What did they say, exactly?"

"Umm, well. Let me see. They said Roger borrowed a book from their friend Jimmy. And that Jimmy was hoping to get it back. I told them I didn't know anything about it, but maybe you did."

"Yeah? And then what?"

"Well, they said they'd have to ask you. And then they said that if I talked to you first, to tell you that you have beautiful children."

The phone slipped from Dannie's hand. Guy quickly picked it up and handed it back to her.

"Elizabeth, don't let them back in the house," Dannie said. "Listen to me. Just lock all the doors and pretend you're not home. Better yet, take the kids out somewhere."

"Dannie, you're scaring me." Elizabeth's voice was shaky. "What's going on?"

"Don't panic—I'll explain everything later. There's just been a mix-up. But just do what I'm telling you, okay?"

"Okay. Okay…"

"Elizabeth, everything will be fine. I'm taking care of it."

"Yes."

Dannie could hear her mother-in-law breathing heavily over the phone.

"Go. I'll call you soon," Dannie said.

Just then the elevator door slid open, and Liliana, Ben Wiser's secretary, emerged with a security guard.

Dannie grabbed Guy's arm and ran with him out of the building.

"What are you doing?" he asked as they jogged down the sidewalk. "Are you crazy?"

Dannie's heart squeezed in her chest. "Can you get in touch with Jimmy Duke?"

GUY HAD PUT IN A CALL to Duke's "assistant," and he and Dannie were now waiting at the diner, Myrna's, where they'd first met, sitting at a booth in front of one of those functional framed windows. *Waiting for a Criminal to Call.*

"Where could he be?" Dannie sucked down her third Coke as she twisted the straw paper between her fingers.

"Hard to say," Guy answered. "He has a house in the Poconos, a suite at a casino in Atlantic City and he owns a piece of a hotel in the Adirondacks."

"Great. We could be here for hours." She waved the waitress over. "Can I get a hot fudge sundae, please?"

"You're kidding. It's eleven o'clock in the morning. Do you really want a sundae?" Guy said.

"Desperately. I've had two hours of sleep in the last thirty-six hours. I need sugar."

"How about a muffin or some oatmeal?"

"Sorry. They don't serve oatmeal in my amusement park."

The waitress ignored Dannie and stared at Guy. Dannie snapped her fingers in front of the woman's face. "Hey. My sundae?"

"Oh, right." She hustled away.

Dannie rolled her eyes.

Guy tapped his cell phone on the table. "Come on. Ring."

"That's good. That'll work," Dannie said sarcastically.

The phone rang.

Guy gave her a triumphant grin and flipped the phone open.

"Hey," he said. "I'm trying to get Jimmy. I have a friend who has something he may be interested in. Uh-huh. Uh-huh. Right." He flipped the phone shut.

"So?"

"That was Francis, Jimmy's assistant."

"And?"

"Jimmy's at Philadelphia Park."

"The racetrack?"

"Apparently he owns a piece of a racehorse that's running there today."

"Yeah?"

"He wants us to meet him there, in his box, at noon."

Dannie's stomach turned. "Oh."

The waitress returned with Dannie's sundae. But for the first time in her life, hot fudge didn't seem like a cure for everything.

She pushed it away. "Come on. Let's get out of here."

Chapter Twenty-One

CARS HAD JUST BEGUN to trickle into the parking lot of Philadelphia Park, filling up the empty spaces like grains of sand in
a giant hourglass.

Dannie grabbed the pink canvas beach bag she'd taken with
her to Wiser-Crenshaw. She got out of the car and slung it over
her arm, taking a deep breath.

The smell of exhaust fumes from Street Road mingled with
the scents of horse and parking-lot dust.

Dannie and Guy entered through the main entrance into
a spacious marble-tiled hall, soon passing through an area
with stacks of simulcast TVs and rows of wagering terminals.
A few men gathered at a table in the handicapping lounge,
drinking beer from plastic cups, their racing forms spread out
on the table.

Dannie and Guy took the escalator up to the mezzanine

level, where rows of window tellers and self-service betting terminals lined the walls.

Several dozen people stood in line at the teller booths waiting to place bets before the post time of the first race. A clock above the terminal showed the time as 11:50 a.m.

"Which way to the box seats?" Guy asked a security guard in a too-tight blue uniform standing beside a bank of betting terminals.

"Next ta da Derby Dining Room." He jabbed a chubby finger in the general direction.

Dannie grabbed Guy's hand to slow him down. "Wait. I have to find a ladies' room."

He nodded in understanding, as if he knew the thought of facing Jimmy Duke could scare the pee out of anyone.

They located the restrooms and Dannie ducked inside. Of course, there was a line.

"Why is there always a line at every ladies' room on the planet?" she asked the woman in front of her. "Right now there's a line at a ladies' room in the Gobi Desert. You know there is."

Dannie danced from foot to foot.

The woman gave her a hostile look. "I'm not letting you in front of me."

The rules of sisterhood didn't apply in restrooms or singles bars.

Dannie concentrated on what she was going to do when this mess was over. She was going to pick up her kids and take them straight to Pizza Pete's, where they would gorge themselves on junk food, play arcade games and ride those little quarter rides until they all threw up.

Then she was going to pick up her big oaf of a dog from Cecilia's, and they were all going to go home and clean up the house and live happily ever after. The End.

A woman stepped into line behind Dannie, rubbing her pregnant belly. "Can you believe this line? I have to go so-o-o bad."

Dannie gave her a sympathetic look. "I feel your pain."

Then a stall opened up, and Dannie sprinted for it.

THE BOX SEATING AREA afforded a spectacular view of the racetrack, the winner's circle and the lakes on the infield. Naturally, Jimmy Duke's box was located front and center.

But even if it were in a less obtrusive location, Jimmy Duke himself would have been hard to miss. Even though Duke was sitting, Dannie could tell he was a tall man. And a large one, too.

Everything about him was large. His shoulders, his hands, his nose. Even the cowboy hat he wore was big. Forget ten gallons. The thing was fifteen, at least.

"Who wears a cowboy hat to a Philadelphia racetrack?" Dannie whispered to Guy as they approached Duke's box.

"Are you kidding? I think he wears it to bed," Guy whispered back. "Somebody told me it's stuffed with money."

"Guy Loughran!" Duke boomed. "How's the spa business?"

"I wouldn't know yet," Guy said, shaking Duke's hand.

"I know. We have to talk about that sometime soon." Duke gave Guy a look full of meaning. "Now, who's this pretty little lady?"

Dannie extended her hand, but instead of shaking it, Duke kissed it.

"I'm Dannie. Dannie Treat."

Duke held on to her hand, even as he motioned with his other one, dismissing the posse of pro-wrestling types who surrounded him. "Well, well. Mrs. Treat. Would you happen to be related to Roger Treat?"

"He was my husband."

"Was, or is?"

"I'm not sure I understand the question. My husband passed away in February."

"Not according to an acquaintance of ours. A Mr. Lyle Faraday?"

"Sadly, I've heard Mr. Faraday is mentally ill," Dannie said.

"I can confirm that," Guy said.

Duke looked at Guy with raised eyebrows. "Just how do you and this little lady know each other?"

"Let's just say Lisa and Roger were…close friends," Guy said.

Duke squinted at him. "I see. Well, have a seat, both of you. My horse is running in the first race. It'll be post time in just a few minutes."

"You own a racehorse?" Dannie said.

"Not a whole one. Just the ass end." Duke laughed, a big, booming, throaty laugh.

Guy and Dannie exchanged nervous glances.

Duke motioned to a small television positioned unobtrusively in the corner of the box. "If you don't want to watch the race live on the track, you can see it on this little bitty TV here. You can also place a bet, if you want."

"What's the name of your horse?" Guy asked.

Duke grinned. "Money Pit. Kinda like that spa of yours, huh?"

Guy's jaw tensed, but he said nothing. Dannie brushed his lower back with her hand, just to remind him she was there.

They both took seats behind Duke, watching as the track staff prepared for the first race, checking the surface for foreign objects, testing the timers at the gate.

After the condition of the track was approved, handlers led the horses for the first race into the gates. The animals were spectacular, their coats shining in the sunlight.

In gate number four, Money Pit, a chestnut filly showing purple and yellow colors, sidestepped and tossed her mane.

Duke rubbed his hands together. "Here we go. Here we go!"

Duke's men materialized, filing into the seats around Dannie and Guy. Dannie wasn't sure if they were there to watch the race or to make sure she and Guy watched the race.

An androgynous voice announced that the betting windows were closed.

After several tense seconds when time seemed to stand still, a loud bell, not unlike the one that had signaled the end of the day at Dannie's old high school, rang out over the track.

The horses shot out of the gate, streaking past the grandstand windows and rounding the turn at the bottom of the track. Dust plumed up behind them, forming whirling dervishes that danced in their wakes.

Money Pit came out of the gate slowly, but caught up to the rest of the runners before the first turn. Duke leaned forward, pumping his fist. "Come on, baby. Come on!"

The horse picked up speed on the far stretch, the jockey riding high on the saddle. Money Pit pulled ahead of the leader.

Duke hefted his considerable frame out of his chair, swiped the hat from his head and slapped it against his thigh.

The horse accelerated and seemed an easy winner until she stumbled fifteen yards from the finish line. She recovered her footing, but managed to garner only a third-place finish.

Duke lurched backward and sank into his seat, mashing his hat back onto his head. "Well, what're you gonna do? It was only her fourth race. Not bad, right?"

"Absolutely, boss," said the man beside Dannie. "She'll do better next time."

The other goons muttered their agreement.

Duke flipped open a cell phone and murmured into it before turning his attention back to Dannie and Guy.

"So, Mrs. Treat. Tell me what I can do for you. Or better yet, what you can do for me."

Dannie gripped the handles of the canvas bag sitting at her feet, taking a few seconds to bolster her nerve. She knew she had to approach this thing the right way if she was going to get what she wanted. She could not show fear.

She looked Duke squarely in the eye. "I think I have something you've been looking for."

"Really? What's that?"

"Are you going to play coy with me, Mr. Duke?"

He laughed. "I've been looking for some records your husband may have...misplaced."

"Your men tore my house apart," she said. "That wasn't nice."

"Those records are very important to me, little lady," Duke said, his face serious this time.

"My home is important to me."

He nodded. "I understand."

She pulled one of the books out of the canvas bag and handed it to Duke.

Duke removed the elastic bands holding it together, and leafed through the pages. "This is it?"

She shook her head. "There's one more. I don't have it with me, but you'll get it after we settle on the terms of our deal."

Guy gave her a questioning look.

"The *terms?*" Duke's face turned red. "Little lady, you got some nerve."

"I don't want anything more than what I'm entitled to," Dannie said. "I want to be safe, and I want to be able to take care of my kids."

Duke regarded her in silence for a minute. "Okay, then. What are your terms?"

"I want this to be the end of the unexpected visits to my home, and my in-laws' home."

Duke nodded. "Of course. There will be no need to keep in touch."

"I want a check from Wiser-Crenshaw for Roger's shares of stock."

"You'll have to take that up with Wiser-Crenshaw," Duke said.

Dannie shook her head. "They won't listen to me, but for some reason I think they'll listen to you."

Duke shrugged. He pulled his cell phone out of his pocket and dialed. "Ben? Jimmy. I have a little lady here says you owe her a check. Her name's Dannie Treat. Pay her, Ben. Today."

Jimmy snapped his cell phone closed. "Done. Now, what about the money your husband stole from me?"

"The money your men took from the hot-dog box in my freezer should cover some of that. And the painting they stole, too. Maybe we can just call the rest my finder's fee."

Dannie held her breath. If Duke called her on the fact that the money was counterfeit, she could play dumb. Pretend she had no idea.

A voice announcing the start of the second race filtered over the intercom above their heads. A waiter came, handing Duke a bourbon on the rocks.

When the waiter had gone, Duke focused his attention back on Dannie. "Anything else?"

Dannie nearly melted with relief. "Just one more thing. I want you to get out of the spa business. Permanently."

Duke broke out into a grin, and looked at Guy. "Well, well. Seems you got yourself a bodyguard, Mr. Loughran."

"Dannie—" Guy said.

"I just don't want to see a friend get into something over his head," Dannie interrupted.

"Don't think I can help you with that one," Duke said. "You see, our friend here owes me a lot of money. I can't just forget about that now, can I?"

"You'll get your money. As soon as the spa is running and Guy can pay you back, he will. Every cent, plus interest. But you have to agree you'll never become a partner, and you have to take him out of those books."

Duke took off his hat and scratched his head. "And if I don't let Mr. Loughran here out of our arrangement?"

Dannie shrugged. "Then I guess our deal is off. I'll just have to take the other journal to the proper authorities."

Duke shook his head. "You're playing a dangerous game, Mrs. Treat."

"It's not a game, Mr. Duke. I give you my word you'll get exactly what I've promised if you agree to my terms. What have you got to lose? A partnership in a spa?"

Duke said nothing.

The bell signaling the start of the second race rang. The announcer's spiel flowed from the intercom as the horses stormed past below the grandstand's windows. Duke stood framed against the track. *Silhouette of a Gambling Man.*

In seconds it was over.

Duke set his hat back on his head and turned to Dannie. "You paint that picture? That lady on the bed?"

Dannie nodded.

"I'm a great admirer of art. When can you get me the other book?"

"So we have a deal?" Dannie stuck out her hand.

This time Duke shook it instead of kissing it. "We have a deal. But only because I admire your spirit, Mrs. Treat. You're a regular filly, you are."

He motioned one of his goons over. "Cecil. Escort Mrs. Treat wherever she needs to go."

"That's not necessary," Guy said. "I can take her."

Duke shook his head. "You're going to stay with me. We need to have a little talk."

Cecil, a bald, flat-nosed, walking refrigerator of a man, swept an arm toward the stairs, motioning Dannie to walk in front of him. She looked over her shoulder at Guy.

He nodded to her. "I'll be right here when you get back."

He sounded as if he might be trying to convince himself as well as her.

Duke's bodyguard shuffled behind Dannie, past the Derby Dining Room, where spectators discussed what horse they wanted in the third race over plates of pasta and chicken cacciatore.

"Where are we going?" Cecil asked, his soft voice diametrically opposed to his big hard body.

"To the ladies' room."

Cecil rolled his eyes, but followed her as she located the same restroom she'd stopped at on the way.

There was a line, of course. She waited, letting a few other women cut the line, until the same stall opened up that she'd used before, on her way to see Jimmy Duke.

Inside the stall she removed the small plastic bag from the trash receptacle that was screwed onto the steel partition. Beneath it lay a paper bag containing Roger's second ledger.

"YOU HID THE OTHER BOOK in the ladies' room?" Guy asked, laughing.

"I just figured if I gave him both of them at once, I wouldn't have any leverage."

"Why didn't you tell me?" he said.

She shrugged. "A girl has to have her secrets."

Guy stopped and kissed her, right in the middle of the parking lot. "Will you tell me some of them?"

She smiled. "If you're a good boy."

They walked a little bit more, the late-October sun glinting off car windshields and mirrors, making the lot look as if it were filled with diamonds.

"I have a question for you, now," she said. "What did Duke say to you while I was gone?"

Guy laughed. "He told me he'd never liked Lisa. He said I should do everything in my power to make you happy, because you're a keeper."

"He said that?"

"Yep. He said you have a rare gift for negotiation."

Dannie laughed, too, giddy with relief and lack of sleep, and the thrill of the deal. She could hardly believe she'd faced down Jimmy Duke and won.

Well, provided that she didn't end up dead tomorrow.

They reached Guy's car, and both of them seemed a little bit amazed that they'd gotten out of the place with their limbs intact.

"What now?" Guy asked.

"Let's go get the kids."

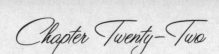

Chapter Twenty-Two

Nine months later

Richard and Betsy ran up and down the hall, past Dannie's paintings that hung on the walls—*Woman With Lily, The Bathing Pool, Green Chair on a White Beach.*

They were subdued pieces. Tasteful. Perfect for the hallways of Guy's day spa, Pink.

Or rather *their* spa, thanks to the money Wiser-Crenshaw had coughed up.

Dannie was mostly a silent partner, providing the artwork for the building and her opinion when Guy asked for it. Guy ran the place, which, although it had opened its doors less than four weeks ago, was booked solid for the first six months of operation.

There was just something about Guy that made women want to put themselves in his hands. Herself included.

Dannie smiled at the thought of the night before. And the night before that, and the night before that…

Turned out Guy was right. A temple could be every bit as much fun as an amusement park.

Dannie snatched up a twin in each arm as they toddled past her. "Richard, come on, honey. We're going to be late for visiting hour. Betsy, put your shirt back on. What did I tell you?"

Betsy sighed. "A girl has to have her secrets."

They trooped out to the front of the spa, to the salon area where Guy had just finished coloring a customer's hair.

Dannie waved to the other stylists, and some of the customers, as Guy followed her out to the parking lot.

"Are you going to see Roger?" he asked.

"Yes."

Though he had escaped Judy Finch's clutches in Cuatro Blanco, Roger had been nailed by Customs when he'd tried to use Lyle's passport to get out of the country. He now awaited trial for insurance fraud at the county lockup. His bail had been set at half a million dollars cash because he was considered a flight risk.

His lawyer was convinced Roger would serve only a couple of months if they could arrange a deal for him to testify against Jimmy Duke, who had been arrested for passing counterfeit money in an FBI sting operation. The investigation had prompted an audit of Duke's finances, which had led to the arrest of a dozen employees of Wiser-Crenshaw, including Ben Wiser himself.

Guy folded Dannie into his arms and squeezed her tight, her cheek pressing against the soft pocket of his pink silk T-shirt. "Guess what? My lawyer called today. Lisa finally signed the divorce papers."

Dannie sighed with relief. Her own divorce had gone

through a couple of months ago, with little protest from Roger. He'd said it was the least he could do.

But Lisa had clung to the misguided notion that Guy would welcome her back with open arms. She'd come home broke, unable to find a job in Cuatro Blanco, and was living with Rose.

"We should celebrate," Dannie said, thinking about the negligee she'd bought that afternoon at the lingerie place next to the Wee Ones Art Studio.

"How about we take the kids to Pizza Pete's?"

Dannie was about to protest, but the thought of cheese-laden pizza and greasy fries made her change her mind. Living with Guy had forced her to cut way down on her junk-food fixes, so she had to take them however she could get them.

"Deal," she said.

ON HER WAY HOME from visiting Roger, Dannie's cell phone rang.

"Hey, Dano!"

"Lyle?"

"God, it's great to hear your voice! Listen, you probably know Roger stole my passport and all of my ID, and of course the embassy here is dragging their feet getting me a new one. I can't get out of this country. It's driving me crazy, Dano. You gotta help me."

Amazing. It was as if he couldn't remember holding a gun to her head.

"Gee, Lyle. I don't know…"

In the background she could hear him shouting, "Come *on*. Don't tell me it's siesta time again!"

Panting, he came back on the line with her. "Dano, you've got to send me my birth certificate. You have a key to my house. Just go over there and get it—"

"Listen, Lyle. You're breaking up. But I hope you're having a great time down there—"

"No! Dannie, don't hang up! I need your help."

"I'm sure you'll figure something out," she said. "And Lyle?"

"What?"

"Take it easy, amigo!"

★ ★ ★ ★ ★

Suburban Secrets

To all the girls who kept my secrets.
We sure had some good times, didn't we?

Chapter 1

Friday, 7:17 a.m.
Weird Eggs

"Kevin, let's move! It's 7:17."

From the bottom of the stairs, Grace Becker heard the telltale thump of a body rolling out of bed. *Jesus.* They had thirteen minutes. She'd better find something he could eat on the way to school.

Megan and Callie were already in the kitchen, poking the food around on their plates.

"Finish your eggs," Grace said.

Callie stuck out her tongue. "What's *in* them?"

"Camembert and shallots," said Grace. "Why? Don't you like it?"

"What's wrong?" said Megan.

"What do you mean, what's wrong?" Grace grabbed a Pop-Tart from the pantry and stuck it in the toaster.

"You always cook weird stuff when you're upset," Megan said. "So, what's wrong?"

Grace bit the inside of her cheek. What was she supposed to say?

Well, girls, I'm upset because your father left me for his older, less attractive assistant; he's been a complete dirtbag about the divorce; we're probably going to lose our house; and the closest thing Mommy's had to a date in the last ten months was drinking a Dixie cup of warm Gatorade with your field hockey coach, Ludmilla?

She sighed. "Nothing's wrong. Eat your breakfast."

"Mom, nobody eats breakfast. And I mean *nobody.*" Megan, at twelve, had some sort of detailed list in her head about what everyone did or did not do, which she checked with agonizing frequency.

"They especially don't eat *eggs* for breakfast," Callie added.

"Yeah?" said Grace. "When I was your age, I would have killed to have eggs for breakfast. But it was cold cereal and a vitamin pill every day for me. Grandma actually had a job."

"*You* could get a job," Callie suggested.

"Be careful what you wish for." Grace tried to draw a deep breath, but it got stuck halfway down.

She *was* going to have to get a job. But where? She hadn't held a position outside her yoga class in thirteen years.

Everything in her life had revolved around Tom, his career and their kids. His bosses had loved her, his coworkers' wives had envied her, and his clients had jockeyed for invitations to Becker parties. She'd been the events coordinator, secretary, moral support beam, taxi service and butt kisser extraordinaire, all without ever drawing a paycheck.

But it was time to face facts. Tom was gone. He was making a new life, with a new woman who would be all those things.

So who would *she* be now?

She forced a smile. "If I get a job, who'll take care of you guys?"

Megan rolled her eyes. "Please, Mom. I'm almost thirteen. I think I can get my own breakfast."

"What? A handful of grapes and a Diet Coke? I don't think so. You're going to have a decent breakfast if I have to give it to you through an IV. You're not going to end up looking like Lara Flynn Boyle."

"Who?" said Callie.

"The walking corpse on *Twin Peaks.*"

"Twin *what?*"

"Never mind. Eat your eggs."

"I'm with Callie. I think you should get a job," said Megan. "You need a change. Don't you want some excitement?"

"There's plenty of excitement around here," Grace said. "Just yesterday while I was folding towels in the laundry room, I saw Mrs. Pollack's dog bite the mailman in the crotch."

"Mother!" Megan jerked her head in Callie's direction. "Was that really an appropriate thing to say in front of the child?"

"Who are you calling a child?" Callie shouted. "I'm almost nine!"

The Pop-Tart started smoking in the toaster just as Kevin flew into the kitchen and slid across the floor in his socks. "Four minutes!" he said, breathlessly.

"Wow, you can hardly tell," Megan said.

Grace examined her son. His hair stuck out from his head like he'd spent the night in electroshock therapy. His shirt was wrinkled, and she was pretty sure he'd taken the jeans he was wearing out of the hamper.

"No way. Get up there and do it right," she said. "Meet us

at the car in—" she checked her watch "—three minutes. I'll have your breakfast with me."

"Why can't I have a Pop-Tart, too?" Callie whined. "You only get something good around here if you're late."

"Is Dad coming to my game this afternoon?" Megan asked.

"I'm sure he is, but I'll ask him when I see him."

She'd be seeing him this morning. Damned Tom and his damned lawyer. Big Prick and Bigger Prick, as she liked to think of them.

They'd scheduled the fifth meeting in two weeks to discuss the settlement. This divorce was such a joke, all they needed to get it onto network TV was a laugh track.

Grace plucked the molten hot Pop-Tart from the toaster and wrapped it in a paper towel. "Okay, let's roll. We have seven minutes to get you to school."

The girls happily dumped the rest of their eggs down the garbage disposal and grabbed their backpacks from the hooks by the door.

Friday, 8:25 a.m.
Foot Powder and the Mouth

The Grocery King piped a Muzak version of U2's "Sunday Bloody Sunday" into the aisles. Grace was just the age to find this both entertaining and disturbing.

She checked her list.

Salmon. Fresh dill. New potatoes. She was going to make herself something special tomorrow night to celebrate her freedom. Her parents were taking the kids for the Columbus Day long weekend and solemnly swore to get them to all extracurricular activities on time and dressed in the correct uniforms.

Maybe it would be good to have a relaxing weekend alone.

Completely alone. She could think about what she was going to do with her life when she was the ex–Mrs. Thomas Becker.

The thought made her break into hives.

She hung a left into the pharmacy aisle and threw things into her cart.

She stopped in front of the Dr. Scholl's display. A lump crept up her throat, and before she could stop them, the tears came. She couldn't believe she hadn't had to buy foot powder in ten months.

Tom had notoriously damp feet. And it wasn't as though she missed his feet—they really were gross—but she'd loved him so much, she'd been able to overlook the grossness. Would she ever feel that way about someone's feet again?

As she fished through her purse for a tissue, she felt a hand on her shoulder. It was Lorraine Dobbs, otherwise known as the Mouth of South Whitpain.

"Grace? Are you all right?"

Grace nodded. Her blouse, now soaked with tears, stuck to her chest. "I think I'm allergic to foot powder."

Lorraine gave her a funny look. "O-*kay,* then. Are you going to Misty's later?"

Grace nodded again.

"Alrighty. See you there." Lorraine hurried off, one of the wheels on her cart shuddering in time with the Muzak version of "Rock the Casbah."

Grace checked her watch. Already nine minutes over her scheduled grocery shopping time.

Friday, 9:33 a.m.
Poster Girl

"We were about to send out the National Guard," said Tammy Lynn. "You're three minutes late."

"I know. I'm *so* sorry." Grace threw her coat and purse on a hook in the closet and rushed over to the chair at Tammy Lynn's station at Beautific, the salon where Grace had been getting her hair done for the past ten years.

"Grace, I'm only kidding," Tammy Lynn said, laughing as she fastened the black polyester cape around Grace's neck.

"Right." Grace laughed with her.

But the thing was, she didn't *really* think it was funny. Punctuality was important. A minute here, two minutes there. They all added up. When you had three kids you learned how to manage your time, or else dinner was chronically late, homework time was chronically late, and you ended up cleaning the bathroom at ten-thirty at night instead of watching the rerun of *Murphy Brown* on Lifetime you'd been looking forward to all day.

Her shoulder muscles bunched painfully. She had to relax. Maybe she could squeeze a few minutes of meditation in before lunch.

"Cover the gray and trim the ends?" Tammy Lynn asked, plucking the barrette from Grace's shoulder-length brown hair.

"Mmm-hmm."

Tammy Lynn spun the chair around to face a poster of a slender, sophisticated woman with a soft, blond, bouncy cut that looked like at least twenty minutes worth of work every morning.

"Wait," Grace said. "I want that."

Tammy Lynn stopped the color bottle in midair. "What? The do on the poster?"

Grace nodded.

"Really? You sure? You gotta blow it out with a brush and curl it. You can't just put it back in a barrette."

Grace studied the poster again.

It wouldn't be a completely off-the-wall thing to do. She'd been blonde once, a long, long time ago. Before Tom had hinted it wasn't quite sophisticated. Not quite who he thought she should be.

Maybe Megan was right. Maybe she needed to shake up her life a little. Hell, she could get up a few minutes earlier.

"Do it," she said.

Friday, 10:58 a.m.
Big and Bigger

As Grace waited for the elevator in the four-story, brick-and-tinted-window building that served as suburban Philadel-phia's answer to the high-rise, she raked the wispy hairs at her neck with her fingernails.

What had she been thinking? She felt naked without her ponytail. And the last thing she wanted to feel around the man who was almost her ex-husband was naked.

She hadn't actually wanted to *be* naked around him, either, for a long time.

She supposed she had a sixth sense that he'd been cheating on her, which was probably why she'd skipped the meeting with the decorator that day and gone straight home, only to find Tom stretched out on their bed, covered with peanut butter. His assistant, Marlene, was on top of him, wearing nothing but a Smucker's negligee. A nauseating sight, consid-ering that on her best day, wearing her best Donna Karan power suit, Marlene looked a lot like a broomstick in a red wig.

Grace had been angry as hell. In retrospect, she realized it was mostly because they'd ruined a pair of really good sheets, but also a little bit because she'd been married to Tom for thirteen years and they'd never made a PB and J sandwich together. The most creative thing they'd ever done in bed was fill out their taxes.

She supposed part of it was her own fault. Tom knew she lived and died by her Day-Timer, and if the Day-Timer said she'd be at the decorator's at two o'clock, then that's where she'd be.

If she'd been a tad more unpredictable, maybe they'd have had "lunch" at Marlene's place instead, and ruined *her* good sheets.

Grace stepped out of the elevator on the fourth floor at Kemper Ivy Kemper, where Tom's lawyer, aka Bigger Prick, practiced. The receptionist directed her to the conference room, where Big Prick, Bigger Prick and Grace's own lawyer, Debra Coyle, waited.

Tom raked his long fingers through salt-and-pepper hair. She could see the tension in his squared jaw. His bone structure was impeccable, really. He would undoubtedly age like Sean Connery, remaining breathtakingly handsome well into his retirement days.

She took a deep breath and pushed the door open.

Big Prick's eyes bugged. "You cut your hair. And it's *blond*."

Bigger Prick flashed his client a look.

Grace felt a moment of grateful relief before she considered where the compliment had come from. She gave Tom a bitchy look. "I'm getting the kids' hair cut, too. I figure we'll save money on shampoo."

"Oh, for God's sake, Grace. You know the children will be well taken care of, and—"

"Just hold on, Tom," his lawyer interrupted. "Debra, will you keep your client quiet for a few minutes?"

"I think she has every right to be pissed, David. Don't you?" Debra motioned to the chair next to hers, and Grace took a seat. "How many times are we going to rehash this pathetic settlement?"

"She signed a prenup, Debra."

"Then what are we doing here?"

"My client just wants to be fair. He wants to do what's right."

Grace snorted. "He should have thought of that before he decided to audition for the role of mascot for Skippy's porn division."

Tom pushed away from the table and stormed out the door.

Grace rubbed her temples. "Can we just get this over with?"

Bigger Prick slid the latest draft of the divorce settlement across the wide conference room table.

"Will you leave us alone for a few minutes?" Debra asked Bigger Prick.

The other lawyer nodded and followed Tom from the room. Grace could see them through the floor-to-ceiling windows, waiting just outside the door.

Upon closer inspection, Tom didn't look well. The bags under his eyes matched the gray suit he was wearing. Maybe the strain of the divorce was catching up to him, too.

Yeah, right. More likely he and Marlene had been dressing up in condiments all night.

A vision of Marlene's bony ass, covered in ketchup, flashed in Grace's mind. *Blech*.

"Grace, I don't think we're going to do much better than this," Debra said. "The terms are shitty, but you did sign a prenup. He gets all property and monies generated by his inheritance, including the house. You get half of what you've both made since you got married."

"You mean half of what *he's* made. He wouldn't let me work, Debra. God, I was so stupid."

Debra reached out and squeezed Grace's hand. "The child support is good. Some would argue that he's being generous."

"Generous? Listen, I don't give a crap about the money. Well, okay, maybe a small crap. But I'm going to lose the *house.* My *kids* are going to lose their house."

"Maybe you could offer to buy him out."

"How? The house is worth three-quarters of a million dollars."

Debra thought for a minute. "Can you borrow it from your parents?"

Grace shook her head. "They don't have that kind of money."

"Do you have anything you can sell? What about stocks? Jewelry?"

She shook her head. "It wouldn't be enough to buy him out." For the second time that day, tears threatened.

She'd worked so hard to make that house a home for Tom and the kids. It was a gorgeous, historic colonial manor house, once owned by William Penn's sous-chef or something. When they'd moved in, it was hardly more than an old pile of bricks. She'd restored it, room by room, over the years, finding authentic fixtures at flea markets and on the Internet. She loved that house, and now she'd never even be able to afford the taxes. But there were more important things than houses.

At least she'd won custody of the kids. Probably because— unlike the house—Marlene didn't want them.

"Screw it," she said. "Give me the papers."

"Are you sure?"

"I'm sure." She signed the papers, and Debra waved Tom and his lawyer back into the room.

"You did the right thing, Grace," Bigger Prick said. "The sooner we end this hostility, the sooner you and Tom can get on with your lives."

Right. Only now, hers would be almost unrecognizable.

Grace rose. "Good luck with Marlene."

Bigger Prick stuck out his hand. Grace ignored it.

She made it to the door before Tom said, "Wait, Grace. I want to talk to you. Alone."

Both lawyers looked stricken. But Grace nodded, and Tom held the door open for her as they left.

"What?" she said. "You want to thank me for signing that piece of shit agreement?"

He came closer. "No. I want to ask a favor of you."

"A *favor?*" She laughed. "You haven't changed a bit, have you?"

Tom closed the distance between them and guided her to an alcove in the lobby. "I need you to do something for me. In return, maybe we could work something out with the house."

She looked into his eyes. "You're serious?"

"Yes." He lowered his voice. "I need you to sign some papers."

"What kind of papers?"

"Work-related stuff."

She narrowed her eyes. "Why would you want *me* to sign work-related papers?"

He reached out, almost touching her hand before pulling back. He whispered, "Not *your* name."

Her insides went liquid. "No-oh. No way. Forget it."

Now he grabbed her hand. His voice was low and quick. Persuasive. His sales voice. "Come on, Gracie. You're the only one I know who can do this for me. You're the best."

"Are you crazy?" Her voice rose, and she made a concerted effort to quiet herself. "Are you nuts? Do you want to send me back to jail?"

"You won't get caught. I promise. It's a one-time deal."

She pulled her hand from his.

"Think about it, Gracie. Five minutes of your time and the house is yours."

"What about Marlene? I thought she wanted the house."

"Yeah, well. She'll just have to live without it."

He must have known how tempting this all would sound to her. He'd always been a great salesman, finding just the right carrot for the mules.

He'd found hers, all right. But it wasn't a big enough carrot.

"I'd want the 'Vette, too," she said. Tom's white 1976 Corvette was basically a fifteen-foot extension of his penis.

He frowned. "Grace—"

"Okay, then." She started walking toward the elevator, and he grabbed her arm.

"Wait. All right. The 'Vette, too."

She realized then that he was really, truly desperate.

She chewed the inside of her cheek. "I'll think about it."

"Think fast, okay? I need this done quickly."

She nodded.

Before she could figure out what his intentions were, he leaned in and kissed her. "I'll call you."

She got almost to the elevator before she remembered to ask him about Megan's field hockey game.

"Hey," she shouted over her shoulder. "You know Megan has a game today?"

"Of course. I'll be there," he said. "I wouldn't miss it."

Grace walked out of the building and into the sunshine. She'd made a decision.

She didn't need meditation. She needed a margarita.

Chapter 1.5

Friday, 11:45 a.m.
Wild Card

Pete Slade popped another Tums and stared out the window of the Melrose Diner in South Philly. He had a bad feeling.

Hell, he'd had a bad feeling since this whole mess began. And the fact that he now had to rely on a sharp-looking kid with a hundred-dollar haircut and a different girl for every night of the week didn't help matters.

Nick Balboa wasn't what you'd call reliable. Not even a little bit. He was a low-level thug with big plans.

A wild card.

And he was gonna screw everything up.

Pete chugged his coffee and threw a couple bucks down on the table for the waitress.

Out on the street, he flipped open his cell phone and called Lou.

"Hey. I got a funny feeling."

"Yeah?" said Lou.

"Yeah. I'm gonna swing by the airport, maybe watch Balboa's car."

He imagined Lou rolling his eyes. But Pete had been doing this long enough to know when to follow his gut. Even when it was rebelling against him.

"Anything you want me to do?" Lou asked.

"Just sit tight. I'll call you if I need you."

Pete disconnected the call and popped another Tums.

Jesus, he couldn't wait for this to be over.

Chapter 2

Friday, 11:56 a.m.
Grazing

Beruglia's was packed, as usual. Businessmen in athletic-cut suits lined the bar, hunched over low-carb beers and plates of South Beach–acceptable protein. Groups of women crowded around tables, grazing on giant bowls of lettuce and sipping water with lemon wedges.

The hostess led Grace to a table against the window. It had taken her a while to get used to eating alone in restaurants, but as long as she didn't see anyone she knew, it was okay.

She unfolded her napkin and laid it in her lap.

"Grace?"

Damn. So much for that.

One of the grazers at the table beside hers was leaning so

far back in her chair Grace was afraid she'd topple over backward. Motherhood had made her hypersensitive to behaviors apt to result in head injury.

"Grace Poleiski?" the woman said.

"Yes?"

"It's me, Roseanna Janosik, from Chesterfield High."

"Roseanna! Wow, how long has it been?"

"Since the last reunion, I guess. What, eight, nine years?" Roseanna squeezed out of her chair and came to sit at Grace's table. "You look great! What's going on with you?"

"Eh, you know. It's always something."

"I hear that. Hey, what're you doing tonight? Some of the girls are getting together at a club downtown. They'd die if you walked in."

Grace thought about the salmon and new potatoes in her fridge. "All the way to Philly? I don't know…"

"Come on. It's fifteen miles, not the other end of the earth. Live a little. Leave the kids home with your husband and come out and play. The club is supposed to be a riot. There's a DJ playing all eighties music. It'll be just like high school."

Grace had a sudden flashback to high school. The sausage-curl hair, giant belts, parachute pants. Smoking in the girls' room. Making lip gloss in science lab. She smiled.

She and Roseanna had been good friends. In fact, she'd had a lot of good friends.

Grace's mother had always told her those were the best days of her life, but she'd never believed it.

How was that possible when one strategically placed blemish could put you on the pariah list for a week? When the wrong look from the right guy could annihilate your confidence for a month? When there was no bigger horror than having your period on gym day and having to take a shower in front of twenty other girls?

God, she missed those days.

It was hard to admit, but her mother had been right.

Roseanna squeezed her hand. "So, what do you say? Wanna come?"

"Why not?" Grace said. "Sounds like fun."

"Great." Roseanna scribbled on a napkin. "Here's the address of the club. Meet us there around nine."

Grace pulled her Day-Timer out of her bag and penciled it in and then ordered a salad.

And a margarita. Rocks. No salt.

Friday, 1:30 p.m.
Slow Brenda

"Look at y-o-o-o-u." Misty Hinkle grabbed Grace's hand and pulled her into a living room the size of a hockey rink, and almost as cold. Six card tables were huddled together in the center of the room. Probably for warmth.

"Look at Gra-a-a-a-ace, everybody. Doesn't she look fa-a-a-abulous?" The women sitting around the tables tore themselves away from the snacks long enough to glance at her.

"Oh, stop it, Misty," Grace said. "It's just a haircut."

"It's not just a haircut. You went blonde." There was an accusatory note in Lorraine's voice.

"I needed a change. What can I say?" Grace caught the knowing glances ricocheting around the room and wondered how long these ladies of modest society would continue to invite her to their functions.

There was currently only one divorced woman in the group, and Grace had a feeling they only kept her around to talk about her behind her back. All the rest of the unfortunately uncoupled had been drummed out of the pack within weeks of their divorces being finalized.

Face it. No one wanted a suddenly single woman running around at one of their holiday parties, talking about how hard it was to get a date when your boobs sagged and your thighs jiggled. Why invite the ghost of Christmas Future?

"I, for one, liked the ponytail," said Brenda McNaull. She pointed to the chair across from hers and motioned for Grace to sit down. "We're partners today."

"Great," Grace said. She should have had a couple more margaritas at lunch. Brenda was the most maddeningly slow card player in the world.

"Pe-e-eople." Misty clapped her hands. "La-a-adies, ple-e-ease. A couple of announcements before we begin."

The room quieted. Slightly.

"Tha-a-an-nk you. Once again, Meredith is looking for volunteers for the Herpes Walk—"

"Hirschsprung's!"

"Sor-r-r-ry—Hirshbaum's Walk. Kathy needs crafts for the Literacy Fair, and Grace is collecting clothes for Goodwill again today. Leave your bags by the door. And I don't mean the ones under your eyes. *Haw haw!* Oka-a-a-ay, ladies. Let's play!"

Brenda examined the tiny glass dish of nuts at the corner of the card table. "Can you believe this chintzy spread?" She plucked an almond from the dish between two long, manicured fingernails and popped it into her mouth.

"So what's the game today?" Grace asked.

"Pinochle," Brenda said.

The two other women at the table rolled their eyes. It was going to be a long afternoon.

Friday, 4:10 p.m.
Date with Ludmilla

The parking lot at Megan's school was nearly empty. Field hockey wasn't exactly a big draw, as witnessed by the fact that the snack bar wasn't even open.

Grace pulled a couple of grocery bags out of the back of the minivan and looked around. No sign of Tom's car.

Not yet, anyway. But Grace knew he'd be there. He hadn't missed one of Meg's home games since she'd started playing field hockey. Or one of Kevin's soccer matches, or one of Callie's band recitals. Grace had to admit, he was a good father. A lousy husband, but a good father.

Grace picked her way to the field, her high heels aerating the grass. She'd forgotten to bring sneakers.

She plunked the grocery bags down on the bench at the sidelines and unloaded the supplies—a giant plastic bag of quartered oranges, homemade chocolate chip cookies, paper cups and two industrial-sized bottles of Gatorade.

Coach Ludmilla, a hairy but not completely unattractive Hungarian woman, winked at her from the center line. Grace waved.

She wondered if theirs could be considered a monogamous relationship. Did Ludmilla wink exclusively at her, or did she wink at every mother who brought cookies and Gatorade? Maybe they were just dating.

Maybe she needed to get a life.

She watched as Megan dribbled the ball down the field and smacked it toward the goal cage. It hit the post and bounced out of bounds. She saw Megan's gaze search the sidelines. Grace waved, but Megan was looking elsewhere.

Grace looked over her shoulder. Sure enough, Tom stood near the risers, alone. He hesitated before heading toward her.

The official blew the whistle to indicate halftime, and Ludmilla trotted over to the bench.

"Sorry I'm late," Grace said. "My afternoon, uh, appointment ran a little long." *Thank you, Brenda.*

"No problem," Ludmilla said. "Thanks for bringing the snacks again, Grace."

"Sure. The team's looking good."

"You bet." Ludmilla sidled next to her. "We're looking for an assistant coach. Someone to carry equipment and keep the stats. You interested?"

"Sorry," Grace said, handing the coach a cup of Gatorade. "I've got too much on my plate right now. Maybe next year."

Ludmilla looked disappointed. "Sure. Well, I've got to get these ladies ready for the second half. Will you pour some drinks for the team?"

"Of course."

While Grace bent over a row of paper cups, she saw Tom's three-hundred-dollar shoes approach. Unfortunately, he was in them.

"Grace, how are you?"

She continued pouring. "Same as this morning."

"Have you thought about what I asked you?"

"You mean how you want me to perform an illegal act that might get me arrested and destroy our children's lives in order to get what I deserve out of this marriage anyway?"

He sighed. "I'm not trying to screw you."

"Really?" She straightened. "Well that's a relief, because I'm pretty sure you got the K-Y in the settlement."

They both clammed up as the girls filed past the bench, inhaling oranges and cookies and Gatorade. In seconds they were gone, leaving nothing but empty plates and crushed cups in their wake.

Tom stuffed his hands in his pockets. "You don't know what's going on, Grace. You don't know what my life is like. I just want—"

"I'm not really interested in what you want, Tom. At this moment, I'm just trying to be here for one of my kids. I hope we can be civil for their sakes, but as far as your wants and needs—well, I guess that's what you've got Marlene for."

Tom's jaw twitched.

Grace wondered if he and Marlene were having problems. So, why should she give a damn? She had her own relationships to worry about.

Ludmilla waved to her from across the field.

Okay. So maybe it was time to reconsider her definition of *relationship*.

She looked over at Megan, chatting with her friends, watching her and Tom out of the corner of her eye. She'd been through so much the past year. They all had.

She didn't want to put the kids through a move, on top of everything else.

"All right," she said, forcing a smile for Megan's benefit. "I'll do it."

"Oh, God. That's great, Gracie. I knew I could count on you." He pulled an envelope from his jacket pocket.

"You brought them *with you?*"

He gave her a sheepish grin. "Just in case."

She looked around nervously, expecting the cops to be waiting for her just outside the fence. But there was no one there.

The game had resumed, and Ludmilla and the team moved to the far end of the field, leaving her and Tom pretty much alone. She spread the papers out on the bench, studying the signature he wanted her to forge.

"Roger Davis," she read. "Isn't that your boss?"

He nodded but didn't offer any more information. And she didn't ask.

She had the feeling she wasn't signing an authorization for an extra day of vacation, but she figured the less she knew about all of this, the better.

"I'll have to practice the signature a few times before I sign them. I'll get them back to you."

"When?"

She pulled her Day-Timer out of her purse and flipped through it.

"Will Marlene be home tomorrow morning?"

"No, I don't think so."

"Good. I'll bring them over then." She shoved the papers back into the envelope and stuck them in her purse. "The kids will be at my mom's this weekend if you want to get in touch with them," she said. "Kevin has a soccer game tomorrow."

"I know," Tom said. "I'll be there."

"How about if we also meet at the notary office Tuesday morning?" she said. "You can bring the papers for the house, and the title to the 'Vette, too."

He gave her a sickly smile.

"Don't worry," she said. "It'll be relatively painless. We'll get it all over with at once. Like pulling off a Band-Aid."

He opened his mouth as if he might say something, but he didn't. He just walked back toward the bleachers, hands in his pockets, his three-hundred-dollar shoes sucking mud.

Chapter 2.5

Friday, 5:58 p.m.
Roadkill

The asshole drove right past their meeting place.

According to the plan, as soon as Balboa arrived in Philly, he was supposed to drive straight to the gym and call from a pay phone. Shit. He was gonna screw them.

Pete had followed Balboa's rented green Taurus all the way from the airport. Balboa's own car, a cherry 1959 Buick, still sat in the VIP parking lot at the airport.

If Pete hadn't suspected Balboa was turning on them and staked out the baggage claim, he'd never even have known the guy was back in town a day early.

He flipped open his cell phone. "Lou. He's back."

"No shit."

"I followed him from the airport. He just passed the gym. I need you to go wait at his house. I doubt he'll show up there, but you never know."

"Right. I'm on it."

Pete snapped the phone closed.

In front of him, the Taurus eased into the exit lane. It looked like Balboa was heading for City Avenue.

Pete jockeyed through four lanes of frantic expressway traffic but just missed the exit.

Damn.

When Pete caught up to him, that son of a bitch Nick Balboa was dead meat.

Chapter 3

Friday, 7:12 p.m.
Oh, Mother!

As she drove toward her childhood home in Ambler, Grace felt younger and younger until, by the time she pulled into her parents' driveway, she was eight again.

In her mind she could hear the sprinklers whirring, and smell the newly cut grass of her youth. She looked across the street, half expecting to see her best friend, Sherri Rasmussen, playing hopscotch on the sidewalk.

"Okay, guys, everybody out of the car. Callie, don't forget your flute."

As the kids dragged their crap up the sidewalk, the door opened and Grace's mother stuck her head out. "My babies are here! Andrew, the children are here! Come help them with their things."

"Hi, Mom." Grace herded the kids into the house and bussed her mother on the cheek. "Thanks for taking them this weekend."

"Well, your father and I can imagine how difficult things must be for you, with the—" she stuck her head out the door and scanned the neighborhood for spies "—*divorce*."

Divorce was one of the words in Grace's mother's vocabulary fit only for whispering.

"You can say it out loud, Mom. It's not a dirty word."

Her mother pulled a face. "Come on in."

"Actually, I was kind of in a hurry."

"So you don't have time for a soda? Come in for a minute. I want to show you something."

Grace sighed. She knew once she got sucked over the threshold, it would be at least a half an hour before she got out of there.

The kids thumped up the stairs, already arguing about who'd get to play her father's Nintendo first. Grace followed her mother to the kitchen and sat on one of the vinyl-covered chairs. They were the same chairs she'd sat on as a child, once sadly out of style but suddenly retro chic.

"Look what I made in craft class," her mother said. She held out a tissue box cover constructed of yarn-covered plastic mesh. God Bless You was cross-stitched into the side in block letters.

"Nice."

"Here, take it. I made it for you. And you know, you can come with me next week. We're making birds out of Styrofoam."

"That's nice, but I can't."

Her mother took a diet soda from the refrigerator. "Why not? Now that Tom is gone, what are you doing with your time?"

Grace got up to get a glass from the cupboard. "I've got plenty to do, Mom."

"Like what?"

"Well, tonight I'm meeting some of my old high school friends for a drink downtown."

Her mother's eyebrows shot up and disappeared beneath her heavily hair-sprayed bangs. "Really? Do I know them?"

Déjà vu. How many times had Grace seen that look growing up? She felt inexplicably guilty, and she hadn't even lied about anything. Yet.

"Roseanna Janosik's going to be there. I ran into her today at Beruglia's."

Her mother sat down at the table. "Roseanna Janosik. Isn't that the girl who got caught smoking at cheerleading camp?" She pulled a face.

"That was Cecilia Stavros. And Jesus, Mom. That was a hundred years ago."

"You're right, of course. People change. Look at you."

"What's that supposed to mean?"

Her mother shrugged. "So who was Roseanna Janosik?" She tapped her chin. "I remember! She was the one who was crazy about that band and followed them everywhere."

"Right. Mullet."

"What? What's a mullet?"

"A bad haircut. And the name of the band Roseanna followed." Grace chugged her soda. "C'mon, tell me. What did you mean I've changed?"

Her mother got up from the table and took Grace's empty glass. "Oh, for heaven's sake, Grace, I didn't mean anything by it. Is that what you're wearing?"

"As a matter of fact, it is." Grace tugged the hem of her black skirt, but it refused to budge. She buttoned the red Chinese silk jacket Tom had given her the Valentine's Day before last. It had been the only thing in her closet remotely resembling club attire.

Her mother raised her eyebrows again. "Well, have fun. Tell Roseanna I said hello."

"Right."

Grace stalked to the bottom of the stairs. "Megan, Callie, Kevin. I'm leaving now!"

Megan and Kevin shouted a muffled goodbye. Callie stuck her head over the second-floor railing. "Bye, Mom. Have fun without us."

Grace tamped down a sudden attack of guilt. "I'll miss you."

"I'll miss you, too. Can we make brownies when I come home?" Callie could sense Grace's subtle vibrations of guilt like a fine-tuned seismograph.

"Sure."

"Grace, are you still here?" her mother called from the kitchen.

If she didn't get out of there soon, her mother would be dragging her up to the guest bathroom to show her the decorative fertility mask she'd made out of half of a bleach bottle.

Grace wiggled her fingers at Callie and slipped out the front door.

Friday, 8:08 p.m.
Killing Me Softly

Grace sped down the Blue Route in the eight-year-old BMW that used to be Tom's but was now hers. He'd insisted on getting a manual transmission, and now she was stuck with it—a real pain in the butt while she was trying to wipe noses and juggle juice boxes.

She much preferred the minivan, but she'd be damned if she was going to pull into a club driving the family taxi.

She fiddled with the radio. Why were all the stations in her car set to soft rock? When, exactly, had her eardrums surrendered?

She searched the dial for the station that played all eighties, all the time. AC/DC's "You Shook Me All Night Long" came on and she smiled. It took her back to when she and her girlfriends would cruise the back roads in an old Dodge Dart looking for keg parties, blasting this song and singing at the top of their lungs.

How sad. Somehow she'd gone from AC/DC to Celine Dion. From keg parties to the occasional glass of chardonnay. Was that what her mother meant? Was that how she'd changed?

She knew it was that, and a whole lot more. She used to have spirit. She used to take risks.

But when she'd married Tom, somehow it had been easy to accept the security and stability he provided in exchange for a few little changes. Higher necklines. Lower hemlines. The Junior League instead of her bowling league.

She drove around for almost an hour, reprogramming the buttons on her radio and thinking about all the crazy things she used to do, forcing herself not to worry that she was going to be late.

Eventually, she pulled into the parking lot of the club. She squinted up at the sign.

Caligula?

She checked the address in her Day-Timer. Sure enough, it was right.

She almost backed out of the lot, but images of her closet filled with navy poly-blend slacks and V-neck sweaters bolstered her nerve.

She could be every bit as crazy as her teenage alter ego. She *could*.

She got out of the car and tugged her skirt down as far as she could.

"Bring on the Romans," she said to the dark.

Friday, 9:13 p.m.
Flaming Togas

"ID, please."

The guy at the door wore baggy jeans and a black T-shirt with a picture of a snarling bulldog. His fingers worked the buttons of a Game Boy with lightning speed.

The B-52's "Love Shack" blasted out through the open door of the club.

Grace leaned in so the bouncer could hear her over the noise. "You're kidding me, right? Have you even *looked* at me? I was twenty-one when this song actually came out."

He shined a flashlight in her face. "Sorry 'bout that. Five bucks."

He stepped aside, and she walked straight into ancient Rome. Or a Hollywood-meets-Las Vegas version of it, anyway.

Buff, gorgeous, toga-clad waiters and waitresses wandered the faux-marble floor carrying trays of colorful drinks. Buff, gorgeous, denim-clad patrons sipped them while leaning against faux-marble columns. They were all so young. Well, most of them, anyway.

Grace had no trouble spotting her old high school friends. They were the only ones not trying to look bored.

Roseanna must have had one eye on the door, because she waved to Grace as soon as she walked in.

"Oh. My. God. It's Grace Poleiski," somebody shrieked.

Grace smiled. "Hi, everybody."

The women at the table jumped up and swarmed around her. She exchanged a quick hug with each of them, blinking back the tears that had inexplicably formed in her eyes.

"Sit," commanded Roseanna. "We just ordered a round of Flaming Togas."

Grace hooked her handbag over the back of a chair and sat

down, taking in all the changes in her friends. "Cecilia, you look great. You lost weight?"

"Forty pounds. Ephedra, until they took it off the market. If I hadn't started smoking again to compensate, I'd probably look like the Michelin Man already. Hey, you're looking good, too, Grace."

"Yeah? I guess you could say I lost some weight, too. About two hundred pounds."

"What! How'd you do that?"

"It just walked away."

It took the girls a minute to figure out what she was talking about.

"Your husband," Roseanna said.

Grace nodded.

Cecilia shook her head. "No shit. When did that happen?"

"January second. Screwing me over was his New Year's resolution, I guess."

A waiter arrived with a tray of pale orange shots and set one in front of each woman. He pulled a pack of matches out of the folds of his toga and lit the shots. Low blue flames danced on the surface of the liquor.

"Don't forget to blow 'em out before you drink 'em," he said. "We've had a couple of mishaps."

Roseanna smiled. "Remember when Dannie accidentally lit her hair on fire while she was smoking a cigarette in the girls' bathroom?"

"What did she expect?" said Cecilia. "She used so much hair spray, her hair wouldn't have moved in a hurricane."

"Come on," Dannie said. "My hair wasn't any worse than anyone else's. In fact, I remember Grace getting hers tangled in the volleyball net in gym class. It had to be at least a foot high."

They all laughed.

Grace ordered a margarita and another round of shots.

The waiter walked away, his tight little butt all but peeking out from under the toga.

Dannie propped her chin up on her hand. "Those look like my sheets he's wearing."

"You wish," Cecilia said.

Grace pulled a bunch of pictures out of her purse and passed them to Roseanna.

She'd found them in a shoe box along with the dance card and tiny pencil from her prom, a football homecoming program and the hunk of yarn she'd used to wrap around her high school boyfriend's class ring.

"Oh, God. I remember this skirt," Roseanna said. "I couldn't get one thigh in there, now."

"Sure you could," Dannie said. "It would be a little tight, though."

"Ha-ha." Roseanna passed the pictures to Cecilia. "Hey, remember when we used to play truth or dare in study hall?"

"Yeah. I think Mr. Montrose almost had a heart attack," said Cecilia. "You'd always dare me to lean over his desk to ask him a question."

"He couldn't stand up for the rest of the class."

"To Mr. Montrose," said Grace, raising the shot the waiter had just delivered. They all toasted Mr. Montrose and blew out their Flaming Togas.

"Let's play," said Roseanna.

"Play what?"

"Truth or dare."

"Here?" Grace said. "You're crazy."

"It'll be fun," said Dannie.

"Why not?" said Cecilia.

Music thumped in the background. Mötley Crüe belted out "Girls, Girls, Girls."

"What the hell," Grace said.

Friday, 11:44 p.m.
Gracie's Secret

Grace was drunk.

Not merely drunk but what they once affectionately called shit-faced.

Roseanna's head rested on the table, surrounded by empty shot glasses. Dannie balanced a straw on her nose. Cecilia puffed on a cigarette, making tiny smoke rings by tapping on her cheek.

Grace had quit smoking soon after she'd married Tom. He disapproved of the habit. Said it made her look cheap. Unlike Marlene, who looked so classy covered in grape jelly.

"Gimme one of those," Grace said.

Cecilia rolled a cigarette across the table. "Okay. Grace's turn. Truth or dare?"

"Truth."

"What's the worst thing you've ever done? And high school shenanigans don't count."

Grace shook her head. "Nothing. I've never done anything remotely bad."

"Oh, come *on*," Dannie said, taking the straw off her nose. "We know you better than that."

"Seriously. I'm the perfect wife. The perfect mother. The perfect daughter. The worst thing I've ever done is wear this skirt, which is definitely too short for me. Gimme a light."

"Dare it is, then," Roseanna said, dragging herself to a sitting position.

"What? I told you—"

"No way. You're lying," said Cecilia. "But that's okay, because I have the perfect dare for you."

Grace raised her eyebrows.

"Go over there and give your underwear—" Cecilia pointed toward the bar "—to him."

Grace sucked in her cheeks.

The guy looked as if he'd stepped off the pages of *GQ*. Black turtleneck. Black leather jacket. Dark, brooding eyes. He sat in a pool of light shining down from the ceiling as if he were some sort of fallen angel. The most gorgeous in-the-flesh man she'd ever seen.

Gorgeous, and young.

"Nun-uh. He's a baby," Grace said.

"All you gotta do is give him your undies, Grace. It's not like you've never given a guy your undies before, right?" Dannie's smile was evil. Evil and smug.

Grace wobbled to her feet. Damn. He might be young, but she wasn't *that* old. She still had decent legs and a not-so-bad ass. "Fine. Consider it done."

She marched to the ladies' room, only to find a line a mile long. While she waited, she had plenty of time to reconsider her decision. There was something slightly sinister about that man.

She could always go back to the table and make up a story for the "truth" portion of the game. Surely she could come up with something suitably shocking.

Grace looked over at her friends, who watched her with a mixture of admiration and disbelief. No. She couldn't lie to them. Way back when, they'd all sworn on their posters of Jon Bon Jovi. No lying at truth or dare. It was a matter of honor.

But there's no way I'm telling them the truth.

Her own parents didn't know about her arrest, and she intended to keep it that way. It had been a youthful indiscretion, and now that she was a hair past youthful, there was absolutely no need to be indiscreet. Especially since she just did it again—and this time, she definitely knew better.

So?

So she'd take the dare and go give *GQ* her underpants.

She slipped into the bathroom and balanced against the toilet paper holder as she stripped off her underpants, happy that she'd worn a decent pair without holes. Sometimes following motherly advice paid off at the oddest moments.

Stuffing the panties deep into her pocket, she fought her way out of the bathroom and through the crowd that had suddenly grown up around the bar. She tried not to look obvious as she slid in next to the Roman god, elbowing a pouty waif off of the bar stool beside him. The girl attempted a threatening look.

Grace laughed. "Please. I've shaved parmesan thicker than you. Get going."

The girl slinked away to a group of equally emaciated friends.

Grace ordered a margarita from the bartender, took the cigarette Cecilia had given her out of her pocket and stuck it between her lips.

"Excuse me, do you have a light?"

Adonis smiled, his teeth shining like Chiclets in the bluish light. "Sure."

He pulled a lighter out of his pocket and sparked it, holding the flame out in front of her. "How you doin', sweetheart?" He pronounced it "sweethawt," in a perfect South Philly accent.

She leaned in and sucked the flames into the cigarette, drawing the smoke deep in her lungs. It wasn't at all as pleasant as she remembered.

"Just a minute," she rasped, holding up a finger while she hacked into her palm. And into her sleeve. And into the hair of the girl next to her.

GQ handed her the margarita and she sucked down half of it.

"Grace."

"What?" he said. He looked confused.

"My name. It's Grace."

"Yeah. I'm Nick. Nick Balboa." He affected a slur and shadowboxed the air. "Youse know, like Rocky?"

"Right. Were you even born when that movie came out?"

"Almost."

She grinned, aware that she probably looked incredibly dopey but for some reason was unable to stop.

Now what?

She decided that since this was a game of truth or dare, she'd just tell him the truth.

"Nick."

"Yeah?"

Damn, he was good-looking. The dimple on his chin momentarily distracted her.

"Nick, I have a confession. Do you see those women over there?" She pointed to her friends. They all stared back like they were watching a bad reality TV show. All except Roseanna, whose head was back on the table.

Nick nodded.

"They dared me to come over here and give you something."

Nick grinned. "Like what?"

"Like my underwear."

He didn't look the slightest bit surprised. She guessed women offered him their underwear on a pretty regular basis, much as they did Tom Jones.

"I have to give you my underwear," she continued, "in order to satisfy some sick need they have to humiliate me."

He shrugged. "Okay."

She sidled closer, and dangled her panties in front of him so the girls could see.

Nick gave her panties an appraising look. He crumpled them up and stuck them in his pocket. Then he grabbed her around the waist and pulled her close. "Wanna give your friends something better to watch?"

Oh, my.

"Like what?"

"Like this." He leaned in close, and she shut her eyes. He smelled of leather, Aramis and tequila—three of her favorite things. She knew what was coming, but she was afraid if she looked she'd chicken out. And she really didn't want to chicken out.

The DJ was playing the Cure's "Just Like Heaven," and the beat reverberated through the bar beneath her elbow. Nick's lips were mere inches away.

What was it the Romans used to say?

Oh, yeah. *Carpe diem.*

Saturday, 12:17 a.m.
Goodbye Girls

When they finally came up for air—about thirteen minutes later—Cecilia was standing behind them.

"You okay?" she asked.

Grace nodded.

"How are you getting home?"

"I'll call a cab."

"Okay." Cecilia winked at Nick. "Nice to meet you."

"Likewise," he said. Rose Frost lipstick smeared his lips.

Cecilia returned to the table and waved to Grace. She made a fist and held it to her cheek like a telephone receiver, mouthing the words, "Call me." Then she and Dannie slung their arms around Roseanna and dragged her through the crowd toward the door.

"Your friends leaving?" Nick asked.

"Apparently."

For a split second Grace thought maybe she should leave with them, but when she tried to stand up, the room spun.

Nick kissed her again, stroking her arms with his palms. It was like kissing Vinnie Barbarino, Scott Baio and Rob Lowe, all rolled into one. Just a teeny bit surreal.

Nick slid his hand down to hers and linked her fingers in his and—

Stopped.

He stopped kissing her.

He brought her left hand up between them and looked at her fingers.

The diamond band Tom had given her for their tenth anniversary refracted the spotlight above them like a disco ball.

"Nice ring. You married?" Nick asked.

Damn. Why had she worn it?

Oh, yeah. To discourage this very thing. After all, she was a sensible lady. A mother. A woman who wasn't quite divorced. She shouldn't be picking up strange men in bars.

The momentary wave of guilt she felt was quickly replaced by drunken defiance.

She slid the ring off her finger and dropped it into Nick's drink. "Not anymore. Now kiss me."

Chapter 3.5

Who was the babe?

Pete watched Balboa with the blonde in the red jacket for almost twenty minutes. He'd never seen her before, but that didn't mean anything. Balboa always had a roll of cash in his pocket and a girl on his arm. Often, both appeared from nowhere.

Problem was, this one didn't quite look like Balboa's type. His recipe for the perfect woman was forty-five percent silicone, forty-five percent collagen and ten percent ink.

This one, while the clothes she wore weren't exactly conservative, they didn't come close to some of the anti-apparel he'd seen before. Her breasts actually looked real, too, and she didn't have one visible tattoo.

Something was up.

As time went on, the crowd at the bar began to thin. Pete moved to a spot behind Balboa and the female. The woman stood to flag down the bartender, and Pete watched as Balboa's hand cupped her rather spectacular ass.

Life could be so unfair.

Pete ordered another club soda from the waitress and leaned against a column.

If he had to guess, he'd say that Balboa had the memory key on him. According to Pete's sources, Balboa had come straight here after meeting with the Russian's competition, Johnny Iatesta, in Trenton. The asshole. Two years of wheeling and dealing, and the guy was going to screw him? No way.

All Pete had to do was stick close until the horny couple left the club.

He yawned. When in the hell were these two going to get a room?

Just then Balboa slipped something into the pocket of the woman's red jacket. Drugs? Money?

The memory key.

Balboa whispered something in her ear, and they sucked face for another five minutes before she broke away.

She headed straight for Pete, brushing his arm with her breasts as she squeezed by him on her way to the can. She smelled fantastic. He thought she might have a pretty face, too, but it was dark and he'd been distracted by the rest of her.

He watched the ladies' room, looking forward to her return trip.

She emerged from the bathroom, but instead of coming back toward him, she headed for the door.

Pete hustled after her, pushing through the ranks of ultrahip boys and girls pretending not to notice each other. He'd almost reached the door when a guy resembling a woolly mammoth in a tuxedo plowed in.

"'Scuse me."

"No problem." Pete tried to get around him, only to discover six more just like him pouring through the door. Seven equally large women in ruffled bridesmaid gowns followed close behind the men.

Pete got caught in the undertow and was pulled back into the club, surfing a wave of Aqua Velva and powder-blue taffeta. Somehow he managed to squeeze through the wedding party and reached the door just in time to see a cab pull away from the curb.

Pete smacked the door with the palm of his hand.

Now what?

He turned and went back into the club. No way was he going to let Balboa disappear.

But by the time he fought his way back into the bar, the only thing left sitting at Balboa's bar stool was a lipstick-smudged margarita glass and an ashtray full of butts.

"Shit," Pete muttered.

It really wasn't his day.

Chapter 4

Saturday, 7:54 a.m.
Turning Japanese

Someone was sticking needles into her eyes. Not sewing needles, but long, thick hypodermics.

Wait. What was that? The smoke detector? The kids!

Grace leaped out of bed and ran for the door, slipping on the silk jacket that lay on the floor, smacking her head on the ceramic cat at the end of the bed.

She lay on her back, staring up at the frosted glass light fixture on the ceiling.

That noise wasn't the smoke detector going off. It was her alarm clock.

"Crap." She winced at the sound of her own voice.

She rolled onto her stomach and pushed up onto all fours. Just the thought of standing left her weak with nausea.

She crawled into the bathroom on her hands and knees and laid her cheek on the cool Japanese porcelain tile floor. Her tongue felt like one of Kevin's gym socks and, she imagined, smelled like it, too.

What have I done to myself?

Her hand bore an ugly blue ink blot—the stamp for the club. And on her palm she'd written a number—1767.

1767? What the hell was that?

A high, wavering voice echoed in her head. "In 1767, the Townshend Acts were implemented by the British on the American colonies…" It was Mrs. Dietz, her ninth-grade American-history teacher.

Grace squinted at the numbers again. Why in the hell would she have written the date of the Townshend Acts on her hand?

She debated taking a shower but imagined the water would probably feel like Niagara Falls beating down on her head. She managed to pull on a sweat suit and comb her new pain-in-the-ass haircut without throwing up.

She took three aspirins and staggered downstairs to check her Day-Timer.

Meals on Wheels, the Goodwill drop and then Tom's.

She'd signed the papers he'd given her. No, she'd *forged* the papers (why not call a spade a spade?), and she just wanted to get rid of them and get on with her life.

Crap.

She dragged a giant green trash bag full of clothes from her closet. In a moment of pique over the bump on her head and her prick of an ex-husband, she stuffed the red silk jacket into the bag.

Saturday, 9:11 a.m.
Mrs. Beeber and Mr. Pickles

"Who is it?" Mrs. Beeber peered at Grace through the smeary film coating the window of the storm door. Her head resembled a small dried apple nestled atop the collar of her purple turtleneck.

"Meals on Wheels, Mrs. Beeber."

"I didn't think you were coming today. You're late."

"I'm not late, Mrs. Beeber. Will you open the door?"

Mrs. Beeber squinted at her watch, and shook her head. "You're eleven minutes late."

One cup of instant coffee—made with hot tap water and consumed while standing over the sink—had not prepared Grace for this day. She took three calming breaths. *Nadi shodhana.* Her yoga instructor would be proud.

"I'm very sorry, Mrs. Beeber. I couldn't find my car keys."

In fact, she hadn't been able to find her purse. She'd scoured the whole house, with no luck. She must have left it at the club.

She'd allowed herself a few minutes of heart-thumping panic. Her cell phone was in there, along with her car keys and house keys (which explained why the panty hose she'd worn last night had been covered with mulch, and the spare key she hid under a rock in the flower bed was now on the table near the back door).

But, worst of all, the papers she was supposed to return to Tom that morning were in that purse.

When she went out to the garage, she realized she had to go back to Caligula anyway, to pick up her car. Surely her purse would be there, safe and snug in the arms of the Game Boy–playing bouncer.

She'd chosen to ignore all logic to the contrary. Her stomach just couldn't take it.

So she'd snagged her spare keys from the hook by the door, and took the minivan for her morning appointments.

"Helloooo?" Mrs. Beeber called her back to Earth, and made a sour face. "Are you coming in with that?"

She held the screen door open and Grace entered, bearing a white tray covered with plastic wrap she'd picked up on her way there.

Mrs. Beeber squinted at the tray. "Is it a kosher meal?"

Grace bit the inside of her cheek. "You aren't Jewish, Mrs. Beeber."

"Yeah, but they give you more with them kosher meals."

Grace set the tray on Mrs. Beeber's mutton-gray Formica countertop. "I'm pretty sure everyone gets the same amount, whether it's kosher or not. Is everything okay with you?"

"As a matter of fact, my sciatica's a bitch and my son never calls me."

"I'm sorry to hear that."

"And I got the runs from that ham casserole you brought the other day."

"I didn't bring you a ham casserole."

"You didn't?"

"No."

Mrs. Beeber scratched her chin. "Now wait, I remember. It wasn't you. It was my neighbor Peggy. I should know better than to eat anything she gives me. One time, oh, I guess it was nineteen seventy-eight or nine…I remember I was watching *Dallas*…she brought me this disgusting meat loaf—"

"Mrs. Beeber, I really have to get going. I have three more meals to deliver."

"Oh. Well. Can you help me with something before you leave?"

"You know I'm not supposed to…"

"But it isn't for me. It's for Mr. Pickles."

Mr. Pickles was Mrs. Beeber's cat, a giant old Persian with male pattern baldness and a lazy eye, who'd hissed at Grace on more than one occasion. Not a huge motivator.

"Please?" Mrs. Beeber's wizened face sank deeper into the turtleneck sweater.

Grace sighed. "Okay. What do you need?"

Saturday, 10:41 a.m.
Shake It Up

"Rough night, eh?"

"Will you just help me, please?" Grace struggled under the weight of the bag filled with clothes, her arms weak from hefting a fifty-pound bag of cat food up forty stairs from Mrs. Beeber's cellar.

Grace doubted Mr. Pickles would live long enough to see the food at the bottom of that bag.

Martha Moradjiewski, the clerk at the Goodwill, grabbed one side of the garbage bag and helped Grace drag it across the floor to the counter.

"You look hungover," the clerk said.

"Just a little."

"Try a vanilla milk shake. They always help me."

Grace imagined Martha drank a lot of milk shakes, what with having a couple of sons who spent the day sniffing nail polish, a live-in mother-in-law with Alzheimer's and a husband who considered pot a major food group.

Grace slid her sunglasses on. "I'll give it a shot."

Six minutes later she pulled out of McDonald's, shake in hand, heading for home. She took a sip, her eyeballs nearly imploding from the suction necessary to draw a mouthful of the stuff.

"Ugh."

She stuck the shake in a cup holder and rolled down the window, trying to clear her head. *What* happened last night?

There were togas, of course. And cigarettes. And primo butts.

She remembered shots. Lots of shots. And lots of margaritas, too.

She remembered talking about movies and music and high school haircuts. And boys. And men.

Beyond that, nothing.

She pulled into her driveway, not too sick to admire the bright red Japanese maple near the front door. She couldn't imagine not seeing that maple every day.

What she'd done in order to keep it crept back into her consciousness. One small act of forgery, and the landscaping was forever hers.

She gagged and shoved a fist into her mouth to keep from barfing into the bushes.

Hey, at least they were *her* bushes. Right?

Saturday, 11:39 a.m.
Lord of the Ring

After the needles in her eyes had been replaced by tiny straight pins and there was absolutely nothing left in her stomach to puke up, Grace made a pot of coffee and braved the thirty seconds of blinding sunlight to fetch the paper from the lawn.

She needed a few minutes to get herself together before she called a cab and went back down to the city for her car.

She sat down with her World's Best Mom mug and opened the obituaries, half expecting to see her own name, when she stopped short.

Her anniversary band.

The twenty-thousand-dollar diamond-and-sapphire Tiffany anniversary band.

It wasn't shooting spectacular prisms of light across the kitchen ceiling. Nor was it catching on the edge of the paper like it always did or digging uncomfortably into the sides of her fingers.

It wasn't there.

She took the stairs two at a time, ignoring the persistent sensation that her head was going to explode.

The crystal dish on her dresser where she usually kept the ring was empty. Beside it lay a red credit card.

No, not a credit card. A hotel room key.

"Jesus." She clutched her head between her palms. The previous night played in her head like a Fellini film.

The last time she had seen her ring, it was lighting up that gorgeous guy's smile. He'd chugged the drink she'd put it in, and caught it in his teeth, like a frat boy playing quarters.

Her stomach churned. Oh, God. What was his name? Nick something. Barlow? Bartlett?

No, something more ethnic.

She squeezed her eyes shut.

Balboa. Like Rocky. Yo, Adrian. That was it!

It all came back to her in a rush. He was staying at the Baccus, a swanky hotel in Center City. He'd invited her back there. But she'd chickened out. Took a powder. Scrammed. Punked out.

Why is the voice in my head talking like Sam Spade?

She took a moment to hyperventilate before she grabbed the room key from the dresser.

Okay. All right.

Just what were the odds a young, gorgeous godlike stud would still be there, waiting for her to show up, with a twenty-thousand-dollar ring between his teeth?

She ran into the bathroom and ralphed in the sink.

Chapter 4.5

Saturday, 11:53 a.m.
Over Easy

It had taken Pete all night, but he'd finally tracked Balboa down at the Baccus. Dumb shit had checked in using a fake name but his own credit card.

Pete stepped into the elevator and flipped open his cell phone.

"Lou. I'm at the Baccus. Any movement from the Russian?"

"Nah. Everything's quiet here. Just the girlfriend coming and going. You shoulda seen what she was wearing last night." Lou whistled into the phone.

"Glad to hear you're having a good time."

"Hey, a man's gotta entertain himself."

"Just make sure you're not 'entertaining' yourself when the Russian makes a move."

Lou laughed, and Pete flipped the phone closed.

The elevator arrived on the seventeenth floor, and Pete unbuttoned his coat to give himself easy access to the weapon in his shoulder holster. He didn't think he would need it. Balboa was a lover, not a fighter. But you never knew.

He walked quickly to Balboa's door and waited there, listening. He didn't hear anything, but that wasn't surprising. Balboa typically slept until noon.

He pounded on the door, watching the peephole for light or movement. Still nothing.

After a cursory look up and down the hall, he pulled a key card from his pocket. The card had been doctored with copper tape, to which he'd attached a wire with a toggle switch hooked to a nine-volt battery. He slid the card into the lock and flipped the switch, holding his breath.

The lock popped, and he pushed the door open.

The room was dark, the curtains still drawn. He flipped the light switch, half expecting to see Balboa snoring in the king-size bed, but he wasn't.

The room was empty.

"Shit."

Pete gave a thorough search through the drawers and the pockets of the clothes hanging in the closet.

He found a pair of pink ladies' underwear and a black handbag which, a search revealed, belonged to one Grace Becker.

The lady in red.

She had darker hair in the picture on her driver's license, and longer, too. But it was definitely the same broad.

He checked her birth date, and whistled through his teeth. Thirty-seven.

Really not Balboa's type.

But he had to admit, she looked good for her age. Hell,

she looked good for any age. Maybe Balboa's taste was improving.

He looked through the handbag again, searching for the memory key, but it wasn't there.

Maybe they'd taken it somewhere. To the Russian or someone else. Iatesta, maybe.

That memory key was worth double what the Russian had agreed to pay for it, and Balboa knew it. He wasn't a stupid guy.

Maybe, if Pete was lucky, Balboa and the lady had just gone to breakfast.

Pete's stomach growled. He should have stopped for something to eat before coming up. A nice plate of eggs and scrapple at the Melrose, or a tall stack of pancakes. Jeez, he could be waiting there all day.

He called Lou again. "Hey, I need you to have someone checked out for me. A Grace Becker." He read the driver's license number and address.

"Right, boss. By the way, the Russian's girlfriend just left again. She was wearing this stretchy blue skirt, like a tie-dyed thing, with these really high heels…"

Pete sighed, suddenly jealous of Lou, with Skobelov's girlfriend coming and going in her crazy stripper outfits. At least Lou had something to look at.

Pete hung up the phone, turned off the lights and flipped on the TV, turning the volume all the way down and hoping he wouldn't have to wait too long.

Chapter 5

It didn't hit her until she was in the elevator at the Baccus Hotel, on her way up to the seventeenth floor, that maybe she should have brought some protection. But what kind?

Mace? Condoms?

Both?

Well, it was too late. If she turned around now, she'd never work up the nerve to come back. Besides, the irresistible combination of bad breath, bloodshot eyes and the baggy yoga pants she wore all but guaranteed Mr. Hottie wouldn't come within six feet of her.

Her Lady Keds were silent on the thick, burgundy carpeting of the hall. What in the hell was she going to say to this man?

Hi. Remember me? I'm the slut who gave you my underwear and played tongue aerobics with you for several hours last night. I'd like my anniversary ring back, please. And as long as I'm here, you wanna make out?

When she arrived at room 1767—she'd finally figured out what the numbers on her palm were—she stopped and took a deep breath. Blood rushed to her head, and she had to squat down for a minute until it rushed back to all the other places it was needed.

She was never going to drink again. Ever.

She tapped lightly on the door. No answer.

Maybe he was still sleeping. Or maybe he'd picked up another woman at the bar. Probably the see-through nymphet who'd been sitting next to him when she'd first approached. Or maybe one of the toga-clad waitresses.

Or waiters.

She started to hyperventilate. Oh, God. She didn't know anything about this man. He'd probably already pawned her ring and spent the money on crack, or heroin or the ponies.

What? Was she living in an HBO documentary now? *Jesus.*

She forced herself to breathe and knocked again.

Nothing.

What if he'd already checked out? She rooted through her pockets, producing the key card he'd slipped her. Saying a tiny prayer to the patron saint of Those with Poor Judgment, she slipped the key card into the handle.

The green light lit up.

She pushed the handle down, and, with an obnoxiously loud clack, the door swung open.

"Hello? Nick?"

The curtains were drawn shut, and the room was dark.

"Nick?" She stepped into the room.

The bathroom was immediately to her left. She turned on the light. A shaving kit stood open on the counter next to the sink. The air was damp and smelled of Aramis. She closed her eyes and breathed it in.

Across from the bathroom, the mirrored closet door was pushed open. Inside hung the pants and shirt Nick had worn at the bar. The leather jacket was missing.

She checked the pockets of the pants and shirt. No ring.

She wandered into the room and turned on the lamp on top of the dresser. The surface was littered with crumpled receipts, soda cans and empty potato chip bags.

Jeez. How did men do it? They could eat crap like this and not gain an ounce. Life was so unfair.

Going against every natural instinct, she resisted the urge to clean up the mess. Instead, she poked through it with the hotel ballpoint.

Like he'd leave a twenty-thousand-dollar diamond ring under a candy wrapper. Right.

Feeling an overwhelming urge to pee, she reached for the top drawer of the dresser. Before she could open it, she caught a movement in the dresser mirror.

She spun around. "Who are you?"

A man in a trench coat sat up against the headboard, his long legs stretched out over the bedspread and crossed at the ankles.

If Nick was *GQ*, this guy was Sears and Roebuck. And he was definitely no hot Italian. His red hair, freckles and glow-in-the-dark white skin reminded her of an overgrown Opie Taylor. Cute, in a forty-year-old boy-next-door sort of way.

"I assume these belong to you?" he said.

Her underpants dangled from the tip of his index finger. But they weren't what caught her attention.

"Is that my purse?"

He lifted his right elbow. "I guess it is, Grace."

"How do you know my name?"

He patted her purse. "Your driver's license. The picture doesn't do you justice."

She steeled her nerves. Then she strode over and snatched the panties from the redhead's finger. "Are you a friend of Nick's?"

He snatched the panties back. "You might say that. Where is he?"

"I don't know."

"I don't believe you."

She shrugged. "It's true."

"Then what's your handbag doing in his room? Not to mention your underwear?"

"I hardly know Nick. I met him last night, at the bar. I didn't spend the night here, either. I just came to see if he'd found my ri— My purse. I thought I left it at the club, but it wasn't there when I went back for it today."

"You aren't Balboa's girlfriend?"

She shook her head.

"You didn't spend the night here?"

"No, I didn't."

"Well then. I guess this isn't yours, either."

"My ring!"

It sparkled on his pinkie, catching the small fragment of light that filtered in through a crack in the curtains.

Opie stood up. He was a full head taller than her, slim and lean and much more intimidating than when he was sitting. He moved closer. "I'll tell you what, Grace. You can have it all back, if you give me what I want."

"Oh-h." She backed toward the door. Her heart clattered in her rib cage. All remnants of her previous hangover were long gone. Damn. Why hadn't she brought her Mace?

He laughed. "Relax. I'm not going to hurt you." He stepped closer. "All I want is the key. Give me the key, and I'll give you your stuff."

"The key?" Relief washed over her. She dug into her pockets and found the room key card, holding it out to him. "No problem. Here."

He stared at it like she'd offered him a severed ear. "What's that?"

"The key card. For the room."

He exhaled through his teeth. "You know damn well that's not the key I want."

"What key do you want?" Her voice climbed higher. She could feel her heels hanging over the edge to hysteria. One more step, and she'd be gone.

"I want the memory key," he said, speaking in tones he might use with a three-year-old. "The one Nick put in your pocket last night."

She shook her head. "This is the only key he put in my pocket."

He pushed his trench coat aside to reveal a pistol strapped to his side.

"Oh, Jesus." She crossed one leg over the other. "I really have to pee."

Opie ignored her. "I saw him put it in your pocket at the bar."

He'd been at the bar. Had she talked to him? She picked through her fuzzy memory but came up with nothing.

"Did we meet last night?" she asked.

He scratched his head. "No. Just give me the friggin' memory key. Or did you and Nick sell it already?"

She laughed. She couldn't help it. It was all so absurd. So surreal. "Is this some kind of joke?" She looked around. "Are Roseanna and Cecilia in on this?"

"No, it isn't a *joke*." He backed her up against the wall.

"Oh, God. I'm sorry. I don't even know what a memory key is."

He studied her, as if debating whether or not to believe her. "Small. Rectangular. About the size of a disposable lighter."

"A lighter?" She rubbed her temples. "Wait. I found a lighter in my pocket last night in the cab. A little black one. But I couldn't figure out how to work it."

Opie looked at her through narrowed eyes.

She said, "Do you think that might have been it?"

"It's a possibility." His tone was steeped in sarcasm.

She'd heard that tone a thousand times before, from Tom. Suddenly she wasn't scared anymore. She was pissed.

"Even if I *do* have this key thing, why would I give it to you?"

"Gee, I don't know. Why would you?" He put a hand on the butt of the gun.

Okay. Back to being scared.

Opie ran his hands over her sides and down her legs, so quickly she didn't have time to react. "You have any weapons?"

"Of course not."

He searched the pockets of her sweat jacket, coming up only with a single car key attached to a square black remote. "It's my spare. My other keys are in the handbag."

"So, where's the funny little lighter?"

"I don't have it with me."

"Where is it?"

She chewed her lip. "I'm not sure. I… I don't remember much from last night."

He stroked the pistol. "Try."

"Oh, God. I really have to pee." She bobbed from one foot to the other. "Okay. Okay. It was in the pocket of my red jacket."

"Where is that? At home?"

She felt the blood rush to her head again. Her stomach

rolled over, and she sank down to a crouch. "No. It's at the Goodwill."

"The Goodwill?"

She nodded. "I put it in the bag I dropped off there this morning."

"Come on." He pulled her up by the collar of her sweat jacket. "You're driving."

"But I have to pee!"

He blew out a breath and dragged her into the bathroom. "Go ahead."

"You're kidding, right? I can't go with you *standing* there."

"Then I guess you're not going."

She gave him what she hoped was a pathetic stare.

"Damn. All right." He collected all sharp objects and threw them into the shaving kit, which he tucked under his arm.

"I'm going to stand out in the hall with my foot in the door so you can't close it. If you try anything funny, I'll shoot right through the door. Understand?"

"Perfectly."

She tried, but she couldn't go. Not with the toe of his big, brown wingtip poking through the crack in the door.

She turned the water on, both for encouragement and to camouflage any sound.

Outside, Opie began to whistle something familiar. What was it? What…?

And suddenly, it struck her.

He was whistling "Somebody's Watching You."

Chapter 5.5

Saturday, 1:17 p.m.
Riding Shotgun

Pete kept his coat pocket unbuttoned so he could get to his gun, half expecting Grace to do something stupid.

He couldn't get a read on her. One minute he'd swear she was playing him, and the next he wasn't so sure. Was it possible she didn't know anything about Balboa, or the memory key?

Nope. No way.

She'd been all over Balboa like Cheez Whiz on a steak sandwich. No way she didn't know him. She had the key to his hotel room.

He had to get the memory key or kick two very long years of work to the can.

He tucked her purse beneath his arm and followed a few

steps behind her, appreciating the view as she led him to a dark green BMW sedan. She unlocked the doors with a blip of the remote.

Then suddenly, the car alarm went off, startling the crap out of him.

Christ! She wasn't as dumb as she pretended to be.

He closed the short distance between them and grabbed her arm. "Turn it off. *Now.*"

"It was a mistake! I'm sorry. It won't happen again."

She punched a button on the remote and the alarm turned off with a blip. Thank God car alarms had become like political promises. Everybody heard 'em, but nobody paid any attention to them anymore.

He walked her to the passenger side door and opened it. "Get in."

She sat in the seat. He squeezed in next to her. "Climb over to the driver's side."

"You're kidding."

"Nope."

He admired her flexibility as she swung a leg over the center console. She settled into the driver's seat and gave him an expectant look.

"Now put the key in the ignition. And if you try anything funny…" He showed her the gun.

"Gee, and I was just about to recite a limerick. Have you ever heard the one that starts 'There once was a girl from Nantucket'?"

He smiled. He couldn't help it. "Listen, all I want is the memory key. You give it to me, we're done. Understand?"

She gave him a look that said she might not believe him.

Chapter 6

Saturday, 1:22 p.m.
Hefty Odds

Okay. This was not a big deal.

She was driving a stranger to the Goodwill. They'd get the thingie he wanted, and then she'd get her ring and her handbag.

Her handbag, which contained the papers she'd forged for Tom.

Oh, dear God.

Her mouth went dry. This. This is what she got for being irresponsible.

She eased the car out of the parking lot, heading up Broad Street toward the Schuylkill Expressway.

Opie fiddled with the buttons on the radio. "What is this crap? Don't you have any stations grown-ups listen to?"

She punched the radio off. "If you don't mind, I'm trying to concentrate."

The traffic was crazy for a Saturday—the Flyers were playing the Rangers—taking her mind, for the moment, off the guy sitting next to her. By the time she pulled into the parking lot of the Goodwill, her hands had almost stopped shaking.

For some reason, despite the fact that he had a gun strapped just inches from her right breast, she actually believed Mr. Sears and Roebuck would do her no harm.

Unless, of course, she couldn't produce that thing he wanted. Then all bets were off.

She wasn't even sure she'd ever had it. Maybe the thing in her pocket last night really *had* been just a lighter. Then what? What were the odds he'd just let her go if she handed him a lighter?

She went woozy and put her head down on the steering wheel.

It had been so stupid to get in the car with this guy. A guy who could be a serial rapist, or a serial killer or some other kind of serial something.

And for what? For a diamond ring that could pay for a year of college? For a bunch of papers that would allow her and her children to keep their home?

Okay. Maybe she could get all that stuff back and get away. It wasn't too late.

Think. *Think.*

She could ram the car into the side of the Dumpster. Maybe the air bag would stun him for a few moments, and she could grab her purse from beside his feet and make a run for it.

"Give me the keys," he said as if he'd just read her mind.

Okay. On to Plan B.

They exited the car on the passenger side, Opie keeping

a light hold on her arm as they walked across the empty parking lot.

Putting a Goodwill in South Whitpain was like putting a Talbots in South Philly. Nobody from the neighborhood would be caught dead shopping there.

She should have taken Opie down with a kick to the groin. A karate chop to the neck. An elbow to the ribs. Any one of the moves she'd mastered after watching the lady detectives in all those late seventies detective shows.

But she didn't.

It was amazing how her inner Good Girl refused to step aside for her inner Charlie's Angel. She wanted to kick ass. She really did.

She just couldn't do anything risky. She would *not* let her children grow up with Tom and Marlene. They were bound to see something scary in that house. Something that would put them off condiments for life.

Right. On to Plan C.

She allowed Opie to escort her, largely due to the protrusion under his trench coat, straight into the building. An old cowbell tied to the door handle jingled when they entered.

She expected to see Martha behind the counter, but instead it was a guy she didn't know, working over a pile of shirts with a pricing gun.

Grace imagined grabbing the pricing gun.

Freeze, sucker. Or I'll mark you down so fast you won't know what hit you.

The clerk looked up from the shirts. "Can I help you?"

"Hi. I, uh, put a jacket into one of the bags by mistake this morning, and I need it back. Can we look for it?"

Grace attempted a psychic connection.

Call 9-1-1. Call 9-1-1!

The clerk didn't seem to get it. He opened the cash register and took a key out of one of the slots. "Donations are in the back room. Follow me."

He led them to the storeroom and opened the door. "There you go."

The floor was a sea of green trash bags that all looked as if they'd been separated at birth.

"We've had quite a few donations this weekend and nobody here to unpack them," the clerk said apologetically.

"Great. Thanks. We can take it from here," Opie said.

Grace caught the clerk's eye, trying to communicate using her eyelids for Morse code. The clerk winked at her and left.

Only a man could mistake desperation for flirting.

"Recognize any of these bags?" Opie said.

"Yeah. The green one."

He smiled. "What time did you bring the stuff in?"

"I don't know. I usually come at ten, but I was running late this morning."

"Too many margaritas last night?"

Was that a snicker? Did she actually hear him *snicker?*

"You sound like that dog on the cartoons. You know, the one who used to have orgasms over his dog treats?"

His face clouded over. "Just find the jacket."

Grace glanced through the narrow window on the storeroom door and saw the clerk talking into the phone.

Look over here. LOOK OVER HERE.

"Get moving," Opie demanded. "Find that jacket."

She bent over and opened a bag. "What's your name, anyway?"

"What's it to you?"

She stood up. "Well, since you've been staring at my ass all afternoon, I figure the least you can do is tell me your name."

He grinned. "It's Pete, all right? Now get down to business."

His eyes crinkled at the edges when he smiled, and Grace realized that if she wasn't afraid he'd cause her bodily harm she might actually find him attractive.

She poked through several bags, hoping she looked productive, still optimistic she'd been able to convey her sense of urgency to the clerk. She was convinced if she just stalled long enough, help would arrive.

Pete rustled through a bag. "Armani. Burberry. Moschino. I've gotta start shopping at this Goodwill." He closed the bag and opened another.

Grace stuck her hand in a bag. "Uh-h!"

"What? Did you find it?"

"No. But I could have sworn I felt something move in there."

Pete straightened, holding something red in his fist. "Is this it?"

Crap, crap, crap! How did he find it so fast? Thirty-eight bags and he nailed it, second one out. She should let him pick her lottery numbers.

She pretended to examine the jacket he held up. "No, I don't think that's mine?"

Pete shook it out and held it open. "Sure it is. I remember this gold snake on the sleeve. And this glittery stuff."

"It's a dragon. And those are called sequins." She snatched it away.

Sirens pealed in the distance. Her stomach did a little flip. It sounded as if they were heading up Monroe, about a mile or so away.

Unfortunately, Pete heard them, too.

He narrowed his eyes. She gave him her most innocent look.

"Shit." He grabbed the jacket from her and rooted through the pockets, pulling out a small, black rectangle from one of them.

"Is that it?" she said.

"Yep." He stuck the memory key in his pocket. "Let's go."

The sirens grew louder. Pete pushed her toward the emergency exit door at the back of the storeroom.

She pushed back against him. If he managed to get her out the door, who knew what would happen in that parking lot? Screw the ring and the papers. At this point, she just wanted to get out of this without an extra hole in her body.

"You said you'd let me go when you had the key."

He grabbed her arm and dragged her to the door. "I can't exactly sit around waiting for a bus back to the city now, can I? If you'd have played nice, you'd be on your way home."

"Then just take the car and leave me here. You have what you want."

"Sorry. I need you."

"For what?"

He pushed open the lever on the emergency door. A bell, like one of those old-fashioned ball-and-hammer school bells, clanged above the door.

"You really screwed up, Grace." He shoved her through the door.

Chapter 6.5

Saturday, 1:35 p.m.
Sticks and Stones

Somehow she'd tipped off the clerk. It was the only explanation. She was smart, he had to give her that. And she had a great ass.

But this was inconvenient. He did *not* have time to deal with cops right now. The meeting between Nick and the Russian was supposed to go down in ten and a half hours, and there was a lot of work to do between now and then.

For one thing, he had to find Nick.

Grace suddenly sat down in the middle of the parking lot. "I'm not going with you. You can shoot me right here, but I'm not getting in that car."

"Yes, you are." He picked her up and threw her over his

shoulder, firefighter style. He grabbed the remote from her hand, bleeped the car door open, then shoved her into the driver's side.

"Why do I have to drive? Just take the car. I have kids."

Outside, the sirens got louder.

He put a hand on the butt of his gun. "Look, Grace. I don't want to hurt you. Just drive the damned car."

Her eyes widened. "You can't drive a stick shift."

He could feel his face heating up, and he knew from experience that soon he'd look like a tomato with eyes. "Just drive. Get me back to the hotel."

The sirens grew louder.

"Will you give me my stuff back and let me go?"

"We'll see."

"I'm not involved in this! I don't even know Nick. I just met him last night."

"If that's true, then you have nothing to worry about. Now drive."

She gave him a defiant look.

Flashing lights reflected off the side of the Goodwill building. A maroon-and-gold police car sped into view.

And then passed.

Pete smiled. "Guess they weren't looking for us, after all."

Grace started the car. "The Baccus?"

"Please."

Chapter 7

Saturday, 2:02 p.m.
Pigs

"What the hell is this?" Pete rolled down the car window and stuck his head out. The slightly off-key strains of "Tusk" drifted in.

"Looks like a parade."

"A parade?"

"The Columbus Day Parade. It goes right up South Broad."

"Jesus H. Christ. You've got to be kidding me."

A giant Porky Pig floated through Marconi Plaza in a sailor suit, curly tail flapping in the breeze.

Sawhorses stretched across Bigler Street, guarded by four uniformed security officers. Although truth be told, there didn't seem to be a danger that anyone would rush a giant, helium-filled pig. Or the float of dancing bananas that followed it.

"What now?" Pete muttered under his breath.

Grace rolled down the window. Pete looked at her.

"What? I'm hot."

She dangled her arm out the window, and below Pete's view waved frantically at one of the guards. He gave her a goofy smile and waved back.

While Pete looked out his window, Grace mouthed the word *help* to the guard.

He mouthed back, "Hello."

"Man!" She slapped the steering wheel.

Pete looked at her.

"I hate being stuck in traffic."

"Turn around," he said.

"You're kidding, right? There are cops right in front of us."

"They're rent-a-cops. They don't have vehicles. And even if they did, I doubt they'd care that we're breaking the U-turn law."

"There are cars behind us."

"So what? Make a K-turn."

"A *K-turn?* What the hell is a K-turn?"

He shook his head. "Don't you have a Pennsylvania driver's license? You had to do a K-turn for the test."

"Oh, yeah. I remember now. It was only twenty-two years ago. The K-turn. How could I forget?"

He shook his head. "You do have a mouth on you, don't you. You are definitely not Balboa's type."

She gave him a stony look.

"Just turn it around. Pull all the way forward. Turn the wheel to the right. Put it in Reverse. Turn the wheel again. See? You're making an invisible *K* with the car's wheels."

"Thank you, Mr. Reynolds."

"Who's Mr. Reynolds?"

"He was my driver's ed instructor in high school. He used to try to peek into my blouse when I was backing up."

Pete grinned his Opie Taylor grin. "An opportunist."

"A pervert."

She made one last attempt to signal the rent-a-cop leaning against the sawhorse, but he just waved again.

She stomped on the gas.

Men were pigs.

Saturday, 2:23 p.m.
X's and O's

Back at the Baccus, they parked next to a blue Ford Taurus. Pete took her keys from the ignition. "Wait here. And no funny business."

Like she was going to break out into a stand-up routine at any moment.

Hey, did you hear the one about the woman who left her twenty-thousand-dollar diamond ring in the mouth of a "mimbo"?

She rubbed her temples. She was actually getting hungry. Unlike normal people, she could eat in any situation.

The bomb—the Big One—could be on its way. While everyone else would be using their last moments to say goodbye to friends and loved ones, she'd be stuffing her face with Tastykakes. She'd be taking full advantage of the fact that no matter what she ate, very soon she'd have the same BMI as a handful of cigarette ashes.

Pete opened the trunk of the Taurus next to her car.

A Taurus? *A Taurus?*

None of the bad guys on crime shows had ever driven a Taurus.

And she was sure none of them would have ever let her pee. How could you fear a guy who drove a Taurus and let you pee?

She watched him for a little while before she realized he'd left her purse sitting on the floor, and she grabbed it. A quick search revealed two disheartening developments. One, her cell phone was dead. Two, the papers were missing.

She wondered if Nick might have them. But why in the hell would he take those and leave her diamond ring? It didn't make sense.

She got out of the car and peered over Pete's shoulder.

The trunk was immaculate. There were four vinyl containers lined up along the back of the space, all tight and spiffy, held down by bungee cords. Grace wondered what was in them.

Pete opened the second one from the left and retrieved a laptop computer from atop a neat pile of technical-looking equipment and cables.

"This is your car?"

He straightened, smacking his head on the trunk. "Hey, get back in the car."

"Relax. I'm not going anywhere. I want my ring back."

"And you shall have it, just as soon as I'm sure this little baby is what I'm looking for." He held up the memory key.

"Why wouldn't it be?"

"I don't know. Maybe you tampered with it."

"That's right. I tampered with it. And then I put it in the pocket of a jacket I was going to give away, knowing full well that you would be in Nick's room today and that you would take me hostage at gunpoint, make me drive you to the Goodwill and force me to look through twenty bags of other people's castoffs before we eventually found it."

"Wiseass."

Pete powered up the laptop and plugged the memory key into a port in the side. He tapped a few keys. "What the hell?"

"What?" She leaned closer, peering over his shoulder at the computer screen.

It was filled with little X's and O's.

"What does that mean?" she asked.

"It means I'm screwed."

Chapter 7.5

Saturday, 2:29 p.m.
Shooting Blanks

Friggin' Balboa.

Pete knew in his gut that Grace wasn't lying. He knew it wasn't her who'd tampered with the key. It was Nick.

Either he'd never checked the memory key when he got it from Morton, or he'd replaced what was on it with crap. But if Balboa knew the key was essentially empty, why would he give it to Grace?

Maybe Balboa had spotted him at the club last night and had put a fake in Grace's pocket to throw him off.

No. Balboa was the kind of guy who bought condoms from a men's room vending machine. He never planned ahead.

It was more likely Morton had given Balboa the bad key to begin with, and Balboa had just never bothered to check it.

Shit. Shit, shit, shit. Two years down the crapper. Two years, and he had nothing.

He looked at Grace.

Well, not exactly nothing. He had Balboa's girlfriend. That had to be worth something.

"Get in the car," he said, deciding to take her BMW since Balboa would recognize the blue Taurus.

"Where are we going?"

"To find your moronic boyfriend."

Chapter 8

Saturday, 2:47 p.m.
Sugar Sugar

Grace edged the BMW around a double-parked delivery truck.

She'd given Pete only a halfhearted argument when he'd told her to get back in the car. She was hungry and hungover and really, if she refused to go and Pete called her bluff, she didn't have much of a bargaining chip unless she was willing to get shot.

She was not. Not on an empty stomach.

She wanted a burger and french fries. She wanted another milk shake.

"Can we drive through somewhere? I'm hungry."

Pete looked at her as if she'd grown another head. "You're kidding me, right?"

She pulled over to the side of the street. "No, I'm not. I

haven't eaten a thing today. I need food. I have a medical condition called hypoglycemia. Low blood sugar."

"Low blood sugar, huh? You know, that's just an excuse women use so they can be bitchy when they're hungry."

"Bitchy?" An image flashed in her mind like a movie trailer. Her, morphing into a vicious werewolf and chewing Pete's head off. "Look. I'm driving you—where?"

"Cottman Avenue."

"I'm driving you all the way across town to Cottman Avenue, largely without complaint. The least you can do is let me take a detour through a Burger King or something."

"We'll eat when we get there."

"And where is *there?*"

"The Cat's Meow."

Saturday, 3:12 p.m.
Dinner Theater

The Cat's Meow, a chartreuse, clapboard building surrounded by warehouses, pay-by-the-hour motels and fast-food joints, announced its presence with a giant pink neon cat in pasties on the roof.

"What is this?"

"One of your boyfriend's favorite hangouts. As if you didn't know."

She took a deep breath, practicing a mini-meditation, clearing all homicidal thoughts from her head. "I told you. I'm not familiar with Nick's hangouts. I'm not familiar with anything about Nick."

"You looked pretty familiar last night." Pete unbuckled his seat belt. "Let's go."

"I'm not leaving my car in this parking lot. It'll never be here when we get back."

"It'll be here."

She pressed the lock button twice, just to be sure, which she figured was about as effective as putting a sign on the window that said Please Don't Steal My Car.

Pete grabbed her purse and hooked it over her shoulder. "Here. You've been a good girl. But I'm keeping the ring for a while."

"Speaking of my things, do you have anything else that belongs to me?"

"Your panties?"

"Something else."

"Like what?"

She glanced over at him. She couldn't tell if he was genuinely curious or fishing for information.

"Never mind," she said.

The first set of double doors led into a small foyer with a pink linoleum floor and silver, cheetah-print wallpaper. A slick-bald bouncer in jeans, a T-shirt and a suit jacket greeted them in front of a second set of doors. Behind him on the wall were handmade posters announcing the appearances of dancers with names like Luscious Lulu and Sierra Starr.

Pete handed the bouncer two twenties—the cover charge, apparently, for the privilege of seeing what was behind Door Number Two, which Pete held open for her.

"Good God."

Can I trade for Door Number Three, Bob?

Because Door Number Two was the booby prize. Literally.

Behind the bar to their right, up on a long, narrow stage, three women of colossal proportions strolled past bar stools filled with patrons—all men—sucking beer and smiling as if they had dreams of being smothered by giant marshmallows.

"Where did they *get* those breasts?"

"Silicone Valley."

A man with slick black hair and a dark spot beneath his nose that may or may not have been a mustache approached.

"Hey, man."

Pete nodded. "Hey, Ferret. You seen Nick Balboa today?"

Ferret shook his head. "Nah. But he might be in later. It ain't like him to miss something like this."

"Go see what you can find out for me, okay?"

Ferret nodded and took off.

Pete took Grace's hand and led her to a booth in the far corner of the club.

Grace couldn't stop staring at the women onstage. It was like a train wreck. No, it was worse than a train wreck.

It was a train wreck with giant breasts.

"It's Mammoth Mammary Day at the Cat's Meow," Pete explained.

"I see that. How do they stand up with all that weight?"

"That's why they put the poles there. To give them something to hang on to. Here." He shoved a menu across the booth.

"I have to pee."

"Again?"

"Hey, you give birth to three kids and tell me how long you can go in between."

"You have three kids?"

"Yes, I do. And I really have to go again."

"In a minute." He handed her a menu. "Figure out what you want to eat before your blood sugar goes too low."

Grace scowled at him and opened the menu, trying not to think about why her fingers were sticking to the plastic cover.

"I'll have a hamburger, French fries and a milk shake."

"They don't have milk shakes here," Pete said.

"Okay, then. A Coke."

"It's a two-drink minimum per table. Why don't you order a beer?"

"Why don't *you* order a beer?"

"I don't drink."

"Neither do I."

He raised his eyebrows.

"Anymore."

A waitress in a hot-pink negligee appeared at the table.

"Hey, honey, how are ya?" She winked at Pete.

"I'm good, Amber. How are you?"

"Hanging in there."

"Are you dancing tonight?" Pete said.

"Yeah. Later. After the cows go home." She jerked a thumb at the women onstage.

"You waitress *and* dance?" Grace asked.

Amber rolled her eyes. "Dincha ever hear of dinner theater?"

"You gonna order?" Pete said to Grace.

Grace gave Amber a fake smile. "I'd like a hamburger, medium, French fries and a Coke."

Amber popped her gum. "…and…a…Coke…" She scribbled on a pad. "Wow, you're brave."

"I'm hungry."

Amber smiled at Pete. "Anything for you, honey?"

"Just coffee. Thanks." Pete's gaze moved over the room.

"Is Nick here?" Grace asked.

"Do you see him?" Pete leaned back against the red vinyl seat.

"I'm afraid to look."

Amber returned with their drinks. Pete stirred a few packets of sugar into his coffee, which looked thick enough to stand a spoon in. "So, how did you get involved with Nick?"

"I'm not involved with Nick."

"You and me, we're not involved, either. Does that mean you're gonna give me your underpants and let me touch your ass?"

"You wish."

Pete took a sip of his coffee. "I want to believe you, Grace. I do. But look at it from my perspective."

She played with the straw in her Coke. "It was a game."

"A game?"

"Yes. Truth or dare. I was at the club last night with some friends from high school, and we decided to play a game of truth or dare. Relive our youth."

"So you gave Nick an expensive diamond ring on a dare?"

"Not the ring, the underwear. I gave him the ring because of the Flaming Togas."

"You're not making any sense."

She sighed. "Shots. I was drunk. I didn't know what I was doing."

"You didn't know you were kissing a stranger? Do you make a habit of kissing men you don't know?"

"No, as a matter of fact, I don't. I was just…" How could she explain what she was feeling to him? How a woman felt when she was fading. Becoming invisible.

No one looked anymore. No one whistled. And it wasn't as if she enjoyed that kind of thing, but she hadn't realized until it was gone how reassuring it had been. "Never mind. You wouldn't understand."

He gave her the strangest look, as if he actually might, and that was worse than if he didn't. She looked away in time to see the skinny guy with the smudge under his nose coming over to the booth.

"Looks like we're getting company," she said.

"Hey, Pete."

Pete made room, and the skinny guy slid onto the seat next to him.

"Grace, this is Ferret. Ferret, Grace."

"Nice to meet you, Mr. Ferret."

Ferret snorted. "Mister Ferret. That's a good one." He pushed a slip of paper over to Pete. "You might be able to find Nick at this address."

Pete nodded, and stuck the paper into his pocket. "This is Nick's girlfriend."

The man's eyes slid over her like fried eggs on Teflon. "She don't look like Nick's type." He waved Amber over. "Gimme a cheese steak and fries. And I'll take a couple beers. You know, to meet the two-drink minimum."

"You got money?" Amber said. "'Cause you ain't working it off at the door like you did last time. You let all your friends in for free."

Ferret jerked his head at Pete. "He's paying for it."

Pete nodded and took another swig of coffee.

"How good could the coffee be at a place like this?" Grace asked as she covered her French fries with watery ketchup.

"Better than that hamburger," he said.

She bit into it.

"Ack." It tasted like roadkill. Or rather, what roadkill would taste like if it were scraped off the street, fried on a grill that hadn't been cleaned in a decade and served on a bun dating back to the Reagan administration.

"This place isn't exactly known for its food," Pete said.

"More for its theater," she said.

Pete smiled. "Right."

She ate the burger anyway, on the theory that it was better than nothing. She suspected she'd pay a hefty price for that theory later.

Ferret kept staring at her boobs, as if he didn't have enough of them to look at on the stage.

"If you gentlemen will excuse me, I have to hit the ladies' room."

"It's back there." Pete jerked a thumb toward the back of the room. "I'll be watching for you." He gave her a look fraught with meaning.

She rolled her eyes.

Saturday, 3:47 p.m.
Flushed

The ladies' room smelled like tangerine Air Wick and abandoned ambitions.

Grace tried not to touch anything. She hovered above the toilet seat, wondering how she got there.

Not only the Cat's Meow but this place where she would rather give a stranger her underwear than tell her once-best-friends that she had made a mistake a long, long time ago.

But it wasn't that long ago, was it? She'd done it again. And this time she couldn't hide behind the excuse that she was a dumb kid.

This time, she had a better excuse. She'd forged those papers for her kids. For their house. They deserved a little stability after everything that had happened this past year.

But she knew she was just sugarcoating things. What she'd done was wrong, her motives be damned.

Suddenly, she felt overwhelmed. Claustrophobic. The walls of the bathroom stall closed in on her. She grabbed one of the sanitary disposal bags stacked on the toilet tank and breathed into it.

When the dizziness passed, she staggered out of the stall. This was crazy. She shouldn't be here. She just wanted to go home and see her kids. She'd never wish for more excitement again.

On the far wall, just below a small window, a condom machine announced its offerings in bold pink letters:

RIBBED
ULTRATHIN
STUDDED
NIGHT-GLOW

Night-glow? *Night-glow?* Who would want to see something that looked like a nuclear waste accident coming at them in the dark?

A draft of cold air tickled her neck. She looked up. The window above the condom machine stood open a crack, allowing a narrow shaft of sunlight into the bathroom. Sunlight that would never get through the dirt-caked frosted glass any other way.

Grace thought she might be able to pull herself up there, and if she could…

She dragged the plastic trash can over to the wall and turned it over, dumping paper towels, lipstick-stained toilet paper and something that looked suspiciously like a body part onto the floor and climbed up on it.

The trash can wobbled. Grace caught herself on the condom machine just as the can slid out from beneath her feet.

She got a foothold on the levers of the machine and heaved herself up to the window, pushing it open with her forehead. Outside, cars raced up and down Cottman Avenue, filled with families on their way home from the mall. Families on their way home from soccer games. Families bickering about what they were going to have for dinner.

God, she wanted that.

She dove for the opening, stopping short when her hips got stuck in the window frame.

Great. She never should have eaten all those fries.

Outside, her head stuck into a sparse, dusty hedge. Inside, her legs dangled on the wall. She kicked, trying to find the condom machine, but no luck.

"You ever seen that Winnie-the-Pooh cartoon, the one where he gets stuck in the rabbit hole? I always loved that one." The voice had a sort of chain-saw-on-metal quality, not quite as melodic as Selma Diamond's from *Night Court*.

"Do you think you could help me?" Grace said.

"I guess."

Hands gripped her ankles.

"Not that way! I'll fall on you. Can you just guide my legs to the condom machine?"

The hands did as they were told.

Grace shinnied down the condom machine, past the picture of a woman who was supposed to be in the throes of an orgasm but who looked more like she was waiting for dental surgery.

She turned and came face-to-face with the oldest stripper she'd ever seen.

She must have been one of the Mammoth Mammary stars, although her mammaries had clearly migrated south, as had most of her contemporaries. Her tasseled pasties dangled just above her belly button.

Hair a bloodcurdling shade of orange stood a foot higher than her scalp, and Grace was pretty sure only a few of her teeth were real.

In that moment Grace realized that her life, which had once, long ago, resembled an episode of *Fantasy Island,* had now deteriorated into an episode of *Moonlighting*.

"Thanks for the help," Grace said.

"Sure, honey. You having a bad date?"

"Something like that." Grace wondered, could a date that was taking place at the Cat's Meow be anything *but* bad?

The dancer withdrew a tube of lipstick from her sequined hot pants and applied it while looking into the cracked mirror above the sink. "Gotta get me some of that collagen in my lips."

Right. Like that's your biggest cosmetic surgery issue.

"Hey, listen," Grace said. "Is there a back way out of here?"

"Sure. Follow me."

The old stripper scuffed along in orthopedic feather-trimmed mules, down a hall decorated with peeling psyche-delic wallpaper. Club music, coming from beyond the wall on their right, thumped and whined like a jet engine.

Grace checked her watch. Four oh-five. Kevin would be on the soccer field, looking for a way to avoid the ball. She wondered if Tom was there, too, looking for a way to avoid her parents and probably looking for her and the forged papers.

The bastard. This was all his fault.

If he had never come selling pharmaceuticals at the doctor's office where she'd worked as a summer temp, she never would have met him. And if he hadn't asked her out the day after she'd seen *Pretty Woman*—he looked a lot like Richard Gere—she never would have gone out with him.

If she hadn't gone out with him, she never would have slept with him, and then she certainly never would have married him, couldn't have found him in flagrante delicto with his as-sistant, wouldn't have divorced him, never would have forged those papers and, thus, never would have felt compelled to let loose with her friends at a cheesy nightclub in a desperate attempt to get the whole damned mess off her mind.

Bastard.

She followed the stripper past a little room off the corridor lined with mirrors and a folding table with a duct-taped leg. Women revealing varying amounts of skin milled about, smoking cigarettes and applying eye makeup.

"That's where we girls get dressed," the stripper informed her.

Wouldn't that be *undressed?* Grace wondered.

They passed an area that was cold and smelled oddly like curry. And at long last they reached an old, gray door. Above it in faded red paint were the words *Fire Exit*.

Nothing like being safety conscious.

"This is it. You sure you want to go out there, honey? Alone?"

"Absolutely."

Grace cracked the door. The fresh air was intoxicating, despite its abundance of fine particulates and nearly double the recommended parts per million of ozone. Philadelphians liked air they could sink their teeth into.

Grace gave the old dancer a nod of thanks and stepped out into the sunshine.

The door slammed shut behind her.

She turned, only to find Pete leaning up against the brick wall, smoking a cigarette. "Well, well. I started to get worried when you didn't come back for dessert. You seem like the kind of woman who eats dessert."

"Shit."

Pete grabbed her arm. "Come on. We have to find your boyfriend, then you're off the hook. Maybe."

"He's not my boyfriend."

"Right." They made their way around the building and back to the parking lot. Pete pushed the button to open the car doors, and the car answered back with a flash of the parking lights.

Tires squealed. Grace and Pete froze, caught in the path of a blue-and-white police cruiser that came to a stop inches in front of them, so close Grace could feel the heat from the car's hood on her thighs.

"Holy—"

Pete clutched her arm.

Cops leaped out of both sides of the car, and two seconds later, another cruiser pulled up behind them.

"Get your hands up." One of the cops, gun drawn, approached them from behind.

"Are you Grace Marie Becker?"

"Yes."

"And who are you?" The cop grabbed Pete's arm and pushed him up on the hood of the car.

"Pete Slade. Can I ask why you're detaining us?"

"Certainly. We got a call from the South Whitpain police, asking for assistance in looking for this woman's car. A clerk at the Goodwill reported suspicious behavior. Said you might be holding this woman against her will."

"I was. I am. But I have good cause."

The cop snorted. "I'll bet you do."

Pete sighed. "I guess we'd better straighten this out at the station."

Chapter 8.5

Saturday, 4:49 p.m.
Coming Out

Pete ground his teeth. He could feel a migraine starting behind his left eye.

Balboa was supposed to meet Skobelov at midnight tonight to give him the memory key. But Pete didn't have Balboa *or* the memory key, and pretty soon he wasn't going to have a job.

The cuffs bit into his wrists as he turned around in the backseat of the cruiser, trying to get a look at the car behind them. The car Grace was riding in.

He wondered what she was telling the cops. And he wondered how she'd tipped off the clerk at the Goodwill.

Damn. He didn't have time for this. And on a holiday weekend, too. Everything was going to take twice as long as it should.

But, hey. Nothing had gone smoothly with this case. Nothing at all. Why should that change now?

Chapter 9

Saturday, 7:37 p.m.
Catching Knives

"You're a *Secret Service* agent?"

"Yep."

Grace gripped the edges of the plastic chair in the small interrogation room where she'd been waiting. "Shouldn't you be guarding the president's dog or something?"

"That's a common misconception. The United States Secret Service has a number of responsibilities."

"But why didn't you tell the police who you were? Why did you let them arrest you?"

"They didn't arrest me. They detained me, which they were going to do anyway until they checked my credentials to make sure I really am who I say. For my own purposes, it was better to be cuffed in front of the Cat's Meow than to be seen showing the cops an ID."

"So why didn't you tell *me* who you were? Where do you get off, dragging me around like you're some sort of dangerous felon, scaring the crap out of me?"

"I'm sorry, Grace. But I had no way of knowing who you were. I would have put myself and the investigation at risk."

"You could have just let me go."

"Why would I do that?"

"Because I don't have anything to do with whatever you're investigating."

"So you claim."

"I've been telling you all along. I don't know Nick Balboa. I went to the hotel to get my stuff. That's all."

Pete straddled the chair across from her at the scarred wooden table. "I'd like to believe that, Grace. But I just can't."

"You can't? Why the hell not?"

"Because, as I said before, the Secret Service is responsible for investigating many types of crimes. Financial institution fraud, computer fraud, money laundering, counterfeiting. Identity theft. Those types of things."

Grace's heart stopped. "What does this have to do with me?"

Pete opened the folder he'd brought in with him. "Grace Marie Poleiski Becker. Born September twenty-first, nineteen—"

"Cut to the chase, please."

He turned the folder around and pushed it toward her. "You have a record for forgery and identification theft."

A pain seared through her stomach. It could have been from the burger she'd eaten at the Cat's Meow, but somehow she doubted it. "That was a long time ago."

"Not long enough, apparently."

"It was a mistake. I was young. We were making IDs so our friends could get into bars."

Pete leaned back in the chair. "Here's the thing, Grace. I used to think you weren't Nick's type, being so ol— Being so mature and all. But, according to your record, it would seem you're exactly his type."

Grace was silent.

"What was the plan? He was going to steal the names on the key, and you were going to help him make up counterfeit identification?"

"What?"

"IDs. False documents. From the names and social security numbers on the memory key."

"I didn't even know what a memory key was before today. I swear."

"But you know what false identification is, don't you? You know how to make it. You know how to forge names."

Grace's throat began to close up. Tears stung the back of her eyelids. "What do you want me to say?"

"I want you to say you'll help me find Nick. And then we'll figure out what to do with you."

"I think I should call my lawyer."

Pete shrugged. "Sure. But you're not officially under arrest yet. If you want to call your lawyer, I'll put you under arrest for suspicion of identification fraud and computer fraud." He looked at the clock. "Being that it's a holiday weekend, you should be out by, say, Tuesday afternoon."

Grace traced her fingertip over a little drawing of Kilroy someone had inked on the table a hundred years ago.

She wanted this all to be a bad dream.

She wanted to wake up next to Tom, with his damp feet and nasal strips, and look out over a backyard littered with soccer balls and hula hoops. In fact, a fourth-grade flute concert was looking pretty good at the moment.

She burst into tears. What was she going to tell the kids?

Pete shifted uncomfortably in his chair. "Come on. Don't cry. I'm not really interested in small fry like you. I'm after the Russian. Even Nick will probably walk, provided he decides to cooperate. I can't get to Skobelov without him. I just need you to convince him to play nice from now on."

"But I told you—"

"Yeah, yeah. I know. You don't know Nick." Pete slammed her file closed in disgust.

Grace rubbed her forehead. "Can I have a minute to think about all this?"

"Sure. But a minute is all we got."

Pete left the room.

Grace swallowed and opened her file. A mug shot of a younger, cockier version of herself stared back at her.

That Grace, twenty-year-old Grace, wouldn't sit here crying. *That* Grace would tell off Pete Slade, Secret Service agent. She'd spend the weekend in jail just to spite him.

But *that* Grace hadn't been to jail yet.

Jail was not a nice place. Just ask Martha Stewart. No matter how hard the maven of style may have tried to make it nice, it just wasn't. Maxi-pad slippers and toilet-paper-roll wreaths couldn't dress the place up enough to hide the cold, gray walls and unbearable loneliness.

And Grace—*today's* Grace—did not want to go back.

She'd only spent three weeks in jail, but to say they were the worst three weeks of her life was like the Black Knight in *Monty Python and the Holy Grail* saying, "It's just a flesh wound!" when his arm was cut off.

And if she opted to stay in jail, she had absolutely no chance of getting those forged papers back from Nick. She definitely did *not* want those floating around. Specifically not now that she knew who Pete was.

Nope. No way. She was not going to sit behind bars and wait for the proverbial shoe to drop.

She couldn't help Pete. She knew that. But he didn't. And if it meant keeping her butt out of jail, she could pretend, couldn't she?

She would just have to look at all of this as an adventure. Flirting with disaster. Like the rush the person hanging on a knife-thrower's spinning target might feel when she sees a nine-inch blade hurtling toward her face.

Grace wiped the tears from her cheeks with the sleeve of her sweatshirt, leaving a streak of black from her mascara.

Pete came back into the room, closing the door behind him. "What'll it be?"

"Okay. I'll give it a shot."

Saturday, 8:08 p.m.
Face-lifting

"Why don't we check the hotel again?" Grace suggested, hoping she could look for her papers. Maybe she'd missed them somewhere in Nick's room.

"Nah. Balboa won't be there," Pete said.

"So, where to then?"

"You tell me."

Grace was just about to reiterate the fact that she had no idea, when one actually came to her.

"What about the address Ferret gave you?"

Pete pulled the slip of paper from his shirt pocket. "Catharine Street."

They drove to the Italian Market area of Philadelphia, which was always busy on the weekends. During the day, vendors sold fresh fruits and vegetables from carts and tables lining the streets. Cheese shops, pasta shops, butchers and bakers propped their doors open for the never-ending stream of customers.

And in the evening, the restaurants came alive.

Grace's stomach growled loudly.

"Don't tell me you want to eat again," Pete said.

She did, but that wasn't why they were there.

"I know where we are," Pete said. "Nick's family owns this place. He told me he liked to hang out here in the kitchen when he was kid. Like five years ago."

"He's not *that* young," Grace said as she searched for a parking spot while diners milled around on the sidewalk in front of a little bistro, waiting to get a seat inside.

"He's not that old, either," Pete retorted.

She worked the BMW into a tight spot near the front of the bistro. She'd always had good parking karma.

"So, go on," Pete said. "Go get him."

"Me?"

"Sure. What do you think he'd do if he saw me?"

"I don't know, and I don't care. I'm not getting involved in this."

Pete snorted. "Lady, you're already involved. You're in so deep you should be wearing diving gear."

"Very funny." She rubbed her forehead. "How am I supposed to get him out here? That is, if he's even in there."

"Not my problem. Just do it quick."

Grace checked her face in the rearview mirror. The makeup she'd so haphazardly applied twelve hours ago, when she'd been hungover and much, much happier, looked ghastly. Her yoga pants were streaked with dirt from her expedition scaling

Mount Trojan, and her sweatshirt sleeves were stained with mascara.

"You look great," said Pete.

She gave him a bitchy look and opened the car door. "How can you be so sure I'm not going to take off?"

"It hasn't seemed to work for you so far."

"Yeah, well, there's a first time for everything."

She slammed the car door shut and pushed her way through the tight crowd on the sidewalk, ignoring dirty looks from hungry women and dodging the men who looked like gropers.

At the hostess station inside the door, a pretty young woman with big, dark curls and deadly looking three-inch spiked heels asked for her name.

"I'm looking for Nick Balboa," Grace said. "He told me he sometimes hangs out here."

"Who are you?"

"I'm his…uh, I'm his girlfriend."

The hostess laughed. "Right."

"I am."

The young woman put a hand on one hip, showcasing long, red nails. "One night of staring at yourself in the mirror above Nick's bed doesn't make you his girlfriend. Besides, aren't you a little old for him?"

"I'm not *that* old." Grace did the instant face-lift thing. The one on the infomercial where some aging soap opera star explains how to tighten certain muscles in your face to look ten years younger in an instant.

Maybe it worked. Or maybe the hostess felt sorry for her because she said, "Hang on. I'll go see if he's here."

A few minutes later, Nick materialized through the swinging door that led to the kitchen. He smiled, and Grace's stomach lurched.

Had she really made out with this demigod? This vision of male perfection?

The thought gave her the shivers.

She did the instant face-lift thing again as he approached.

"Man, am I glad to see you," he said. "Where did you disappear to last night?"

The scent of garlic and Bolognese clung to him like cologne. She moved closer. It was even better than Aramis. "I had to get home. Emergency."

He nodded. "I think I put something in your pocket by mistake."

She went for an innocent look, hoping she could pull it off while still face-lifting. "That little black thingie?"

"Yeah. Exactly. You still got it?"

She nodded. "It's at my place. Why?"

"I need it as soon as possible."

"Do you have my purse? And my ring?"

"They're back at my room."

She tucked a finger under the collar of his shirt. "I'll tell you what. We'll go by the hotel and pick up my stuff, and then I'll take you back to my place and get that thing for you."

"Sounds like a plan." Nick smiled. The wattage could have put a disco ball to shame.

When they passed the hostess station, Nick said, "Hey, Elaina. Tell Aunt Aida I'll be back in a little while."

"Sure." Elaina gave Grace a shrug and a look that implied wonders never ceased.

Nick put his hand on her waist as they hit the sidewalk and guided her through the crowd of waiting patrons. Grace's stomach fluttered, as much from Nick's touch as from the fact that she knew what was going to happen.

Or was it?

Pete wasn't waiting in the car.

What was she supposed to do now? Throw Nick down on the sidewalk and tie him up with her shoelaces?

Come to think of it, the idea did have its merits. But this was neither the time nor the place...

"Hello, Nick." Pete's voice came from behind them.

"Damn," said Nick.

"Funny, that was my thought exactly when you didn't call me this morning. Where are the names you're supposed to have for Skobelov tonight?"

"You know, funny thing. I didn't get the memory key. Morton never met me in Boise."

"Bullshit."

"He wasn't at the motel. I—"

"Cut the crap, Nick. I saw you put the memory key into Mrs. Robinson's pocket last night at Caligula. And I got the feeling you knew I was watching you, or you wouldn't have done it."

Nick shrugged. "Then I guess you got the names."

"No. I got the memory key, but there weren't any names on it. Just a love note from Morton for Skobelov. Lots of *X*'s and *O*'s."

"You're kidding." Nick looked genuinely stunned. "But I checked the key at the hotel. The names were there."

"You checked it?"

"Of course. What do you think? I'm stupid?"

Pete exhaled. "You checked it, and then you never let it out of your sight?"

"No—" Nick stopped short. "Damn. That little weasel. I can't believe he double-crossed me."

"Just like you double-crossed me?"

Nick held out his arms. "Hey, Pete. It wasn't like that."

"Then explain it to me, Nick. Because from where I stand

it looks like you were gonna take the names for yourself and maybe get a little side business going with your girlfriend here."

Nick looked at Grace and then back at Pete. "Nah. I was just gonna sell the key to the highest bidder."

"Thank *you*," Grace said. "The truth finally comes out. I *told* you I had nothing to do with this."

Pete shrugged. "We'll see."

"What now?" Nick asked. "You gonna arrest me?"

Pete opened the back door of the BMW. "I don't know. Get in."

Chapter 9.5

Saturday, 8:21 p.m.
Gin Fizz

Pete felt like his head had gone through a garbage disposal. But that was the least of his worries.

He had an informant he couldn't trust, a case he didn't think was strong enough and a woman he didn't know, period.

If things didn't come together soon, they were going to blow apart. It was the law of Order and Chaos. Either this all was meant to be, or it wasn't. And the next twenty-four hours were going to decide that.

Up front, Nick slipped his arm over the back of Grace's seat and sang some song that Pete vaguely remembered. Something from his early college days. Van Halen. "Why Can't This Be Love."

Pete remembered it because he'd sung it, in a drunken

stupor, to a gorgeous Phi Mu named Barbara at the one and only fraternity party he'd ever attended.

He'd thought the sun rose on her gorgeous pair of breasts and set on her luscious behind. She'd thought he was a hopeless loser, unfit even to lick the gin fizz she'd spilled on her white cowboy boots.

Her boyfriend apparently had thought so, too.

Pete had ended up hanging upside down from the frat house flagpole, his pants in a knot around his neck and his mouth duct taped shut.

It was a moment of supreme humiliation but also one of self-realization.

If he were to ever make it through college and, indeed, the "real world" alive, he would definitely have to become the strong, silent type.

It had worked, for the most part.

But, every once in a while, he was tempted to lick the gin fizz off of some woman's boots and tell her the "mook" she was with wasn't worth the cologne he was steeped in.

Nick twirled a lock of Grace's hair between his fingers, and Pete looked away. He swallowed a couple of Tylenol, dry, and chased them with a Tums.

Screw it. He'd spent the last two years alone, focusing completely on this case. And now, so close to the end, he wanted to risk getting run up the flagpole for some broad with a smart mouth and a nice smile?

Forget about it.

It was time to get his head back in the game.

Chapter 10

Saturday, 8:36 p.m.
Getting Hot

They drove only a few blocks from the Italian Market before Pete told Grace to park.

"Where are we?" she asked.

"My place."

Grace and Nick followed Pete half a block to a redbrick row house, with one red door and one blue. He opened the blue one with a key, and stuck his head in the door. "Louis, it's me."

Pete led them into a foyer with wide wood-plank floors and silver-blue painted walls. Decoupage wall sconces cast indirect light onto the ceiling, giving the entryway a warm feel despite the cool colors.

"Who's Louis?" Nick sniggered. "Your life partner?"

Pete looked over Nick's shoulder. "Hey, Lou. You my life partner?"

A man slightly smaller than the Chrysler Building, with a stare that could freeze antifreeze, filled the hallway.

Nick postured for a few seconds, but when Louis trained hard, black eyes on him, all the wind went out of Nick's sails.

Pete clapped his hand on Nick's shoulder and said to Louis, "This is the jerk-wad who screwed up two friggin' years of work."

"Hey, watch the shirt," Nick said, without much conviction.

"So what do we do now, boss?" Louis asked.

"I don't know. I need a beer."

"I thought you said you didn't drink," said Grace.

"I'm making an exception," said Pete.

They all filed into a neat little galley kitchen with maple cabinets and stainless-steel appliances that looked brand-new. Set up on a small table in the corner was enough electronic equipment to make the place look like the *Star Trek* command center.

"Anything going on?" Pete said to Louis.

"Nah. The Russian left his apartment about an hour ago."

"You got the place bugged?" Nick said.

Pete and Louis ignored him.

Pete opened up the refrigerator, revealing two six-packs of beer, a bottle of ketchup, an open can of succotash and something lying on the bottom shelf that looked like it could win the starring role in the next *Alien* movie.

Grace itched to get her fingers on Pete's appliances. What she couldn't do with a double convection oven.

Okay. How sad was that? The thought of using a guy's stove was making her hot. She unzipped her sweatshirt.

Three pairs of male eyes immediately focused on her chest. She zipped her sweatshirt back up.

They all sat on wrought-iron bar stools around the tiny breakfast bar.

Pete passed the beers around. "Okay, here's how I see it. Nick has to keep the meeting with Skobelov. Business as usual, just like we planned."

"But I don't have the memory key," Nick protested. "And even if I did, didn't you just tell me there was nothing on it?"

"Yeah, but you've got to convince him he's still going to get the names."

Nick shook his head. "No way. I'm not gonna lie to Viktor Skobelov. He's fucking scary, man."

"Oh, but you were going to steal thirty thousand names and social security numbers out from under him? What if he knew that, Nick, huh? What if he knew you were gonna cross him?" Pete took a swig of his beer.

"You wouldn't…" Nick looked at Pete and then at Louis. Louis was smiling.

Nick pulled on his earlobe. "What if I say no?"

Pete shrugged. "You can do that. We'll just have to get you into witness protection as soon as possible, so you can testify against Skobelov when I finally do manage to make a case against him, probably in two years or so. You'll love Kansas, Nick."

"What if I say no?"

"Not an option. It's testifying or jail. That was our deal, Nick. And believe me, the Secret Service does not take kindly to those who mess up our cases. We'll push for the maximum sentence. Right, Lou?"

Louis iced Nick with his stare.

Nick looked at Grace. "What do you think I should do, honey?"

"Me?"

"I'm not talking to Louis."

Grace gave Nick the evil eye. "Can I see you in the other room, *honey?*"

Saturday, 8:54 p.m.
The Viagra Papers

"Are you out of your mind?" Grace said through clenched teeth. "Why are you dragging me into this?"

Nick raised one shoulder. "I just wanted your opinion."

"You want my opinion? Why?"

"I don't know. You seem like you got a good head on your shoulders."

"Oh, sure." She had a feeling Nick missed the sarcasm in her reply.

"Listen," Nick said. "This wasn't the way things were supposed to go between us. Why didn't you meet me back at the room?"

"Because I came to my senses."

Nick ran his hands through his hair. "You were supposed to come back to the room with the memory key. If you had, none of this would've happened."

"Well, why'd you put it in my pocket to begin with? What made you so sure I was going to come to your room?"

Nick gave her a look she hadn't seen since the Fonz on *Happy Days.* She imagined him in a leather jacket, hair slicked back, saying "A-a-ay-y-y."

Grace put her hand on her hip. "Oh, I get it. *Of course* I would come back to your room. A middle-aged soccer mom desperate for a hot night with a young stud. Is that it?"

Nick shrugged. "I thought we had something going."

Grace took a deep, cleansing breath. And another and another. "You said you want my opinion? If I were you, I'd just cooperate with them. Do whatever they want."

"Why?"

"Why?"

"Yeah, why?"

"Because… Because it's the right thing to do."

Nick smiled. "You always do the right thing?"

"I try to."

"Uh-huh."

"What's that supposed to mean?"

Nick reached out and tucked a curl behind her ear. "Let's just say I got a look at some papers that might prove differently."

Grace's body began to buzz. "Papers?"

"Papers that release a large quantity of Viagra to a new 'vendor.'"

Viagra? Was that what this whole thing was about? Tom needed Viagra?

She hadn't read the papers before she signed them. She didn't want to know what he was up to. But this was crazy. It didn't make any sense. Tom would never risk all of this for Viagra. Would he?

An image of him with Marlene and a giant tub of mayonnaise flashed through her head.

That asshole. That stupid asshole.

"I don't know what papers you're talking about," she said to Nick.

"The ones you forged, Grace."

"Prove it."

Nick grinned. "I have a ringing endorsement from your husband."

"Tom?"

"You have another husband?" Nick slid his hand behind her neck and pulled her close, kissing her lightly. "Do you think meeting me was an accident?" he whispered.

"Oh, God…" She didn't want to hear this. "How—?"

"Hey!" Pete shouted from the kitchen. "You done in there? 'Cause we've got to have an answer. Now."

Chapter 10.5

Saturday, 9:08 p.m.
X Factor

C'mon, Balboa. Gimme the right answer.

Pete picked at the label on his beer bottle and tried to look bored.

The truth was, without Nick Balboa, he didn't have much of a case. They could get the Russian, Skobelov, on a few minor fraud charges, but they needed the big pop.

The Russian was too well-protected. Pete knew he was involved in some pretty heavy stuff: money laundering, immigration violations, Internet drug sales. But the only thing Pete cared about was the identification fraud. It was the cornerstone of his investigation. All the rest was gravy.

The Russian had put up sixty grand for names he'd bought

from Morton, a computer geek who worked at a credit card processing center in Boise, Idaho.

The plan was simple. Balboa was supposed to fly out to Boise, pick up the memory key from Morton and bring it back to Philly. Then Pete would copy the information, enter it into evidence and, when Skobelov used the names for fraudulent purposes, they'd have him dead to rights.

But without Balboa, he couldn't pull it off. Balboa was his inside man. The only one he knew who could get close to Skobelov.

But even if Balboa agreed to stay in, who was to say he wouldn't cross them again? He was the loose cannon. The X factor.

Right now, the stupid jerk had his hand linked in Grace's, who looked like she might chew her arm off to get away from him. Pete himself could have happily ripped Balboa's head off.

He'd really begun to hope Grace wasn't a part of all this. He'd wanted to believe her, but her arrest record made it unlikely. He was inexplicably disappointed.

"Well, what's it gonna be, Nick?"

Balboa sucked down the last of his beer and plunked the bottle down on the counter. "I'll do it."

Chapter 11

Saturday, 9:35 p.m.
Big Red Nose

"I have to make a call."

Pete looked at her like she was insane.

"I have to call my kids. My mother. They'll be worried if I don't."

Pete thought for a minute. "Lou, go with her. Let her use the kitchen phone." He went back to hooking a small device to the inside of Nick's collar.

Grace followed Louis to the kitchen, where he pointed to an old-fashioned wall phone with a long, curly cord. It was exactly like the phone her parents used to have in their kitchen. Grace used to stretch it into the pantry, where she'd close the door, eat Oreos and talk to Cecilia and Dannie all night.

"Make it quick," Louis said.

Grace dialed slowly, trying to think of what she was going to say. Her heart bounced around in her chest like a Super Ball. Megan answered the phone.

"Hi, sweetie. How's it going?"

"Pretty lame. Grandma wouldn't even let me go to the mall, and I *have* to get a dress for homecoming. I mean, *when* am I supposed to do *that?*"

"We'll go on Tuesday, okay?"

As long as I'm not in jail. Or swimming with the fishes.

Grace's voice broke. "I promise we'll go. Just you and me."

"Jeez, Mom. It's only a dress. You don't have to cry about it."

Grace wiped her nose on her sleeve. "Is Grandma there?"

"Yeah, hang on."

The phone clunked. A television blared in the background, and it was several minutes before her mother came on.

"Hello, dear."

"Hi, Mom. Am I interrupting something?"

"No, no. We're just watching *Terms of Endearment.* It's almost to the part where Shirley MacLaine's yelling at the nurses, 'Give her the shot! Give my daughter the shot!' So sad."

"How are the kids?"

"They're fine. How was your night out with your friends?"

"Interesting, I guess."

"Does Cecilia still have such a fresh mouth? I remember she once told me to—"

"Mom, that was twenty years ago."

"Well, still. You never get over something like that. By the way, I tried to call your cell phone, but I got the voice mail."

"Yeah. It wasn't charged up."

"I was getting worried. Tom's been calling here for you." She lowered her voice to a whisper. "I can't believe he has the nerve."

Louis nudged Grace with his elbow.

"Listen, Mom. I have to get going—"

"Oh, look. It's the part where Debra Winger is telling the little boy she won't be coming home. You always cry at this part, and your nose gets all big and red."

"Mom, I really have to go."

Her mother sighed. "Okay, then. Callie and Kevin are in bed, but do you want to talk to Megan again?"

"Sure. Real quick." She dodged Louis's elbow and gave him a look.

Megan came on the line. "Yes, Mother?"

"Megan, I want you to help Grandma with Callie and Kevin." The tears started again, and Grace imagined her nose swelling to twice its size.

"Mom, are you crying again? Jeez, take a pill."

"Just be good, okay?"

"Like, when am I ever not good? Can I go now?"

Grace sniffed. "Go ahead. Tell Grandma I said goodbye."

Grace hung up the phone and looked at Louis. "What's in these cabinets? I really need to cook something."

Saturday, 10:44 p.m.
Rash Thoughts

"This is awesome." Nick shoveled food into his mouth while bent over the sink, a paper napkin tucked into his collar so as not to short out the body bug he was wearing.

Grace had discovered a pound of hamburger in the freezer and an onion in the hydrator tray. Along with a couple of cans of succotash and a few squirts of ketchup, she'd managed to pull together a half-decent goulash. But the urge to cook still hadn't subsided.

"Not bad, Gracie," Pete said. "You a professional chef or something?"

"No. And please don't call me that."

"What? Gracie?"

"My ex-husband calls me Gracie. I can't stand it."

"Is he the one who gave you this nice diamond ring? 'Cause I know it wasn't Nick here." Pete wiggled the ring on his finger.

"Hey," Nick said. "It could've been me."

Louis's spoon stopped midway to his mouth. "Heh."

Nick shook his head. "Why is it so hard to believe that I gave my lady friend here a gift?"

"I am not your 'lady friend,'" Grace said.

"Okay, okay. My *woman.*"

The protest was on her lips, but before she could get the words out, Nick leaned over and kissed her.

The scent of Aramis rendered her momentarily unable to function. She sat there, helpless, as Nick's bionic lips moved over hers.

When Nick finally pulled away, Pete's expression was black. "Save it for later. We gotta roll."

"How about giving me my ring back now?" Grace said.

"Later." Pete put the ring in his pants pocket. "Insurance."

Pete and Louis collected some complicated-looking electronic gadgets and loaded them into a big, black duffel bag.

"We'll stop by the hotel first, so I can get my car," Pete said. "Then Lou will take the two of you on to the meeting place."

"Where are *you* going?" Grace said.

"Boise. See if I can track down Morton."

"I hope you find him," Grace said. "I really do." Because maybe then she could go home.

The thought brought relief and just a teeny sliver of regret. She had to admit, she hadn't felt this alive in a long, long time.

Her role as Tom's wife required a sophisticated hostess, not a party girl. A woman who could hold a conversation, not one who could tell jokes.

But, sometime in the last twenty-four hours, her impulsive side had been resuscitated.

The four of them piled into Grace's car and drove to the Baccus Hotel. Pete and Nick went in and retrieved the rest of Nick's things. Pete put everything into the trunk of Grace's car and leaned in the driver's side window to talk to Louis.

He smelled of decent cologne. It was no Aramis, true. But Grace was surprised by his choice. He had the beginnings of reddish beard stubble growing on his chin, like an unkempt version of David Caruso. It was the kind of stubble that could give a girl a nasty rash…

Whoa. Where had that *come from?*

She already had one more imaginary boyfriend than she wanted. The thought of getting a rash, or anything else, from Pete Slade was strictly verboten.

"Don't screw this up," Pete said to Nick. "Louis will be listening. If you get into trouble, remember the emergency word."

"Pineapple."

"Right. But only if you're in trouble. Convince him, Nick. Convince Skobelov the names are on the way."

"Sure."

Grace could see Nick's face in the rearview mirror. He didn't look so sure. In fact, he looked like he was about to puke.

Pete slapped the roof of the car. "Go get 'em."

Saturday, 11:51 p.m.
Eavesdropping

Back to the Cat's Meow.

The neon cat on the roof seemed to be running out of juice,

its winking eye more closely resembling a palsy twitch than a seductive gesture.

"What time is it?" Nick asked.

"Five of," Louis said. "You ready?"

"Yeah." Nick got out of the car and leaned in Grace's window, just as Pete had done. "Can I have a kiss for good luck?"

Her stomach knotted. "You're kidding me, right?"

Nick flashed his thousand-watt smile. "You want me to be kidding you?"

She hit the button to roll up the window.

Nick straightened his collar and headed for the door of the club. Grace had a hard time keeping her eyes off his butt.

"Now what?" she said to Louis.

He rooted through the bag and pulled out a black box the size of a hardcover book and plugged it into the cigarette lighter with an adapter. "Now, we listen."

"What is that thing?"

"A receiver. It records everything that comes over the body wire."

Louis opened the lid of the box, revealing a row of knobs and buttons. He hit one and it crackled to life, lights jumping in little bars across the face of a tiny screen. A rhythmic sound spewed from the box.

"What's that noise?" Grace said.

"Nick's breathing. I guess that's a good thing, huh?" He snickered to himself. Just then it struck her who Louis reminded her of. The old detective Fish, from *Barney Miller.*

They heard "Hey, Nick."

"The bouncer at the door," Louis said.

Blaring music. The Pussycat Dolls.

"Hi, Nicky."

"Hey, Shannon. Looking good."

"Hey, Nick."

"Lisa, wow. Nice dress."

"He's smooth," Louis said. Grace thought she detected a tiny note of admiration in his tone.

"Nicky, where you been?"

"Hey, Maria. Where's the boss?"

"He's waiting for you at the back booth."

"Thanks."

"Here we go," Nick muttered under his breath.

For a few moments, all they could hear was the sound of dance music pumping in the background.

"Nicholas. How is the car running?"

"It's the Russian," said Louis to Grace, as if she couldn't hear the accent.

"Car's running great," they heard Nick say. "Just got some new rims. I'm gonna show her at the Classic Car Expo."

"Good. Good. She's a beauty." Belch. "You remember Tina?"

"Of course. How are you, honey?"

"Couldn't be better."

"So, Nicky," said Skobelov. "How was your trip? You got something for me?"

Nick beat a rhythm on the table with his fingers. "Morton screwed us over, Viktor."

Bass thumped in the background. "What you mean, screwed us over? You don't have?"

"Nah. I got to the hotel near the airport and Morton wasn't there. Maybe he was being followed or something. I have a friend working on it."

"A friend?"

"Yes. A good friend. One who can be trusted."

"I don't trust nobody. I don't trust you."

"You can trust me, Viktor. I'll get the names."

"I should kill you. You know that?"

"I know. I know. But it wasn't my fault. I'll have what you want by tomorrow."

A long pause. "What you think, Tina?"

"Ah, give him till tomorrow. What's it gonna hurt?"

Ice cubes clinking in a glass. Music thumping.

"Tomorrow," Skobelov said. "If you got no names, I won't be happy. First, I cut your fingers off. Then your pretty nose. Then we see what else stick out, eh?"

Skobelov's laughter faded and the music grew louder. Grace could hear the sound of Nick walking away from the table. Fast.

"Nice guy," Louis said, switching off the receiver as Nick emerged from the club's front door. He hightailed it across the parking lot and climbed into the backseat of Grace's car.

Nobody said anything.

Grace wondered what the men were thinking. Because she knew what she was thinking.

Holy shit.

Sunday, 2:35 a.m.
The Chopping Block

They were about a block from Pete's place when they passed the all-night supermarket. Louis was in the driver's seat. Grace didn't think her nerves could handle it.

"Pull over here," Grace said.

"What for?" Louis asked.

"You have to eat, don't you? And I have to cook. But just about all that's left in that kitchen are a few packets of soy sauce and a banana. Even I can't do much with that."

"You heard her. Pull over, Louis," said Nick. "The lady needs to cook."

Louis double-parked in front of the grocery store.

Grace was in and out in fifteen minutes, struggling to the car with three big paper bags of groceries.

"What'd you get?" said Louis, grabbing the bags and throwing them in the backseat next to Nick.

"You'll see."

Back at Pete's, Grace shed her coat and shoes, poured herself a glass of wine before she remembered her vow never to drink again and went to work. She watched Nick out of the corner of her eye, waiting for a chance to talk to him when Louis wasn't lurking nearby.

"You want to help me chop here?" she said to Nick.

"Sure." He unbuttoned the sleeves of his silk shirt and rolled them up to his elbows.

She never knew a man's wrists could be so sexy. She took a gulp of wine.

In the other corner of the kitchen, near the command center, Louis turned on a small television set and flipped through the channels before settling on a late-night western. He propped his feet up on a chair and opened a bag of potato chips.

Trying to keep her voice beneath the sound of galloping horses and the *ping-pings* of gunshots, Grace said to Nick, "Maybe we should finish our conversation from before."

"What conversation?"

"Hello? The one where you insinuated you know my ex-husband?"

"I didn't insinuate anything. I do know your ex-husband. I met him at a car show about six months ago. He's the one who got me thinking that we should hook up."

"*What?*"

"That you and I should get together."

"Jesus! Does he think I'm so desperate for a date that *he* has to set me up? What a sick f—"

"Hey, he didn't try to set us up like *that*." Nick grinned. "That was my idea."

Now she was confused. "I'm not following you."

Nick looked over at Louis. He'd fallen asleep, head tipped back, mouth open, potato chip crumbs on his shirt.

"Tom and I were talking one time about your…*skills*. I got to thinking that maybe I could use you for a little plan I cooked up." He checked on Louis again and lowered his voice to a whisper. "I was gonna get these names, see, and set up a little business for myself with the help of a friend in Trenton. Maybe fill out some credit applications, or make some fake ID's. Tom happened to mention once that you were an expert at forging names."

Grace got a cold, hollow feeling in the pit of her stomach. She couldn't believe she was hearing this. The cabbage she was cutting suddenly looked an awful lot like Tom's head. She gave it a solid whack with the knife.

"So what you're telling me is that you met Tom at a car show, and he started off the conversation by telling you I have a record for forgery and ID theft?"

"Nah. Nothing like that. We didn't have that conversation until after…"

"After what?"

Nick stopped chopping. "What are you so shocked about? Like I said last night, did you think it was a coincidence that we hooked up at the club?"

"But *I* came to *you*. On a dare."

He raised his eyebrows. "Okay. Think about this. There were a hundred guys at that club. Why'd you come to me?"

"Because…"

Because you are so much sexier than Ludmilla. Because your eyes make me want to do things that might be a teensy bit illegal. Because I was feeling obsolete, and you made me feel like a teenager again.

"Because you were looking at me." Realization hit her like a softball to the head. "You knew if I saw you looking at me, I'd come over."

Damn. It had all been a setup.

Her throat tightened. She chopped unmercifully at the cabbage. *Die. Die!*

"How did you know I'd be there?" she asked.

Nick shrugged. "I followed you from your house."

"You know where I live?" She took a deep breath. "Then why didn't you just come to the house to get the damned computer key this morning?"

"I did, but you were gone already."

Chop, chop, chop.

"Hey." Nick gently removed the knife from her hands and took her by the shoulders, turning her to face him. "I was looking at you because I wanted you to come over. But I kissed you because I couldn't help myself."

She couldn't move. The combination of Nick's beautiful hands on her, his gorgeous eyes staring into hers and the smell of food drove her over the edge.

"Kiss me one more time," she said, and closed her eyes.

Chapter 11.5

Sunday, 5:45 a.m.
Taking a Dive

Pete pressed the buzzer screwed on to the check-in desk at the Sleep-In Motel, three miles from the Boise airport on Interstate 85.

He'd checked the room Balboa had said Morton was in, but it was empty, the open curtains revealing no sign of occupancy. He wasn't surprised.

Pete yawned. He would have liked nothing better than to check into one of these rooms, as skeevy as it might be, and sleep for ten hours. But he wasn't there to sleep. He was geek hunting.

The night manager staggered out of the room behind the desk in a bathrobe that looked like it hadn't been washed since…well, ever. His hair stuck up on one side at a ninety-degree angle.

"Hey, Gumby. Where's Pokey?" Pete said.

The manager gave him a blank look. "Help you?"

"Yeah. I'm looking for someone." He pulled a grainy picture of Morton out of his pocket.

The manager shook his head without even looking at the picture.

"His mother's been in an accident. I need to find him."

"I can't help you, sir. Our guest register is confidential."

"Why? Is the president staying here?"

The night manager shook his head and again turned to go back to his room.

Pete pulled a crisp fifty out of his wallet and snapped it. "Hey. I've got a president right here. President Ulysses S. Grant. Can he check in?"

Gumby rubbed the back of his neck, and turned around. "Okay. Let me have a look at the picture." He stuffed the fifty into the pocket of his robe and held the photo of Morton up to the light.

"Uh-huh. This guy checked in a couple of days ago. With a girl."

"He still here?"

"Nope. Only stayed one night."

Which proved Morton had had no intention of waiting around for Nick to deliver the key to Skobelov, and for Skobelov to courier him a check for the goods. He knew there'd be no check for an empty key.

"How'd he pay?" Pete asked.

"Credit card, I think."

Oh, the irony. "Can you look it up for me?"

The manager flashed him a look of annoyance. "Come on, man. I'm tired."

Pete slid a twenty onto the counter. "Here. Andrew Jackson wants to check in, too."

Gumby powered on the old computer behind the desk. The hard disk whined and clicked as he tapped on the keys. Eventually, the printer behind him spat out a sheet of paper. He tore it off, gave it a quick look and handed it to Pete. "Can I go back to bed now?"

"Just one more thing. Where does the trash from the rooms end up?"

"In the Dumpster behind room sixteen."

"Has it been taken away in the last two days?"

"No. Pickup is Monday and Thursday mornings. Your guy checked out Friday."

"Mind if I take a look?"

"In the trash? Knock yourself out."

Pete located room sixteen with little problem. The Sleep-In was laid out like a horseshoe that started with the office and ended at a maintenance unit across the wide driveway. The rooms were numbered one to twenty-six, excluding thirteen. He guessed anyone unfortunate enough to have to stay at this dump already had all the bad luck they could handle.

Room sixteen was located on the curve of the horseshoe, next to a narrow alley containing vending machines and an ice maker. The alley led through to the back of the building, where the Dumpster stood beside an access road off the main highway. A regular rodent fast-food drive-through.

Pete shinnied up the side and peered in. The Dumpster was nearly full.

"Great. Just great."

He climbed into the Dumpster and poked through a few bags, soon realizing he was going to have to dig deeper. He covered his face with the collar of his coat, and worked his way down through the refuse.

How did Ferret do this for a living? A professional Dumpster diver—a guy who dug information on individuals and businesses out of the trash—Ferret spent the majority of his nights knee-deep in other people's Chinese takeout, used tissues and liquefied vegetables.

It was definitely freaking Pete out.

He hacked down through the refuse, ripping open dozens of large trash bags until he found one that contained a bunch of smaller bags—the kind that lined little motel room trash cans.

He began ripping them open, like small piñatas filled with delightful prizes. Beer cans. Coke cans. Tissues. CornNut wrappers. Half-eaten donuts. And—

Pete gave an involuntary shudder.

Used condoms.

He was about to give up when he struck pay dirt.

A Sleep-In notepad with several phone numbers starting with a 215 area code. Southeast Pennsylvania. And a 609 area code. Central New Jersey.

In the same bag he found a list of airlines and flight times, and it didn't take an agent's intuition to guess where the flights were landing.

Morton was playing games. And he was playing them right in Pete's backyard.

Pete pocketed his treasures and climbed out of the Dumpster, picking a crumpled Band-Aid off of his shoe.

He flicked open his cell phone.

"United Air Lines. How can I help you?" The voice on the other end of the line was annoyingly chipper for—he looked at his watch—six-fifteen in the morning.

"I need to get on the next flight to Philadelphia."

Chapter 12

Sunday, 6:50 a.m.
Kulebiaka and Bad Boys

By the time breakfast rolled around, Grace had worked up a pretty good appetite chopping and trying to quell the sexual tension that had built up between her and Nick.

Louis awoke refreshed from his nap, and Grace served up a huge platter of flaky pastries filled with eggs, meat, cabbage and rice.

"What is this stuff?" Nick asked through a mouthful of food.

"*Kulebiaka*. It's an Eastern European dish."

"Where'd you learn to cook like this?"

Grace finished off her third glass of wine, ignoring the little voice that told her she'd pay for this tomorrow. Or rather, later today. "An executive at Tom's company was Russian. I took lessons so I could have him and his wife over for dinner. Impress them."

"Mmmph." Louis bent over his plate like a vulture protecting a zebra carcass.

"You did all that for your husband?" said Nick.

"It was important to him."

"Was it important to you?"

Grace thought about that.

She supposed it was important, at the time. Very important. Her whole life had revolved around the ability to make a good impression. To make Tom happy.

But looking back on things now, she wished she hadn't been so obsessed with making everything perfect. She wished she would have had more fun, like she did in her life before marriage.

She said, "Tom was important to me. And my kids were. *Are.* They're the most important."

"But what do *you* want, Grace? For yourself?" Nick's heavy-lidded gaze felt like a thousand tiny fingers on her skin. She turned away, not wanting him to see her blush.

She'd been asking herself that very question for months now.

"I don't know." She stood and began clearing the plates.

"Don't worry about that," Nick said. "Lou will get the dishes."

Louis grunted again.

Nick poured her another glass of wine and took her arm, leading her into the small living room, where he sat beside her on the sofa.

Close.

Too close.

She edged away and took a swig of wine.

Nick reached out and twirled a piece of her hair in his fingers. "I like you, Grace. Even though you're not my type."

"So I've been told." Grace tried to breathe slowly. She

recited her mantra in her head. *Namu Amida Butsu. Namu Amida Butsu.*

Despite the fact that being with Nick would be wrong on so many levels, Grace's heartbeat quickened. It was like the time in high school when she had gone beneath the bleachers at a football game to look for the pencil she'd dropped—the one with a troll doll on the top. Bobby Gaither was already down there, leaning up against one of the metal supports, smoking a cigarette. He had looked so cool in his Members Only jacket, with his hair hanging over dark, dark eyes.

"Come here," he'd said. And because she hadn't wanted to look chicken, she'd gone over.

"You want a cigarette?" He'd held out a pack of Newports. And because she hadn't wanted to look dorky, she'd said yes.

It was the first cigarette she'd ever smoked. She'd coughed a little bit and her eyes had watered, and when she had finished she'd been light-headed and had felt like she might throw up. It was a feeling she'd have around men many times to come.

"You wanna make out?" Bobby had asked. And because she hadn't wanted to look like a goody-goody, she'd complied.

The ground had lurched, and above her the bleachers had spun like they were caught in a tornado. Bobby's tongue had slid over hers, tasting of cigarettes and Pop Rocks from the concession stand.

She'd felt bad, and wild, and her lips had burned deliciously. She'd forgotten all about the troll pencil. She'd gone below the bleachers a girl, and had returned a woman. Or, almost a woman. She was changed.

That Monday, Bobby had lied to all the boys in wood shop that he'd gone to second base with her. She hadn't bothered to deny it. Those few, carefree minutes when she hadn't thought of anything else but the way she'd been feeling with Bobby had been worth the smudge on her reputation.

Nick moved closer to her on the sofa, and she realized she could have that again. Right now. A few transcendent minutes in the arms of a bad, bad boy.

He leaned in and kissed her, and she felt herself letting go.

She pulled away. "I'm going to bed now."

Nick grinned. He stood when she did, but she shook her head. She realized she'd had just about enough of bad boys.

"Let me clarify," she said. "I'm going to bed now. Alone."

Sunday, 2:29 p.m.
Primates

Grace woke up drooling on a strange pillow, in a room decorated with subdued animal patterns and framed prints of African savannahs in gold-gilt frames.

She was sprawled on a bed in her underwear, her sweatshirt and yoga pants lying in a heap beside the bed. Downstairs, she could hear the sound of men arguing.

She looked at her watch and realized Kevin would be finishing up his soccer tournament about now.

She pulled on her clothes, combed her hair with her fingers and marched downstairs to the living room, where Pete and Nick were facing off against each other like a pair of apes in the wild, posturing and beating their chests.

Pete looked wiped out. "Didn't you even bother to check the damned key before you took it from Morton?" he snapped.

"Hell, yes. What do you think I am? Stupid?"

"You said it, not me."

"I told you, I checked the damned key. The names, the social security numbers, they were all there."

"Then what the hell happened?"

Nick rubbed the stubble on his chin. "I don't know. Maybe he switched it with another key or something before I left."

"Well, did you give him an opportunity to do that? Did you leave him alone with the key?"

"No." But Nick's face flushed.

"What?" said Pete.

"I don't know. Maybe…" He sighed.

"What happened?" said Pete.

"There was a girl in the room with Morton. Great hair, long legs. Stacked." Nick lit a cigarette. "She followed me into the bathroom, and one thing led to another…"

Pete gave Grace a sympathetic look.

"What?" she said. "I don't care what he does."

Pete turned back to Nick. "And then what? You did her in the bathroom?"

"Nah. Nothing like that. We just fooled around a little."

"And during that time, Morton was alone with the key?"

"Well, yeah. But how would I know he'd pull something funny? He was there to sell me the damn thing. Why would he tamper with it?"

Pete flopped down into a chair. "I don't know."

Nick crushed out his cigarette in an ashtray on the coffee table. "Now what? I told Viktor I'd have the names for him by tonight."

"Well, you won't. Even if we could set up a fake key, it would take time." Pete buried his face in his hands. "Shit."

Louis came in to the room. "Fegley wants you to call him, Pete."

"Of course he does."

"Who's Fegley?" said Grace.

"My boss." Pete pulled his cell phone out of his pocket. "I

guess I'll have to tell him we're done. Finished. I'll have him set Balboa up in witness protection, and we'll pull out."

"Ho, hey." Nick snatched the phone from Pete. "Not so fast."

"Listen," Pete said. "I know you're not thrilled with the prospect of entering the program, but you're my only chance of making a case against Skobelov. I won't have much now, but if I can't get anything on him at all, I've wasted two years. And I can't risk you getting popped or taking off on me before I have the chance to build the case."

Nick held his arms out. "I wouldn't take off on you."

"I'm supposed to take your word after what you pulled Friday? You'd screw me in a heartbeat."

Nick grinned. "Nah. You're not my type."

Pete grabbed his cell phone back from Nick.

Nick drummed his fingers on the coffee table. "Maybe I could make it up to you."

Pete shook his head. "It's over."

"What if I could buy some more time? Another day or two? Just enough time for you to find Morton or put something else together."

Pete was quiet for a while. "How?"

Nick jerked his head at Grace. "Her."

Grace sat up straight. "Me? What about me?"

"What about her?" Pete said.

"Her cooking." Nick stood up and began to pace behind the sofa. "The only thing the Russian loves more than money is food. He's always complaining he can't get a decent Russian meal in Philadelphia." He pointed at Grace. "She can give it to him."

Louis nodded. "She's good, Pete."

"What, that hamburger stuff?"

"Nah," said Lou. "That was bush-league. She's been making some great food here. You missed it while you were out in Boise."

"Viktor would do anything for good borscht," Nick said, his voice rising with excitement. "He'd definitely give us more time."

"Uh-uh. No way," Pete said.

"No way," Grace agreed. Her arms broke out in gooseflesh just remembering Skobelov's evil laugh.

"See?" Pete said. "She's just a suburban housewife. She's not up for something like that."

A tiny spark flared in the back of Grace's brain. "Excuse me? How do you know what I'm up for?"

She knew it was crazy, but them were fightin' words.

As "just a suburban housewife," she'd battled forty-one hours of childbirth labor, months of colic, years of poopy diapers, endless nights of croup, homework, broken hearts and broken bones.

She'd cooked, cleaned, finessed, flattered, cajoled, faked orgasms, faked joy over crappy anniversary gifts and faked holding it all together when Tom walked out on them.

Surely, she could survive cooking for one maniacal Russian mobster for a day or two.

Despite earlier vows to go back to her mundane life, she discovered she really *did* want to do this. Her inner Charlie's Angel begged to be free.

"I'd be there," Nick argued. "I'd protect her."

Pete snorted. "Right."

But Grace could tell by the look in his eye that he might at least consider the idea.

She touched his arm. "I want to do it."

Chapter 12.5

Sunday, 3:22 p.m.
Salvage Work

Grace was clearly out of her mind.

The Russian was volatile. Dangerous. Three hundred pounds of menacing flesh.

If she were tougher, more familiar with the underworld, he might consider it. But it had become clear to him that what Grace had been saying all along was true. She really wasn't Nick's girlfriend.

He knew, because there wasn't a woman alive who could hear her boyfriend confess to making out in a sleazy motel bathroom with another woman and not bat an eyelash. If he knew nothing else about women, he knew that.

He still wasn't completely sure she had nothing to do with

this case—he couldn't completely ignore her record, after all. But putting her in close quarters with Skobelov?

He couldn't do it.

He looked down at her hand, so pale and fragile looking, resting on his arm. Her touch was gentle, and he felt a surge of uncharacteristic protectiveness.

Damn. What was he getting all sappy about? She was the one offering to put her neck on the line. She knew what she was getting into, and if she could possibly save his case, why shouldn't he take her up on the offer?

Grace and Nick and Lou looked at him like they were waiting for him to sing something from *Yentl* or start spinning plates on broomsticks.

His cell phone buzzed in his hand. He looked down at the number.

Fegley. Crap.

He took a deep breath and flipped open his phone. "Fegley? Hey, there might be a way to salvage this thing after all."

Chapter 13

Sunday, 4:40 p.m.
Tangled Up

Pete followed her through the front door of her house, into the foyer.

"Nice place. How long have you lived here?"

"Fourteen years. My ex-husband inherited it from his aunt. When we got it, it was just about falling down, so we had our work cut out for us."

He strolled into the living room, hands behind his back, peering at everything as if he were a detective in an old-fashioned mystery. He pointed to the walk-in fireplace. "Is the cartouche original?"

"Most of it. But a few of the pieces had to be recreated." The fleur-de-lis shield beneath the mantel had been a pet project of hers. It had taken weeks of research and phone calls to find the perfect craftsmen to handle the restoration. But it had been worth it. In Grace's opinion, the cartouche was the heart of the house. She'd remodeled the entire interior around that design.

Pete strolled to the cabinet in the corner. "Nice étagère."

What was this guy, gay? Nobody knew what an étagère was, except for interior designers and gay men.

"Tom always called it the junk cabinet. He can't stand knickknacks."

"Those are hardly knickknacks. I see some Lladró there. Royal Copenhagen. And is that Lalique?"

Definitely gay.

"Do you collect figurines?" she asked.

Red crept up from beneath his collar like the liquid in a thermometer, turning his entire face the mottled color of a bruised apple. "My mother does. I get her one every Christmas."

"So how do you know so much about the other stuff? Cartouches and étagères?"

"My sister's an interior decorator. I guess I just picked up some of the terminology."

Grace was inexplicably relieved that he wasn't gay. "Did your sister decorate your house in Philadelphia?"

If possible, his face grew even redder. "No. I decorated it myself. I guess I picked up a little more than terminology." He cleared his throat. "Are you gonna go pack some clothes, or what?"

"Do I have time to take a quick shower?"

He looked at his watch. "Make it fast."

"There are drinks in the fridge if you want something." She ran up the steps, avoiding the squeaky one, the third from the top, out of habit.

Her bedroom was at the end of the hall, through ivory-painted French doors. She and Tom had combined two smaller bedrooms to create a modestly sized but luxurious master suite with a fireplace at either end; a large bathroom with a clawfoot spa tub, shower and double sink; and a huge walk-in closet and dressing area.

It was the one part of the house that didn't have an authentic colonial feel. But she was addicted to long, hot baths, and she had a lot of clothes and shoes, things that weren't exactly priorities in colonial times.

She locked the door to the bathroom and stripped off the dirty yoga pants and sweatshirt. She hadn't showered or used deodorant in nearly three days—a bodily state unknown to her since her brief membership in an environmental group her freshman year in college.

She and a bunch of fellow EarthSavers had camped out with video cameras in the woods next to a fertilizer plant to prove phosphate chemicals were being dumped into a nearby stream. But instead of nailing corporate America, the trip had pretty much turned into an excuse to drink a lot of beer and nail each other.

She'd left pretty quickly, since she really had no desire to make naughty videos with people who hadn't showered or brushed their teeth in several days.

Now, she showered in record time, then attempted to blow-dry her new coif with the round bristle brush Tammy had given her. Halfway through, the brush got hopelessly tangled in her hair. She turned off the dryer and cursed the time-sucking style.

She could only hope it would turn out to be her biggest regret of the weekend.

Pete called to her from downstairs.

"Gimme five minutes!" she yelled.

She sprinted from the bathroom to her closet, where she dug through a drawer full of "functional" undergarments until she found a pair of underwear and a matching bra. Tom's idea of a nice Mother's Day gift.

She leafed through the hangers, picking out a pair of black Liz Claiborne pants and a pink, loose-weave sweater. She had the sweater halfway over her head when she heard the squeaky step and realized that Pete was upstairs. And that she'd left the door to her bedroom open.

"I'll be right out!" She tried to pull the sweater on, but it got stuck halfway over her head.

The brush! The brush was still tangled in her hair!

She bent over and clawed at the sweater, which only became more and more snarled in the brush the harder she tried to get it off.

"Grace?" Pete's voice came from inside her bedroom.

Pleasepleaseplease. Don't let him see me like this.

Why? What do you care?

I don't.

Yes, you do. And you were just kissing Nick last night.

So what? I can kiss whomever I want.

Slut.

Prude.

Hey. Both of you. You do realize you're talking to yourself.

"Grace?"

"Don't come in!"

A warm hand touched the small of her back. "Too late. Can I help you?"

"No!" She wrestled with the sweater some more but only succeeded in getting out of breath. She stood up and peered out at him through an armhole.

One side of Pete's mouth was curled up into a smirk. "Let me get it. There's a piece of wood sticking out through the sweater."

Pete worked the sweater over her head, leaving her standing

there in her closet in nothing but her underwear. Why, oh, why couldn't she have worn a camisole to cover the road map of stretch marks across her belly?

Luckily, there was something to distract Pete.

"What's that thing in your hair?" he said.

"A hairbrush."

"Mmm. Are you just going to leave it there?"

"Yes. It's an accessory." She pulled on her pants. "What are you doing in my bedroom?"

"Your phone was ringing. Someone left you a message, and it sounded like it might be important."

"You listened to my message?"

"I couldn't help it. I was sitting right next to the answering machine."

"Get out."

"Hurry up."

She pushed Pete out of the closet and slammed the door.

"You *were* kidding about the hairbrush, weren't you?" he said from the other side.

Sunday, 5:23 p.m.
Feeding Dracula

By the time she came back downstairs, Pete was sitting on the sofa leafing through her wedding album.

"Where did you get that?"

"On the bookshelf over there. Behind *Divorce for Dummies* and *A Hundred Healthy Ways to Channel Your Rage*. Who's the guy in the tux?"

"That would be my husband."

"You mean your ex-husband."

"He wasn't my ex-husband at the time, obviously."

"You didn't look very happy on your wedding day."

"Yeah, well. I had PMS."

"Must have been a fun honeymoon."

She snatched the book from his lap. "Are you ready?"

"What about your message?"

"Right." She stuffed the wedding album under the sofa, and went over to the answering machine on the mahogany console table.

Three messages.

The first was from Kevin. "Hi, Mom. Grandma said your cell phone wasn't working. Guess what? We won! Dad took us out for pizza after. Don't forget to feed Dracula. Bye."

Oh, crap. She'd forgotten about Dracula. She hit the pause button.

"Dracula?" said Pete.

"Kevin's frog. I was supposed to pick up some crickets at the pet store yesterday."

"You want me to go check on the frog? I mean, just in case he's…"

"Okay. That would be good. If he *is*…you know, there's a shoe box under Kevin's bed. If he's not, there's a container up there that might have a few crickets left in it. Just put them in the frog's tank."

"Where's Kevin's room?"

"Up the stairs, make a left, second door on the right."

Pete headed for Kevin's room, and she unpaused the answering machine.

The second message was from Lorraine. "Grace. How *are* you? I'm calling to remind you that you're up next to host cards. I know things are hard for you right now. Call me if you need a friend, okay?"

Sure. Will do. Because I'd like my business broadcast to every woman in South Whitpain in the eighteen to forty-five demographic.

Third message. "Grace? Pick up, Gracie." Tom's perfect diction streamed out from the machine. "Did you sign those papers yet? I really, really need them. Call me as soon as you get this."

She punched the erase button, wishing there was a button big enough to erase Tom himself.

Chapter 13.5

Sunday, 5:32 p.m.
Three-hour Tour

Pete listened to Grace play the message he'd just heard come in, wondering who the guy with the Cary Grant voice was. Her ex-husband, probably. Didn't she say he called her Gracie?

He felt a twinge of something low in his gut that felt suspiciously like jealousy. Her ex was a good-looking guy. An all-star quarterback type. Prom king. Class president. At least, that's the way he looked in the wedding pictures.

But hey, a lot could change in fourteen years. He could have gained fifty pounds. Come down with some horrible skin disease. Lost his hair.

Pete raked his fingers through his own dark red mop. At least he didn't have to worry about *that* anytime soon.

He sucked in his stomach and walked into the living room. "Good news. The frog's still kicking. You ready to go?"

Grace spun around, wiping a tear from her cheek.

No. No, no, no. No tears. "You okay?"

"Yeah. I just miss my kids."

"Hey, listen." He touched her arm. "You don't have to do this."

She shook her head. "No. I want to."

"I'm gonna warn you again. Skobelov is a dangerous man."

"But you'll be listening in, right? You'll have Nick wired. And all I'm going to do is cook for him."

"You could get caught in the middle of something."

She smiled. "I'll be careful."

"Good." And the next thing he knew, he was kissing her.

It started as hardly more than a peck, the kind of kiss he might give his sister. But the heat hit him like a nuclear blast, and soon he pulled her closer, losing himself in the taste of her lips. The flowery scent of her shampoo.

She melted against him and made little kitten sounds.

And then, as if she'd suddenly found herself embracing a tiger, she backed slowly out of his arms.

"Well."

"Grace, I'm sorry. I shouldn't have done that. It was completely inappropriate."

"No. No problem. We should go."

Damn. He screwed up. "Grace—"

"Pete, it's okay. It wasn't just you. It was me, too." She pushed the hair out of her eyes. "Will you help me with my bag?"

A big blue duffel sat near the door. He got a hernia just picking it up.

"What the— What's in this thing?"

She shrugged. "I didn't know what to pack. I mean, what does one wear to cook *rasstegai* for a Russian mobster?"

"You're only going to be there a day. Maybe two."

"I can't help it. It's Three-hour Tour Syndrome."

"What?"

"Like on *Gilligan's Island*. Three-hour Tour Syndrome. They brought enough clothes for several months, even though they were only supposed to be going on a three-hour boat cruise."

"Yeah, but the Skipper and Gilligan only had one set of clothes."

"That's why I never dated a sailor."

He hefted the duffel over his shoulder. "You're an interesting woman, Grace Becker."

Chapter 14

Sunday, 6:10 p.m.
Channeling Nancy Drew

As Pete's Taurus sped toward Philadelphia, Grace couldn't help but think about how different things were—how different *she* was—less than forty-eight hours ago.

She'd been picked up by a Secret Service agent, had hung out at a strip club, had been recruited to cook for a Russian mobster and had kissed two different men—two very different men—all in two days' time.

If only Cecilia and Dannie and Roseanna could see her now. This was turning out to be an unbelievable game of truth or dare.

In fact, she'd begun to look at it all like a test. A measure of her ability to change and adapt. She would definitely need it in the days and weeks to come, as she tried to put her life back together.

She switched on the radio. The easy-listening station filtered out from the speakers. She gave Pete a sad, knowing look. "Mind if I change the station?"

"Go ahead."

She flipped through until she heard Elvis Costello singing "Radio Radio."

Pete drummed on the steering wheel.

He had nice hands. Long, straight fingers with just a few freckles. No knobby joints, hairy knuckles or chewed nails.

The rest of him wasn't bad, either. He had a sprinkling of freckles across his nose and the beginnings of a ginger-colored five o'clock shadow.

While Nick was Death by Chocolate, Pete was a cinnamon bun.

And she was developing quite an appetite.

She rolled down the window and let the wind ruffle her new, short haircut. She hadn't felt this wild, this free, since her college days. She, Grace Poleiski, was going to help the Secret Service crack a case.

"Uh-oh," Pete said.

"What?"

"I recognize that look."

"What look?"

"That Nancy Drew, Girl Detective look."

She looked out the window. "Don't be ridiculous. I was a Hardy Boys fan."

"When you get in there," Pete said, "I want you to keep your mouth shut. You're there to cook. This isn't amateur night at the detective agency."

"I get it."

Pete switched off the radio. "I mean it, Grace. The best thing you can do for this case is to leave everything up to Nick."

"I can't even believe you can say those words with a straight face." She stared out the window.

Pete took the next exit and pulled over onto the side of the road. "Look. I know Nick isn't the most reliable informant, but he's all I've got. You're not going to help me by sticking your neck out, and possibly putting an already nervous perpetrator on alert. And I don't want to have to worry about you."

He'd worry about her?

She rolled this around in her mind for a moment, just to see how she felt about it. It had been a long time since anyone, including Tom, had worried about her. Besides her mother, that is.

She smiled. "I'll behave. I promise."

"Good."

They drove to a vacant lot on the border of West Philadelphia. Broken glass glittered under the streetlight like diamonds on black velvet, and plastic trash bags danced across the space, only to be trapped up against a sagging chain-link fence. Tufts of straggly weeds growing up through the cracks in the macadam offered proof that surviving in this part of town wasn't impossible, it just took persistence.

Pete put the car in Park but left it running for the heat. They sat listening to the radio in comfortable silence.

A few minutes later, Lou and Nick pulled up in front of them in a baby-blue-and-white 1959 Buick LeSabre with miles of fin and chrome.

"Wow," Grace said. "Nice car."

Pete grunted and opened the car door. "Come on."

He swung around the back of the Taurus to get Grace's duffel bag out of the trunk, while she went over to admire the LeSabre.

Louis sat in the car talking on his cell phone, but Nick got out and came around, patting the roof of the Buick.

Grace ran her hand over chrome on the massive fin in the back. "Beautiful."

"You like classic cars?" Nick asked.

"I learned to appreciate them. I went to a lot of car shows with Tom. He has a '76 Corvette."

"Yeah. I know."

Grace looked up at him. "I guess you would."

Nick stuffed his hands in the pockets of his leather jacket and shrugged.

"Did you ever show the car?" she asked.

"A couple times. But I don't like other people touching my girl."

Grace snatched her hand off the fin.

Nick laughed. "It's okay. I don't mind if you do."

Louis got out of the car. "Okay. You ready?"

Nick nodded. He looked at Grace. "How about you?"

"I'm ready."

Pete came over to the car with Grace's bag, and Nick opened the trunk.

"Remember," Pete said to Nick. "Try to get him to talk about his various business ventures, especially the identification fraud. And if anything goes wrong, you know the code word?"

"Pineapple."

"Right. Just say *pineapple* and we'll be there, with an army of cops. Don't take any chances." Pete looked at Grace. "No chances."

"Got it," Nick said.

"Don't screw me over, Nick. This is your last chance."

"Yeah, yeah." Nick threw the bag in the trunk and slammed it shut with the kind of sonorous *kathunk* only a 1950s Buick could make.

Grace sensed some tension beneath Nick's bravado. She wondered how he'd gotten involved in all of this in the first place, and what his expectations had been.

Then again, she was a fine one to talk when she didn't even know what her own expectations should be.

Sunday, 6:32 p.m.
Feminine Protection

A few minutes later, Grace and Nick drove up in front of an old, run-down brick building less than half a block from the railroad tracks. The place looked as if it might have housed some sort of manufacturing plant.

"Feminine products," Nick said.

"What?"

"It was a feminine products plant." He got out and came around to open her door.

"Like a tampon factory?"

The tips of his ears turned red, and he shrugged. "I guess so. Jeez."

She almost laughed. Here was a man who wasn't bothered by guns or Secret Service agents or crazy Russians, but the word *tampon* could kill him with embarrassment.

Pete should have made that his secret word instead of *pineapple.*

"What are we doing here?" she said.

"You'll see." They walked toward a door beside a fenced-off parking lot littered with potholes and pigeon droppings.

Grace's stomach fluttered. Not the good kind of flutter, like when you get the first three out of five numbers on lotto or when you see an old boyfriend at a class reunion. It was the bad kind of flutter, like when the phone rings at three in the morning or when the doctor leaves a message on your machine saying he wants to discuss the results of your STD test.

"What about my stuff?" Grace said. "This doesn't exactly seem like the safest of areas. I'd rather not leave it in the car. And come to think of it, you might not want to leave your *car*."

"Don't worry. There are people watching."

She breathed deeply, and tried to calm herself with the thought that Pete was listening in on everything. She wondered what would happen if *she* shouted the word *pineapple*. Would Pete and Louis rush to her rescue, too? Or would she just look like a lunatic shouting "pineapple" at Nick's chest?

Nick took her hand and gave it a squeeze. "Don't worry, babe. I'm right here. I'll protect you."

That wasn't as comforting a thought as she'd have liked.

He pressed a small, lit doorbell beside a big, glass door. A buzzer sounded, and Nick pushed open the door and led her into the lobby of the tampon plant.

A brick wall with a handlebar mustache and a pit-bull scowl sat behind a semicircular receptionist's desk, watching football on a small television. Behind him Grace could make out the shadow of the word *Femm-Care* where the letters had been removed from the wall.

"Hey, Benny. Who's winning?" Nick said.

"Stinking Giants."

"Damn. I got a nickel on the Eagles."

Benny grunted and pressed a button on the desk. A dark brown elevator door opened on the other side of the lobby.

Nick dragged Grace into the elevator and punched Four, the highest floor on the panel.

"Why are we here?" she whispered. "It looks abandoned."

Nick shook his head and looked up at the corner of the elevator, where a security camera stared back at her.

The elevator grunted and wheezed and finally ground to a halt on the fourth floor. The lit button went out with a ding that sounded like a bad note struck on a toddler's xylophone.

The door opened, and Grace stifled a gasp. Not a tampon in sight.

Instead, she and Nick stepped off the elevator into a gorgeous entrance hall with a parquet floor and a lush fresh-flower arrangement on a marble credenza that stood taller than her.

To the left were two white doors trimmed in gold. They reminded her of doors that might lead to a French courtier's boudoir.

"I get the feeling we're not in Femm-Care anymore, Toto," she said.

Nick smiled. "The plant is pretty much empty, except for this. This is Skobelov's apartment. It's modeled after the Emperor's Suite at Caesars Palace in Las Vegas. Look." He pointed to the ceiling.

A reproduction of Michelangelo's *The Creation of Adam* was painted on the ceiling.

"What do you think?"

"Unbelievable."

Nick slung his arm over her shoulders. "You ready?"

She nodded.

He knocked on the door.

A woman in black stretch pants and a leopard-skin tank top opened the door. Her strawberry-blond hair turned under just before it touched her shoulders, and spiky bangs brushed the tops of her penciled eyebrows.

The arch of those eyebrows gave the woman an innocent expression, and if it weren't for the cynical set of her lips, Grace might have thought she'd been kidnapped and stuffed into these clothes for some sort of bizarre episode of *Candid Camera*.

"Hey, Tina. The Russian here?"

"Where else would he be? He has a nickel on the Eagles, so he's in a rotten mood."

"Hey, this is my girlfriend, Grace."

Tina's gaze ran from Grace's hair to her toes and back. "Oh, yeah? She looks a little uptight for you, Nicky."

"You think? She's kind of a surprise for Viktor."

"Oh, yeah?" She put a hand on the curve of her hip.

"Not *that* kind of surprise," Grace said quickly.

Tina shrugged. "He's in the TV room." She drifted away, her high heels clicking on the marble floor.

Grace followed Nick into the apartment. The marble floor gave way to gold-and-black carpet in a living room dominated by a buttery leather sectional couch. Heavy gold drapes hid the functional factory windows, while a stunning crystal chandelier in the middle of the high ceiling gave the room a soft glow.

A seventy-two-inch flat-screen plasma television hung on a distant wall, broadcasting the Eagles-Giants game in digital splendor. The players looked so crisp, so real, Grace felt as if she could reach out and pinch their butts while they huddled up.

In contrast to the players, the man who watched the game hardly seemed real at all.

Viktor Skobelov was a cross between Jabba the Hutt and Chewbacca. A fat, furry, noxious blob, spread out like molasses along the length of the sectional. Grace wouldn't have been at all surprised to see Princess Leia in a gold bikini chained to the coffee table.

The Russian let out a belch and hit the mute button on the TV. "You have something for me, Nicky? I am not in good mood."

His words seemed like an effort. Slurred. Yakov Smirnoff on Quaaludes.

Grace might have laughed if she hadn't been so terrified. She had to pee, but she knew it was an inopportune moment.

"I don't have the names just yet," Nick said.

The Russian shook his head. "I am not happy, Nicky. What we going to do?"

"I'm working on it."

"You say that yesterday."

"I know, I know. I'm getting close. But in the meantime, I brought you something else. A gift. Something to keep you happy while I get the names." Nick dragged Grace in front of him like a human shield. "This is my girlfriend, Grace."

The Russian's tiny eyes raked over her like he was inspecting a side of beef. She gave an involuntary shiver.

"What you do?" he said.

She stared dumbly at him, mesmerized by the trembling of his jowls.

"What you do?" he repeated. "You do leather? Rubber?" He looked at Nick. "She's a little old."

Old?

Grace opened her mouth to inform the fat bastard that she wouldn't touch him with somebody *else's* hands let alone her own. But Nick gave her arm a hard squeeze before she could get the words out.

"No, no. She's not that kind of gift," Nick said quickly. "She cooks."

"She cooks? What? That freaking noodles and tomatoes you call food?"

Nick grinned. "Nope. Eastern European cuisine."

The Russian's eyebrows shot up. "Like what?"

"*Kulebiaka. Borscht. Kulich. Rasstegai. Okroshka,*" Grace answered.

The Russian leaned back on the couch and trained his gaze

on her as if were so hungry he might devour her words. Or maybe her.

Her toes curled, and not in a good way, but she met his gaze without blinking.

"You better hope she good, Nicky," Skobelov said. "Real good. If not, you are dead man."

Chapter 14.5

Sunday, 7:02 p.m.
Happy Noodle

Pete checked his watch for the eightieth time. He picked up his cell phone and hit the speed dial for Lou's number.

"Yo."

"Any sign of Morton?"

"Not yet. But lots of party girls walking around this part of town. Christ, who dresses these ladies?"

"Lou, you're so friggin' interested in women's clothes, you should be a designer. You could create a whole line of clothes just for hookers and strippers."

"*Hmp.*" Lou sounded as if he might actually consider that career change.

"Let me know when Morton and the girl show up."

"Right." Louis hung up.

While Pete listened in on Nick and Grace, Louis was staking out the hotel that matched the phone number Pete had found in the Dumpster in Boise. It had turned out to be a low-rent establishment in Northeast Philly that was one step away from renting rooms by the hour.

The desk clerk confirmed that Morton had checked in the day before with a cute little brunette in tow but they hadn't been around much.

Pete figured the girl for the one Nick had groped in the bathroom of the Sleep-In.

He wondered how the two had been spending their time. Checking out the Liberty Bell? Maybe the Betsy Ross House? He doubted it.

He adjusted the frequency on the receivers for Balboa's body wire.

Damn. Balboa and Grace had separated. Grace had left the living room and Nick. Pete could hear only the football game—he had a nickel on the Eagles—and Balboa's incessant humming, which Pete suspected was a calculated effort to make him crazy.

He wondered if he shouldn't have put a wire on Grace, too, just in case.

The thought of her trapped in a room with Skobelov or that gorilla he called a bodyguard made Pete sick.

His cell phone launched into Wild Cherry's "Play That Funky Music," and he flipped it open. "Yeah?"

"Morton's here with the girl. Just went upstairs with a bag of takeout from Happy Noodle."

"Good. Let's try to get a bug in there. Let me know if he goes anywhere."

Pete flipped the phone shut and propped his feet up on the dash, just as the announcer signed off on the football game.

Stinking Giants.

Chapter 15

Sunday, 8:18 p.m.
Wild One

The Russian's kitchen was a cook's nirvana, with a Viking stove, Sub-Zero refrigerator, granite countertops, Judge cookware and a spice rack that included obscure spices sold only by men in trench coats in the alleys of Chinatown.

Unlike Pete's bare refrigerator, Skobelov's was stocked with everything imaginable, from Caviar to cottage cheese.

The SieMatic cabinets held seven different kinds of rice, four kinds of flour, six kinds of honey and a bag of dried something called Hu-Hu that she suspected might be related to the insect family.

And for her listening pleasure, there was even a Bose Wave system mounted beneath one of the cabinets. Grace located the remote and tuned it to an eighties station, mostly to serve as a reminder of how she ended up there in that kitchen. Madonna, asking the all-important question, "Who's That Girl?"

"I don't know. I just don't know," Grace answered back.

She'd sent Nick out to the car for her bag, thankful that at the last minute she'd remembered to pack a couple of cookbooks. She wasn't sure she had the presence of mind to remember anything but her name right now. And even that was fuzzy.

She figured she'd start with some salted herring and a rich meat soup called *solyanka* for the first course. For a main dish, she'd chosen *golubtsy*—cabbage leaves stuffed with ground beef, rice and vegetables—easy to make but very tasty. And she'd decided to finish it off with a simple Ukranian honey cake.

An hour later, she was so engrossed in cooking she didn't even hear Tina clatter into the kitchen on her stilts.

"What are you doing?" Tina said.

Grace flung the cup of dried beans she was measuring in the air, and they rained down on the granite countertop like black hail. "Jesus. You scared me."

"Nervous type, huh?"

"Just a little."

The young woman chewed a long, red nail. "You don't look like Nick's kind of girl."

"So I've heard." Grace collected the spilled beans and swept them into the garbage disposal.

"Where'dja meet him?"

"Caligula."

"Ah. Eighties night." Tina nodded, as if that explained everything.

Grace put a hand on her hip. "Did you want something?"

"Nope."

Tina examined her cleavage and pulled a bra strap out from beneath the tank top, adjusting the slider before letting it snap back into place.

She was pretty, in a little-girl-in-the-big-wide-world kind of way. Nice skin, clear blue eyes. What was a pretty young woman like her doing with a pig like Skobelov?

Grace shook her head and turned back to the beans.

Tina slid onto a chair at the table, a massive golden oak affair with six chunky chairs. She straightened a leg and wiggled her ankle. "My dogs are barking. You mind if I take off my shoes?"

"Be my guest. I don't know how you can walk in those things."

"It sucks. But Viktor likes them. So do the men at the club."

"The club?"

"The Cat's Meow. I'm a dancer."

Aha. That explained it.

After a while, Grace said, "So how did you get into that line of work?"

Tina shrugged. "Just lucky, I guess. I was in my senior year of high school when I met this guy who ran a club. He said I had a good look, and I could make a lot of money. Way more than working at the mall or waitressing or something. So I started dancing on the weekends, and I eventually just quit school. I mean, what was the point? I figure I can always get my GED when my boobs start to sag."

Grace looked down at her own chest. She wanted to say, "That'll come sooner than you think," but she knew it was futile. The road to thirty was a long, slow, bumpy ride, and then after that it was nothing but freeway. You sped toward middle age doing ninety, stopping only for more and more frequent bathroom breaks.

"So what do you do?" Tina said.

"I'm a mother." Grace's tone was defensive, she knew, born from years of comments like "Oh, well. That's *okay*." Or, "Don't worry, you can always have a career when the children get a little older." People tended to look at stay-at-home mothers as if their heads were freakishly large or they were covered in boils.

Since when was being a mother such an easy job?

It wasn't. It was a lot like being a wilderness survival guide. She'd like to see those tight-ass executives sticking their hands in the toilet to remove a Barbie head, or reading *Goodnight Moon* seventeen times in a steam-filled bathroom with a coughing infant.

She sighed. "I'm a mother," she said again, this time without all the venom.

"Cool," said Tina. And she looked as if she actually meant it.

Grace could have hugged her.

She whisked a few eggs in a bowl and slowly added some flour, blending it to form a sticky dough. She turned the dough out onto a floured board and began to knead.

"You need some help?" Tina said.

"You can cut up that cabbage if you want."

Tina jumped up from the table and came over to the counter. "Where are the knives?"

"You don't know? I thought you lived here."

"I do, but, Viktor has a girl come in to cook a couple of nights a week. The rest of the time we eat at the club. I don't really cook."

"That's a shame. It can be very relaxing."

"Yeah?"

"Sure. Here, I'll show you."

For the next hour, Grace showed Tina how to chop vegetables, roll out dough and measure spices by using the palm of her hand. And as they cooked, the two met on that age-old common ground. Busting on their men.

"You should have seen him with that car," Grace said. "Every Sunday without fail, out in the garage rubbing it with a diaper. He imported his car wax from Australia."

Tina snorted. "You're exaggerating."

"Nope. He wouldn't even touch the thing without wearing a pair of white gloves. He looked like Mary Poppins."

"Yeah, well I got a good one about him." She jerked her head toward the television room.

"What's that?"

"He never misses an episode of *The Golden Girls*."

"You're kidding. *The Golden Girls?*"

"Yep. I think he has the hots for Bea Arthur." Tina chopped quietly for a moment. "I don't sleep with him, you know."

"It's really none of my business."

"He just keeps me around for show. Likes people to think we're a couple. But he's into weird stuff, ya know?"

"I got that impression."

Tina shrugged. "You wouldn't believe some of the shit I've seen."

Grace was suddenly queasy. "Is there any wine around here?"

Tina put her hands on her hips. "You know, you've got nice boobs. I have a shirt that would look great on you."

She practically skipped from the room, and Grace smiled. It was nice to have someone to talk to. A distraction.

She pulled the Ukranian honey cake out of the oven and put it on a wire rack to cool.

Tina was a good listener. She had a natural curiosity, asking all kinds of questions, and Grace wondered if maybe Tina was feeling unsettled with her life. Maybe wishing she was doing something more than dancing on a pole.

But, hey. At least she had a job. Grace had no idea what she'd be doing for money a couple of months from now. Maybe she'd be wishing for a pole and for anyone interested enough to watch her dance on it.

She hoisted her boobs higher. Maybe she could spend some of her settlement on some implants and get in on the Mammoth Mammary action at the Cat's Meow.

Tina came back to the kitchen with an armload of clothes, which she dumped on the kitchen table. She picked out an electric-pink wraparound blouse and held it up to Grace as she stirred the pot of *solyanka*.

"What do you think?" Tina said.

"It looks kind of…revealing for me."

Tina rolled her eyes. "You gotta advertise, Grace. Believe me, not many women have such a nice rack." She rooted through the pile and came out with a pair of pink-and-gold leopard-print pants.

"I don't know…"

"What?"

"Leopard print? It's not really me."

"It's cheetah. And animal patterns are classic. They never go out of style. You know why?"

Grace shook her head.

"Because they make women feel wild. Like they're hard to handle. Don't you want to feel wild sometimes?"

"If you only knew."

Tina rummaged through the pile again, digging out a pair of hot-pink high-heeled stilettos. "I brought shoes, too. It looks like we're about the same size."

"Tina, I appreciate the gesture. But—"

Tina snatched the wooden spoon from Grace and shoved the clothes in her arms. "Go on. Go try them on. The bathroom's that way."

Sunday, 9:45 p.m.
Little Red

The bathroom looked more like a day spa, complete with massage table, pedicure chair and several stainless-steel gadgets that could have been some sort of weird torture devices.

The room was bigger than her bedroom, with dark marble floors and an entire mirrored wall. The white whirlpool tub on the far side seated four. Or one big, fat Russian.

A double-wide white chaise longue rested in the corner atop a fuzzy white rug, with an overflowing basket of magazines beside it. *Vogue. Cosmopolitan. Us. People.*

Grace shed her own carefully chosen clothes and folded them neatly before slipping on the pink wraparound. She fastened the buttons, pulling the blouse tightly across her chest.

It was a top not constructed for those who wore a bra.

She removed hers and refastened the shirt, enjoying the newfound freedom. She couldn't remember the last time she'd gone without a bra. Probably at the same EarthSavers outing where she hadn't showered.

She squeezed into the cheetah-print pants, which had apparently been constructed of some miracle space-age fabric able to stretch enough to accommodate her more generous proportions. But there, too, underpants were *vestis non grata.*

She doffed her panties and stuffed them into the pocket of her folded pants, as she did at the gynecologist's office. Because, of course, unlike a full-on assault by the parts they covered, her underthings would be an affront to a gynecologist's delicate sensibilities.

Clothing in place, she slid her feet into Tina's shoes before turning to face herself in the mirrored wall. For a second she thought there was someone else in the bathroom with her. Then she realized that wild woman in the mirror was *her*.

She smoothed the blouse over her belly and turned from side to side, marveling at the way Tina's clothes hugged her curves and the way the high heels shaped her calves. Though she never hesitated to show off her legs, lately she'd taken to wearing loose shirts and baggy jackets to hide the rest of her.

This getup didn't leave much to the imagination. And, she thought with satisfaction, that was okay. As long as she could stay here in the bathroom.

True, no one would ever mistake her for a model or actress, but she didn't look too bad. She wondered what Lorraine and Misty and Brenda would think if they saw her in this getup.

It would definitely *not* get her invited to the Christmas party.

She took one last look at herself and gathered up her clothes. On her way out of the bathroom, she ran into Nick in the hallway.

He gave a low whistle. "Look at you." He ran a finger over her jawline and down her throat, stopping just before he reached her cleavage. "Smoking clothes, baby."

She leaned in for a fix of Aramis, coming dangerously close to bursting into flames. "Tina lent them to me."

"Nice."

For a split second he morphed into the wolf in the story of *Little Red Riding Hood*.

My, what big teeth you have.

She backed away slowly. No sudden moves. "Dinner will be ready in a few minutes. Think Mr. Skobelov is ready to eat?"

Nick laughed. It was a low, sexy sound that went straight to her toes. "He's always ready to eat."

"Right. Good. Okay." She tried to ease by, but he stood right in the middle of the hallway, forcing her to brush up against him.

He stuck out an arm and blocked her from passing, brushing his lips against her earlobe. "Let me tell you what *I'm* hungry for."

Then he whispered something so sinful, so physically convoluted and deliciously amoral, she couldn't even repeat it to herself.

She fanned herself with her hand, wondering if the laws of physics would even permit such a suggestion.

"Listen," she whispered. "I know you want Skobelov to think we're together. I understand that. But we aren't. So keep your…your *appetite* to yourself. Okay?"

She teetered off toward the kitchen in Tina's high heels, praying her knees would hold her up, at least until she was out of his sight.

Chapter 15.5

Sunday, 9:56 p.m.
Little Red Redux

Did he hear that right?

Pete adjusted the volume on the receiver. He wondered where Nick came up with this stuff. But more importantly, he wondered what Grace was wearing to elicit such a creative proposition.

Damn.

He shouldn't have let her go in there.

No, that was just Little Petey talking. He wanted Grace. Didn't want Balboa to have her.

Balboa was the type of guy who always got the girl. And Pete was the kind who pretended he didn't care. But he did.

Especially with this girl.

She was what his mother would call "well crafted," both

inside and out. Intelligent, funny, beautiful. The kind of woman who didn't notice men like him.

That was the story of his life. He was the guy all the girls wanted in high school—for a lab partner. The kind all the girls wanted in college—for a buddy.

He suspected his ex-wife had married him because he made her feel safe. He took care of her. Held her arm when they crossed the road. Checked out the house when she heard noises at night. But in the end, it wasn't enough.

She'd divorced him and married a karate instructor.

He hadn't even attempted to date since then. The past two years had been consumed with the Skobelov investigation, so there hadn't been much of a conflict. But now. Now, there was Grace.

He sighed and unfolded the papers he'd found in her purse in the hotel room. Release forms from a pharmaceutical distribution company for a large amount of Viagra to be shipped to an address in Lodi, California. But why would Grace have them?

He didn't even want to think about it.

His cell phone rang, and he flipped it open.

"Yeah, Lou."

"Morton's on the move."

"Great. Stay with him. Let me know where he ends up."

"Will do."

The toilet flushed in Pete's ear, and Balboa started humming again. Pete rubbed his eyes. He couldn't wait for this assignment to be over. He'd had about all the dealings with Nick Balboa he could take.

Chapter 16

Sunday, 10:48 p.m.
Fighting Squirrels

"What did I tell you? You look great." Tina turned Grace around in the kitchen and examined her from every angle. "How do you feel?"

"I have to admit, I feel pretty good. Just like you said. Wild. Sexy."

"Uh-huh. And the guys couldn't take their eyes off you at dinner."

"I've got news for you. It wasn't *me* they were looking at. It was the girls here." She hefted her bra-free bosom.

"You. The girls. What's the difference?"

Grace sighed. "I don't want to get attention that way. It's wrong."

Tina looked hurt. "You saying what I do is wrong?"

"No. It's just wrong for me."

Tina shook her head. "Lots of people judge me, ya know. They think I'm some kind of slut. But I'm not. I'm a dancer. And just because I'm proud of my body and I show it off doesn't mean I don't respect myself."

"I didn't mean to… I'm sorry, Tina. I'm not judging you. Really. I guess I'm just not comfortable putting myself out there like that."

"But you said yourself you feel good. What's wrong with that?"

"I don't know."

What *was* wrong with that? She hadn't always been so uptight about her body. When she was young—and much closer to perfect—she'd had no qualms about showing a little T and A. But now that she was older, now that her body had gone through perfectly normal changes, she was ashamed of it. Well, that just sucked.

Meanwhile, most men could walk around in a Speedo, with a package that jiggled like fighting squirrels and a belly like the Pillsbury Doughboy, and wouldn't think twice about the way they looked.

It just wasn't fair.

Grace and Tina loaded the dishwasher and scrubbed the pots in silence.

Nick came into the kitchen. "Well, you did it, baby."

"Did what?"

"Viktor. He loved the food."

"Yeah, he did," said Tina. "I haven't seen him so happy since he stopped having his back waxed."

"Eew."

Nick wrapped his arms around her waist and pulled her close. "Bottom line is you bought us some more time. Good job."

Tina gave her a questioning look, which she ignored. She

had no idea how much the young woman knew about Skobelov's business, but she sure wasn't going to be the one to clue her in on anything. The less Tina knew, the better.

Ditto for herself.

Grace peeled Nick off of her. "That's great. But we've got to clean up in here."

Nick nodded. "Viktor and I are gonna go out for a while. You two girls behave yourselves."

"Oh, goody," Tina said. "I want to do Grace's makeup."

Grace gave her a smile she hoped looked a little more enthusiastic than she felt. "Can't wait."

Sunday, 11:29 p.m.
Tattoo You

Tina's bedroom was done up in gold brocade and black lacquer, with a king-size bed, her own bathroom and a walk-in closet that would have housed a family of four in New York City.

She hustled Grace into the bathroom, sat her down in front of the mirror and poured her a glass of wine from a bottle she'd retrieved from a little refrigerator near the tub.

"Isn't this fun?" She picked up a hairbrush and started teasing Grace's hair. "When I was little, I got this big Barbie head for Christmas that you could put makeup on and fix her hair. I loved that thing."

"Maybe you'd be a good cosmetologist or a makeup artist."

Tina smiled. "You really are a mother, aren't you?"

"Can't help it."

"So what was all that about with Nick? What did he mean that you bought him more time?"

"He's working on a project for your…for Mr. Skobelov, and he needed a little more time."

"What kind of project?"

"I'm not sure, really. I don't ask."

Tina nodded. "I hear you. I don't really want to know about Viktor's business, ya know? What should we do with your eyes?"

"Do we have to do anything? Aren't they okay the way they are?"

"Don't be chicken. How about some Wild Heather eyeliner?"

"Sounds wonderful."

Apparently, Tina didn't get the sarcasm in her tone because she tilted Grace's head back and started penciling purple along her lids.

While her neck was busy cramping up, Grace thought she'd ask a few questions of her own.

"So how did you hook up with Viktor?"

Tina popped her gum. "I guess I just got lucky."

"Hmm. Yeah, but how did you meet him?"

Tina hesitated. "A mutual friend introduced us."

"Ah." Nick. It had to be. How many people had told her Nick preferred a girl like Tina?

"Are you from Philadelphia?"

"Uh-uh. Baltimore." Tina selected some eye shadow from her makeup case and held it up beside Grace's eyes. "Misty Mauve or Irish Rose?"

Because she wanted nothing more than to get her nose out of Tina's cleavage, she muttered, "May as well stick with the flower theme and go with Irish Rose."

"Good choice."

It seemed so odd to hear someone say that. She didn't feel like she'd made a good choice in quite a while. Most certainly not this weekend.

A good choice would have been to keep her simple hairstyle. A good choice would have been to say no to Tom when he'd asked her to sign the papers.

A good choice would have been to pick "truth" instead of "dare."

Well, hell. She'd made what she'd thought were good choices her whole life. Majoring in marketing when she really loved dance. Marrying Tom when she'd been enjoying her freedom. Natural childbirth.

In retrospect, they'd all left something to be desired. But at least they'd *seemed* like good choices at the time. Responsible choices.

The choices she'd made this weekend? Well, they hadn't even seemed good when she'd made them, but at least they made life a hell of a lot more stimulating.

"I doubt the guys will be home anytime soon," Tina said, looking at her watch. "How about a henna tattoo?"

Hmm. A henna tattoo? Not a good choice.

"Go for it."

Tina grinned. "I like you, Grace."

"I like you, too."

Tina rooted through a makeup case the size of a steamer trunk and pulled out her henna kit.

She poured Grace another glass of wine. "After we do tattoos, I'll teach you some dance moves."

"Can't wait."

Monday, 6:43 a.m.
Bungee Jumping

Momentary panic engulfed Grace when she opened her eyes to the dark red chain links encircling her bicep.

Had she met a sailor in Tina's bathroom? Had she joined the Navy?

Then she remembered. The tattoo wasn't real. Unlike the nasty headache, which definitely was.

She had to stop drinking. Really.

So far this weekend alone, she'd given away her panties and a twenty-thousand-dollar ring, made out with two complete strangers, agreed to cook for an insane Russian mobster, got a tattoo and learned how to dance like a stripper. What was next? Jumping out of a cake at a bachelor party? Bungee jumping naked off the Betsy Ross Bridge?

She dragged her ass out of bed and down the hall to the bathroom, where she splashed some cold water on her face and caught her reflection in the mirror.

She looked like a psychotic raccoon.

She grabbed her cell phone out of the charger, which she'd thankfully remembered to bring, and slunk out to the kitchen. No one else was up, which didn't surprise her. Nick and Skobelov hadn't returned until after three, and Tina had drunk as much wine as she had.

If the batter for the blini she planned to make this morning didn't have to rise twice, she wouldn't be up herself. But she had to hold up her end of the bargain—distract Skobelov with carbs and butter.

It seemed silly, but she didn't want to let Pete down.

She wondered if he and Louis had located the computer key yet. From the conversation she'd overheard last night between Skobelov and Nick, time was running out. The Russian was getting antsy, and no amount of *rasstegai* or *solyanka* was going to help.

She had to admit that Skobelov scared her, more than just a little. It was less what he said than how he said it. Less how he looked at her than what she saw in his eyes. Nothing. Absolutely nothing. Not a touch of humor. No forgiveness. Not a modicum of understanding or compassion.

He was like a sadistic little kid with a magnifying glass, and everyone else was just an ant on the sidewalk. Everyone near him walked around in fear, wondering when they were going to get fried. Even Nick seemed a little intimidated.

Grace wondered what had made him decide to become an informant. He had to know what would happen if Skobelov found out.

She finished the blini batter and removed a package of smoked salmon from the refrigerator. It tasted better at room temperature. Then she boiled the eggs for the *okroshka* she planned to make for lunch.

At 8:01 a.m. she decided it was late enough to call her mother.

She poured another cup of coffee and settled into the breakfast nook with her cell phone. When she flipped it open, she saw that she had a message from Tom. She punched in the access code for her voice mail.

"Gracie, where in the hell are you? I need to talk to you. I need those papers. Call me, please."

His typical composure, and the clipped diction that had first impressed her and then later driven her crazy, were gone. He sounded on edge. Nervous, even. And Tom didn't get nervous.

She called his cell phone, but he didn't answer. She refused to call his home phone. No way did she want to talk to Marlene.

Besides, he really wasn't going to be happy when he found out that she no longer had the papers and wasn't sure where they were.

She hit the speed dial for her parents' number.

"Hi, Mom."

"Grace! I left a couple of messages on your home phone. Did you get them?"

"Actually, I haven't been home. I spent the night at a friend's house."

"A friend?"

Did she detect a note of disapproval in her mother's tone?

A *note?* Hell, it was more like an entire symphony.

"Yes, a *friend*. Her name is Tina."

"Oh, do I know her?"

"No. I'm pretty sure you don't."

"What does *she* do?"

Ever since her mother had gone back to work part-time at the Wicks 'n' Sticks in the mall, she'd become a real career woman.

"She's, ah…she's in the entertainment business."

"Oh? What, like the record business or something?"

"No. Dinner theater."

"Interesting. Maybe your father and I could go see her sometime. We love the theater, you know."

By "the theater" her mother meant the First Presbyterian Players' production of *Oklahoma*.

"I'll try to get you tickets. I'm sure you'd enjoy the show. How are the kids?"

"They're fine. Megan is on the phone all the time, though. Did you know she talks to boys?"

"I suspected as much."

"And you approve of that?"

Grace sighed. "Mom, if I could have, I would have kept them all in diapers for the rest of their lives. But they have to grow up, don't they? Whether we like it or not."

Her mother was uncharacteristically silent for a moment. "I suppose they do."

Grace had no doubt her mother was remembering *her* in diapers and wondering where the years went. She could hear the nostalgia seeping through the quiet hum of the phone line.

"I love you, Mom," Grace said.

"I love you, too."

"Can you keep the kids one more night? Take them to school tomorrow morning? I'll pick them up after."

"Of course, dear. I know you have a lot on your mind."

"You have no idea."

Chapter 16.5

Monday, 8:22 a.m.
Champagne Hangover

Pete fell out of the chair in which he'd fallen asleep listening to Balboa's snoring, after Balboa had apparently fallen asleep in Skobelov's living room with his face right near the bug.

Pete picked himself up off the floor and wiped the drool from the corners of his mouth, stumbling toward the kitchen to make a pot of coffee.

He loaded the filter to the brim. The blacker the better.

Maybe he could just skip the middleman and snort the coffee grounds instead.

He guessed that Nick would be asleep for a few more hours at least, considering the night he'd had at the Cat's Meow. A night that yielded absolutely nothing in the way of usable information against Skobelov but plenty of moans and sighs from the ladies giving lap dances in the Champagne Room.

The Russian must have been licking his wounds from the Eagles' loss to the Giants and brought Nick along for the ride. Literally.

Unfortunately, Pete had been stuck in his car in the parking lot with the body wire receiver all night, with nothing to think about except what Grace might be doing back at the apartment.

At least he hadn't been worried about her safety. With Nick and Skobelov at the Cat's Meow, there wasn't a whole lot to worry about.

He yawned and wondered if he had enough time to take a shower before Nick woke up. He checked to make sure the feed from the bug was being recorded and trudged upstairs, coffee mug in hand.

Just before he stepped into the shower, his cell phone rang. "Yeah?"

"It's Lou. Morton's on the move. He left the chippie in the hotel room and he's driving into Jersey in a little rented piece of crap. Friggin' tin can with wheels."

"He heading north or south?"

"North. Could be going to New York."

"Nah. I don't think so. If he had business in New York, why wouldn't he have flown into New York? Why would he be staying near Philadelphia?"

"You seen the price of a hotel room in New York?"

"Maybe he's got something set up with Johnny Iatesta in Trenton," Pete said.

Lou was silent for a minute. "Makes sense. Iatesta does a good business with counterfeit credit cards."

"Yeah. And the state police in Jersey have been on him for immigration violations. Fake social security cards, that kind of thing."

"Think Morton's trying to get a bidding war going between Iatesta and Skobelov?"

"That would be my guess. Just stay on him, okay? Let me know what happens."

"Right. Later."

Chapter 17

Monday, 9:30 a.m.
Charo's Blouse

When Grace got back to her bedroom after taking a shower, Tina was sitting on her bed, her wallet in hand.

"Oh, sorry." Tina blushed. "I just... I thought you might have some pictures of your kids. I didn't have any brothers and sisters growing up, and I—"

"It's okay. Here." She took the wallet from Tina and opened up a little snap to reveal an accordion of snapshots. "This is Megan, my oldest. And this is Kevin. He's ten. And this is Callie, my youngest."

"This your husband?" Tina pointed to a picture of Tom standing beside his Corvette.

"My ex. Yeah."

Tina had a funny look on her face.

"What's the matter?"

"Nothing." She sighed. "I just wonder if I'll ever have that. A husband and a family and all that. Dancers don't have the most stable lives, ya know?"

Grace sat down on the bed beside the younger woman. "You don't have to be a dancer forever."

Tina smiled. "Thanks, *Mom*."

"What can I say? Dress me like a wild woman, but underneath I'm still a mother."

"Speaking of wild women, what are you going to wear today?"

Grace pulled a pair of chinos and a lavender scoop-neck T-shirt out of her bag.

"No, no, no-o-o." Tina stuffed the clothes back into her bag. "That shirt won't even show your tattoo. Come on, I'll fix you up."

"You don't have to do that, Tina. Really."

"Oh, I don't mind. I have tons of clothes. Viktor really spoils me that way. He likes me to look good."

"Yeah, but—"

Tina grabbed her hand and pulled her off the bed. "I'll do your hair, too, while we're at it."

Grace bit her tongue.

She wouldn't pooh-pooh an offer of help in that area. She guessed the trade-off for hair that didn't have a brush tangled in it would have to be clothes that looked like they'd been worn in a Whitesnake video.

Tina led her down the long hall and into her own bedroom, disappearing into the huge walk-in closet. Grace sat down on the bed—which she was surprised to find neatly made—and examined her surroundings.

There seemed to be very little of a personal nature in Tina's room. No framed photographs on the nightstand. No bric-a-brac. No jewelry lying around.

"How long did you say you've lived here?" Grace said.

Tina's voice sounded as if it were coming from a cave. "About six months, I guess."

"Where did you live before that?"

"Here and there. Nowhere special." Tina emerged from her closet with several garments draped over her arm. She held up the clothes. "I found the perfect outfit for you."

Grace eyed the blue lamé rhumba blouse and black cigarette pants. "Wow. That's something else."

"Isn't it? I'll get you some shoes."

Grace held the ruffled blouse up to her chest and looked in the mirror.

"Did you get this shirt off of eBay or something? It was Charo's, right?"

"Who's Charo?"

Grace shook her head. At least she wouldn't see anyone she knew. It was unlikely Misty or Brenda or Lorraine would be walking around this part of town.

"Cuchi-cuchi," she muttered beneath her breath.

Monday, 11:44 a.m.
Lucky

In the middle of breakfast, the phone rang.

Skobelov, his mouth stuffed with blini, looked at Nick.

"You want me to get it?" Nick said.

Skobelov nodded.

Nick wiped his hands on his pants and picked up the phone. "Yo."

He listened for a while and then put his hand over the mouthpiece of the phone. "It's Morton," he said to Skobelov. "He's in Philadelphia. He wants to meet you. Says he got an offer from Johnny Iatesta for the files and wants to give you a chance to make a counteroffer."

"I already paid him. What? He offer me my own damn property now?"

"I'll take care of it," Nick said.

"No. You take care of enough already. I have another thing for you." Skobelov wiped his mouth.

"Another thing?" said Nick.

Skobelov pointed to the phone. "Tell him I'll meet him. At the club." He looked at his watch. "Two o'clock."

Nick put the phone to his ear. "He says he'll meet you. Two o'clock at a club called the Cat's Meow, on Cottman Avenue. You got a car? Okay. Okay."

Nick hung up the phone. "He'll be there."

Skobelov nodded.

"You sure you don't want me to go with you?" Nick said.

"Nah. You blow this once already. I got another job for you." Skobelov motioned to Tina. "Get me pen."

He scribbled on an envelope and handed it to Nick. "You know this guy. Go get him. He is being very difficult. I need to talk to him."

Nick looked at the envelope and then at Grace.

She raised her eyebrows.

Nick gave her a little shrug. To Skobelov he said, "Where do you want me to take him?"

"To the club also. Today I take care of two assholes at once, no?" He laughed and stuffed his mouth with another forkful of blini.

"I'm going with you, Vik," Tina said. "I have to work at three." To Grace, she said, "You wanna come along?"

Grace's cell phone rang, and she pulled it out of the back pocket of the cigarette pants.

"Hello?"

"Don't go." Pete's voice was low and calm. "Make an excuse."

She hesitated. "Okay. I'll be sure to do that."

"Call me back after they leave."

"Will do. Okay. Bye."

She closed the cell phone and it slipped out of her nervous hands, skittering beneath the table. She went down on her hands and knees and crawled under the table, coming face-to-face with the Russian's fat knees.

Figured. He had two different-colored socks on.

She retrieved the phone and resurfaced.

"Who was that?" Tina asked.

"Oh. My mom. She wants to borrow my, uh…my lobster pot."

"You got a lobster pot?" Tina said.

"Sure, doesn't everybody?"

Tina shrugged.

Skobelov looked at Nick. "What you waiting for?"

Nick hesitated and looked at Grace.

"You hump your girlfriend later, eh? Go."

Nick gave Grace one last, lingering look as he left the kitchen.

"So, you wanna go with us or what?" Tina asked Grace.

"Actually, I think I'll hang out here. Do the dishes, get a start on dinner. Is there anything special you want, Mr. Skobelov?"

The Russian rubbed his jaw. "You make *pelmeni*?"

"Of course. It's my specialty."

Skobelov smiled, showing tiny brown teeth that looked like dried mung beans. "Nicky is lucky man."

"Why?" Grace said, completely forgetting that she and Nick were supposed to be an item.

Skobelov laughed, but Grace caught Tina staring at her, an unidentifiable look in her eyes.

Not for the first time, she wondered if Tina might not be as ditzy as she pretended to be.

A few minutes later, Grace watched from the window as Skobelov's long black Cadillac emerged from one of the over-sized doors of the building's four-thousand-square-foot garage. From her vantage point, she could see Benny the Brick Wall driving. She wondered if there was anyone guarding the desk in the lobby or if she was all alone in the building.

Not a comforting thought.

She ran into her bedroom and locked the door before picking up her phone and dialing Pete's number.

"Yeah." Pete's voice nearly made her sob with relief, and she realized just how insecure she'd been feeling without him around.

"They're gone."

"All of them?"

"Nick, Skobelov and Tina. And a guy named Benny was driving them. I don't know if there's anyone else in the building."

"Good. Get your stuff together. It's time to get you out of there. I'll meet you out at the corner in ten minutes."

"Right."

She stuffed her cell phone in her purse, on the verge of tears. She didn't know if it was because she was relieved to be leaving or sad that she wasn't going to make *pelmeni*.

Probably both. It felt good to cook for people who really appreciated it, even if they were felons.

Monday, 12:26 p.m.
Ch-ch-changes

On her way out the door, Grace realized she hadn't changed. She was still wearing Tina's clothes.

Well, it was too late now.

She doubted Tina would miss them, but she still vowed to somehow get the clothes back to her.

She wondered if Tina would get arrested along with Skobelov and felt a pang of regret for the younger woman, whose only mistake had been to give in to the lure of a tampon-factory penthouse and a Frederick's of Hollywood credit card with no limit.

Grace gave the place one last look and locked the door behind her, admiring the Michelangelo again as she waited for the elevator. Which didn't come.

She pushed the button again, but then noticed she needed a key to operate the elevator.

Crap.

An examination of the little vestibule revealed a door that led to a dim, concrete stairwell.

Noise echoed eerily off the putty-colored cinder block walls, making her own breathing sound like a pit full of vipers. At ground level she peered through the narrow glass window, out into a deserted lobby.

The heavy door groaned on its hinges as she emerged from the stairwell. She took shallow breaths, waiting for someone to pop up from behind the desk like an oversize jack-in-the-box with multiple piercings and a scary clown tattoo.

But the place remained quiet as a…well, as a deserted tampon factory. She hustled to the door she and Nick had entered, past the camera mounted above the desk. The bright sunlight outside threw her. Though she knew it was only midday, it felt as if it should be dark. She'd been at Skobelov's for less than twenty-four hours, but it had felt like a week.

Resisting the urge to look behind her just in case someone was watching, she hung a right and walked calmly to the corner. A chilly wind made the ruffles on the Charo blouse dance, and she realized she'd forgotten her coat in the hall closet.

A bright pink flier skittered up the sidewalk and pasted itself to her leg. She bent down and peeled it off her calf. A two-for-one special at Paco Taco.

She crumpled it up and then realized she didn't have any pockets, so she bent down and unzipped the duffel and stuffed it in.

When she stood up, Pete's Taurus was driving past.

"Hey!"

His car jerked to a stop and then backed up. He unrolled the passenger side window.

Her stomach did a little flip.

He leaned over on the seat and said, "Sorry. I didn't realize that was you."

"You were looking right at me. Who did you think it was?"

Two bright spots of color emerged on his cheeks. "Never mind."

She opened the car door and threw her bag into the backseat before sliding in beside him in the front.

"You look…different," he said. "Is that a tattoo?"

"Tina gave me a makeover. What do you think?"

"I think the 'Chiquita Banana' girl wants her shirt back."

Chapter 17.5

Monday, 12:28 p.m.
Wet Dreams

Pete had to fight to keep his eyes on the road.

What was she wearing?

He wasn't lying when he said he didn't see her back there. What he'd seen was the stuff of his adolescent wet dreams—a cross between Carmen Miranda, Cheryl Ladd and a Times Square hooker who would do anything for fifteen bucks.

The ruffly shirt was killing him.

"Where are we going?" she asked.

"Back to my place. We have to wait to hear from Nick."

"Isn't he wired?"

"Yeah, but he's way out of range. Besides, he's nowhere near Morton, and that's who we're interested in."

"Who's Nick with?"

Pete debated how much he should tell her.

Just then his phone rang. Saved by the bell. Or rather, by the sound of Wild Cherry.

"Yeah."

"It's Lou. Morton's leaving the motel."

"Okay. Keep me posted. I'm going to drop Grace off at my place. Let me know when he gets to the club."

Pete felt a rush of adrenaline. This was it. The payoff was so close he could practically taste the celebratory champagne.

As soon as he had Skobelov, Morton and the memory key in the same place at the same time, his case would be made. With Nick's corroboration, the wiretap and bug recordings, along with some physical evidence, they'd get the Russian on numerous fraud and identity theft charges.

Soon, all of this would be a memory.

He looked at Grace in her ruffly shirt and thought about how some things would be much easier to remember than others.

Of all the cases he'd worked, none had been as aggravating, or as interesting, as this one. And the "interesting" part was largely due to the woman sitting beside him.

It was going to be tough saying goodbye to her. He reached over to touch her shoulder as she looked out the window, but snatched his hand back before he made contact.

Jesus. When had he turned into such a schmuck? Maybe it was time to seriously consider retiring. When a man couldn't let go of a case without an ache in his gut, something was seriously wrong.

Chapter 18

Pete dropped Grace's duffel inside his front door. "Here you go. I'll talk to you later."

"No way. I want to go with you."

Pete sighed. "You're imagining you're Nancy Drew again."

"Oh, come on. You can't just leave me here."

"You're right." He fished her keys from his pants pocket and dropped them into her palm. "Go home. But don't leave the country. I may need you later on."

"Pete—"

"I'm going to the Cat's Meow. If you show up there, how are you going to explain your presence to Skobelov? You didn't have a car while you were at his apartment."

She hesitated. "Good point."

"If things end the way I think they will, it could get dangerous, Grace." He touched her face. "You were a big help, but your part is over now."

She was worried about Tina, and Pete, too. And even a little bit about Nick. But she knew Pete was right. She was a mother, for God's sake. She should go home. Call her kids. Take a nice hot bath.

She nodded. "Okay. Will you call me when it's over? Let me know how it went?"

"Won't Nick do that?"

"Aagh." She growled with frustration. "For the last time, Nick is *not* my boyfriend."

But Pete was already smiling. "I know. He was wearing a wire, remember? I heard you send him packing."

He slid his fingers over her cheek into her hair, pulling her close. His lips covered hers. His kiss took her breath away. She closed her eyes, and wrapped her arms around his neck.

The kiss seemed to go on forever. Pete ran a hand down her side and settled it on her hip. She leaned against him, but before she could get comfortable, he pulled away.

"I have to go."

"You're leaving me here alone?"

"I trust you. Just make sure the door is locked when you leave."

She nodded. "Be careful."

"I will. Go home."

"I will."

He gave her one last, quick kiss, and then he was gone.

She stood there for a moment in Pete's small foyer, letting her heart settle into a regular beat. It seemed as if she'd been on edge for so long, she wondered if her adrenaline levels would ever be normal again.

She decided a drink of water might help slake the seemingly unquenchable thirst she'd had the whole weekend.

In the kitchen, red lights glowed all over the receivers on the table, and Grace knew from watching Lou that they were recording whatever was going on in Skobelov's living room and on Nick's wire.

She grabbed a glass from the cabinet beside the sink and ran some tap water in it. While she was drinking, the receiver for Nick's wire let out a startling squawk.

Grace dropped the glass into the sink with a thunk.

Nick must have just come back within range of the receiver.

She heard his voice over the receiver. "Grace has them. They're in her purse. I saw them."

"When did you see Grace?" said another voice. A defensive voice, with neat, clipped diction.

Tom.

Could Tom be the guy Skobelov had sent Nick to pick up?

She knew Tom was acquainted with Nick, but with Skobelov? Why? How?

She hurried over to the receiver, straining to hear the conversation that was interrupted by fits of static.

"…no big deal. We met at a club."

"Wasn't that a coincidence?" Tom said, a note of suspicion in his voice.

"Listen, man. I'm trying to help you. Skobelov isn't happy with you."

"You're sure Grace has the papers?" Tom said.

"She did Friday night."

There was a long silence. Then Tom said, "Did you hook up with my wife?"

"Wouldn't that be your *ex*-wife?" Nick said. "And why shouldn't I hook up with her? She's hot."

Grace couldn't help but smile. What she wouldn't give to see Tom's face at that moment.

"You goddamned sh—"

"Relax, man," Nick said. "I just wanted to talk to her about a business proposition."

"A business proposition? What the hell?" Now Tom was getting out of control. "If you've dragged my wife into something—"

"Hey. Let's not talk about this right now, okay?"

"Bullshit. We are going to talk about it."

"I'd advise against it," Nick said.

"I don't care what you'd advise against, you *a*-hole."

"A-hole?" Nick sounded amused. "Okay, then, *Tom Becker*. Let's talk about it." Nick spoke slowly and clearly. "If you don't deliver the shipment of Viagra you promised Skobelov, you better kiss your ass goodbye."

Silence, and then Tom's voice, quiet and tired. "Christ. How did I ever get into this?"

The Viagra wasn't for Tom, Grace realized. It was for Skobelov.

And she suspected it wasn't for his personal use. She wondered exactly how much Viagra those papers were meant to release.

Hadn't Pete said that Skobelov was involved in all kinds of things? Things like Internet drug sales, maybe?

How *had* Tom gotten into that?

Goddamned Marlene. She'd bet on it. Marlene and her insatiable desire for designer clothes and five-star vacations. And Tom was just stupid enough to do it for her, too.

"Listen," she heard Nick say. "We'll swing by Skobelov's. Grace is there. You'll get the papers, show them to Viktor, tell him you'll have the stuff by Monday, and that's that. No big deal."

"Grace is at Skobelov's?" Tom had gone from defeated to incredulous.

It was amazing how much emotion you could hear in somebody's voice. She'd never realized how much before. Then again, she'd never listened to conversations over a body wire before.

And that's when she realized that the whole conversation Tom and Nick just had—the one where they discussed her forging papers and Tom's involvement in procuring Viagra—had been recorded.

Was *still* being recorded. Right there, in Pete's kitchen.

She dove for her phone and dialed Tom's cell number. It rang once, twice, three times—a ring she couldn't hear over Nick's wire—until finally someone answered.

"Hello?"

Shit. Marlene.

"Hello? Hello!"

Grace closed her eyes and counted to three. "Marlene, it's Grace."

"Oh. Grace. Tom isn't here."

"I know. I need to get a message to him. It's urgent—"

"Urgent. I see." Marlene sighed. "Grace, aren't you tired of all the theatrics?" Marlene spoke slowly and calmly, as if she were dealing with an escaped mental patient.

"Marlene, listen to me. If Tom calls, you have to tell him—"

"I'm sorry, Grace. I don't have to tell him anything. I'm not your messenger girl, and I refuse to let you drag me into the middle of your problems."

Wha-a-at? Grace's mouth fell open. "Excuse me, but you *created* my problems when you decided to coat yourself in jelly and roll around on my good Ralph Lauren sheets."

Marlene sighed again. "Must we point fingers, Grace? Do we have to rehash that scene over and over?"

"I'm not reha—"

"I can't believe you're so petty."

"So *petty?* Are you *kidding* me?" *Breathe. Breathe. Breathe.* "Listen, Marlene. If Tom calls you, just tell him to call me on my cell phone as soon as possible."

"Right. I'll tell him it's *urgent.*"

"You little—" A very bad word came to Grace's lips, but before she could release it into the cellular universe, Marlene had already hung up.

Grace squeezed the phone, imagining it was Marlene's wrinkled little neck.

Think, think.

She wished she had Nick's cell phone number, but she didn't.

She could call Pete, but then what? She would have to tell him that Tom was working with Skobolev—that is, if he didn't already know.

"…want to get her involved," Tom said.

What?

Grace turned up the volume on the receiver.

"I mean, she's the mother of my children," Tom went on. "I never should have asked her to sign those papers."

"Hey," said Nick. "Why not? She's got a God-given talent. Why not have her use it?"

"That's what you were going to do, wasn't it?"

"Listen," Nick said. "I was just gonna capitalize on an opportunity. What's wrong with that?"

"What's wrong is that Grace is a good person. I didn't tell you that stuff about her so you could recruit her for some scheme. I just… I just wanted you to think I was, you know, cool. That I understood all this underworld crap because I had a wife who'd done time for forgery." Tom sighed. "If I'd have known you would try to use her…"

"Like you did?" Nick said.

"I really have been a shit." Tom's breathing came heavy. "I

pretty much forced her into signing those papers. I used my kids' security as a carrot. I'm such an asshole."

Imagine that. Tom wasn't as big a prick as she'd thought.

She bit her lip to keep from crying.

"So, what? You don't want to go get Grace?" Nick said. "See if she has the papers?"

"No. Just take me to Skobelov."

Monday, 12:52 p.m.
In the Grinder

No, no, no.

She couldn't let it happen. She'd seen Skobelov. She knew what he was like.

He was like a shark.

She shivered.

She had to get to Tom. Tell him to get out of the ocean. Stay away from the shark.

As soon as Pete arrested Skobelov, Tom would be out of danger.

Wait. Not true.

She looked at the receiver on the table. Everything Tom and Nick had just said had been recorded on the machine. Tom was in this way too deep to get out of it unscathed. There was no way to erase what he'd said. It was burned onto a CD.

She could take the disk, but she had no idea what else was on it or what might need to be recorded later. It could mean the difference between Skobelov getting what he deserved or getting away with everything.

She couldn't take that chance. She wouldn't endanger Pete's investigation.

But she could at least save Tom from getting his ass kicked

by the Russian. As for her own ass, there was no doubt it would be in the grinder as soon as Pete heard those recordings.

She grabbed her bag and headed for the door, hoping she could make it to the Cat's Meow before they did.

Chapter 18.5

Monday, 12:52 p.m.
Tunnel Vision

Lou had already arrived at the Cat's Meow by the time Pete got there. He pulled into a spot near the end of the parking lot, next to Lou's Chrysler sedan, and took a deep breath.

This was it. This was *it*.

The Russian and Morton together under one roof, negotiating a price for thirty thousand names and social security numbers.

But where in the hell was Balboa and his body wire? Without proof that this meeting had gone down, the event would be as believable as Bigfoot meeting the Loch Ness Monster. No matter how many witnesses there were, it was only a myth until hard proof could be offered up.

He couldn't take a chance that Balboa would be a no-show.

He popped the trunk latch for the Taurus and went around to the back of the car. Opening one of the large plastic containers, he removed a palm-size black box. Attached by a short wire to the box was a tiny camera lens, no bigger than the tip of a pen.

He taped the box to the inside of a black Flyers baseball cap and threaded the camera lens through a small hole, until it rested on the brim of the cap. It was virtually invisible against the black-and-orange lettering on the cap.

In the event that Nick didn't show, Pete would at least have a video of the meeting. No audio, though. He didn't want to get too close.

He pulled the cap onto his head and adjusted the brim before setting up a small video receiver in the trunk and plugging it into a power inverter. He turned it on, and a picture of his trunk sprang to life on the screen.

He turned his head this way and that, checking to make sure the receiver picked up a clean signal when he moved.

When he was certain everything worked, he turned the recording device on and shut the trunk.

He smiled. He'd heard about this. The brass ring. The silver lining. The light at the end of the tunnel.

And in a case that had been nothing but a train wreck, that light sure looked good about now.

He just hoped the light wasn't attached to a train that was gonna hit him head-on.

Chapter 19

The parking lot was full. One-fifteen on a Monday afternoon, and the parking lot was friggin' full.

Who *were* these men who hung out at a strip joint on a Monday afternoon?

She doubled back through the parking lot and around the rear of the Cat's Meow, taking a detour through the alley where Pete had caught her leaving the club the day before.

As she entered the alley, the back door opened and three men emerged. Two extra-large and one medium.

The first extra-large was Benny the Brick Wall, sporting a black cowboy hat, a scowl and a healthy bulge beneath the too-tight gray sport coat he wore. The second extra-large was more monolith than a brick wall. He resembled a statue on Easter Island, broad and flat and seemingly chiseled out of stone.

And the unfortunate medium being muscled along between them was—

Oh, boy.

It was Tom.

As she drove past, Grace ducked down as far as she could behind the steering wheel. But like typical men, they weren't looking at her, they were looking at the Beemer. That marvel of German engineering.

She'd like to put a 540i onstage in the club and see which the boys were more likely to ogle—half-naked girls or thirty-seven hundred pounds of sculpted steel.

Whether or not Tom recognized the car as hers was anybody's guess. She imagined he was pretty nervous. But if he *had* recognized it, or her, he'd given no outward indication.

She cruised past and watched in the rearview mirror as the three men disappeared into the building across the alley from the club.

Damn. That couldn't be good.

She circled the lot again, forced to wait until a guy in a pickup truck lit a cigarette, dialed his cell phone and fiddled with the radio before finally giving up his parking spot.

Heels clicking on the macadam, she hurried into the alley. Now the Cat's Meow was to her right, and the building where Benny and his Easter Island friend had taken Tom was to the left.

She debated what to do. Should she try to go into the Cat's Meow and get help? But who would help her?

Nick? He was the one who'd brought Tom here in the first place.

Pete? She wasn't even sure he was here. But even if he was,

she doubted he'd be willing to mess up his investigation to save her ex-husband's ass.

And that left…

Nobody.

Nobody but her.

Tom's ass was in her hands.

She shuddered at the thought. But still, she had to do *something*. After all, he may have screwed up royally but he was still the father of her children.

She veered left, edging her way along the tan corrugated siding until she reached a narrow slit of a window, about chin high, that stretched for about three or four feet. She tried to look in, but the window had been covered with brown butcher paper from the inside.

She made it to the door and pressed her ear against the cold metal, but she couldn't hear a thing through the industrial-weight door. She rattled the door handle, which was, of course, locked.

Now what, Nancy Drew?

The answer was simple. Knock. But she needed something first.

She searched the alley until she found what she was looking for. A small square of cardboard the size of a playing card. She slipped it down the front of her blouse and pounded on the door.

No one answered.

She pounded again, harder.

Benny opened the door a half minute later, minus the cowboy hat but still wearing the scowl. The light of recognition flashed in his bulldog eyes.

"Hi. Benny, isn't it? I'm looking for Nick Balboa. Is he with you?"

"No, he ain't with me. Get outta here." He started back in.

"Wait! Can you tell me where Nick is?"

"Not my turn to be his babysitter."

Nice guy.

Benny disappeared and the door swung shut, but not before Grace was able to get the cardboard in between the door and the latch, so it closed but couldn't lock.

Now all she had to do was wait until Benny had gone back to whatever it was he'd been doing.

As she waited, her bladder sprang to life the way it always did when she played warden with the neighborhood kids. Warden was a rather sadistic, preteen version of hide-and-seek, played in the dark with flashlights over a whole neighborhood block. One kid would be the warden, the others would be inmates who'd escaped from prison. The prisoners would have to hide and, once in a spot, could not leave that spot until they were found or called in for dinner by their mothers.

Without fail, Grace would have to pee almost as soon as the game had begun. She'd sit beneath a shrub in torturous pain until she finally had to quit and run home.

Wouldn't it be great if she could run home right now? But that was, of course, out of the question. This time, she was the warden.

So she opened the door and stepped into what appeared to be some sort of evil genius's laboratory.

Monday, 1:28 p.m.
WWCAD?

A machine that looked like an oversize roller-coaster car sat in the middle of the floor, surrounded by a low scaffolding platform. The row of fluorescent lights hanging above it were unlit; a noisy humming sound emanated from the thing, as if it were growling at her.

Tall shelves that stretched from floor to ceiling, loaded with boxes of unidentifiable content, lined the long wall beside it. A chemical odor hung in the air, reminding her of the smell of her fourth-grade classroom after the teacher had handed out freshly mimeographed math quizzes.

Just as stupid women in horror movies will do, instead of turning tail and running, she wandered farther in and let the door close behind her.

The place was dim except for a flood of bright light spilling over the floor from an open doorway at the end of the wall. An occasional shadow broke the strip of light, and she knew from watching too many detective shows that that had to be where she would find Tom.

She pulled off one of Tina's shoes, testing the heft in her hand, slashing the spiked heel down in front of her like a butcher knife.

Not bad. She could definitely put an eye out.

She removed the other shoe and crept toward the light, avoiding the growling monstrosity in the center of the cold cement floor. After what seemed an eternity, she reached the door. She flattened herself against the wall and leaned in, peeking around the doorjamb.

The room was a small office, furnished only with a couple of filing cabinets, a chrome-and-particle-board desk and a battered chair on wheels. Tom sat on the chair, elbows resting on the desk, his head in his hands.

His right eye was centered in a big red circle, which was sure to become a big black circle by tomorrow. A small trickle of blood had escaped his nose.

It looked like Benny and his friend had wasted no time.

Suddenly, the machine let out a big, long hiss and went quiet. The place turned eerily silent. The kind of silent where you think you might have died and just didn't know it yet, and you wanted to make some noise—any noise—to prove that theory wrong.

Grace jerked away from the doorway and stood completely still, her heart pounding painfully in her chest.

"Finally," Benny said from within the office. "I hate that friggin' noise. Now, where were we?"

"Our friend was gonna call his distribution center," said the other simian. "Weren't cha?"

"No," Tom said. "I wasn't. I told you, I don't have the authority to release large amounts of pharmaceuticals. Not without an order from a legitimate distributor and a signed release form from my boss. And I can't get that. At least not today."

"Like I said," Benny said, "every day Mr. Skobelov's clients have to go without the valuable medication you supply, they suffer horrible anguish. Do you know what it's like not to be able to bone your girlfriend?"

"I could hazard a guess," Tom said.

He could? Grace idly wondered if he'd ever had trouble boning Marlene.

Yuck.

"And every day Mr. Skobelov's clients can't get the medication they need is one more day Mr. Skobelov's reputation suffers. Which means *you* have to suffer. Understand?"

"I get it," Tom said. "But I'm telling you, there's nothing I can do. The procedures have changed. I don't have access to the stuff anymore. I'm afraid I'm going to have to bow out of this deal."

Benny and his friend yukked it up, as if someone had just told a joke about a rabbi, a priest and a duck going into a bar.

"He's gonna hafta bow out," said Benny.

"Yeah," said the monolith. "Bow out."

"I'll tell you what," said Benny. "Why don't I help you *bow out*."

Grace heard the wheels of the chair squeak and then a pounding sound she suspected was Tom's head bouncing off the desk.

She grimaced.

"Zat a good bow?" Benny asked. "You like that?"

Tom groaned.

Grace moved into the doorway, brandishing her size-eight pumps. Unfortunately, the simians had their backs toward her, which completely blew her big entrance.

Even more unfortunately, Easter Island had one of Tom's legs in his hand. Benny raised a foot and stomped on it, and there was a sickening crack.

Grace stumbled away from the door. Now would be the time to do something, wouldn't it? Now would be the time to ask *WWCAD?*

What Would Charlie's Angels Do?

Clearly, this situation called for a distraction.

Where was Farrah Fawcett and her little white tennis skirt when you needed her?

The sound of Tom's groans making her increasingly nervous, Grace scanned the warehouse for something, anything, she could use to create a diversion.

She circled the machine, locating a control desk on the far end with about sixty lit buttons and a network of switches and levers. The word *Heidelberg* stretched across the top of the machine in silver letters.

Heidelberg? Why did that sound familiar?

She figured one of the buttons had to turn the thing on, so she began pressing them.

The machine roared to life with an earsplitting squeal, hissing and groaning even louder than it had before.

Within seconds, Benny and Easter Island shot from the

office. The looks on their faces would have been comical if they hadn't been spattered with blood.

The blood that, by rights, was *hers* to spill. And if she'd managed to restrain herself from spilling it through fourteen years of marriage and a venomous divorce, it wasn't fair that they'd gone and done it.

The two men ran toward the machine. Grace circled it, and when they'd reached the control panel she waved at them from the other end.

"Hey. Over here." Her voice echoed through the building.

The simians charged, coming at her with speed that belied their blocky physiques. Before she could get out, they got between her and the door, trapping her inside the warehouse. With a sick feeling growing in the pit of her stomach, she realized her mistake.

Faulty math.

While there were three Angels, there was only one of her. On the show, the bad guys always had to split up to chase the Angels, but in this case it was two on one.

Which, if she remembered simple fractions correctly, two on one gave her only half a chance to get away.

Chapter 19.5

Pete sipped his coffee and tried to keep his eye on the dancers, instead of on Skobelov's booth in the back of the club.

The Russian's girlfriend had just left the table, so Skobelov was there with Morton, Ferret and Balboa, who had arrived about ten minutes ago. As long as he kept his cool and kept the camera trained on the Russian's table, they'd have enough to prove the two were dealing.

One of the dancers, a girl in a Wonder Woman costume, hopped off the stage and tried to lasso him with her gold rope. A bunch of young guys in the corner cheered. But Pete wasn't worried about being noticed at the Cat's Meow. He'd frequented the club for nearly six months now, getting to know the regulars and the girls, making himself inconspicuous by his habitual presence.

That's how he'd gotten to Balboa. And that was how he was going to nail Skobelov.

Lou was seated at the bar not ten feet away from the Russian's group, tucking dollar bills into a dancer's G-string and, presumably, keeping tabs on what was happening.

Lou had a tiny receiver in his ear that would pick up the sound from Balboa's bug, so he could monitor the conversation. As soon as Lou gave the signal, Pete would call the cops for backup.

Wonder Woman left him and climbed back up onstage, shedding the gold bustier she'd been wearing to reveal a set of red tassled pasties.

Pete felt bad for the girls. Most of them were really sweet, just hard workers trying to feed their kids or pay the mortgage or send money home to their families in other countries.

When Skobelov was taken down they'd all be out of jobs, since the Russian owned the club. But there wasn't anything Pete could do about that. It was an unfortunate side effect of his work.

But it wouldn't be an issue after today.

Pete had already decided it was time to retire. Get a civilian job, maybe start up a security consulting business. Buy that 1965 Mustang he'd always dreamed about.

He moved the baseball cap slightly, lining up the eye of the camera with Skobelov's big blob of a body.

He was close now.

So close.

Chapter 20

They were close. So close.

The simians charged. Grace retreated.

She flew past the open office door—where Tom lay on the floor, groaning—and around the perimeter of the building, desperately searching for another way out of the warehouse.

Benny and Easter Island split up, coming at her from opposite sides. Apparently, they weren't as dumb as they looked. *They* understood division.

She was trapped.

She backed up against the shelves on the wall, groping for the tire iron that, according to all cheesy detective show scripts, should conveniently have been there.

It wasn't.

The only things on the shelves were a bunch of boxes.

If this were an episode of *Charlie's Angels* and she was Jill Munroe, those boxes would conveniently be filled with knives, or marbles, or tiny goon-seeking missiles.

They weren't.

They were filled with paper.

Easter Island was still chugging his way around the machine, but Benny was close. Too close.

She had to do something fast.

Grace couldn't go right or left or down. The only way to go was up. She started up the shelves, but Benny reached her before she was out of range.

He grabbed her ankle. She gave him a kick, drilling him in the temple with her high heel. He let out a squeal that didn't sound like anything issued from a man his size.

She reached the top shelf and wedged herself behind the boxes, crawling on her hands and knees like a hamster in a tube. She could hear Benny, and now the monolith, too, pacing beneath her.

Okay, now what?

She reached into one of the boxes and pulled out a handful of paper.

She could throw it. Maybe cause a wicked paper cut.

All right. No. That was ridiculous.

She looked at the paper in her hands. Blue, with red circles. Familiar.

Was it…?

She squinted at it in the dim light.

Damn. It was.

Sheets and sheets of social security cards. There had to be thousands of them.

And then she remembered what Heidelberg was. A company that manufactured printing presses.

Somebody was making their own social security cards.

Her stomach rolled. She didn't want to see this. Didn't want to know about it. She just wanted to get out of there and get some help for Tom.

At the moment it seemed unlikely, considering the fact that she had roughly five hundred pounds of goon below her, waiting for her to come down.

What she needed was the element of surprise.

Closing her eyes, she said a little prayer. Then she pushed one of the boxes over the edge of the shelf with her shoulder.

It landed with a thunk.

She looked down over the edge to see Benny sprawled on the ground, surrounded by a pool of blue paper.

Bull's-eye!

The monolith looked up at her, stunned.

She let another bomb drop. It missed the mark but sent the goon scrambling for cover.

She clambered down the shelves and bolted for the door, not daring to look behind her.

She imagined she could feel hot breath on the back of her neck as she burst into the alley and sped toward the club.

The cold air seared her lungs as Easter Island chased her around the Cat's Meow for the second time. She realized she couldn't risk trying to get to her car. If he caught up with her in the parking lot, she was dead meat.

She lost him around the corner, and once she had a decent lead on him, ducked into the front door of the club.

"Twenty bucks, please," said the bouncer.

Damn.

"I don't have any money," she said. "I mean, I'm a dancer. I'm new, and I'm late for my shift."

"You're a dancer?" He looked her over. "You look a little ol—"

"I have a specialty. Ya know?" She winked at him but suspected it looked about as cute as the spastic cat's eye winking on the roof.

"I guess." But he looked like he didn't guess at all.

"Can I go in?"

He shrugged and held the door open. "Break a leg."

She shuddered.

Inside the club, she walked straight into a table while her eyes fought to adjust to the dark. A cold draft of air at her ankles told her someone else had just entered the small vestibule in the club, and by the way her hair stood up on the back of her neck, she strongly suspected it was Benny's friend.

Keeping to the shadows on the outskirts of the room, she made her way toward the back door.

She had to get help. Poor Tom. God only knew what damage those thugs had done.

Benny's friend emerged at the front door and squinted into the darkness. He set off in the opposite direction from her, toward Skobelov's booth.

Grace spotted Louis at the bar. She tried to get his attention, but his eyes were glued to the women on the stage.

Wasn't he supposed to be working?

Men.

She couldn't just go to him, either. Easter Island was sure to see her if she got near the lights of the stage.

She walked past the row of booths and through an area of freestanding tables, where a rowdy bunch of young guys— college students, she guessed—had camped out. Empty beer pitchers and shot glasses littered the tables.

The guys made catcalls at Grace as she passed.

They had definitely met their two-drink minimums.

"You going on next, honey?" one of the kids yelled to her. A kid who looked a lot like her nephew.

A kid who *was* her nephew!

"Michael?"

The kid belched. "Aunt Grace?"

"Jesus!" Grace made a beeline for the table. "What are you doing here?"

"I…" He glanced sheepishly at the stage. "Uh, it's for a report."

Grace gave him the sternest face she could muster. "Michael, how did you get in here? You're underage. Your mother would kill you. Not to mention Grandma."

Another kid walked over. "Hey, Mike. Who's the MILF?"

"Dude, chill. This is my *aunt*." Michael shook his head. "Man, what a bonehead."

"What's a MILF?" Grace said.

The other kid grinned. "A Mother I'd Like to F—"

"Dude," Grace said.

Michael plopped into a chair. "You gonna tell my mom, Aunt Grace?"

Grace sighed. "No. Just… No more beer for you. Drink some water. A lot of water. And get out of here right now."

He pointed at his friends. "But I came with them, and they aren't gonna want to leave until they see the one who dresses like Supergirl."

"Gotta stay for Supergirl," the other kid agreed. "She's the best. She does this thing with her kryptonite that'll blow your mind."

Michael looked up at Grace with bleary eyes. "We'll leave right after that, I promise."

"Is there a designated driver?" Grace asked.

Michael shrugged.

Grace looked around for Easter Island, but he had disappeared. "Don't go anywhere with anyone. I'll handle this."

"Cool." Michael went back to his table with the rest of the boneheads, and Grace made a beeline for the back hallway.

She wound her way through the serpentine corridors, trying to remember how to get to the back door. The club music thumped, reaching decibels that could rival the noise from the Heidelberg next door.

And suddenly Benny was there, plugging up the hallway as effectively as a cork in a bottle of wine. He must have come in through the back door.

Fortunately his back was to her, and she slipped into the ladies' room.

And let's face it. At that point, it wasn't the worst place she could hide.

Monday, 1:59 p.m.
The Justice League

When Grace peeked out into the hall again, Benny was gone.

She crept along the maze of hallways, wishing she had a compass. Or better yet, OnStar navigation system.

Hello, ma'am, can I help you? the perky-yet-soothing OnStar voice would say.

Yes, I'm trying to get to the alley, but I'm afraid I'm a little lost.

Well, we can certainly help you! Just make a left at the storage closet, a right at the alcove that smells like a dead rat, and go straight through the section of hallway painted that lovely shade of earwax-yellow.

After a few minutes of aimless wandering, Grace passed a door that looked familiar.

The changing room.

She slipped inside, thinking she might find a cell phone or maybe a Sherpa who could guide her out of the place.

A dark-haired dancer in a blue silk robe stood in front of the mirror, applying her lipstick.

"Excuse me…" Grace said.

The dancer turned. "Grace?"

"Tina! I didn't even recognize you."

"It's the black wig. What's going on? You look like hell."

Grace burst into tears. "This Easter Island guy broke Tom's leg, and Michael is here and he shouldn't be here, and Benny's after me and I'm scared. I can't help it. I tried to be brave but I'm done. I'm just scared."

"Wait. Hold on a minute. Who's Tom? Who's Michael?"

Grace's breaths came in fits and starts. "Tom, my ex-husband. I don't know. Somehow he's involved with Viktor. And Michael is my nephew. He's underage, shouldn't be here, but he is. He's right out there! I—"

"Shh. It's okay. Tell me again about Tom."

Grace sank into one of the folding chairs. "He's across the street, in this big warehouse. Benny and some other guy took him there and beat the crap out of him. I'm pretty sure they broke his leg. I'm afraid they're going to kill him. And me."

Grace stopped. Why was she telling Skobelov's girlfriend all of this? It was crazy.

But it wasn't. Because right now, Tina was the only person she had any hope of trusting. The only one who could help her.

Tina handed her a tissue. "You say Tom's across the alley?"

Grace nodded. "In the warehouse, in the back office."

"And your nephew, where is he? What does he look like?"

"Curly brown hair, Temple University sweatshirt. He's with a bunch of frat boys on the left side of the club."

Tina pulled off her wig and tossed it on her dressing table.

"Okay, just stay put. I'll take care of everything." She gave Grace a quick hug and hurried out the door.

Grace grabbed another tissue and blew her nose. She took a few cleansing breaths to try to stop her hands from shaking.

Tina would help her. She had to.

A door off to her right—one she hadn't even noticed before—burst open. Grace nearly fell off her chair. Music blared as three dancers hurried into the changing room, and Grace realized the door must lead directly to the stage.

"What a crowd today," said one of the women, a short blonde in a Batgirl costume. She spoke with a thick accent and looked as if she couldn't be a minute older than sixteen. "I dance my tits off, and for what?" She pulled a handful of dollar bills out of her underwear. "Ten…eleven…twelve. Twelve dollars. I could have stayed home and watched *When Harry Met Sally* on cable."

"It's all those freakin' college students," said another, an unnatural redhead dressed as Aquagirl. "They expect you to let them cop a feel every time they put a dollar in your pants."

An older, more worldly-looking Catwoman, who was at least twenty-three, shook her head. "Some days just suck." As if she'd just noticed Grace, she said, "You better get going, girl. The natives are getting restless."

"Oh, I'm not… My shift hasn't started."

The girl shrugged.

"Hey, do any of you have a cell phone?" Grace asked.

"They don't work in here," said Aquagirl. "Don't you know this is the pit of hell?"

The others laughed.

"There's a pay phone in the hall," one offered.

"Great. Anybody have a couple quarters I can borrow?"

The girl with the accent handed Grace one of the dollars she'd pulled out of her G-string. "You'll have to get change."

Grace thanked her and went to the door that led into the hallway, opening it just a crack. Benny stood less than two feet away.

Damn.

She closed the door softly. If he decided to poke his head in there, she was a goner. She was trapped like a rat in a trash can.

No, that wasn't quite true.

She looked at the stage door.

There was another way out.

Chapter 20.5

"Su-per-girl. Su-per-girl." The kids in the back chanted at the empty stage.

Usually Pete enjoyed Masked Mondays. It was something a little different, watching the surrogates of his boyhood fantasies come alive onstage. But not today.

Today, he'd already had all the excitement he could handle, and then some.

His chest squeezed, and he wondered idly if he might be having a heart attack. Even if he was, it wouldn't matter. He was gonna sit right there in that chair, still as stone, until Lou gave him the goddamned signal.

"Come on, Lou," he muttered under his breath.

At Skobelov's table, things were heating up.

The Russian wore a flat look, which Pete knew from experience was his look of rage. His Chernobyl look.

Morton, oblivious to the impending explosion, continued to shake his head. Pete tried to focus on Lou instead of the unfolding scene, but he found he couldn't look away.

Skobelov leaned back in his seat and looked at Nick.

Nick leaned forward and spoke to Morton, who shook his head again.

Skobelov's goon moved to the table and stood behind Morton.

Pete held his breath.

He willed Morton to back down. The man couldn't testify with his balls in his throat.

Skobelov turned redder and redder. Borscht-red.

Morton said something else, and Skobelov smiled. He waved his goon off and lit a cigar.

Pete wiped the sweat off his forehead with his sleeve. Morton would live to see the next minute, at least.

From the corner of the club, a cheer went up.

Supergirl had arrived.

Chapter 21

Monday, 2:05 p.m.
Kryptonite

Grace stumbled into the light, tugging at the sequined bra that barely covered her boobs.

In the corner the boneheads cheered wildly. She prayed Michael was no longer among them. Wasn't there a law against letting your nephew see you in a G-string?

This was insane.

All the other stuff—giving Nick her panties, cooking for Skobelov, trying to save Tom—that stuff was crazy. But this? This was certifiably insane.

"Psst. Hey, Supergirl. You forgot something." A dancer just off the stage tossed Grace a big, blue, phallic-looking chunk of plastic.

Grace caught it in one hand. "What is it?"

"Your kryptonite."

Another cheer went up from the frat boys.

You should see what she does with her kryptonite.

"Ugh."

Music blared over the speakers behind her, but beyond the lights she could see anticipation in the eyes that stared up at her. They were waiting for her.

Actually, they were waiting for Tina, but they were gonna get her, at least for a minute or two. Just until she could make sure Benny and his friend weren't around and she could get off the stage and get out of this place.

She hoped the black wig she was wearing changed her appearance as much as it had changed Tina's.

She shimmied out to one of the poles as the music changed from pulsing techno to a sensuous rhythm-and-blues thing with lots of sax. She scanned the faces in the crowd, spotting Benny.

He squinted at her as if trying to figure out how he knew her, and she realized if she didn't start moving soon, he'd figure it out pretty quickly.

So she closed her eyes and grabbed the nearest pole, leaning her back against it so she didn't pass out or fall over or something.

Grace did a couple of squats and then spun around and hooked an elbow around the pole, spinning until she was dizzy. She opened her eyes a crack and saw that the men at the bar along the stage were looking at her as if they expected something more.

Benny had moved closer, and she began to panic.

Her movements felt stiff, even to her, and she suspected she looked something like a corpse humping a pole. She forced herself to loosen up. Go with the flow. Listen to the music.

She'd done this before. Tina had taught her all the moves in the big white bathroom at Skobelov's place. She'd done fine there, and she could do it again.

But the lights, the music, the eyes. They conspired against her.

She knew then that she was about to relive one of the most embarrassing moments of her life. A humiliation so acute, it had taken many dozens of cupcakes to repair the damage to her reputation at William Marker Elementary School, and several months' worth of therapy later in life to repair the damage to her psyche.

It was the fourth-grade talent show, and she had forgotten every single step of the jazz dance routine she'd practiced for months. So she'd ended up performing the only dance she could remember at the time—the one the kids on the *Brady Bunch* had done for *their* talent show when they'd sung that groovy song "Keep On."

The humiliation had been utter and complete.

And now, in a horrifying echo of that day, she did the only moves she could remember.

Yoga poses.

She threw the kryptonite on the floor and sank to her knees, striking the lion pose. To her surprise, the crowd cheered. Maybe because her left breast had nearly popped out of her bra.

But, hey, it had worked.

She transitioned into cobra pose and then rolled onto her back, bringing her feet over her head into plow pose. The crowd cheered again.

Who knew yoga could be so sexy?

Getting into it now, she did the full sun salutation sequence into scorpion pose, standing on her elbows, back arched, her legs dangling above her head.

"Hey, come on over here, honey!" a guy called from the bar. She crawled over to him on her hands and knees, retrieving the kryptonite on the way and rubbing it sensuously over his bald head. The crowd went wild.

The guy stuffed a couple dollar bills into her bra, and she almost punched him until she remembered she was supposed to be grateful.

She scanned the room again and noticed that Benny had moved back by the DJ booth.

She struck a shooting bow pose before crawling along the edge of the bar. More bills were stuffed into places she didn't want to think about, before she finally made it to the edge of the stage and dropped down to the floor.

It was now or never.

She started off toward the front door, but just then Easter Island materialized there. His beady little eyes came to rest on her, so she danced toward the tables.

Easter Island moved closer.

She turned her back to him, and straddled the lap of a guy wearing a Flyers cap.

"Not now, honey." He tried to push her off.

"Hey, cowboy. Don't you want a special dance?"

The guy tensed. "Grace?"

Oh, my God.

"Pete?"

"What in the *hell* are you doing here?" he growled. "What's with that getup?"

"I—"

"Wait. No. I don't even want to know. Just get the hell out of here, right—"

"Freeze! Everybody stay where you are!"

Men in uniforms and blue jackets poured in through the

front door and from the back hallway, surrounding the stage and the DJ booth, blocking the exits.

"God*damn* it," Pete swore.

"What? You didn't call them?" Grace said.

Pete shook his head. "I don't even know if we got what we needed yet."

Grace's stomach turned. She could have made a wild guess as to who had called the cops. She looked around but didn't see Tina anywhere.

Much to her relief, Michael was gone, too. A few police officers had rounded up the boneheads and were checking their IDs.

Numerous police officers and a group of men in dark blue windbreakers with the letters USCIS emblazoned in yellow on the back surrounded Skobelov's booth.

Grace's close proximity to Pete—and she couldn't get much closer than straddling his lap—allowed her to see the anger and disappointment in his eyes.

She took his face in her hands. "I'm sorry."

And she really, truly was.

Pete shook his head. "It's not your fault. Just bad luck." He lifted her off his lap. "By the way, you look pretty hot."

"You think?"

"Definitely."

He left her standing there and went over to where Louis was talking to the men in the blue windbreakers.

"Ma'am?" An officer approached her. "You're going to have to come with me."

"But I'm not a dancer. I don't really work here."

He glanced sideways at her. "Yes, ma'am."

"No, I'm serious!" She reached up and tugged the black wig off. "I don't work here."

"Yes, ma'am."

She sighed. "Can I at least get the money out of my bra? It's itching like crazy."

The cop led her through the hallway and past the changing room, where the other members of the Justice League were also being fitted with beautiful plastic bracelets. Most of them were speaking in rapid-fire Russian.

Grace and her escort soon emerged into the alley, which was jammed with police cars and vans and dark blue government-issue vehicles.

The door to the warehouse next door was closed, taped over with yellow crime tape.

The cop led her by the arm toward one of the police vans—the paddy wagon, she guessed—but before they'd reached it, the door to one of the unmarked cars swung open.

"Wait," said a female voice. "I'll handle her."

Tina emerged from the backseat of the vehicle, wearing jeans and a blue windbreaker. She gave a low whistle. "Look at you. Taking the wild thing a bit far, aren't you, Grace?"

Grace's mouth fell open. "Are you…?"

Tina nodded. "U.S. Citizenship and Immigration Services."

Grace shook her head. "That explains a lot. Did I ruin your case, too?"

Tina looked confused. "No, you didn't ruin our case. We had to move a little early, but we were ready."

"I guess you found Tom." She nodded toward the warehouse.

"Yeah." Tina took her to the car.

Grace got into the backseat and Tina slid in beside her.

"Your ex-husband was in pretty bad shape. They took him to Penn."

Grace's stomach churned. "Is he going to be okay?"

"I talked to the EMT. She said his vitals were relatively stable. He was hurting, but he should be all right. You cold?"

Grace nodded.

Tina grabbed a USCIS windbreaker from the front seat and wrapped it around Grace's shoulders. "Your nephew is back at the dorm safe and sound, probably sleeping it off."

"Thank you. I don't know how I can ever repay you."

Tina smiled. "Cook me dinner sometime?"

"Absolutely. And then maybe afterward we can play charades. I bet you'd be good at it."

Tina winked. "You're a good woman, Grace Becker. Promise me you'll be careful who you get involved with in the future?"

Grace nodded. "I will."

Tina opened the car door. "Wait here. I'll go get your stuff out of the club."

Chapter 21.5

Monday, 3:14 p.m.
Home Videos

Pete scoured the club for Grace, but she was nowhere to be found. Some of the dancers had been taken out of the club by Immigration Services, and he was worried Grace had been picked up along with them.

But when he'd spoken to the guy in charge for the USCIS, he couldn't locate her. Ditto for the Philly PD.

And he hadn't even said goodbye.

Once Pete had spoken to Lou, he discovered that they'd managed to get all the evidence they needed. Skobelov had agreed to pay Morton eighty thousand dollars for the memory key, topping Iatesta's bid of seventy grand.

Most of the conversation had been caught on Nick's wire,

as well as on the video feed in Pete's cap. At least it was, up until the point Grace had sat on his lap and blocked the action.

Man, he couldn't wait to get a look at that recording. A vision of Grace in that scorching Supergirl costume flashed through his mind. A vision he had to get out of his mind, pronto, unless he wanted to find himself sporting wood for the walk out to the parking lot.

He shook his head.

He was glad it was over, but he wasn't looking forward to the next few months.

Now, the grunt work for the case began. Submitting evidence, writing reports, working with federal prosecutors to build a case against Skobelov.

At least there would be no problem with that. Especially since somebody had located a counterfeiting operation across the alley, with a printing press, boxes of counterfeit social security cards and an office full of papers with Skobelov's name all over them.

How Pete and Lou had never gotten wind of the counterfeit operation was a mystery. And why Balboa had never told them about it was something that would definitely be addressed when they discussed his cooperation in the case with the prosecutor.

Lou came over and clapped Pete on the shoulder. "How 'bout a drink and some dinner?"

"Nah. I got a lot to do."

Lou nodded. "Guess I should get to work, too. Besides, nothing's gonna taste as good as Grace's cooking."

"Yeah."

"That Grace was one hell of a woman, eh, boss?"

Pete rubbed the back of his neck. "She sure was."

Chapter 22

Monday, 6:35 p.m.
Burn Baby Burn

Grace rubbed a small circle in the steam on her bathroom mirror.

All her makeup was gone. The henna tattoo had already begun to fade. And she had no idea how long it would take her to style her hair.

She sighed.

Goodbye, wild woman.

She bundled up in a thick white robe and slippers and scuffled down the stairs to make a cup of tea.

The kids' backpacks hung by the door, and a frisson of worry ran down her spine. What if Tom's conversation with Nick, the one that was recorded from the body wire, got her in trouble?

It seemed unlikely since the papers she'd signed had never

actually been used, and were, in fact, missing. But still, it was a possibility.

She didn't regret not taking the CD from the recorder at Pete's house, though. Skobelov was a despicable and dangerous man, who had undoubtedly ruined many lives. He deserved to go to prison for a long, long time.

Grace had called the hospital, but they wouldn't let her speak with Tom until the police had a chance to interview him.

Grace took her cup of tea into the living room and lit a fire.

She was sitting on the couch debating whether or not she should call her lawyer, when the doorbell rang.

Through the peephole, she could see Pete's red hair and the collar of his trench coat. Her heart jumped.

He turned when she opened the door, and smiled.

"I didn't think I'd see you so soon," she said. Or ever.

"Yeah, well, I wanted to return a few things." He pulled her panties out of his pocket and dangled them on his finger.

She grabbed his wrist and pulled him inside the house, her cheeks burning.

"Thanks," she said, plucking the panties from his finger and stuffing them into the pocket of her robe. "Do you have anything else? Something a little more sparkly, perhaps?"

He produced her ring from his other pocket and slipped it onto her finger. He cupped his hand over hers, giving it a squeeze.

"Thanks for your help, Grace. I'm sorry if I was… Well, if I wasn't always a gentleman."

"You were fine. You were doing your job. Did you get everything you needed on Skobelov?"

He shrugged. "It didn't turn out exactly as planned, but we got enough to put him out of business. Along with the immigration violations and Internet drug sales, he's going away for a long time."

"What about Nick?"

"He's under witness protection until the trial. After that, we'll see. He's got some things to answer for with the USCIS, too."

"So you were working with Tina all along?"

"Actually, no. We didn't even know about the immigration investigation. It was purely a coincidence they wrapped up their case the same time we were finishing ours."

Grace wondered if she should tell him that it wasn't quite the coincidence he thought, but she decided against it. "How could that have happened? I mean, how could you all not have known about each other?"

"It isn't all that uncommon, to tell you the truth. Lots of times different organizations will be working on the same guy or the same group, and they don't even know it. It's the secretive nature of the business, I guess."

"Hmm." She stared at her anniversary band. "What's going to happen to my ex-husband?"

"I'm not sure. We'll have to go through the evidence, see what comes up. If he agrees to testify, things might not be too bad for him."

She nodded.

"By the way, his girlfriend was arrested on conspiracy drug charges, too. They just picked her up half an hour ago."

"Marlene?"

He nodded.

Grace smiled. Finally, a bright spot in all this mess.

Pete hooked her chin with his fingers and tilted her head until she looked into his eyes. "I have something else."

He reached into the inside pocket of the trench coat and pulled out an envelope.

She opened it and removed the papers inside. The bottom of her stomach dropped out.

"I know what they are, Grace," Pete said quietly.

She nodded. What could she say? She'd been nailed. She just hoped she and Tom wouldn't be in jail at the same time.

Her poor kids. She could only imagine what their lives would be like.

Friend: Hey, Kevin, wanna go skateboarding on Saturday?

Kevin: Nah, I can't. Gotta go to Riker's Island and see my mom and dad.

Her eyes filled with tears. She'd really screwed up this time.

"Hey," Pete said, pulling her close and kissing her forehead. "As far as I'm concerned, I have no idea what those are. They're yours. Do what you want with them."

"Really?"

"Really." He brushed a tear from her cheek. "I know why you did it, Grace. And if anyone asks, I don't have any idea what Tom was talking about on that recording. But I hope you understand that nothing is worth this kind of risk."

"I know. Believe me, I know."

"And I suggest you don't leave those lying around."

She went to the fireplace and threw the papers in, watching as they curled and blackened and turned to ash.

Goodbye, house.

Pete came up behind her and wrapped his arms around her waist. She turned, curling her fingers in his hair and bringing his mouth to hers.

It was a make-out session to rival the one she'd had with Robbie Freeman when they'd played seven minutes in heaven at Cecilia's fifteenth birthday party. She couldn't figure out what was making her hotter—Pete or the fire.

He pulled away and took a deep breath. "I forgot to tell you. We found out that Skobelov isn't Russian after all. He's Polish."

She laughed. "I guess no one was really who they seemed to be in this mess, huh?"

"Nobody except you."

She looked away. "I don't know. I seem to have a little problem figuring out who I am these days."

"You're the genuine article, Grace." He hugged her, resting his chin on the top of her head. "So what are you going to do now?"

She sighed. "I've been thinking about that. I decided I'm going to try and start my own catering company."

"You're quite a cook."

"Among other things." She smiled. Maybe the wild woman hadn't completely disappeared, after all. She kissed him again. "Want to come upstairs with me? I'll model these for you." She pulled the panties out of the pocket of her robe.

Pete turned the color of a tomato. "I shouldn't. I mean, I really shouldn't get involved with someone from the case."

She kissed him again and twirled the panties on her finger as she headed for the stairs. "Why don't you just pretend I'm someone else?"

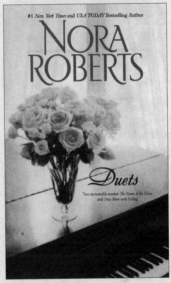

Bundle up and get cozy with three new stories
from *USA TODAY* bestselling authors
Jennifer Greene and Merline Lovelace,
and reader favorite Cindi Myers!

USA TODAY Bestselling Author
JENNIFER GREENE

USA TODAY Bestselling Author
MERLINE LOVELACE

CINDI MYERS

Baby,
It's Cold Outside

A little ice...adds spice!

Baby, It's Cold Outside

A little ice…is sure to add some spice!

Be sure to catch this
heartwarming collection in stores today!

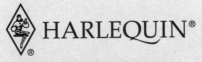